01024634

A Thousand Perfect Things

CALGARY PUBLIC LIBRARY

DEC ⁻ 2013

A THOUSAND PERFECT THINGS

by

KAY KENYON

Premier Digital Publishing - Los Angeles

A THOUSAND PERFECT THINGS

Copyright © 2013 Kay Kenyon

All rights reserved. No part of this book may be reproduced or transmitted
in any form or by any means, electronic or mechanical, including photocopying,
recording, or by any information storage and retrieval system, without written
permission from the publisher, except where permitted by law.

eISBN: 978-1-62467-095-4
Print ISBN: 1624670954

Published by Premier Digital Publishing
www.PremierDigitalPublishing.com
Follow us on Twitter @PDigitalPub
Follow us on Facebook: Premier Digital Publishing

This is a work of fiction. Names, characters, places, and incidents either are
the product of the author's imagination or are used fictitiously. Any resemblance
to actual persons, living or dead, events, or locales is entirely coincidental.

Acknowledgments

In sketching an imaginary India, I am very much indebted to a number of authors, books and friends. A special thanks to Natarajan Janarthanan for his guidance on India and the Hindi language. I hope that my admiration for India and its cultures shines through despite the transmutations of fantasy. The following books inspired and guided me, providing a jumping off point for research: *Dry Storeroom No. 1: The Secret Life of the Natural History Museum* by Richard Fortey; *Raj: The Making and Unmaking of British India* by Lawrence James; *Charles Darwin: The Power of Place* by Janet Browne. For assistance and astute suggestions I am also indebted to Bairavi Vijay, Donald Maass, Louise Marley, Neil Noah, and my agent Ethan Ellenberg for his faith in this story and his work on its behalf. My thanks to everyone at Premier Digital Publishing. I also wish to thank my husband Thomas Overcast for his unwavering support and patient re-readings of the manuscript. All distortions of fact—which can't be ascribed to magic—are, in the end, mine. Research must someday end or books would never be published.

PROLOGUE

January 18, 1857

Lord Nelson's statue perched on its granite column in the square, but to Edwina Banning it appeared that his shoulders stooped, as though he were weary of the heroic pose. It might have been a trick of the light.

Presently satisfied that the great naval hero was not drooping—and how, indeed, could a statue droop—Edwina tipped her parasol back into place and turned to watch six-year old Anna who was feeding pigeons with her father. The day darkened as a sudden high cloud tented the sky wintry gray. A horse pulling a coach shied in its traces, for a moment disrupting the decorous progression of carriages. Anna's father pulled her close.

But the grand square with its flags and well-dressed gentlemen—all these lent Londinium a reassuring presence, an everyday glory, well-earned. Scotland was long subdued, the famous naval victory at the Firth of Clyde having united the island after centuries of war. And as to the mystic continent with its troubling ways, it was now possible for traders to reach it in ninety days and never worry about winds or kraken—thanks to that wonder of engineering, the Great Bridge.

"Papa," Anna said, pointing at Lord Nelson on his column, "the statue is bleeding."

Mr. Banning held his top hat on as he craned his neck to see. "Pigeons do make rather a mess," he said.

"But the mess is *red.*"

Edwina Banning turned to look, noting with alarm a red slime oozing down the column. Just as she was trying to imagine how this could be, she stared hard at one of the lions anchoring a corner of the plinth. The metal

1

sculpture opened its mouth in a cavernous yawn. It was said that the iron lions had been cast from Scottish cannons. She had always found satisfaction in that story, and therefore it took her a moment before she entirely grasped that the animals were awake.

They stirred.

As Mr. and Mrs. Banning gaped in stunned denial, blood oozed from under Nelson's coat and dribbled down the granite column.

Edwina's lips parted for a scream just as one of the lions—the one facing the church of St. Martin's-in-the-Fields—leapt through the air and landed on a peanut vendor, crushing him to the ground. Then the second lion found its prey: a top-hatted gentleman with a cane. The cane crashed down on the beast's head, but as the lion was made of iron, it had no effect. The square erupted with shouts and screams. Pigeons flew up in a clatter of wings and demented cooing.

Lord Nelson sagged and fell to one knee, clutching his chest.

The rampage began. The lions rushed to the slaughter, breaking necks with mighty paws and tearing at throats. They did not linger to feed, but turned from one victim to the next, finding their quarry closely packed in the square, though trying to flee. The fastest among them got as far as the steps of the National Gallery before falling.

Mr. Banning yanked open the door of a carriage, and surprised the lady inside by throwing his daughter into her lap and shoving his wife in as far as he could. He jumped inside and slammed the door closed. As terrified horses charged away, their careening carriages in tow, people in the square threw themselves on top of the conveyances, or clung to riding boards.

From the floor of the carriage where she huddled with her mother little Anna whispered, "They're not real lions, though."

Edwina clutched her daughter tightly. They weren't, they weren't at all.

But they killed.

"It's terrorism, and straight from Bharata." Lord Palmerston said. "They grow stronger, your majesty."

King Albert nodded at the Prime Minister. Bharata and its damned mysticism. He turned to face Arthur Helps, Clerk of the Privy Council. "We have traded with the continent for 200 years. Why should their priests of magic decide to turn against us now?"

Helps said, "It's the Bridge. We were fine before the Bridge."

"And the lions are all... dead?" The Prime Minister asked.

"Yes," Helps answered. "It took a full company of Grenadiers, but they prevailed. Threw them into the estuary for good measure."

The king shook his head, muttering, "Good God. Forty people torn limb from limb." Nor had it been a proper military attack. It was a damnable convulsion, an intrusion of magic from a land devoid of science, religion or decency.

Helps piped up. "It began with the Bridge."

The king sighed. "So you have said, sir. On numerous occasions."

"Please pardon me, Your Majesty. I only meant—"

"Yes," the Prime Minister said, crossing a leg and assuming that bland look he had perfected over his long government career. "That the Great Bridge causes the realms to mix. But the Bridge also smoothes the way for imports upon which our nation utterly depends. Need I remind you? Lumber, cotton, diamonds, tea..."

"And blood," Helps added.

"Blood is always the price of prosperity."

The king flicked his wrist in dismissal. "Gentlemen. The Bridge is here. It has been accomplished. Spilt milk to lament it now."

He went on, "We must convert them to our way of thinking, and then we shall have peace." He moved to the window of his audience room, hands clasped behind his back, gazing out on St. James Park. "My speech to Parliament must be along those lines." Magic would only give way to scientific rationalism when the people of Bharata enjoyed the benefits of education and civilization.

"Yes, Your Majesty," came Helps's tepid response.

King Albert rounded on the man. "Well? Out with it. You are our advisor. Let us be advised."

"We could sink the Bridge."

The Prime Minister rolled his eyes and crossed his legs in the other direction. The king stared at Helps in high distaste. Sink the Bridge? But it had only just opened!

Part I: A Contagion of Magic

1

In the greenhouse cottage, Grandpapa kept the curtains drawn against the winter chill and against watchers in the trees. Tori suppressed the urge to throw open the drapes and casements of the study to freshen the air, heavy with the smell of greenhouse specimens. But she did not want, any more than her grandpapa did, to face the thing in the tree.

Sir Charles's pen scratched across his notebook, a beloved and familiar sound. He knew how to write with one hand while leaning into the eyepiece of his microscope, a feat Tori greatly admired. At nineteen, she had learned taxonomy, botany, illustration, three languages and the art of preserving plants in a herbarium book. But as for writing while not looking; that she had yet to master.

He glanced up, sensing her gaze upon him.

She tucked back into her illustration of the sweet pea *Lathyrus brevis,* discomfited to have been caught watching him. They all watched him these days—her parents, her sister, the servants—alert for signs of confusion. He was determined to thwart them, however, and in this Tori was his most staunch ally. It was insufferable for Sir Charles to have his capabilities called into question when science and the Crown had bestowed every scientific honor upon him including a knighthood.

This was why he couldn't admit that he had seen something very odd in the sycamore tree. It was often there—as it was right now—but just as often it was not. So if one were to alert the household, and if say, Papa came to investigate, it would not look well to have the thing gone.

That the watcher in the tree had returned again today was disturbing. Not because it was likely a magical being, but because it did not seem a *neutral* magic. That is, it did not seem well-meaning. Not that anyone in Anglica truly understood magic and its workings.

Nor was this the worst of Tori's worries. It was her grandpapa's state of health.

She could not deny that at seventy-eight Sir Charles was slipping away from everyday things. Even today, his normally punctilious habit of dress was marred by a stain of morning porridge on his cravat. And worse, at times he lost hold on what year it was—indeed, what decade—and spoke of things long past as though they had just happened. Thus one could never be sure whether he was speaking of things real or less so.

The watcher in the tree, however, that was genuine.

Tori had never before been afraid of magic. True, always before it had been something that intruded in Londinium and centers of commerce, not in pastoral Shropshire, at Glyndehill Manor with its well-ordered fields and orchards. Furthermore, magic was the subject of their current venture, the treatise upon the golden lotus. And since magic was the very theme of their inquiry, it was unseemly to fear it.

Sir Charles took off his glasses, rubbing the profound indentation in his nose. "You might open the window, *piari*. An inch. No more." She loved that he called her *piari*—dear, in Bharati, her third language after Latin.

She managed to push the casement ajar without opening the drape.

As she turned back, Sir Charles was regarding her. On either side of him lay the morning's accumulated herbarium volumes, closing him in like giant bookends. He cleaned his spectacles on his handkerchief, his hands steady, still capable of that lovely script in which he catalogued his herbarium.

"You've finished *Lathyrus brevis*?"

"Yes, Grandpapa, roots and all." She was a competent illustrator, but she would much rather do real science. *Brevis* was a variety of sweet pea Sir Charles had developed; it grew only a foot high, but carried a profusion of flowers. Now it was time to put *brevis* on the map.

Plucking a pin from the tray, she turned to the wall. Here was a faded, yellowish map, with the world's two continents placed side-by-side as though mirror images of each other, although their shapes were distinct, with Anglica's lobed oblong and Bharata's nearly diamond shape. The world ocean narrowed between the two continents to a mere eleven hundred miles. Tori placed her finger on the spot where the new pin would reside, in the pin-rich environs of

Glyndehill Manor, West Midlands, Anglica. She paused for Grandpapa to give her the nod, then stabbed in the pin, certifying that the sweet pea specimen had been properly curated with taxonomy, herbarium sheet and sketch. Tori had begun the pin map as a child, chronicling her grandpapa's botanical discoveries and neither one of them had outgrown it.

"I don't suppose I may pin up *aureus*?"

Leaning in to his microscope, he said—as he had so many times before—"We have no sketch."

Scanning the continent of Bharata—its provinces and states demarcated with a child's colored pencils, Tori knew just where the pin for *Nelumbo aureus* would go: south and west in the great land mass, in the princely state of Nanpura. There were many pins in the Bharata map. Sir Charles's old expedition had shipped back four hundred and three heretofore undiscovered plant species, but after fifty years, one botanical treasure still remained aloof from her pin project and from Sir Charles's highest hopes: the golden lotus.

No sketch.

This summed up the missing prerequisite for a pin in the map: after taxonomy and a real specimen must come the sketch. Grandpapa had named the genus long ago: *Nelumbo* for species lotus. *Aureus* for its color. They had, of course, a petal specimen preserved on a herbarium page, but even Sir Charles had never seen an entire golden lotus. He had acquired the petal on his famous Bharata expedition, but had not actually seen a full specimen, the thousand-petaled lotus which—if legend followed fact—was the color of the sun. With most unusual properties.

"But we know it exists," Tori persisted. "We have a lotus petal as long as my arm." She wanted to say, *and it is my map. I have kept it up for fifteen years. I know what every pin signifies and which herbarium book the specimen rests in. The pin should be there.*

A pin in a map would not convince the scientific world. Those who believed that science had no room for magic had heaped derision on Sir Charles for even suggesting the lotus existed. But at least here in the greenhouse cottage, couldn't Tori have it all as it ideally should be?

Grandpapa looked up again and sighed. "The ways of science are exact, *piari*. If they were not, we would have everyone with opinions, and no one the wiser for proofs. One must show respect for learned traditions, even when turning them on their heads. There are things which one must be careful to couch in the terms of the day, you see. We do not rush into the fray making claims and upsetting all that has gone before."

"But surely that is what your monograph will do?"

He smiled, making a notation in his notebook. "Yes, but prudently. Prudently, as Darwin did with his transmutation of the species."

It befitted the age of science in which Anglica now found itself, and Tori was thankful that religion put no constraints on scientific investigation. Yet people managed to impose an orthodoxy in any case.

From outside, someone called. It was her sister. Jessa always called out, thinking it less intrusive to Sir Charles than a knock on the door. Tori slipped out to intercept her, clunking out the library door and into the greenhouse proper, past the tables of seedlings and jars of specimens too large to compress in sheets.

She met Jessa on the walkway between the greenhouse cottage and the great house.

"A visitor!" Jessa declared, waving a note. "Arriving this afternoon."

Tori felt a crimp of disappointment that she would not have her afternoon free to read *The Natural History of Oxfordshire*, recently arrived by mail coach. "Who?"

"Captain Edmond Muir-Smith. He's coming to visit Papa."

Tori vaguely remembered that a Muir-Smith had served under her father in the Pict campaign.

Jessa's color was high. "Mama's in a tempest, though he's just an army officer. One to whom I suppose papa will try to marry me off."

With her sister's recent broken engagement tarnishing her prospects, any eligible male visitor raised immediate interest. "How old is this one?"

"Um. Not old."

For all that Jessa was making light of the visit, her cheeks did have a flush. "How not old?"

"Twenty-eight. A captain in the King's Company of the fusiliers. Mama says he's first in line for a baronetcy. Just returned from a voyage to Bharata. Papa says he's a pleasant looking chap. He dislikes whist but plays backgammon." She finished, "And he's taller than I am."

Tori felt a smile break out. "How long do we have to tear apart the closet to find something to wear?"

Jessa grinned. "Not long enough."

Looking at her sister, younger by one year, Tori could not imagine that she wouldn't impress the captain no matter what she wore, with her light brown tresses framing a heart-shaped face, and that full figure that neither her sister nor her mother shared, both slender and willowy as they were.

Looking back toward the library, Tori said, "I'll be right up."

Jessa laid a hand on her arm. "Mama said perhaps not Sir Charles this time."

Tori bristled. She wished that Jessa would speak up for him, and not always defer to mother whose highest ambition seemed to be avoiding discord at tea.

"I'll just see if he he'd like to stop in to join us. You go on."

As Jessa ran off, Tori paused, glancing up at the roof of the greenhouse cottage over which the sycamore tree loomed. She moved to the end of the path and turned to face the great, spreading tree. The sycamore always managed to gather shadows this time of day. With its flaking bark and patches of dusty green algae it was easy to see in it something that wasn't there.

Oh, but this time, it was. Her throat went dry.

It perched on a branch quite close to the trunk of the nearest tree. At first impression, it was an owl with bluish purple feathers. Its rotund body was very bird-like, but it wasn't a natural creature, not with that visage. The face was almost human. A bulbous nose flabbed down the length of its face so that both human and owl aspects were equally repugnant.

Its head rotated around to her. Large eyes, chillingly light-filled, met hers. She backed up a step. It was... it had to be, a manifestation of magic. *Do not be afraid,* she charged herself. Every child learned there was magic in the world, but far away, in the other continent, in Bharata.

She shivered under that maladroit gaze. Sometimes magic killed, Anglics had come to learn. Such visitations from Bharata were called *contagions,* a term that so perfectly represented Anglic fear of the unscientific. Sometimes contagions presaged a malign event: for example last month's attack in Londinium, or the disaster in Oxfordshire when the train went off its tracks and went four miles before plunging over a cliff. But that said nothing about magic as a practice, for any endeavor might be turned to horrid purpose by those who abused knowledge. She did not wish to judge the intrusion in the sycamore. But the *face...*

It looked away, as though to prove it had other business. But then, slowly, the head swiveled back in her direction. Her stomach tightened. Oh, it looked at her. *Assessed* her. She yanked her gaze away, lest its eyes drag something out of her—she knew not what.

Why had it come? Oh, leave us in peace, she wanted to plead, but found herself unable to speak. Backing up, she felt a most unseemly haste to be away from it, and turning, rushed up the walkway. She hurried back through the greenhouse—though with a club foot, such haste was neither very fast nor easy to manage.

In the library she found Sir Charles asleep, stretched out on the window seat.

The curtain was open a few inches. So he had checked outside. She leaned over him to look for herself. As she did so, Grandpapa's eyes fluttered open. "*Daitya*," he whispered.

"*Daitya?*" It was a Bharati word. Demon. "*Daitya*, Grandpapa?"

"Yes, child." He gazed past her to the draped window. "Down to hell. The last kingdom, isn't it?"

Tori looked at him in dismay. "No, Grandpapa. There is no such thing."

"To be fair," he said, in sudden clarity and looking directly at her, "you haven't been there."

"But we are safe at home now," she whispered.

He groaned softly in protest. "Looks like a..."

She leaned in closer to hear him. "Like a what?" she asked.

"Like one of those... you know. *Daityas*." His eyes slid closed.

Carefully, Tori reached over him and pulled the drape aside.

The shadowy owl had vanished.

2

"Tori, dear, can you wear the mauve?" In the upstairs hall, Tori and her mother had chanced to meet. "The mauve gown becomes you," Mrs. Harding said.

The dreadful thing made her look like a giant peony. "I haven't seen it in ages."

"Oh, but I laid it out on your bed."

The two women faced off, at odds already and they hadn't spoken since breakfast. Olivia and Tori Harding were in many respects similar to each other: slender and dark, with wide mouth and a nearly aquiline nose. Of course her mother did not clunk when she walked, there was that difference.

"Jessa needs me." Tori turned to enter her sister's room.

"You invited Sir Charles."

Turning back, Tori steeled herself for a disagreeable conversation. "He knows we're having company."

Mrs. Harding frowned. "This is an important acquaintance for your sister. Colonel Harding *particularly* invited him."

"Then our visitor should certainly meet the whole family."

Mrs. Harding's frown sank deeper, but she refrained from argument, leaving Tori having to be unpleasant all on her own.

"Let's say they get engaged and then Grandpapa suddenly appears at tea in his pajamas. Why not drag out the hidden family all at once?"

Jessa threw open the door, standing in her under slip. "Tori, are you ever coming?" She glanced from mother to sister and back again, falling silent.

Mrs. Harding put starch in her tone. "They will meet, but not this afternoon."

Making a pleading face at Jessa, Tori carefully drew the door shut again.

She knew it was best to accept her mother's edicts since she was famously immovable. But hopeless causes did have their attraction. "Must I pretend no one is coming?"

"My dear, he won't ask. And if you tell him, he won't remember." She paused. "Do you think this is easy for me?"

It was horrible for everyone. But the rest of the family could only see Grandpapa's lapses. They didn't devote the time with him to be amazed by what he knew, to page through his herbarium books, to hear his stories of discovery. To acknowledge what remained.

Lowering her voice lest Jessa hear through the door, she said to her mother, "The more desperate you act, the more anxious she becomes. Whoever she finds, can't we just let it happen?"

"You don't let things happen. You make them. That is the lesson from Sir Charles's long career and your father's. The women of this house do the same."

Tori watched in consternation as her mother retreated down the hallway. A discussion of even such a thing as wardrobe turned so quickly to marriage!

In Jessa's room she found gowns thrown on the settee, the bed, the chest and the dressing table.

"I can't decide," Jessa admitted ruefully.

"You don't say."

Jessa waved her maid out of the room. "We'll manage, Ginny." To her sister: "You had words with Mama about Grandpapa again."

"Yes, and with the usual result." She brought the conversation back to Jessa's dilemma of the gowns, snatching up a cream-colored frock with yellow silk bodice. "Try this."

She ballooned the dress over Jessa's head, and her sister wiggled into it. As they stood in front of the mirror, Tori thought Jessa would make a kitchen apron look fine.

As Tori laced up the back, Jessa asked, "Is it too much?"

"Not in the least. It suits you so well!"

An array of opened shoe boxes littered the floor and bed, spilling out slippers in silk and creamy leather. Tori's own shoes were specially made, thick and black. But she cared nothing for fashion. Her hope was to someday achieve membership in scientific circles; in a learned society. The Linnean, for example, or The Royal Society. Women must someday be allowed into their ranks, but it would come only from a great accomplishment in natural history. And while that might appear unlikely, hadn't she received her training from the foremost botanist in Anglica?

"Mother says you will wear the mauve," Jessa said, still turning to and fro in front of the mirror.

"The dark blue, I think."

"But it is too plain, surely?"

Tori ignored her, searching for shoes that might match Jessa's dress.

"Perhaps Muir-Smith will prefer *you*."

Tori looked up from her position on the floor among the shoe boxes. "I wouldn't care if he did. Which he won't."

"Papa says Muir-Smith considers himself quite the naturalist. You'll have things to talk about."

"Well, I'll speak to him in Latin, then!"

After a pause, Jessa said, "You mustn't give up, Tori."

"Well, but you know what I want."

"Yes. You want to publish papers and collect your specimens."

"If they let me."

"Oh, but if you do it well, they have to let you."

It was sweet of Jessa to declare herself a supporter, but she had little grasp of the difficulties, first, in being a woman, and second, the controversial subject matter of Sir Charles's latest hypothesis. She and her grandfather would both be tarred by the same brush if the scientific disciplines balked at it.

"The idea goes harder than we had looked for."

"The idea," Jessa stoutly recited, "that magic can give benefit to science."

"Yes. That it is a way of knowing, just as science is, and while they may take different paths, they may each one cast light on the other."

"Who could take exception to such a gentle proposition?"

"Sir Charles's colleagues, at least a few. Some people take pride in recalcitrance."

"Narrow-minded and dreadful old men," Jessa murmured.

It would be mean-spirited to point out that their own family lacked somewhat of an open mind, so Tori only said, "Grandpapa says we must be sure to frame the argument so that it is the more readily accepted. The same as Darwin did with religion and science, befriending the archbishop, who is now a firm champion of the scientific approach."

Jessa eagerly concurred with this pleasant summation. "That's it exactly!"

Tori held up a pair of butter-yellow shoes. "These will suit, I think."

She knelt before the divan and helped Jessa into the slippers, lovely, but so impractical, of course.

Jessa rose, taking Tori's hands and bringing her up. "Thank you. This will be such fun." Her smile wobbled.

"You're nervous, aren't you?"

"Horribly."

"Sea monsters, by God," Colonel Harding said. "Glad to see you safely home, Edmond."

Mrs. Harding, commanding the divan which she shared with Jessa, poured tea for Muir-Smith. "Indeed, we must be thankful your ship did so well, Captain."

Captain Muir-Smith accepted the cup. "We left the altercation one mast short, but I think the kraken came off the worse for it." He had a knack for self-deprecating good humor, and used it to fine effect. No doubt it was the result of dozens of match-making teas, where he must be agreeable without presuming on a lady's affections.

"What do they look like, Captain?" Jessa asked. "As fierce as the drawings in the *Times?*"

"All drawn from vivid imagination, Miss Harding, but not an ounce of truth, I'm afraid," Muir-Smith responded. "The creatures are more like a snake than a whale, with strong jaws filled with teeth."

"Oh," Jessa said, overwhelmed by the story and Muir-Smith's sandy-haired good looks. Tori had to admit his army uniform was a bit dashing, but she wished Jessa had not given over to adoration so quickly. He was decidedly pleasant-looking, and both her sister and her mother clearly had their noses into the wind.

"Perhaps it goes as well on land, like an amphibian," Tori said.

Colonel Harding laughed. "This is a kraken, my dear, not a frog."

Muir-Smith pronounced, "Yet who can say whether they might venture ashore like seals? We know nothing of their natural habits." He turned back to Colonel Harding. "Your daughter has a fair point."

Tori noted how the captain was at pains to make everyone feel well-regarded. She hoped that Jessa would not make too much of his easy pleasantry. Her father caught Tori's eye, not bothering to hide a small smile of pride.

Turning to Muir-Smith, he said, "I'm glad to see you none the worse for the wear, Edmond." A moment's silence swept the room. Colonel Harding had informed the family of the death of Muir-Smith's brother, a navy officer lost in a kraken battle last year. "We must welcome the Bridge. The beasts can't sink *that*, by God. It will last the ages, make no mistake."

Muir-Smith murmured, "It's a marvel of engineering."

Colonel Harding accepted a slice of cake from Mrs. Harding. "Bharata reachable by coach and wagon! Engineers are now foremost in science, and Henry Culp the most brilliant among them. I attended his knighting at Buckingham." He shook his head. "A thousand miles, and all on pontoons."

Jessa slid a glance at her mother, fretting that a topic to which she could not contribute was not yet exhausted.

"The key insight," Muir-Smith said, "was to create the understructure of wood—heavily treated against rot—while the surface is girded with iron."

Heedless of Mrs. Harding's pointed look, Colonel Harding went on, "I've heard some surmise that the Bridge permits magic to flow unnaturally in our direction."

Muir-Smith nodded. "The altercation in Londinium."

Tori did wonder if magic passed over the Bridge as a natural phenomenon, or if magical practitioners found the great Bridge inimical to their interests and were inspired to use it as a road for mischief.

She ventured, "We have seen more contagions since the Bridge opened."

Muir-Smith turned a surprised look in her direction. "There are always fanatics. Some of them look on everything foreign as contamination. But theirs is a hopeless cause. The princely states depend on Anglic trade."

"I beg your pardon, Captain," Tori said, "but do not some people find an over-matched cause fuels their resolve?"

He frowned. "The resolve of so few can hardly shake our purpose."

"But perhaps we might take the trouble to learn their doctrine, lest our recalcitrance makes us near-sighted."

"I think it is not *we* who are near-sighted, Miss Harding."

Into the subsequent gaping pause Mrs. Harding interjected, "Oh, but let us go to pleasanter things!"

Father clapped his hand on his thigh, saying, "You must stay to dinner, Edmond, and we'll hear more of your adventures."

"I certainly hope," Mrs. Harding was swift to say, "we may enjoy your company for another day. Can your regiment spare you?"

Muir-Smith set down his plate. "I'm hard-pressed to imagine a more delightful respite, Mrs. Harding, but I fear I'm expected in Londinium."

"But we must hear your Bharata stories! The girls are counting on it."

"Olivia, the man has his duties." Colonel Harding stood up. "I'll have Jackson bring my walking boots, and we'll stroll down to the meadow, Edmond, if you like."

Jessa bit her lip in dismay but her mother could hardly argue.

While Colonel Harding went out to change, and with the gathering ready to adjourn, Jessa led the captain to the bow window overlooking the garden.

Tori and her mother were left with the remnants of tea. Mrs. Harding would not stand yet, for fear Tori would abandon her demure pose on the wing-backed chair and go clomping about the room.

"A shame we are not to hear Bharata stories," her mother murmured.

"I don't doubt he has an excess of them," Tori murmured back.

"And we should be most grateful if he stayed to share them." Mrs. Harding lowered her voice even further. "Tori dear, try to be agreeable."

She allowed herself to be schooled. This was Jessa's chance. And she supposed Muir-Smith could not be blamed for his airy confidence in Anglica's *open mind*. Restless, she stood up and made for the bookcase, ignoring Mrs. Harding's irritated glance. She would have thought that by now her mother would be reconciled to having a daughter who made noise when she walked.

She reached for an early favorite of hers, *Frogs, Newts and Salamanders of Halifax County*. Turning the pages, she looked at the pen and ink illustrations.

"Sketched by the author, do you think?" Muir-Smith stood at her side, looking at the drawing of a salamander.

His return had taken her by surprise. "Oh no, Mabry hired an artist. This illustration is lovely, is it not?"

"I never thought a salamander lovely."

"But pray look closer, Captain. See how close the legs are to resembling flippers. Mr. Darwin says that the species transmutate, and here one can well imagine it." She glanced up at him. "You are familiar with the theory?"

"Somewhat. It is far to go. Do you hold with Mr. Darwin, Miss Harding?"

"Grandpapa and I do, indeed. How else account for the varieties, unless you believe God took the time to work out flippers and feet."

"*Deus crevait*," he said.

"Yes, God created, but He must have created things to transmutate!" She looked at him with a slightly higher regard. "You know your Latin, sir."

"A few phrases, no more. Your father says you have the language."

"Sir Charles insisted that I learn the language of science. Is it not singular, Captain, that such a great civilization that could have spoken Latin passed from our continent as though it had never been?"

"Indeed, I have often thought the same. I've joined expeditions to dig for artifacts." He shrugged. "A hobby of mine, along with natural science. I see that the latter is yours as well."

"Oh, sir, no one trained by Sir Charles could possibly think it a hobby!" A glance to the divan, and she found both her mother and Jessa staring at her and no doubt hoping she would not resume her argument. "You may borrow the portfolio if you like, Captain."

She lurched away from the bookcase, leaving Muir-Smith with the dilemma of whether he must prove his interest by borrowing the book or not. He put it down. So much for natural history.

Colonel Harding appeared at the hall door. "Ready, then, Edmond?" The barking of the dogs echoed through the hall where Jackson kept them from charging through the front door.

Muir-Smith bowed to the three Harding women, and followed Colonel Harding out of the room, perhaps relieved to be free, if Tori read him aright.

When they heard the front door close, a flushed Jessa exclaimed, "Oh my."

"Indeed," Mrs. Harding said, beaming.

3

In the end, Colonel Harding persuaded Edmond Muir-Smith to spend the night, offering his personal carriage for an early morning departure. That settled, the evening had progressed from pudding to port wine and thence to backgammon. Jessa was holding up well, conversing without fawning and Captain Muir-Smith showing himself quite charming to Jessa.

Of course this stasis could not last with Mrs. Harding in the room. We must make things happen, after all. Thus it was that her mother maneuvered herself to the piano and the singing began.

Tori was beginning to enjoy the evening, producing a harmony under Jessa's soprano. "Splendid, Miss Harding," Muir-Smith exclaimed.

It was startling how much the compliment meant, this merely polite expression from a guest—unless he had meant it for the other Miss Harding. But a few more songs and Tori's voice had quite warmed up, until she felt she could sing all night.

"And now a dance!" Mrs. Harding announced, turning her fingers to a waltz.

After papa took a turn around the floor with Jessa, it was Muir-Smith's turn. He cut a fine figure in the turning waltz, and Jessa was grace itself. They pirouetted around each other, a swirling mixture of hot red uniform with its braid and buttons, the cream colored gown…

By the time the couple had completed one circuit of the gaming room, Tori had excused herself and stood outside in the hallway, her skin flaming, thoughts black. She stood with her back to the door, listening to the pounding piano, feeling a strange pressure in her chest.

Jackson was nearby. "Miss, is anything needed?"

"No," she exclaimed. "Nothing." Then softening, "We have all we need, Jackson, thank you."

Furiously, she rushed across the atrium and down the side hallway. Reaching the back door she found her cloak hung on its habitual rung. Pausing, she stretched out her leg and drew back her skirt to view the despised left foot. Why did she have a malady such as this that must mark her entirely? One could not expect an answer to such a question, but really, *why?*

Throwing her cloak over her shoulders, she yanked the ties into a knot.

She pushed out through the back door heading toward the greenhouse cottage. It was an implacable truth that her swaying gait would make a mockery of the dance. It could not be otherwise, and perhaps it was better thus. If her mother had not despaired of her domestic future, there would have been dancing and music lessons and the social season, with no time for Latin and taxonomy, chemistry and curating. How could one exchange the exhilarating precincts of natural history for marriage's stale round?

Always in her grandfather's company, she had understood that her calling was for greater things. She went to him now.

The greenhouse study was empty. A sheet of manuscript was loaded into Grandpapa's prized new machine, a Remington type-writing device. His treatise on the golden lotus was now up to page forty-four, she noted. Next to it, lay an open herbarium volume. She recognized the specimen at once, its golden petal long since faded to the color of sherry. *Nelumbo aureus.*

The petal had been cut in two to occupy adjacent pages. And still it was only a partial cutting. Sir Charles estimated that the whole golden lotus must be at least five feet in diameter, surely the largest flower in the world. To watch it unfurl must be a wonder of the earth, and indeed, in Bharata their religionists said that the flower's emergence from the sacred ocean was like the rising of the sun.

Behind her, the door opened. Anna stood on the library threshold. "Pardon, Miss, but Sir Charles was here, so I thought."

"No, Anna. He must have gone to bed."

"Pardon, but I can't find him anywhere, Miss. I been looking."

Tori now gazed about the room and saw that the drapes were thrown open. She went to the window overlooking the sycamore trees, finding the latch not fully closed. A sliver of wind spilled through the gap. She pressed the latch into place.

Turning back to the maid, she said, "I'll find him. Thank you for letting me know."

With Anna gone, Tori went out by the front door of the greenhouse and entered the pruned-back perennial garden, pulling her cape close against gusts of wind. Piano music trickled out from the parlor. Light poured through the windows of the great house faintly highlighting the sycamore trees. Empty.

She hurried past the gardener's cottage—dark since he and his wife were on spring holiday—and on to the stables. In her rush, she produced a rolling gait that she had grown quite accustomed to. A few drops of rain needled in on the wind. Her grandpapa could be anywhere, and it was very cold, even for February.

With the great house now far enough behind to prevent hearing, Tori called for her grandfather, receiving no answer. He could be anywhere, but surely he had not gone so far. She should sneak back and take the rear stairs lest anyone think she had run recklessly outdoors in the conviction that Sir Charles had begun wandering. He was surely in his room now. However, just then she spied a gleam in the distance—a lantern—perhaps in the apple orchard. She hurried on, scrambling over the stile in the split log fence and into the barley pasture, undulating and sere in the moonlight. Clouds scudded and stacked above her, bringing harder rain and flickers of lightning. By its sickly light, she saw her way through the stubble.

A lantern flashed again among the trees. Following the light, she entered the orchard and spied her grandfather immediately. He was dressed for an evening's work at the cottage, without hat or overcoat. The wind whipped at his hair and his cravat had come undone, flapping at his throat.

Turning around and around under the fruit trees, he held the lantern aloft, and cried out, "You would have lost it all! All! I did what I had to, what I thought was best."

Oh, he was raving. The image stabbed at her most forcefully, her grandfather raising his lantern, talking to trees. Oh, Grandpapa… but he would catch his death, she must guide him back, and quickly.

Turning about, still looking above, receiving the now pelting rain in his face, he shouted, "Easy to make judgments now! But were you there? Were you? It was war, I tell you. The forest would have taken it, taken it all!"

As she came into his lantern light, he looked at her as though he didn't recognize her. "Grandpapa. What are you doing?"

His hair was matted down, his top coat slicked to his frame, so much thinner than she had realized.

"All of you," he muttered in her direction. "You all stand in judgment."

Her cloak was soaked through, lying upon her back like a saturated pelt. If she was this cold, he must be frightfully exposed. "Let us go back!"

"Back!" he scoffed. Staggering away, he strode farther into the grove, gesturing wildly. "Look at this orchard!" He held up his lantern. "Do you see apples? No, you do not. But when they come in their season, how do they know what to do and when?"

Plunging after him, she tried to take his arm, but he evaded her.

He stalked on, deeper into the orchard, under the arbor of branches. They were no drier for that; the rain crept down in a steady progression from a thousand twigs. "They have their green ways, *piari,* their own knowledge."

Here in the midst of the storm his voice grew calm and pedantic. "The ways of natural science. Yet science is full of mystery. We search for truths, but we are often wrong, pursuing dead ends. Is it not credible that God has given us magic to ease the path? That if we combine the disciplines, we shall know more than with each one separately?"

"Yes, Grandpapa, of course you are right. We shall write our paper!" For a moment the trees with their gnarly arms took on a decidedly purple cast. This was not a good place to be. "Pray come back, now," she said. "We'll catch our death."

His voice grew suddenly tender. "Don't be afraid," he said.

"No. But we must go home." She tugged on his arm. Amid the patter of rain, she thought she heard claws crabbing along a branch. "Please, Grandpapa!"

His mood swerving, he wrenched his arm away. "You want the safety of the old ways."

"No, Grandpapa, but pray let us leave!"

The lantern had given its last and the flame guttered out. In the darkness came his voice, calm and penetrating: "I think it has come for me."

She looked up in alarm. Above her the canopy was black, a greasy wet tangle.

"Do you not see it?"

The trees were masses of tossing black branches, but as they swayed, after-images of purple remained. She whispered, "It is something strange, but I know not what. The colors…"

Suddenly she was in a very great hurry to be away. This place could hide any mayhem the thing had in mind. They must get into the open. She snatched the dead lantern from Sir Charles and let it drop to the ground.

Though the house was too far to see, she took her grandpapa's elbow, and pulled him in the direction of the meadow. "Hurry," she urged him, practically dragging him along.

At the edge of the trees, there interposed a gully that she had not crossed to get there. She could hear its runoff sluicing through. Heedless of the muddy bank, she descended with Sir Charles in tow, but he slipped, landing in the water.

"Help over here! Help!" she cried.

"*Piari*," he said as he sat in the mud. "There is decorum to be observed in the Society."

Crouching, she helped Sir Charles stand and they clambered up the other side, thoroughly begrimed. She looked about her, concerned now whether he could walk back unaided. "Help in the orchard!" she called out again, even while despairing of being heard.

A "halloo" from across the pasture; they had been found. Anna must have alerted her father after all.

She and Sir Charles held on to each other, managing between them to make progress across the meadow. Over there, swaying lanterns pricked the darkness. The two of them staggered on in the increasingly heavy rain, Grandpapa leaning heavily on her arm. He stopped now and then to look behind, as though expecting the shadowy owl to come bursting out of the apple trees, claws extended.

Oh! Here was someone coming with a lantern, someone looming large in a great oiled cloak. It was Captain Muir-Smith.

Seeing them, he hurried forward. "Miss Harding! Are you all right?"

"Yes, we are… we are… Please help Sir Charles."

Muir-Smith put one arm around Sir Charles, while with his other hand holding the lantern aloft, he gave his elbow to Tori.

"They send magic," Sir Charles cried amid the exertion of walking. "Does it go over the Bridge, do you think?"

"We shall get you home and dry, sir," Muir-Smith said, "it's not far now."

Sir Charles turned querulous. "I said, is it over the Bridge, or is it not?"

Struggling on, Muir-Smith said, "I know not, sir, but you'll do better with a sip of brandy and a good fire." They had come to the stile in the fence. Muir-Smith passed the lantern to Tori and effortlessly lifted Sir Charles over.

As he did so, Tori looked back to the orchard.

In a trembling flash of lightning, the orchard filled with light. But it was not an orchard any longer. Each tree branch was replaced with lances, or skewers, long and thin. They spread out in vase-like formation from the trunks, pointing in all directions, gleaming blue and gray and purple; a horrifying transmutation.

Sir Charles caught a glimpse of this—of something—and grimaced, his face taking on a reflection of faint purple. Oh, were the grotesqueries never to end?

Deposited on the other side of the stile, Sir Charles yanked his arm away from the captain. "'Tis magic. But one has to *look*. You're not one who looks, that is plain!"

Staring at the altered trees in dread, Tori turned away and clambered over the stile, eager for a barrier between her and the orchard, even if only a log fence.

Muir-Smith said, "Can you take his arm? I fear he is quite chilled through. Calm him, if you can."

"He doesn't need to be calm." She looked at the captain, and his sturdy common sense grated exceedingly. "Can't someone listen to him?" she demanded. "There is magic over there!" She pointed wildly, and Muir-Smith looked, but now all was in shadow, devoid of lightning, without the lances. Frustrated and shaken, she exclaimed, "There is magic in the world. But you all refuse to see—it's just as he said!" To her dismay, she found herself quite undone. Thankfully the rain hid the tears that now ran down her cheeks.

Muir-Smith reached out to her, saying, "First, out of the rain, Miss Harding." He took her forearm and turned her toward the path, gathering a now belligerent Sir Charles firmly by the waist.

"Sensible girl. Resist the bully!" Sir Charles cried. "Teach a soldier about courage, by God!"

"We will stake our claims upon courage or not," Muir-Smith said, "but we will do so in the parlor. I must insist." And with that, he had them both in tow. Tori acquiesced, embarrassed at her outburst. She almost caught the captain by the arm to say, *Look, Captain. Look. Let down your guard and* see, *really see!* But digging for buried truths was but a hobby to him.

Sir Charles growled, "The *parlor*, he says. The *parlor*..."

Now more lights, with Jackson running across the front lawn toward them and Papa just rounding the gardener's shed. Tori was highly aware that the sight greeting them was mad: she and Sir Charles spattered with mud and brambles, drenched to the bone and shivering.

Tori gripped Muir-Smith's arm, desperate to salvage what she could of the affair. "Pray do not mention *magic*, Captain... that Sir Charles said it was in the orchard."

Her grandfather teetered.

"I will carry you, sir," Muir-Smith said to him.

"Keep away, by God!" Sir Charles shouted.

But taking a few steps forward, Sir Charles collapsed, caught by the captain. He carried Sir Charles toward the house.

Her father was at her side. "Astoria. Why didn't you call me? My dear, come inside." His arm went around her shoulder and he would have led her in Muir-Smith's wake, but she caught a glimpse of something in the cottage window. An outline, moving.

"I left a lantern in the cottage. I'll be in the parlor directly!" She peeled away before it could be suggested that she send a maid.

Hoping her father wouldn't follow her—she did not want her lie about the lantern exposed—she rushed toward the cottage.

Entering the library, she quickly found the lantern and lit it with a packet of strikables. The room was empty. She went through to the greenhouse. Round the long trestle tables with their pots and trays of seedlings, she searched most thoroughly. Nothing but *Solanum lycopersicum,* tomatoes, the various species of *Lathyrus*, sweet pea, and the hundreds more of Sir Charles's nursery.

Returning to the library, she stopped in surprise before the herbarium book. There was a sprinkling of soil on the page. Then she noticed that the Remington was no longer loaded with a sheet of manuscript as it had been before. The monograph lay to one side. She picked up the top page, page forty-four, and stared at the corner. It was torn and wrinkled, as though someone had not known how to extract the page from the roller.

Her stomach had been slowly twisting and now wrung into a deeper clench.

Tori saw the tracks, faint but unmistakable. Across the table, heading to and from the direction of the window, were wet tracks, four inches across, of three toes forward, one back.

Using a cloth, she wiped everything clean. There were marks left behind on the wood. Faint scratches from the claws could not be rubbed out. Hands shaking, heart still thrumming in her chest, she went to the window to secure it, pulling the latch down—unnecessarily, for it was already closed.

A noise at the outside door caused her a most acute start. Colonel Harding stood there.

He surveyed the library which he did not often visit. "Why didn't you summon me? I may be fairly useless in the lives of my young ladies, but I like to think I would be suited to running across a pasture with a lantern."

"I thought he was just in the rose garden, and then I went a little further..." Her voice was hoarse and shaking.

"Across the barley fields to the apple orchard. In the pelting rain."

"I should not have done," she whispered. "I apologize, Papa."

"No need, my dear." He put his arm through hers and led her out through the cottage and into the great house where Prue and her mother's maid were waiting with blankets and a great fuss.

"Grandpapa..." she croaked, with all that was left of her voice.

"He's bundled off to bed, miss," Prue said. "Rest will do him a world of good, I'm sure."

Tori determined that she would keep a vigil by her grandfather's bed tonight. Something had entered his library a few moments ago through a window that had been latched. It had come in dripping rainwater and bits of bark. She believed it to have been the owl.

But whatever it was, it could read.

$$\sim\!\partial\!\ell\!\sim$$
4
$$\sim\!\partial\!\delta\!\sim$$

Mahindra had not been in the Gangadhar *Mahal* for many years. Why would anyone come here when the *rana* himself did not see fit to banish creeping vines and monkeys from its halls, and had not looked upon it since his grandsire's day? In fifty years the Gangadhar had seen little but ghosts.

Old Dulal leaned upon his stick. "This way, *baba*."

He led the way through the Elephant Gate, broad enough for two bull elephants to enter side by side through the great arch. At once the ripe heat of the day fell away, leaving Mahindra's bare arms and feet cold.

Passing through the inner gate, set at right angles from the outer in the ancient ploy to pick off assaulting armies, they entered the antechamber, called the Night Pavilion, with its vaulted ceiling inlaid with thousands of mirrors. Though now the mirrors were dim with grime, in the old days it was said that at night a single candle could light the entire chamber.

From the upper floors came the hooting of monkeys amplified by the marble pathways and galleries. Dulal paused; their presence was an intrusion in a place the monkeys had long had to themselves.

"Show me," Mahindra urged.

The old servant looked pained, but led on.

Dulal need not fear admonishment from Mahindra. He had led a righteous life and had done no evil, except to conceal for so long an event of great import.

It was a deep palace, yet not dark, with halls narrow enough that light from the windows on each side met in the middle. Thus exhibits placed in the middle of the hallways could be shown to good effect. In the old *rana's* time—before Mahindra's, but not before Dulal's—the museum's treasures had been displayed in a spine of elaborate wooden cabinets. Before it had been a museum, it had been an elaborate *zenana*. And before that, the first fortress of Kathore, in the days of glory, before strangers came among them and explained how Bharata must be improved.

Mahindra knew it was his personal defect to prefer the past. He must not dwell upon what had been. He had become a renunciate in the hopes of escaping the past, and also of surrendering the future. It left one with a small space indeed: the present moment. He had lived within this fleeting, narrow slot for fifteen years and been comforted. Now in the Gangadhar, Mahindra felt his blood rushing in a state of excitation. Dulal's tale of seeing the divine flower had aroused an old longing.

They entered the west gallery, one of four that comprised the Gangadhar and enclosed the central garden. In these galleries and those of the matching floor above had been displayed the plant and animal treasures of Nanpura. The mahogany cabinets on their carved legs still remained, some fallen like wounded deer, some invaded by vines crawling from the courtyard garden.

The setting sun glared onto the arched ceilings, the hall mosaics and the wooden cases. It was a time of spirits, this last hour of day, when shimmering presences mixed with the earthly. Mahindra could almost see the interloper, the white man in his frocked coat, slipping through these marble halls like a demon parting a virtuous woman's thighs, and taking possession of something so much more valuable than a maidenhead: a piece of the very body of the golden lotus, if Dulal was to be believed.

"Here, *baba*," Dulal said. "This is the one."

The mahogany case gleamed like a polished bier. Mahindra stepped forward as his servant carefully slid open the drawer, wide and deep. A shudder came over Mahindra and he made *namaste* to the place where the petal had lain. He had not foreseen how the sight of the thing would overcome him.

Seeing this gesture, Dulal fell to his knees and sobbed. "*Baba*, it is gone, gone."

Mahindra put his hand on the old man's shoulder. "It has been gone many years." Hearing this, Dulal bent low, head in hands, though Mahindra had meant to comfort him.

The drawer lay open, its very emptiness giving rise to imaginations.

Once, in the days of the museum, a servant of the former *rana*—a prince who coveted a royal collection of the wonders of his realm—this servant had found a very large yellow flower. He must have taken a cutting. Had the man been so ignorant as to not recognize that it came from a golden lotus, never seen in the world of men? Did he not know that when Prajapati desired to evolve the universe, the cosmic waters grew a thousand-petaled lotus, golden in color? If the specimen had issued from the golden lotus, then the holy flower existed. Somewhere, even at this moment, it grew.

And Mahindra must have it.

Long ago the Anglic scholar had come looking in the Gangadhar for precisely that specimen. What did he know? Why had he come here, out of all the hidden places of Bharata? The specimen was gone, but surely the plant itself must lie enfolded in these sacred hills. The *rana* must hear of this surmise. He must be made to pause in his boar hunts and consider what this gift from the gods might mean.

Mahindra helped Dulal to his feet. "Come, my son. We shall not weep. We will not speak of this to any man. But I see a time when we will have holiness in our presence once more." Dulal nodded in a combination of misery and hope which was, after all, the condition of man's life.

They reemerged by the Elephant Gate into the hot dusk. As Dulal led the way across the great square to the shrine, washer women, potters and mahouts made *namaste*, and Mahindra blessed them. Among them, other *sadhus*, come to perform devotions at the shrine. They were wild-looking, with uncut hair and ochre on their faces. Some *sadhus*—he did not know which ones—hating the Bridge and its wide road of foreign influence, meddled in terrorism, bringing their bloody magics to Londinium. But their displays were futile, conjured from timid austerities. It took more than throwing pebbles to tame the Anglic lion. Mahindra made *namaste* to them as he passed.

Under the balcony in the deep shade of the gallery, something moved. Ah, here was Sahaj, the *rana's* son. Alongside him, his pets, the white tigers. He had raised the females from kits, and they loved him. But Mahindra had seen Sahaj overcome with hashish, lecherous with wine and cruel to the servants. Mahindra had often pondered this *yuvraj* prince, the next in line. With proper instruction, might Sahaj become a worthy successor to his royal father? Mahindra looked up to the balcony where the *rana* sometimes gave audience. Though robust to outward appearances, he was unaware of what Mahindra perceived, that he had growing within him a deadly canker.

In the time remaining, the *rana* must be persuaded to a great undertaking. And the Anglic scholar must be made to help them, whether he wished to or not. Assuredly he would not wish to. The *rana* must play his part, and perhaps his son Sahaj. So many threads. To hold them all, one must perform austerities.

His steps slowed as he neared the shrine. Within, the skewers waited for him, resting on a silver tray. He was no stranger to them; they knew he was not timid.

~

February 12, 1857
Francis Lyell, President
Royal Society
Somerset House
Strand, London

My Dear Sir,
I have just returned from the duty which you set upon me, to visit our esteemed colleague, Sir Charles Littlewood. I must report that pneumonia has quite conquered his lungs, and the family does not have great hope for a recovery.

It quite saddens me to report that Sir Charles is a man much reduced in capacity. To hear him take his usual interest in botanical subjects and yet stray so far from reason gave me a most difficult hour. Yet, in consideration of Sir Charles's interest in publishing a scientific paper, I have taken what measure I am able of his thesis. Sir, it is untenable.

I feel that I should produce a more coherent report if I explain in some detail how our meeting unfolded. I arrived at Glyndehill in late afternoon and was met with great civility by Colonel Terrence Harding, Sir Charles's son-in-law. I found the household much subdued, as Mrs. Harding led me to Sir Charles's room. There, to my surprise, I found Sir Charles sitting up in bed furiously writing in a notebook and surrounded by papers. At his bedside, his granddaughter sat at a small desk and poked at a Remington machine. Sir Charles welcomed me warmly and after introducing me to his granddaughter, Astoria, the two of us proceeded to renew our acquaintance with talk of the Society and the latest presentations.

At this time Miss Harding made bold to mention that the monograph summarizing Sir Charles's views was now almost ready and it only needed another pass through the machine before it would be complete.

With this introduction of the subject, Sir Charles commenced to press me hard on his ideas of spiritualist methods in pursuit of science. He came to the idea during his early expedition to Bharata. It was the first time I had heard him recount the details of his adventure which, to be brief, included many interviews with native holy men who had knowledge of local botanicals. Traveling through the northern regions of Bharata, he encountered a priest-practitioner who showed him paintings of a very large lotus, a mythical representation. (The natives set great store upon the lotus's growth habits of beginning in watery mire and rising to the surface and the light of day—a pleasing conceit for attaining spiritual wisdom.) This priest, however, claimed that the flower was not merely a religious idea, but actually existed. He went on to confirm what Sir Charles had also heard from others on his expedition, that touching the plant itself conferred visions, and here is the heart of it: visions that bestow useful knowledge.

The bush priest claimed that the Rana of Nanpura had such a plant in his possession. A long journey south led Sir Charles to a museum at the Kathore fortress in Nanpura province. He befriended the prince who owned the museum, but found curated there only one petal of a yellowish flower.

Now Miss Harding brought forward two herbarium pages showing a bisected petal that bore all the hallmarks of Nelumbo. *Its proportions did indeed suggest a lotus of enormous size. Sir Charles concluded it was a new species. He named it* Nelumbo aureus. *But he was unable to determine whether such plants still existed in the wild. Events called him away; his chance to drive home his thesis was therein lost.*

I was far from ready to believe in the specimen's mystical properties. I ventured that it was an exceptional philosophical assertion, and one that might have difficulty conforming to scientific proof.

Most difficult, Sir Charles conceded. He seemed ready to say more, but a fit of coughing rendered him prostrate for a time. While Sir Charles settled, Miss Harding asked whether any harm would be done to entertain a new question in scientific circles, for if unusual questions could not be considered, would it not dampen scientific inquiry?

I assured her that no harm could come of questions, but I explained that the scientific method is based upon the proposition that experimental proceedings can be reliably conducted.

She readily agreed, suggesting that a search for the plant was necessary in order to discern its properties. Of course such an investigation would need a champion, and sadly it could not be Sir Charles at the present time.

To my dismay I realized that she was indirectly asking for Society sponsorship of an expedition.

Miss Harding read my reaction quite accurately and suggested that it would depend on the Society finding merit in Sir Charles's new theory and that must begin with publication of the monograph.

Obviously, Sir Charles had coached her well. It pained me not to show more keenness for the proposition. "Is not the thesis," I said, "plainly put thus: that there are magical paths of knowing that lead to empirical truth?" She agreed that was a fair summary.

"The problem, then, Miss Harding, is that magic and science contradict each other, one being subjective, and one impartial, dependent upon natural law."

Miss Harding responded. "As to magic being subjective, that is the very question we must pursue!"

She pointed out that Bharata convulsions in Anglica proved supernatural powers existed. While acknowledging the truth of this, I countered that it might be too great a leap to ask that we, as Anglics, engage such powers ourselves, and yet a greater stretch to posit that those powers might be useful to science.

The room was thrown into late afternoon gloom. Sir Charles was exhausted from our conversation, and I saw that he was saddened by my failure to be won over. The great man wanted a last legacy; I saw it most clearly. I assured him that his place in history was undoubtedly quite secure.

As I took my leave, Sir Charles extracted a promise from me to read his abstract and make comments when the final copy was ready.

When I took my leave, Miss Harding accompanied me down the hall. She manages with a skeletal infirmity which limits her gait. I do not doubt that her energies have been diverted from more feminine pursuits to natural history.

On the way to the drawing room she asked if I would send my comments on the monograph to her, as she handled many details of Sir Charles's investigations. When I looked at her with some surprise, she assured me that she had received training of her grandfather and was conversant in the chemistry and structure of flowering plants. I was saddened to intuit that her hopes had settled upon a scientific career, an ambition that can only prove an embarrassment.

I remember her final pleading words: "What greatness could not be achieved once the laborious workings of the scientific method are abetted by magical paths of knowledge?"

"Miss Harding," I said, "pray do not distress yourself over these matters. We will discuss scientific principles in the proper forums. You must trust to learned men to weigh the merits of ideas."

I think she took heart from this.

Should you wish further details of my meeting with Sir Charles, I am at your disposal. We shall read this paper, of course. But I fear it will prove to be a reproof to a man whose reputation must rest upon his past accomplishments, not the new.

I remain, yours faithfully,
Allen Goodwin

$\sim\!\mathcal{O}\!\mathcal{C}\!\sim$
5

"Ah, *babaji*, you know how it pains me to deny you."

The *Rana* of Nanpura stood in his royal quarters as his servant, standing on a drum, wound his turban.

Mahindra bowed in a show of submission. In his heart, though, desire raged. For the first time in many years Mahindra wanted something. It was an intimate, startling thing, one that would not lie still.

Even dressed in simple attire for his hunt today, Prince Uttam looked every inch a ruler. He was a big man, broad-chested, with a manly belly filling out the *achkan* that extended to his knees. In contrast, Mahindra had but half of his prince's weight, as befitted a *sadhu* who had long ago tasted his last *jellabies*. Though the two men had been raised together in the palace and had been friends from boyhood, their paths had always been different: Uttam raised to rule, and Mahindra, the son of a chamberlain, destined to study.

Escorted by more servants, they walked to the courtyard where the hunting party awaited. Mahindra murmured, "My prince, does not this flower portend the favor of the gods?" They must be careful not to mention within the servants' hearing *which* flower, lest rumors take hold that the holy golden lotus had been sighted. Religious fervor over the lotus would fit well into Mahindra's plans, but not yet. Of course, Uttam had been told of the holy flower's likely tangible existence. But now his first reaction of amazement had cooled to doubt and perhaps fear.

Mahindra went on, "The flower can be our banner. The princes throughout the land—even the lowly villagers—will stir once they have this proof of their nobility."

Uttam frowned. "Must we have a flower to be noble?"

"For a great nation, a symbol is needed."

"Ah. Your high enterprise." Uttam cut an ironic look at his friend. "Which you propose to make *my* enterprise: a Bharata under one *rana*, without Anglic soldiers. Without, too, Anglic mechanicals from which we prosper." Uttam had affection for the trains, clocks, masted ships and the steam shovels of his copper mines.

Mahindra ventured, "We prosper. But our sons abandon their parents' ways. They play cricket and are strangers to our temples and our gods. The Anglic teachers are a hidden army, opening the gates to the minds of our children." The *rana* allowed no Anglic schools at Kathore, though the school rooms spread through the province like a pox. In cities like Chidiwal and Poondras and across the land, young men rushed to assume Anglic ways, shaming their ancestors and mocked, Mahindra knew, by the very men whom they wished to emulate.

Uttam said, "You yourself went to Anglic teachers, *babaji.* Now you scorn them?"

Mahindra raised his hand in acknowledgment. "I was young." In those days he had thought he would prosper by knowing the foreigners' language, the foreigners' ways. He had loved all things Anglic, to his shame.

Uttam cut a glance at him. "My friend, are you hounded by the things that the Anglics took from you? Is it for Nanpura or yourself that we must challenge the Anglic lion?"

"Never for myself, Highness." His narrow life held no room for such bloated things as revenge.

"Forgive me *babaji*, but a *raja* must weigh all."

"My prince, it is time for our great enterprise. If the gods bless us with the flower of legend. One word from you, and we shall pursue it."

They had come to the palace quadrangle where the *rana's* hunting party was gathered. Uttam stepped into the heavy sun, looking up to the balcony where, behind the fretted screen, his wife Kavya had come to watch her husband depart. He smiled at her, pleased that she had arisen from her couch. Ah, Mahindra thought, the poor *ranee*. Her sons were disappointments, but one of her daughters was the delight of her heart. She saw this daughter every day though a thousand miles separated them. Her *sadhus* conjured a fire dream, so that from her couch Kavya could gain the presence of her child. Sometimes it seemed to Mahindra that the whole of Bharata lay half-dreaming like Kavya.

It was time to awake.

The *rana* turned to the hunting party: the elephants rocking in their pickets, his guards armed with Anglic rifles, standing by their swift ostrich mounts. Upon seeing the prince, the great elephant Iravatha raised his trunk and then laid it upon the ground, in a gesture very like a bow. Uttam smiled at his favorite, one of the largest elephants of Nanpura, with magnificent ears which could meet when brought together across his face. Uttam strode out to Iravatha.

"My prince," Mahindra murmured. "You have not said."

Placing his hand on Iravatha's trunk, Uttam gazed into Mahindra's eyes. "I say. Only bring me the flower, *babaji*."

Mahindra bowed deeply. So it would be war. At last they would gut the Anglic lion. His heart soared. "Highness. May your glory never end."

The *rana* grunted in response. "May it not. But I would be happy for a fat boar."

Then, as Mahindra had arranged, Sahaj appeared through the side gate, come to bid his father a profitable hunt. He wore an embroidered coat and silk trousers, looking more the *rana* than the father did. Mahindra had been clear with Sahaj that he was not to have the tigers, but here they were, padding softly at his side.

Seeing the tigers, Iravatha trumpeted and shied. The elephant thrust back down the knee which he had raised to let Uttam climb.

Uttam scowled. "Look, my foolish son gives me a bad beginning." Sahaj noted that his entrance had not been received favorably, and held back.

As the *mahout* calmed Iravatha, Mahindra murmured, "My prince, surely here is a young man who needs a worthy duty." Sahaj would be the one to lead the army, for Mahindra feared Uttam's fighting days were past.

"Duty," spat Uttam. "To spread his seed and multiply his bastards." Iravatha offered his knee once more and the *rana* climbed up to the howdah.

Mahindra looked up at him. "Highness, since Sahaj is the heir you prayed for, keep him closer to your side. Show the people that he has your favor. When the time comes, Sahaj will be a sword in your hand."

Uttam looked back at his son and this time nodded to a slight degree, bringing a smile of gratitude in return.

"Take him with you on the hunt, Highness. Let the people see him with you."

"No. My son wants the hunt to be easy. He would let his tigers stalk the boar." Uttam touched the side of Iravatha's face with his stick, and they moved forward, followed by three more elephants and a dozen fierce hunters on their birds.

Sahaj joined the *sadhu* in the courtyard. The tigers strained at their leashes, watching Mahindra with ebony eyes. Black stripes slashed their silver fur.

"You said he wanted to see me, but he did not," Sahaj muttered, resentful that his greeting had nearly been snubbed. The *yuvraj* prince just missed being handsome, with a too-round face and heavy eyelids.

"I did not say he wanted to see you, my son, but that he *needed* to." Mahindra almost put his hand on Sahaj's arm, but one of the tigers lifted her ears in full alert.

Sahaj scratched the head of the nearest cat. "He is afraid of my tigers."

"No, Iravatha is afraid of them. Do not confuse your father with his elephant."

Uttam was still a great leader. He had just proven that, giving permission for their noble mission to proceed.

I say. Only bring me the flower.

Soon.

∽

"Astoria." A gentle hand shook Tori's shoulder. Her mother's voice: "Wake up, Astoria. It's time."

Two candles pierced the darkness of Sir Charles's room, barely showing the outline of the bed and the figures gathered around. Tori sat bolt upright from the chaise lounge where she had dropped into a desperate sleep after watching two nights at her grandfather's side.

Dismay clutched at her. "He has not…"

"No dear," Mrs. Harding whispered, "but Doctor Seibert says he is going."

As Tori hurried to the bedside, Jessa gave up her chair, her eyes glistening with tears. Papa put his arm around Jessa's shoulders. Before he led her from the room, he said to Tori, "We have said our goodbyes, my dear. These last moments shall be yours." Mama pressed a hand onto Tori's arm and she and Dr. Seibert followed Colonel Harding out of the room.

Sitting at the bedside, Tori was unable to accept Sir Charles's demise, though she had known it was coming. That his spirit would vanish from her life was inexpressibly hard, and quite possibly, wrong.

"Oh, Grandpapa," she whispered.

She had had two weeks to regret that she hadn't roused the household to find him earlier the night of the storm. Papa had assured her that Sir Charles would have been caught in the downpour even a half-hour earlier, but she had relived the evening many times. Ever the gentleman, Captain Muir-Smith had said nothing of Sir Charles's outburst about magic in the orchard. A few days later he had sent to express his concern about Sir Charles's condition, a gesture by which Jessa set great store.

Tori held Grandpapa's thin hand. "Do you remember when we turned over the big rock in the pasture? So many worms! We calculated the weight of the mass of the earth's worms from the evidence in the field." In her mind's eye she saw Sir Charles in his impeccably cut frock coat, strolling with her through the barley field, exclaiming on the wonders of the vascular systems of trees and the mating habits of snails. "One million tons," she whispered.

"One point three million," came his rasping voice.

Startled, Tori leaned forward, pressing her hands around his. "Grandpapa!"

"So dark," he whispered. "You'll ruin your eyes."

She nudged the candle closer on the bed stand.

"It's not done yet," he said. "So much work…"

"I've finished the abstract, Grandpapa," she murmured past her swollen throat. "It's perfect. Sixty-eight pages."

Though his breath came in labored puffs, he gripped her hand tightly. "You shall count the world, *piari*. All the parts, even the magical. You… carry on."

"Oh, I shall try, Grandpapa."

"Don't let them… *seduce* you," he whispered. He fixed her with a bright, watery look. "Young men, young captains… but marriage… a state of slavery for such as you. Slavery!" A cough struggled up through his chest. "Do not let them take science from you. Promise me."

She had promised this so many times. The paths of science led to an infinite pursuit. There was no room for husbands who demanded a domestic manager. "Never, Grandpapa. I shall never marry."

She waited with him as he gathered his next effort to speak.

Finally, in a soft rasp, he said, "I have not told you all. My visions… of the lotus."

"Your visions?" Had he had experience of them himself?

"I was not careful," he whispered. "No gloves. I allowed its resins to… come into me. I saw truths."

Truths… oh, but which? "Surely you could say so in your monograph. Would it not be your strongest argument?"

"They would call it hallucination. No proof. Without proof, the owl marks us as ravers.…"

So he *had* seen it. "Grandpapa," she said tenderly, "what truths did you see?"

"Oh *piari*," he said, his voice warbling. "We cannot… tell all."

"Then just to me," she whispered, leaning in close.

He struggled to say something, but no sound came. Finally, with great effort came his whisper. "They. Stole. It."

"Stole what, grandpapa?"

"It. The…" He gestured vaguely behind her. His eyes fluttered closed, and his chest sank as though he had been exerting an effort he could now release. Oh, he was going.

"I love you," she whispered to him. "I shall always love you."

She felt that her devotion might hold him for a few moments more, seep into him and give him another few breaths. She could not imagine it otherwise, but his grip on her arm gradually subsided, then fell away.

"Not yet, Grandpapa. Pray stay awhile," she whispered, tears streaming. "Just a little while…"

He spoke no more. She put her hand on his chest, desperate to feel it rise. But he was gone.

For a long while she lay with her head on his chest, sobbing. She could not bear it should anyone came into the room, but they did not.

Finally she stood and smoothed the covers around his form, laying his arms gracefully along his sides. It was very hard to compose herself, but she did so, moving to the pitcher on the side table for a drink of water. But something was not right. She stopped in confusion by the typewriter stand. The abstract was gone. The neat stack of sixty-eight pages that had lain on the desk since she finished typing them two days ago had vanished. *They stole it.*

She looked around the room, her mind numb. The typewriting machine sat upon the small table; she was sure she had left the manuscript there. A terrible suspicion welled up, displacing for the moment the great passing she had just witnessed.

The hallway was dim, with only a few sconces lit by Jackson, who had rightly guessed this night would be long. Tori walked down the hall in a daze, moving to the narrow back stairs that, on the floor below, gave on to the garden walkway. She should announce Sir Charles's passing; Papa would be awake in his study, she knew. But down the stairwell she went, leaning heavily on the railing against the chance of tripping. Here on the servant staircase and she came upon Prue, coming up with a tray of leftovers.

"Miss?"

Tori paused, looking down on the servant. She blurted out, "Prue, Sir Charles has passed."

"Oh, Miss," the young servant said, forgetting in the bald moment of the death announcement how unlikely it was for her to receive such news from one of the Misses Harding.

Tori did not move. "I will miss him so."

"Oh Miss," Prue said again. "I'm right sorry. So terrible for the house and all."

"Yes, terrible." The understanding in Prue's eyes almost undid her, but she had no time for grief, not yet. She pressed against the railing and Prue managed to squeeze by.

The cold outside air let her breathe again. There was not a shred of light on the pathway, but she knew the way by heart and went through the greenhouse into the library, every step bringing deeper foreboding.

In the library, it was as she had feared. The herbarium book was gone. It, too, was stolen, just as Grandpapa had said.

Her mind churning with panic, Tori rushed out through the greenhouse and down the path toward the house.

When she put her hand on the latch of her father's study door, she closed her eyes, summoning a calming breath. Opening the door, she found her parents seated together in front of the hearth fire. Colonel Harding rose as she entered.

She blurted out, "I've been searching for the typed abstract that I left on the table in Grandpapa's room. Do either of you know where it is?"

No one spoke.

She forced her voice into a reasonable tone. "Have you seen it, Papa?"

Mrs. Harding said, "Astoria, dear, pray sit down." She gestured to the seat next to her.

"Papa?" Tori persisted.

He looked all of his fifty-seven years. "It cannot be published, Tori."

"Surely we may let the Royal Society decide that?"

Mrs. Harding said, "It's not his best work. Mr. Goodwin agreed."

"But, Mama, Mr. Goodwin has not *read* the paper. He gave me his word that he *would* read it."

Father held her gaze. "The paper will not be sent. Your mother and I have decided that Sir Charles's unfinished notes do not rise to the level of publication."

"But the abstract was *finished*, Papa."

He looked away. This would be their answer: silence. But she would make them utter the things they conspired to do. She stepped farther into the room. Her mother looked at her with that pleading look. *Sit down, be quiet, don't make a scene.* And: *Has he gone?* But that last was something she could withhold from them, and for a few more minutes she would.

"It is his last wish, Mama. To publish the Bharata paper. Can you claim to judge what is scientific and what is not?"

Colonel Harding frowned. "Tori, do not be rude."

"Is it rude to cast doubt on my mother's scientific understanding, when you both have discounted *mine*? Oh, but this is not about science, at all, is it? This is about society's regard and the family reputation."

"Your grandfather's reputation," Mrs. Harding shot back. "He spent his *life* in science and now you wish him to be known for *magic*?"

"But there *is* magic in the world!"

"The tools of bush priests and terrorists…"

Tori blurted: "But they pervert what could be useful, even noble!"

Colonel Harding shook his head. "Tori, please see reason. The Bharata theory can hardly prosper without Sir Charles present to rally scientific support. It's too far a leap."

They had not even considered that she might make a contribution. It was deeply mortifying. Tori glanced from one to the other. "Have you never imagined me having something of value to offer?"

"Whatever you do in science, Astoria," Mrs. Harding said, "it shall not be for that dreadful water lily."

"It is *not* a water lily. It's a genus unto itself. Let's be clear, as we brush aside Sir Charles's most cherished theory, just which plant we have concluded does not exist!"

Colonel Harding raised his chin in that way he had of bringing conversation to a close. "We will not have a scene, Tori. I'm afraid the matter is settled." He turned his back on her, gazing at the fire.

"How singular it is," she said, just to make sure there *would* be a scene, "that a man with only hours to live still dared so much. *He*, at least, was not afraid of controversy."

"*Was?*" her mother said, her voice faint.

Tori swung around. "Oh, he's dead, Mama. Didn't I say?"

"Tori!" her father barked. "Recollect yourself." Then, shaking his head: "I had thought better of you."

She could utter no apology. "Papa. Where is the lotus petal?"

She followed his gaze to the library table. There the herbarium book lay open, pages obviously torn out. Then Colonel Harding looked to the fire in the grate.

An intake of breath, and Tori rushed to the hearth, falling on her knees.

The fire leapt high over inches of hot coals, the skeleton of papers still visible in the inferno.

"Oh, no, oh no!" she cried. It was the petal, the abstract, everything. Lunging forward, she threw the fire screen aside. Where was the poker? There. She thrust her hand out to grab it, but now her father was dragging her away from the flames. The poker clattered on the hearth with a sound like the world cracking open.

Struggling, they were both on their knees. He held her as she writhed to get back to the hearth. "Tori," came his choked whisper.

She managed to yank away from him. "You couldn't wait for him to die. He knew that you had taken it. You gave him misery in his last hour. Oh, well done!" She staggered backward as she got to her feet, knocking against a side table, sending it crashing to the floor. Mrs. Harding had risen, reaching out for her daughter, her face stricken.

But Tori was backing up toward the door. It was too monstrous. Too much to bear, this hateful room. The smoking grate, its ghastly flames.

Her mother was crying. Tori shook her head. "How dare you cry for him! How dare you."

She turned and raced from the study, jolting from side to side as she reached the great staircase, and clambering up the stairs toward her room.

6

In the shade of the ancient fig tree, old Dulal took stock of his beloved garden.
At the entrance to the shrine of Vishnu was an open arched gateway painted
yellow and white. To the sides spread a low wall embracing the garden within
and the shrine at the rear. The care of this garden had been his duty for forty
years, but now the beds of jasmine and marigolds were desecrated by a gaping
hole, getting larger every day.

The workers who dug claimed they did not know the purpose of the hole.
Nor could Dulal ask the *sadhu*, for he was meditating within, having undertaken
high austerities these past six days.

What could be the reason for the hole?

A commotion in the square caught his attention and he watched as the *rana*
approached with his retinue. Dulal bowed low as Prince Uttam passed through
the gateway and proceeded into the shrine, leaving his courtiers and guards in
the mutilated garden.

Staring at the hole, Dulal feared its purpose, almost too terrible to
contemplate.

What had he set in motion? The *sadhu* had promised him he had not sinned,
but as wise as Mahindra was, he might be wrong. For fifty years Dulal had kept
his secret of the golden lotus—fearing the wrath of the old *rana* and then the
wrath of the new one. The petal was gone. It was Dulal's fault. For that he
might have lost his life. In the old days his wife had been still at his side, and

though they had been childless, he had loved her and their simple life together. This attachment caused him to be cowardly, afraid to divulge his failure.

And now retribution was on its way.

Did not wrong action pursue one through the karmic cycle? Did not the *ranee*, in her malady, pay for the sin of requiring her *sadhus* to undergo pain to produce the fire dream?

Dulal took his broom and resumed sweeping the paths—a task made more meritorious by its hopelessness. He served the *sadhu*. It might be enough.

But in his heart, he knew it was not.

Mahindra sat upon the platform, legs crossed beneath him. He had been sitting so long he could no longer feel the pain. Servants came in and out, sunlight alternated with dark, princes came and went. Sometimes devotees came to place a gift of a flower or trinket in his lap, where a white *dhoti* covered his legs. They believed that through such gifts they acquired spiritual merit, and this Mahindra also believed.

Now there was another worshipper.

"*Babaji*, it is enough."

Ah. The *rana*.

"You are so thin. You have few reserves for fasting. Six days, it is enough."

Uttam could not be what Mahindra was, devoting his hours to illumination and liberation. He still wished to enjoy his young wives and engage in the usual wars. He was not ready for *Sanyasa*, the life of detachment. So he could not know what was enough.

Uttam's voice came to him as though far away. "You were always stronger than others. Even in the old days. A stronger scholar, a stronger fighter. Your blood is a deeper red." He sighed. "I could command you."

Mahindra felt his eyelids flutter. Had it been six days?

"You go too far. Consider all you have lost from extremes. Your sons, alas."

My sons. My sons.

"*Babaji*, are you still in the tree? In the land of the Anglics, keeping watch?"

Uttam went on. "Littlewood is dead. You said so. What good is the child that you seek for her to come? She is only a girl, she cannot help us find the holy flower. Besides, if she comes, her sire will come. If her sire comes, he will bring regiments, thousands of soldiers. We will be weaker than ever."

Mahindra whispered, "For us to find the flower, they must come."

"They have many rifles."

Mahindra opened his eyes at last, looking on Uttam with great compassion. His prince stood before him, unattended, wearing simple white trousers and achkan. "How can 10,000 rule 100 million?"

"They do not rule!" Uttam protested.

Reluctantly, Mahindra came fully into body. His body was full of pain. "They decide the quotas for cotton and mahogany, do they not, Highness? They tell us the cities in which they must have their schools, the locations of the posting houses, the train stations, the cantonments of the regiments."

"Trading matters," Uttam snapped.

"Ah, but Highness, it can all be ours. Once we have the flower, we will drive the usurpers into the sea."

"Beginning with a girl? What does she even know?"

"She was loved by the adventurer. I believe he put great things upon her shoulders. She may have touched the holy lotus, even if only a petal. Such an occurrence marks her to our cause."

Uttam looked to the door, where Dulal had nosed in seeking to care for Mahindra. "Let this fast end, *babaji*. If it is their will, the gods will bring her to us."

"The gods give us wisdom to act for ourselves. We will bring the Anglic regiments here. Among them will be the girl's father. And she will come with him."

Uttam snorted. "Do we summon them with a letter?"

"We will put a thorn in the paw of the Anglic lion. A great display of magical destruction that even their fat king cannot ignore."

"How, *babaji*?"

Mahindra picked at a flower blossom in his lap. Then he pulled aside the white cloth and its burden of offerings.

Uttam frowned at what the cloth had hidden.

Mahindra sat cross-legged in the half-lotus position. Protruding from his feet were a dozen thin, long skewers. Some pierced all the way through his foot, and some his toes. The ground beneath was deeply stained. Now that he was fully present, there was pain.

"The waters will rise," Mahindra said, "to the very feet of the Anglic king."

⁓

The St. Katherine Docks on the Thames employed nearly 3,000 men for the discharging of cargo on ships laden from Bharata, Scotland, and such outlying provinces as Northumberland, Yorkshire and Wales. Fortunately on this early spring day there was an east wind that kept many ships from docking, or the employment levels and therefore loss of life on the quays would have been vastly greater.

Under an open blue sky, Sam Biggs took stock of the gang of fifty men hired that day to get out a cargo from the *Exeter*. The tallow and wine casks would be lifted by steam-powered winches directly from the ship to the warehouses, but the engines needed tending and some items must be discharged by hand. Biggs kept a strict watch on the motley dock laborers: old soldiers, publicans down on their luck, suspended government clerks, bankrupt grocers, discharged lawyers' clerks, broken-down gentlemen, and thieves—all willing to work for five pence an hour. It was this watchfulness that at first distracted Biggs from what one of the laborers pointed at. When he finally turned to see the cause of an increasing commotion, he saw a strange peaked wave moving slowly upriver. It surely was a ship disguised by the glint of the sun. But of course no ship was so thin.

Nor did a ship have eyes.

In the Blackfriars button factory Livy was already coughing from the acrid fumes and it was only eight o'clock. She still had another twelve hours to work. The foreman had opened the south window, and she made bold to grab a breath of air—stinking though it was—before returning to the dye work, matching button colors to fabric. A quick glance revealed the curve of the Thames. But something protruded from the water—a narrow pole moving up the river, as tall as a masted ship. Moving at the pace of a barge, the shape was watery gray, as though made of glass. It weren't possible, Livy thought. As she stared, gap-mouthed, the shape stopped moving. It was at that moment that she realized it had a head, or a top portion that appeared to have a mouth and eyes. The shape now turned to and fro, swaying, obviously searching for something.

"'Ere, now, back to work with you!" the foreman snapped. He was charging around the button table toward her. Livy pointed out the window.

At first he saw nothing, but Livy wouldn't budge until he looked.

When he did, he leaned on the casement, peering in amazement. "By Christ," he whispered. "It's a snake."

"But no snake was ever so big, was it?" Livy asked.

The foreman ogled the bizarre sight, shaking his head over and over. He'd served years ago with the lancers in Bharata and knew the creature. "Bloody hell, if it ain't a cobra!"

Livy looked at him uncomprehendingly.

Sam Biggs watched as the head of the water spout stopped swaying. It was then that the first part of the disaster struck.

Biggs saw the water leaving the docks, pouring out of the docklands south of the Tower of Londinium like milk sucked through a straw. The outrushing water abandoned the ships in their wet docks, tilting the masted ships first toward the dock, then toward each other. In a sickening, slow motion explosion, thirty ships including the *Exeter* tipped over on their keels, masts colliding. Men screamed as casks—suspended from pulleys—fell from their ropes and cascaded down the docks, ramming into the steam winches, gangs, and warehousemen. Sam Biggs stood in frozen horror. As the water rushed toward—and into—the towering snake, it caused the creature to loom higher, now as tall as the Tower itself. Briggs knew better than to run. The colossus was turning its hooded face this way and that, as though looking for prey.

A tongue forked out in the direction of St. James Park. Then the snake started to move up the river again, toward Westminster Bridge, growing taller, thicker, as it sucked the Thames into itself.

The dock laborers were as amazed by the empty Thames as they were by the waterspout. Rushing from the twisted ships and wobbling, crashing docks, they scrambled down the banks into the muddy river bed, milling about like lunatics, stunned, contending with fish and debris left stranded in the estuary.

At Buckingham Palace, King Albert sat at table alone, about to partake of his breakfast of plum cake, buttered eggs in cream and anchovy, compote of pigeons, and thick Kentish bacon. It was his favorite meal of the day, not the least reason being the superb marmalade which his butler would spread on his toast a half inch thick.

As he took the fork which his butler proffered him on a doily-clad plate, the king stopped. Through the stone walls of the palace, he heard a far off tumult, very like distant screams, but also like thunder. He turned to the south window, where sun streamed onto the green damask drapes. Then a great shadow fell over the windows.

At that moment the king's Captain of the Guards burst into the room. Rushing up to the table, he pulled on the king's person, a most shocking and illegal act. Albert's lace breakfast napkin fell to the floor as the king rose in outrage. Nonsensically, the captain asserted that a great wave threatened. He pointed at the windows. Shaking off the captain, the king strode to the windows to look out. Behind him, the doors of his morning room flew open and more guards rushed toward him.

Nevertheless, for another second King Albert stood alone at the south window of Buckingham Palace, his gaze caught by the return glower of an impossible snake towering over the palace. The creature had a flaring hood, a reddish forked tongue, and eyes as large as a kraken's—eyes glittering with what Albert would later define as joy.

For a split second, the snake hovered. Then it disintegrated. It fell toward the palace.

Now the guards bore the king back across the room, saving his life, but not his silk morning jacket and impeccably cut trousers, which were about to be saturated with Thames filth.

The windows shattered, and the explosion of water and sewage caught the fleeing king from behind. The guards just managed to slam the inner doors shut against the flood. Behind the doors, amid the swirling effluvium, broken table, priceless paintings and skittering silver-plate, Albert heard servants screaming. The captain shouted for the guards to help his majesty to reach the inner rooms.

But Buckingham palace had quieted. It was a strong and fortified building, and had suffered all that it was going to that day.

Outside on the Thames was a different matter.

The entire contents of the collapsed snake now rushed toward the riverbed, through the surrounding greensward, decimating St. James Park, and streaming onto Palace Road and Vauxhall, taking with it houses, hovels, merchant stalls, taverns, whorehouses and all their occupants. Onward the flow rushed, no longer sentient, no longer directed, seeking only its home in the river.

There it found Sam Briggs and some thousand others stranded in the mud, rushing to scramble up the banks of the Thames, but unable to do so in the press of bodies and mud slurry. Sam looked up to see a wall of water thundering toward him. The wave carried some of the city with it, including a lamp post that struck Sam in the chest, killing him instantly and saving him from the arguably more unpleasant death of drowning.

In the button factory, Livy and the foreman watched in stupefaction as the flood hit the Londinium Bridge in a broad and hammering wave. It swept on, leaving the bridge standing, but so bestrewn with ship pieces, trees, hansom cabs, bodies, mud and flotsam as to be unrecognizable. The wave continued down the estuary, losing power as it discharged its energy, becoming in the end a shallow, humped wave that gently lifted the boats at Dover and then—with what some bystanders there described as a sigh—merged with the ocean.

3,117 people had lost their lives in the flood.

And the king had missed breakfast.

7

Within two days Parliament had thunderously called for a retaliatory expedition to Bharata; the foreign secretary warned against it, claiming that the actions of renegade bush priests should not be placed upon honest Bharatis; but the Prime Minister had disagreed, and as his first action, recalled the Governor General, replacing him with a more aggressive viceroy. He prevailed on the king to approve an expeditionary force, thus quelling any voices of moderation that might have sided with the foreign secretary. Albert sighed. He had not taken an interest in Government since the untimely death of his dear wife four years ago.

But walking through the sun-streaked gallery overlooking the gardens of Balmoral, King Albert pondered the price the Crown would have to pay for adventurism. If shaking the mailed fist did not persuade Bharata to stand down, it could come to war. It was a shame to escalate a conflict that, until the Londinium flood, had been confined to minor, if dramatic, acts of terrorism. Of course there was no recourse, now that the bombastic speeches in Parliament had inflamed the public against the magical continent. The Government would act.

As the king strolled through the sumptuous hall, a piece of artwork on a sideboard caught his eye. The object, formed from purple glass, represented a badly formed owl. Albert had not seen the piece before and while it was appallingly ugly, it also quite arrested one's attention. After a time, he realized he had been gazing at the owl in a peculiar reverie.

As he moved on, the king considered how the Londinium crisis might profit from a steady hand in Bharata. There was the excellent Colonel Terrence Harding, whom he'd met at some function or other. Son-in-law, wasn't he, to Sir Charles Littlewood? At the time Albert had not quite taken in how impressive a leader the colonel was, but it came to him quite forcibly now. A man not given to the brash and dramatic, but rather the measured and judicious. If Harding could be coaxed from retirement, he would be just the one to take on the governorship of Nanpura province, a key princely state with a friendly ruler.

The king did not normally take an interest in mundane appointments, but the thought now struck him with some urgency, that Colonel Harding must be pressed into service at Poondras. He would speak to the Foreign Secretary to see what might be done about it.

Meanwhile he planned to enjoy a stroll on the terrace. It would be a long time before he could return to Buckingham Palace. It stank most dreadfully. Albert wondered if the old stones could ever be entirely cleaned of the abominable filth. Henceforth, his favorite residence would be Balmoral. But even here the king would from time to time feel uneasy.

Ever afterward, even in the Scottish castle's manicured gardens, there were times when Albert would look up and remember for a heart-stopping instant the swaying tower of water with the glittering eyes.

On the headland overlooking the beach at Hastings, Tori gazed out on a calm Ancific Ocean across which, incredibly, she would be taking a coach.

From the seashore below the braying of horses and shouts of men came to her ears like a battle scene. There on the broad beach milled a great press of supply wagons, oxen, water tanks, passenger coaches and masses of soldiers and pack horses. She could not see how they would bring order out of the expedition, but already the first detachments had begun the line of march to Bharata, pushed along by a stiff April wind at their backs.

She had been awake since well before dawn, and now, wrapped in a heavy shawl against the morning chill, she viewed in wonder that stupendous sight, the lifetime achievement of Sir Henry Culp, the Great Bridge.

Thirty-eight feet wide, the great construct snaked over the water, its jointed segments floating on the ocean swells. It undulated into the distance, disappearing into the misty horizon. To Tori's mind, it pointed due east like a great finger, commanding her to go. Colonel Harding had already set out in the advance party with his secretaries and advisors. His family would presently follow.

In the near distance, from the lodging door, Jessa called. "Tori! It's time!"

Their coach awaited, with Jackson in charge of bringing the sisters down to the Bridge gateway where Mrs. Harding waited for them after seeing Colonel Harding off. Tori was not sure how she could endure her mother's close company for three months, but she'd given over a large share of her travel chests to books, including a copy of *A Geology of the Mystic Continent* and a rare edition of Blackwell's *A Compendium of Bharati Vocabulary*, which should more than serve for decent company.

Waving wildly, Jessa practically lifted from her feet in her excitement. Jessa had been the driving force behind Colonel Harding's decision to take his family to his new posting. When news had arrived that Muir-Smith's regiment would be on the expedition, the matter was quickly settled. The cantonment at Fort Poondras would be a fine place for an unmarried woman to find a husband.

Tori had let it be known that she would be on the lookout for a match, as well. Had there been a moment's pain in her father's eyes when he heard such a forlorn hope? But she could not, of course, admit her true purpose.

Oh, it was time to go. Sir Charles seemed so very close to her at this moment, impeccably dressed, white hair blown back in the wind. He urged her on.

Jackson helped the two young women into the coach, along with her mother's maid. The cabman, sharing a seat with Jackson high and in back, jangled the reins, and the horses set out at a brisk trot for the beach road.

Fidgeting in her seat, Jessa looked out, exclaiming on the long lines of soldiers marching two abreast on the side of the road, filling the beach, replacing those who had already set out onto the Bridge.

"Tori, isn't it grand, simply grand?" Jessa had given up on all dignity and was now craning her neck to see everything. The ocean, for a few moments hidden by the bluffs as the road cut downward, was now in sight, with *HMS Caledonia* in the harbor. The warship was surrounded by Royal Navy frigates and schooners that would provide a ceremonial escort for the first miles.

"It *is* wonderful," Tori said. Her heart was beating so fast she thought it must be audible. Today, within the hour, they would begin their thousand-mile journey.

"There is the Bridge itself," Jessa whispered in awe. A frown creased her forehead. "Oh, it looks so very small. Narrow as a ribbon."

"On the ocean, it is better to be small than great. And see how the segments flex and let the ocean pass unaware?"

"Oh yes," Jessa said, biting her lip.

Tori took her hand. The Bridge did look narrow indeed, nor could one note its undulations without imagining things spilling from it.

Ignoring the maid's presence, Jessa murmured, "Tori, it's very handsome of you to set aside your quarrel. Mama is so glad to have your kind regard again."

Tori squeezed her sister's hand. She could not confide to Jessa in this matter. Her parents' behavior that awful night did not bear close examination, but her sister should not have to share her distress. And indeed, if her new plan came off, she could forgive all.

The sloping causeway led to the staging area, where already they were assaulted with a gamy tang of manure, saddle soap, wood fires and rotting kelp. Their coach pulled out to a loading zone where soldiers organized the civilian rigs for the order of march. They all debarked to await Mrs. Harding, the party quite staring at the enormous arching gateway that presided over the Bridge's western terminus. Iron and brass ornamentation loomed high, forming an arch embellished with Anglic heraldic patterns and a suggestion of eastern mythology. At the summit, a lion supine, the symbol of King Albert, whose royal mastery allowed him to rest even while safeguarding the kingdom. Tori wondered if the great water serpent in Londinium suggested that the lion ought to adopt a more fearsome stance. But with this force of four thousand soldiers the lion was now on the move.

Tori spied Muir-Smith at some distance away. "Pray do not faint, Jessa, but there is Captain Muir-Smith."

Jessa tucked back a wind-blown strand of hair. "Is he approaching?"

"Yes, he's seen us. I believe that is his cousin with him. You remember that mama said Elizabeth Platt will be crossing over to take on a school."

Other carriages were also arriving and queuing up in readiness to cross, including a nicely appointed coach with the letter "H" emblazoned on the side.

"Good morning!" Muir-Smith hailed the sisters. "You've safely arrived amid the chaos, I see." He bowed to them. "You've not met my cousin, I think. Allow me to present Elizabeth Platt, of Cornwall."

Elizabeth Platt, some seven or eight years older than Tori and her sister, wore sturdy brown muslin with a brimmed hat tied with ribbons.

Her smile was immediate. "Ladies! I am uncommonly glad to make your acquaintance! I'll have company on the journey, thank goodness. Edmond has told me so much about you. "

The sisters greeted her with enthusiasm. Tori said, "What an adventure, to be a teacher in Bharata!"

Elizabeth nodded. "Eight year-olds are the same the world over. I shall be prepared! And there"— she pointed to a wagon laden and battened down with oilcloth—"are my books!"

"A wagon load of books," Jessa remarked with a notable lack of keenness, as though she might be assigned to read them.

"You would find them dull, Miss Harding," Muir-Smith said. "They are children's books for the Bharati schools."

Elizabeth's ready smile widened when she spied the nearby coach with its embellished "H" on the side, now divesting itself of its passengers, among whom was a striking young woman dressed in a velvet traveling ensemble.

"Now then, Edmond, pay attention. There is the girl you must marry. Cora Hamilton. Admit it, you like her!"

"Her family has been more than gracious to me."

A peal of laughter from Elizabeth. "Yes, and she vouchsafed you four dances at her coming out."

"Two, I believe."

"Ah, so you kept count!" The oxen pulling the book wagon just then stepped off the graveled staging area and sank to their fetlocks in the sand. "Here now!" Elizabeth shouted and rushed forward to regale the cart man.

Muir-Smith said to the sisters, "Allow me to express my condolences for the loss of your grandfather."

"Oh," Jessa was swift to say, "thank you, Captain. It was very hard. We will all miss him so desperately but Mama is being very brave of course. It was very kind of you to send a note."

The breeze blew Tori's hat ribbons into her face, giving her a moment to recover from the tears that always seemed ready at the subject of her grandfather. Muir-Smith was responding to Jessa, which gave Tori a moment to compose her face.

Elizabeth rejoined them now that the oxen had climbed back to the harder surface. "They say Sir Henry Culp is on the reviewing stand, and the Duke of Edinburgh, too. We shall see them as we pass!"

It was time to go. Elizabeth and the sisters arranged to meet for supper at the first camp and the captain moved off with his cousin to escort her to her party. Tori noted that they stopped to greet the Hamilton girl.

Tori put a hand on Jessa's arm: "Onward to the bridge. We shall both find husbands at Fort Poondras, I have little doubt!"

"But you've always said you wouldn't marry." Jessa's eyes narrowed. "Is it rather the case that you're here for Grandpapa's sake?"

"What if I'm going for myself? For scientific purposes."

Jessa lowered her voice. "Not that flower, Tori! Besides, where can you find one flower in all of Bharata!"

They spotted Mrs. Harding approaching.

Tori whispered, "Well, I wasn't going to find it in Shropshire, was I?"

Jessa sighed. "Papa will be *very* upset."

"That is why we mustn't tell him."

Arriving in her travel dress of green wool, Mrs. Harding demanded, "Mustn't tell who what?"

Tori hastened to say, "Must not tell Muir-Smith that Cora Hamilton is quite the shrew."

Mrs. Harding narrowed her eyes in the direction of the Hamilton coach. "Cora is a delightful child, of course. Don't be dreadful." She took Jessa's arm in her hers, and murmured, "But you will make friends with Elizabeth Platt, of course, and thus we'll be seeing rather a lot of him."

She needn't say the man's name. Of course her mother had already met Elizabeth and would no doubt use this to advantage. Olivia Harding arranged things. Well, Tori thought with a small shiver of excitement from her subterfuge, the rest of the Harding women could do no less!

Jackson reported that they were to join the queue and there was a great commotion of settling into the coach for departure, with Jessa and Mama chatting excitedly. But Tori paid scant attention to them. She would not come home with a husband. She would come home with something far more valuable: proof of *Nelumbo aureus*. A partial specimen, and its sketch, as Grandpapa had demanded. This was her chance—delivered by the ghastly but providential water serpent. She was going not just to Bharata, but to the very province where Sir Charles had found the petal. If she could not wrest a scientific breakthrough from such an opportunity, then she did not deserve to attain membership in the Royal Society.

She, Jessa, Mrs. Harding and the maid boarded the coach with Jackson sharing the cab seat above, and the driver brought the conveyance into line, heading for the bridge gateway.

The *Caledonia*, now engulfed in white smoke, discharged its guns again and again in a royal salute. They passed the reviewing stand with Henry Culp standing at attention, the Duke looking very martial, hand on dress sword. The soldiers still on the beach set up a great hurrah, and Sir Henry took off his hat and waved, as though the gun barrage were for him. Tori wanted to take off her own hat and wave it wildly, but young ladies did not.

Amid the roar of the *Caledonia* and the cheering soldiers, they passed through the portal and onto the Bridge.

PART II: THE PALACE OF THE LOTUS

8

They had been out of sight of land for two days. Their caravan extended for miles, including the line of foot soldiers, coaches for officers and their families, supply wagons for food and water, and a small herd of cows that formed the rear component upon which the expedition would rely for fresh meat.

Today Elizabeth Platt rode on the book wagon next to the driver, having fled the coach where two of her fellow teachers complained constantly of bilious stomachs from the rocking Bridge. With eighty-five days' journey still ahead, Elizabeth thought her companions must adjust or be carried prostrate in the wagons.

That was the one thing they never said about the Bridge, how it *swayed.* The other was how exposed to the ocean one must feel, and how *small.* The mass of soldiers, pack animals, wagons and coaches, so teeming on the beaches of Hastings, now seemed a thin procession indeed.

"The rocking don't make you sick, then," the wagon driver, Newsome, had said when she joined him, as though he wished it *would* so he might be relieved of her company. He didn't speak again and that was just as well, for Elizabeth was eager to read her letter from the Chidiwal school that had just arrived on a mail coach headed west. If a caravan of wagons approached from Bharata, the shouted order was to "fall right," and the troops would narrow their line of march all down the line in a sinuous curve, allowing traffic to pass.

Mr. Ramanath, the teacher at Chidiwal who would be her assistant, wrote a very nice letter indeed, saying how much he and his students looked forward to her arrival:

I believe and hope that you will find everything very much proper. We have just completed a garden wall to enclose the game field where the children can be learning your excellent sport of cricket. We have also repaired the roof which unfortunately became torn off by an enraged elephant. Please do not worry. The elephants have a very temperate mood except when maddened by bees.

Elizabeth put down the letter for a moment. Elephants, indeed! She could scarcely imagine the place; even the name possessed an oriental charm: Chidiwal. She had thought of little else in the five months since her promotion to head mistress.

Yesterday the children learned by memory all the Anglica provinces from A to M! They are eager to be showing you. I have explained that when you arrive you will be bringing biscuits in a tin and a framed picture of King Albert. Oh, the smiles on their faces. I am proud to say that one of the best families has consented to send two youngest sons to our classroom, bringing our numbers to forty-seven!

Forty-seven? That was somewhat smaller than she had looked for. Chidiwal was the flagship Anglic school for Nanpura province. Well, more room for improvement, then. She had marched for universal schooling and worked tirelessly in the movement to increase children's legal age for physical labor from nine years to eleven. Bharata was a fresh slate.

Mr. Ramanath closed with hearty wishes for her safe crossing of "the perilous bridge," with its "sea monsters and storms." She did not at all care for the idea of storms. Just then an ocean swell carried the Bridge up its broad back, setting the wagon a temporary hill. The oxen strained, but soon found the wave's downhill side, and plodded on. The horses, however, faired poorly on the rising and falling plates.

The chop of the ocean glinted and winked, suggesting backs of serpents curled into a dive. "Have you ever seen a kraken, Mr. Newsome?"

The driver cut a glance at her. "They don't dare show with a full Anglic regiment to meet 'em."

The wagon jolted a little at the juncture of bridge plates. Each seam marked a pontoon crossed and each jolt brought them nearer the spiritual continent. But how many plates it took to span the ocean! It did not seem possible that enough iron and wood could be found to construct such a thing, not to mention the staggering cost. But for wood, they must depend on Bharata, and indeed groaning wagons of raw lumber passed them every few days, often in caravan with ore cars and securely bound wagons of cotton, tea and spices—all hauled by the sturdy, ubiquitous oxen. Ingeniously, their droppings were eventually washed away by stray waves percolating down through holes.

"Elizabeth!"

She looked up to find Edmond riding up on his horse. The poor animal looked half crazed with uncertainty where to step or when the ground would heave.

When Edmond came abreast of the wagon, they kept pace for a while as Elizabeth told him of her letter from Chidiwal and the estimable Mr. Ramanath. She was pleased to learn that Edmond had been assigned to accompany her to Chidiwal once they had attained the shore at Poondras, but wondered at the need.

"I don't need a military escort, surely."

"No, cousin, but there are troublemakers. The appearance of our forces may provoke some reaction."

"Oh, pray do not see everything as a battle, Edmond!"

"But neither is the world a schoolroom," he returned with feeling.

Edmond was always looking left and right, scanning the ocean. So serious he was. Of course his brother's death in a kraken battle must weigh upon him now. Turning back to her he said, "I've come to convey an invitation from the Misses Harding for you to join them in their carriage."

"Oh, kindly tell them I am delighted to accept!"

"Excellent, cousin. It will ease my mind to have you inside a carriage." He nodded to her and cantered off, keeping tight rein on his horse.

She shot a glance at the driver. "I trust you will fend off any attacks on my books, Mr. Newsome!"

He only shook the reins and gave a look that said, *We got a regiment to greet 'em.*

"Tori, my dear."

A spectacular sunset in gold and orange had been mesmerizing Tori at the Bridge railing, but she turned upon hearing her father's voice. She had been avoiding him for weeks, and now they looked at each other in discomfort.

He joined her at the rail, gazing out on the lavish display of color that painted the horizon and its escort of stacked clouds. It was lovely, and also reminiscent of the dreadful fire in the grate of the study.

"My dear," he began. "I can't put out of my mind that we are not easy with each other."

How awful it was to bear a grudge; and yet it was very hard to think him fair minded in the events of that night in his study. "Pray forgive me," she dutifully said.

"No, do not apologize. It was a difficult night. None of us carried ourselves well."

She did not care for the phrase. There was theft and burning, to be precise.

He went on, "You may not wish to hear what I have to say. Do let me finish before you judge me." He paused, gazing out over the deeply stained waters. "Mrs. Harding and I have had our differences in our years together."

She cast him an ironic look.

"She may sometimes appear more forthright than one could wish." He quirked a smile in Tori's direction. "A quality that appears to have been handed down in our family. But, my dear, you must remember the great underlying fact of our lives: Sir Charles Littlewood was a scientist of profound standing. It is upon Mrs. Harding that his legacy depends—" He put up a hand to forestall her objection, "—both from his body of published work and from those theories that he had not the time to fully develop. Your mother wished to shield Sir Charles's reputation from what she considered damaging principles. I had long since abandoned my hope to share such decisions with her."

"So you didn't agree to it!"

He turned to face her. "Tori, I did not oppose it. For your sake; because I love you. Perhaps inadequately in your estimation, but most profoundly in mine."

He went on, "My acquiescence in this matter was all for you. Permit me to say that in regard to the theory of magic, Sir Charles did not adequately think through the implications for a young woman such as yourself."

"But you don't understand his theory. You never inquired, you never—"

"—Be so kind as to allow me to finish. Your mother and I have little experience of magical phenomena, but we know that our land is under attack by spiritual terrorists. Furthermore, if the scientific world would heap derision upon the notion of magical paths of knowing, this cannot be your route to a place in natural history. Find another approach and I shall help you all that I can, your mother notwithstanding."

She could not bear to argue with him. Oh, to have a reconciliation, even if it was one that lacked somewhat of candor!

Candor, of course, was impossible. Her goal to seek the flower specimen entailed a great deception: To make her way from Fort Poondras, under the guise of innocent curiosity, to the great museum in Kathore. How she would persuade her father to this journey, she didn't know. But could he deny her permission once she was so close to Sir Charles's old haunt? At the Gangadhar museum she would find Sir Charles's field notebook containing a record of his search for *Nelumbo aureus*. There had been no time for him to retrieve it when he left.

But he had told Tori exactly where it was.

As she looked into her father's eyes she felt a most unwelcome stab of guilt. He took her hands in his, and she allowed it. "Pray do not let what happened that night come between us, my dear. For anything that Mrs. Harding and I have done hastily or without regard to your feelings, I do ask your forgiveness."

She went into his arms. "It is given, Papa."

"And for your mother…"

"I will endeavor to have a better opinion of her."

Holding her at arms' length, he produced a small smile. "One might hope for more."

She smiled back. "One will try."

$$\infty$$

"I don't hold with blackamoors," a sergeant growled.

The comment was within earshot of Tori and Elizabeth as they stood with Jessa next to their coach.

The caravan had come to a stop. Bharatis were laboring to fix a broken lumber wagon, assisted by a dozen Anglic soldiers, none of them happy to be working in the sweltering heat. Bharati laborers not involved with the lumber offloading were heating their thin lunch patties over portable cooking pots. The lumber caravan had been passing alongside for an hour when one of the long, groaning wagons lost a wheel. The great mahogany trunks had to be offloaded to make repairs, forcing the eastbound line to a pinch point.

"Ask me," the sergeant went on, speaking louder now for Elizabeth's benefit, "the blackmen pulled the wheel off so's to rest and cook their stinking meal."

Tori put a hand on Elizabeth's arm to restrain her—she knew her well enough after a week of close travel—but Elizabeth took a step forward. "Hold your tongue. We want none of your scurrilous name-calling!"

The sergeant grinned. "*Scurr-i-lous*, is it?"

"I'll have your apology," Elizabeth pressed on.

"I don't owe none to a school marm."

"You will ask her pardon, sergeant." Edmond had come upon them. The sergeant obeyed, and Edmond escorted the three women to the far side of their coach.

He squinted against the westering sun. "They have low manners, cousin. I'm sorry it distressed you."

"As it should us all," Elizabeth responded. "Equality is the call of the new age. We must live side-by-side, with fewer distinctions and more compassion."

"That man isn't your equal and can't be held to your standard. Surely you admit that."

"Indeed, I do not."

Tori marveled that Elizabeth would argue such a point, but was enjoying the heated discussion.

Elizabeth went on, "It must begin with the lower classes for they far out-number the gentry. Education is the key."

Jessa said, "But there must be distinctions among men, else how could affairs be ordered, if all could do what they would?"

Edmond gave her an approving nod. "Jessa has the right of it. Do you argue against the privileges of name and wealth? Surely we can't all lead, nor have parliament stocked with the common sort."

Elizabeth turned in frustration to Tori. "Well, pray give us your opinion, Astoria, since we have all given ours!"

Tori found herself thinking of *distinctions* in quite another context. She had often wondered if the general exclusion of women in high scientific enterprises was sheer recalcitrance or based upon a firmer social premise. Not that women of science were unknown; there was Mary Anning, of fossil-hunting fame. But even she was not admitted to learned circles.

"Well?" Elizabeth prodded.

"I think it is women whose affairs are curtailed and should not be."

Jessa laughed. "Well, I'm sure *I* do not feel deprived!"

Captain Muir-Smith's expression turned cool. "I've always thought that women enjoy a greater measure of respect—beyond what a man can command with worldly affairs."

Tori fixed him with her gaze. "Have you indeed."

"The fairer sex is thus excused from the rigors of a harsh world."

"And excused also from accomplishment."

Jessa piped up: "My sister will give a paper someday at the Royal Society."

Edmond blinked in surprise. "I did not understand that that august body had gone so far in their thinking."

Tori was mortified to have her hopes thrown into a public conversation, but she could hardly remain silent. "They do not hold with female membership, it is true. Shall I give over to them, do you think, Captain?"

"I would not like to see you disappointed, Miss Harding."

"Splendid. Another vote for my hopeless cause. I thank you, sir."

Elizabeth saw that topic had become difficult and fashioned an excuse to lead Edmond away. Jessa found reason to join them, and soon Tori was left alone to consider how hard it was, indeed, to find supporters of her cause.

Jackson, who had gone forward to see what arrangements would be made for supper with Colonel and Mrs. Harding, now returned, reporting that the march would bivouac early with an early start set for morrow.

A blur of wings took Tori's attention, as a bird hovered over them, flapping in place and then alighting on the Bridge rail some distance away. Jackson noted her gaze. "We don't see any albatrosses that are blue, Miss."

"Yes, come to think on it, they're always white."

"Well, that one rides on our carriage sometimes."

Tori looked back at the bird, her stomach plummeting. *Daitya.* She searched for any shade of purple in its quivering feathers. "Does it, indeed?" she managed to say.

The head swiveled in her direction. It stared at her.

"A regular pet, it is; and gets a share of the driver's afternoon biscuit, too."

In a perfectly natural movement, the albatross tucked its head inside a wing. Surely its stare had not held any meaning. She must not ascribe imaginative characteristics to things. But at the same time she must not remain blind when presented with magical occurrences. Everything depended upon her willingness to *see*, as Grandpapa had said.

She now allowed the question to come to the fore, the one that had been trailing her all the way from Glyndehill Manor: Why had the shadowy owl come to Grandpapa in the first place? Why had he thought it a demon?

Or had it, indeed, come instead to *her*?

9

"Took a whole cow?" Jessa exclaimed when Muir-Smith joined them at their dinner circle and revealed that the first sightings of kraken had been made. Jessa was wide-eyed with alarm, but Tori relished the prospect of seeing a kraken.

"Yes, Miss Harding, at the rear of the line, the last cow. By all accounts, the kraken snatched it from the herd like a seagull snatching a fish. Its jaws went round the neck, and the cow loomed high in the air, kicking wildly, before it was plunged down into the abyss."

"Oh, the poor creature!" Jessa exclaimed.

Elizabeth leaned forward, cradling her plate of mutton. "What of our stalwart soldiers during this thievery?" She was still smarting over her altercation with the sergeant.

Muir-Smith produced a wry face. "Well, no one thought to guard the cows. We will now."

Tori asked, "Are you sure it wasn't a convulsion, Captain? How can we discern whether it was natural or magical?"

Elizabeth pounced on the idea. "Oh! By those lights we could any of us be a bush priest in disguise." She tucked back into her stew. "I shall be vigilant, you may be sure."

Jessa ventured, "Do you think, Captain, that this appearance—if it was a kraken—means we enter a more dangerous territory?"

"I do, Miss Harding. We expected the beasts would make a showing but we're well prepared." Turning to Tori, he said, "When animals are conjured, they have an off-color at the least. These sea beasts were the normal greenish-blue. Nor do I think a magical serpent could devour a cow."

Tori murmured, "There was the curious case of the cast iron lions wreaking havoc in Londinium, of course."

Elizabeth declared, "Wouldn't it be sensible to fight magic with magic? You've been to Bharata, cousin. How is it that the priests of that continent have the powers of magic, whereas we Anglics do not?"

Muir-Smith paused. "Their methods for accruing such powers are distasteful, and contrary to the Church."

"Do you say that mysticism," Elizabeth asked, "is forbidden by our Lord, with all the articles of faith and miracles we are asked to believe?"

"No. But to control elemental powers requires that Bharatis undergo austerities, even to harming their own flesh. The Church decries such mortifications of the body, and rightly so."

Though Tori had heard of this practice from Sir Charles, it was not the whole story. "But, to be fair, the holy men don't always rely on bodily harm. Sometimes they renounce food and water and worldly possessions."

"Yes," Muir-Smith admitted. "There are degrees of abstinence, but the creation of great displays of magic requires more severe austerities."

"It would exclude pleasures of the flesh, then," Elizabeth said. "Isn't that right, cousin?"

Jessa blurted, "How strange! They don't marry, then?"

"No." Captain Muir-Smith fell silent.

Tori was delighted to see that his easy manner had found its limit. She liked him rather better when he faltered; in fact she felt his appeal more strongly at this moment than she could have wished for Jessa's sake. She could not help it when out came, "It would take a man of fierce intention, certainly. Procreation is an instinct common to every animal, civilized or not. I think you wouldn't be a candidate as a bush priest, Captain."

The group turned to him, but Muir-Smith was rescued from having to answer by the appearance of Colonel and Mrs. Harding strolling down the Bridge deck. Muir-Smith stood with alacrity to greet them.

"I see you're holding our young ladies rapt with your stories, Edmond." Colonel Harding smiled at his daughters and Elizabeth. He said to Muir-Smith, "Will you join us for a stroll? Jessa?"

That was neatly orchestrated, Tori thought. Muir-Smith gave his arm to

Jessa, who said half-heartedly that they must all come along and, Elizabeth and Tori demurring, the two couples set off.

Elizabeth watched them go. "I had never remarked upon it before, but my cousin and your sister make a handsome couple."

"Oh, yes." She very much wished she could feel more glad about it, however.

"Forgive me if I am being forward, Astoria, but may I ask if it's a great difficulty for you to walk for a length of time?"

Tori paused. People did not often mention her walk. "No, it is not difficult, as I am completely accustomed to it."

"I'm a teacher and student of some medicinal subjects. I would take it as a great indulgence if you allowed me to examine your foot. But I don't wish to embarrass you."

"I don't mind. We could do so now, if you like."

Seated on the bench in the coach, her skirt hitched up to mid-calf, Tori straightened her legs to look at her two bare feet. The right foot, straight and perfect, with delicate, rounded toes. The left was a half inch shorter than the other and curled toward the instep, forcing the foot into a slight "c" configuration that demanded she walk on the outside of her foot.

"It's not a profound case," Elizabeth said. "Your left leg is shorter than your right? That's usually the case."

"Yes, a fraction smaller. Thus the heel of my shoe is higher on that side."

"The heel also allows for the Achilles tendon to have relief from stretching. That's also usual with the condition." She looked up from her position on the floor of the coach where she kneeled in front of Tori. "I hope this examination isn't awkward for you."

"I thought it would be," Tori said. "But no one except my doctor has ever looked at my foot without... pity. It's rather refreshing."

Elizabeth nodded. "The shoe is very nicely made. Does it pain you to wear it all day?"

"Indeed not. It's barefoot that causes difficulty." Tori went on, "I've been told that the condition passes down in the family line, but none has ever had the malady in ours."

"Oh, but sometimes it is due to the unborn child held in an adverse position in the womb. We can't know. May I touch your foot?"

Tori nodded. Elizabeth extended the left foot down and up, putting her other hand on the back of Tori's leg, gauging the foreshortening there. "It's amazing, isn't it, Astoria, how much the human body can compensate and do perfectly well when required?"

"Oh, I've always thought so! But Mr. Darwin says that natural selection favors the well-formed."

Elizabeth took it upon herself to fit on Tori's stockings and then each shoe. She said at last, "I would venture to say that you are well-formed in most ways. No one person is the precise ideal, yet we find our way. I'm not comely—as you and your sister are—yet I have turned down three suitors! And well that I did, for if I had accepted one, would I be having such an adventure as this great Bridge and going to teach among Bharatis and elephants?"

"But," Tori murmured, "have you never wished to know of the intimacy between man and wife?"

Elizabeth shrugged. "Oh, my dear, it's the most common thing! Men will always welcome a woman to bed and they are seldom lacking in partners, believe me."

It came to Tori most startlingly, that Elizabeth had experienced sexual relations. "Have you fallen in love, then, Elizabeth?"

Her friend raised her chin. "Certainly not! One may have a bed partner at night, and barely stand the sight of him the next day. That is usually the case, in fact. Men in particular set no great store of love upon a willing vessel, I assure you."

"Ah. So it is a physical thing and not of the heart?"

Elizabeth shook her head in wonder. "Oh my dear. How far Shropshire is from the actual world! Men sleep with every willing maiden, and never count their partners. Indeed, for the lusty sort, it might be hundreds."

A hillock of water passed under the Bridge, tossing Tori's stomach into further turmoil as she considered these most interesting matters. The sea was up; disconcertingly so. But the plates of the Bridge were wondrous sturdy.

Elizabeth went on, "Of course, one's eventual husband may notice that a visitor has gone before, but that cannot be helped." She laughed silently at Tori's widened eyes. "But as for bearing children, there is indeed help for that. Most women have to hand a tincture of zinc sulfate. One rinse, and there will be no conception!"

Finishing the buttoning of Tori's shoe, she gave it a pat. "But pray do not rush out and seduce the butler. One must not be *caught*, that is the game."

Great rolling waves swept across the sea, creating hills and vales upon the Bridge, taxing the caravan's footing and will.

Mrs. Harding, trying to rest against the corner of the coach, moaned. Four times this afternoon it had been necessary to bring the coach to a halt so that she could descend to void her stomach. And here came another mountain of water moving under them, lifting the bridge and plunging it down again.

"Ohh," Mrs. Harding groaned.

Her face was a most alarming shade of yellow. "My dear," Colonel Harding said, grasping her hand. "It will pass."

"But when!" she cried.

He did not know. The wind was likely the forerunner of a bigger storm. They were in no danger, for the Bridge had endured all that the Ancific could muster in seven months of testing against the elements.

He returned to his letter from Sir John Beaumont, the retiring Governor of Nanpura Province. Dated some six weeks ago, it had just been given into his hands from the mail coach out of Poondras.

By telegram from Whitehall I have been informed that the occasion of militarily reinforcing the Bharati theatre will coincide with my retirement from command here. Please accept my congratulations and my welcome. I will listen with great interest to your account of your crossing of the Great Bridge, pray God a peaceful one.

Mrs. Harding groaned and spit into her handkerchief.

Provincial affairs have remained stable here these few weeks since a raid at our outpost in Sirinshwari. The raid was touched off by word of the terrorist flood in Londinium. The natives celebrated, taking the opportunity to loot the granary and shoot off muskets, killing several of their own number before falling to our superior guns. The arrival of the regiments under your command will properly show the mailed fist.

As to the fanatical bush priests responsible for the convulsions, we have been unable to identify them. I doubt they reside in Nanpura. Prince Uttam is a firm ally. He beats back border intrusions with effective force, in which endeavors we have given him free rein. Our interests and his coincide in protecting against neighboring princes who cast covetous eyes upon his holdings, especially the highly productive Jhir Ghoda diamond mine, subject of course to Anglic taxes.

The political officer attached to Kathore, Prince Uttam's royal seat, has informed me that Uttam has a fatal cancer though the palace doctors are not admitting it. This will surely mean the succession of his son Sahaj, who is considered unreliable. (Political officer Lieutenant Conolly will be your indispensable guide to Kathore.) If the worst happens, it will be your prerogative to place what pressures you deem fit to influence the succession; however the second son is a hemophiliac and not in favor with his father. The prince has three daughters. So there is the situation, tipping toward instability.

To round out this quick assessment, I will point to some success in our village educational programs. It is the Crown's policy to encourage the rise in middle-class families who enter their sons in productive vocations and as well, to moderate rash elements of Bharati spiritualism. A naive hope, but you must forward these programs as I have. The princes play both sides, allowing us entry into virgin territories while appearing to place limits on us in order to save face with the extremists. You will tease out these issues with Prince Uttam, and you will find Lieutenant Conolly's local knowledge vital to your success.

I most heartily look forward to greeting you at Poondras. Send ahead, of course, for anything that I may do to assure your family's comfort on their arrival. The memsahibs like their creature comforts, and I have found that when my own dear wife is happy, so goes my own peace of mind.

Yours sincerely,

Sir John Beaumont, KCB., CMG.

Colonel Harding folded the letter. Spatters of rain now pelted the window of the carriage, disguising the hills and valleys of the perturbed ocean. He would call an early halt to the day's march, as it looked like they must hunker down for a sustained blow.

His thoughts turned to Tori, as they so often did. He doubted her stated intention to find a husband in Poondras, because surely she had come to revisit the land of Sir Charles's famous voyage. It was his fervent wish that her stay in Bharata would help her find peace with her grandfather's past. In particular, he hoped she would come to understand how the magical practices of the continent could not be admired.

As for Jessa, he was not insensible of her disappointments, either. Mrs. Harding set great store by the Muir-Smith match, but it appeared so had Cora Hamilton's family. From the frequency of their luncheons with Muir-Smith, he was a great favorite.

Mrs. Harding moaned again. He leaned toward her. "My dear, how are you?"

"Bggt." She mumbled.

"My dear?"

"Bugget," came her garbled reply.

He reached for the bucket and held it for her while she retched.

Battling heaving seas and hard wind, the caravan had come to a stop for the day. Alone for once in the coach, Tori had just closed the hinged coach seat after picking through Elizabeth's portmanteau when she heard a tap at the door. Startled, she swerved around to see Captain Muir-Smith standing outside.

What had he seen?

As she opened the door, the wind lashed in along with droplets of rain.

"Miss Harding. My men have found an extraordinary creature washed in. I thought you'd like to see it, if you think the storm isn't too high."

"What creature is it?"

"I believe it's an octopus, Miss Harding. Do not worry, it is dead." In the wind his rain cape flapped about like sopping wet wings. Behind him, the ocean and air were gray against gray.

She unfolded her hooded cloak. "Very kind, Captain. I should love to see it."

Muir-Smith handed her down from the carriage and they made their way on the span as the Bridge bucked and rolled. Seeing the captain and Tori approach, a group of soldiers stood back from where they had been prodding at the beached creature.

"He ain't moved, Captain," one of the soldiers shouted. It was necessary now to raise one's voice to be heard in the rising wind.

Tori pulled her cape more securely around her, staring in delight at the monster. The tentacles extended to nearly a man's height, with suckers gracing the bottom layer. Its bulbous head lay almost flattened against the heaving deck leaving one eye exposed, as large as a big man's fist.

"How remarkable!" Tori exclaimed.

Muir-Smith went to one knee, lifting a tentacle. "They have no bones in them, but they are prodigiously strong."

"To be in the grip of such appendages would make a quick end, I'm sure," Tori said. "Look, here is the siphon, where the octopus thrusts water out in locomotion. It's quite ingenious."

The captain noted a rent in the head sac. "The men cut on this one, but we can see the most of it."

"Do have them extend the cut, and we shall see into the mantle."

Muir-Smith turned to one of the soldiers. "Your knife, here, Barker."

The slit now extended, Tori kneeled to spread the gap wider. A drool of black liquid began to pool inside.

"See, he has pierced the ink sac. They are so strong, yet use a cloak of black ink to escape an unnecessary fight. Grandpapa said that octopuses are quite intelligent, isn't that marvelous?"

"It is indeed. One can't judge such hidden gifts by anatomy." He peered closer, pointing. "And here, this is evidence of its last meal, if we have pierced the stomach."

The wind gusted, blowing Tori's hood back, splattering her with spume off a wave. She leaned closer to the octopus.

"Oh. This is most interesting. It is not the stomach, but the womb. This octopus is female and has eggs. See?" She thrust her hands in, to hold back the organs that Muir-Smith might glimpse the egg sac.

Muir-Smith looked closely and then, noting her soiled hands, unwound his neck scarf and handed it to her to clean up.

She caught his gaze as he did so, and felt a furious blush crest over her face. It seemed to her a most personal moment: she, with his neck scarf wiping her hands clean, and him taking the kerchief back soiled, and tucking it in a pocket. Covering her embarrassment, she said, "I misspoke when I called it the creature's womb. They don't bear young of course, but lay eggs."

"Quite right, of course," he said handing the borrowed knife to his man.

He escorted her back to the coach, but she did not accept his arm. Jessa was smitten with him; that was certain. It would not do to have these thoughts, her sudden warm thoughts of the captain, it would not at all do. She had never cared to have a suitor, and she did not have one now, of course. But the company of an interesting man had taken her quite off guard. *Married slavery...* Grandpapa's phrase came to her mind. It refreshed her very much to remember that she did not care to turn into her mother no matter how noble the groom.

Ahead, Jackson was waiting at the coach with towels and frowns.

She and Muir-Smith bade each other good day. It was then that she noted that next to the lantern the blue albatross had found a cranny in which to shelter from the rain.

As she looked, the little clawed feet became hands clutching the lantern standard. Her indrawn breath could not pass unnoticed. "Is there something?" Muir-Smith asked.

"No," she barely managed to say. Now the bird's feet looked perfectly correct. An albatross's. But she felt that her stare had unnerved the creature, causing it to lose its form. For the moment, having a thesis helped very much to steady her.

Muir-Smith glanced at the bird, which was endeavoring to tuck itself behind the lantern. "Is it the albatross?"

"Oh, it's a curious hue, that's all."

"Well, some depart from the general color."

He had noticed nothing, that was clear. Grandpapa had been right; he was one who did not *see*. It rendered him quite composed at all times, which, after all, was a most necessary trait for a man in his Majesty's service. Jessa must love that in him.

10

The women's tent shuddered in the gusts. Jessa had been reading aloud to the other two women by the lamplight, but Elizabeth felt uneasy. With the wind whipping about, she had visions of the book wagon's tarp coming undone and the rain doing its worst. The original batons had been very secure, but with Mrs. Harding riding prostrate in the book wagon during the days, Elizabeth worried that the tarps might now be neglected.

"I'll be gone only a few minutes," she declared, rising from her seat and throwing on her rain cape.

"You must let Jackson escort you," Jessa said, thinking she meant to make use of the privy.

Elizabeth ducked into the storm, pulling her hood securely over her head, and peered into the rain. Jackson was in the servant tent, no doubt, but she had only a few paces to go to check on the book wagon. No one was anywhere visible, not even the soldiers, having all retreated to tents. They had lanterns within, which threw a pallid light on her path. The Bridge rose and fell like an animal striving to be free of bondage. On her way she staggered against the carriage and careened on, growing more and more concerned for her books as the wind whipped stray cords and sent litter scudding.

At the book wagon, the tarps were holding, but one end flapped a little loose. She wished she had packed the books in another layer of oil-cloth. She had not foreseen that to make room for Mrs. Harding to lie down during her nauseous bouts, they would have to restack the books to make room down the middle, bringing the book stacks higher than the sides of the wagon. She untied the cords at the corner, bending to the task of making a good square knot.

It was just then that she felt more than heard a disturbance a dozen yards from her, out in the water. The ocean rose up, turning a most curious shade of turquoise. By all that was holy, it was an animal, rising from the water. Might this be an octopus such as Tori had seen? But in her heart, Elizabeth knew what it was. Slowly, she lifted her chin to look up into the eyes of an enormous kraken.

It was black against black, impossible to clearly see, yet its presence was palpable. Her mind, stunned in fear, yet noted odd details: the scales glowing green, the slick fin on its back, a wide face looking down on her. Surely it must be a phantom produced by her imagination. For if it was a beast, how could it maintain its position in the thrashing ocean?

With a sickening thump, it threw a great paw on the bridge railing. She was going to die.

Well then, she vowed, the books must not be forfeit. She gave a stout pull on the knot, drawing the cover down to protect the lovely paper. But flesh was weaker, exposed. To die in the jaws of the kraken would be merciful compared with the fate of the cow which had been hauled into the air and then submerged in the endless depths. She pressed trembling against the wagon, realizing with dismay that if she had not secured the knot, she might have thrust aside the edge of the tarp and scrambled into the wagon. Drawing breath, she prepared to scream to draw the guards.

A flash of sheet lightning.

Her scream died. She saw the kraken most clearly. The creature had let go its hold on the rail of the bridge and sank down a few feet, bringing its vast face on a level with her own. Oh, it was not a phantom, it was all animal, all teeth and nostrils and eyes, eyes like lanterns lit by the storm, its whiskers cascading water. It regarded her, oh indeed it did, with the delight of a lord about to enjoy a favorite repast.

That was her first thought. Her second was that it had seen enough and would proceed on its way.

And it did. It fell away as though it had never been. She thought—though the lightning had passed—that she saw a coiling tail humping up and slithering down.

Elizabeth fell to her knees. A moaning sound came to her ears. She was making a most remarkable sound, a guttural cry of terror and relief that soon subsided into a whimper. That would not do. Elizabeth Platt did not *whimper,* not in the face of a classroom of unruly tenement children nor a kraken from the abyss.

After a few minutes she heard Jackson calling for her. She stood up, smoothing her dress, trying to think how she would explain her dreadful state, her sopping hair, her shaken visage.

"Miss Platt," Jackson said as he hurried forward.

Cracks of rifle fire came from down the Bridge.

A shout from nearby as a sergeant rushed half-dressed from the nearest tent, pulling up his trousers. Then on every side the tents erupted with soldiers bearing rifles and swords. Officers shouted their men into formations.

Underneath yells of the troops and the howl of wind, from the distance came wild bellows like foghorns gone mad.

Colonel Harding leapt onto a stack of crates to get a view over the rail, into the churn of the sea. Cries of "kraken" came from all sides, but he could see none in the dark; he heard them, though, trumpeting at a distance.

Down the line, an explosion lit the Bridge, a magazine having caught fire. A tent burned, crackling and hissing. By this light he saw a dozen soldiers keeping formation, firing in sequence into the blackness, pray God finding a target. Heavy rifle fire came from forward on the line. There must be several of the monsters, all probing for weakness.

"How many?" Colonel Harding demanded as his adjutant rushed up to him.

"Five or fifty, sir, I do not know! They no more than rise up, than they're gone again!"

Harding felt the Bridge shudder. Good God, were the creatures attacking the Bridge deck itself? That was a greater peril than any other. "Shoot through the deck holes!" he shouted at soldiers who now swarmed around him. He jumped down, determined to get off a shot at the next passage of a kraken.

The deck rose up like a peaked roof. From under the grating came a grinding rattle that shook the pontoon, skewing it nearly out of line with the next segment. Soldiers fell, muskets clattering aside just as a foaming wave rushed over the lowest point, sweeping up his adjutant and carrying him away. Harding heard his scream as the surge threw his body against the rail and unto the very back of the kraken that now emerged from its passage under the Bridge.

The creature's long neck and head swiveled. Its jaws clasped down on the major's head and shoulders, snapping his bones.

"God damn it, shoot!" Colonel Harding cried at the stupefied men. He rushed to the railing which had now settled into mere humping chaos, and fired into the monster's neck, but his adjutant was gone. The kraken plunged down.

All along the bridge, ragged volleys spewed out but likely with little effect, as their kraken targets were one with the turbulent ocean, their movements cloaked in storm and waves.

Harding gathered the men near him and raced with them toward the civilian camp, but even as they drew near, they heard high-pitched screams.

Rifle fire was thick outside Tori and Jessa's tent, and the air filled with acrid smoke. Elizabeth was out there somewhere, alone. Tori rushed to the tent flap. "Stay here!"

Jessa threw herself forward, grabbing Tori's arm. "No! You can't go out!"

"Stay here!" Tori wrenched away and shoved out the tent flap into the storm. Wind-blown waves scudded over the rails, and men knelt by the carriages, shooting into the black, boiling sea. Fire engulfed a tent, barely slapped down by the salt water that seemed to come from every direction.

"Elizabeth!" she shouted. It was fruitless to call, so great was the roar of sea and fire and rifles. But there, just beyond the tent, she glimpsed her, bonnet gone, hair whipping around her, helped along by Jackson, as they labored to make progress up the Bridge. Tori was soaked through, her clothes weighing her down like an anchor, but she lurched forward to help. Then came a sound like the very mouth of the sea, a roar from a throat that must be many yards long, half-howl, half-screech. It brought Tori to her knees, as though a blow had struck her. The howl went on and on, filling her mind with its nightmare strength. How was it possible for an animal to produce such a sound?

Around her, soldiers were firing up at an apparition, but it was like shooting peas at a maddened bear. Hunkered down, face pressed into the heaving deck, she could not bear to look up at the thing.

And then she did. A great head and body towered over the bridge. Oh, it was all scales and cascading water, and whiskers jutting like lances. Somehow the kraken rose very high in the sea, balanced over the scurrying life forms under it. It paused horribly, looking down on the burning tent. God in heaven, it was going to devour the tent, and Elizabeth was right in the path. Tori sprang up, staggering, wildly lurching, and ran. She did not know why, nor what she could do, but she screamed for Elizabeth to back away, to dive clear of the descending jaws.

But it was too late.

Down they came. Serrated teeth tore at the flaming tent and hoisted it into the air and thence into the sea. Tori rushed through the cascading, flaming remnants, aware that she would die, stunned by the prospect of death at sea, death at all.

Crashing forward in Elizabeth's direction, she came upon her, huddling with Jackson against a coach wheel. She collapsed onto the bridge deck, throwing her arms around them both.

"Oh, Miss!" Jackson exclaimed, gathering her in.

The kraken bellowed a gargling rumble, long and satisfied and every bit as loud as before. Oh, if the noise might end! Tori felt she could endure anything if only this roar might subside.

Then the kraken bent sideways to dive away, forming a great glistening, turquoise arch above the sea. Yards and yards of hide snaked past, until at last it was gone.

The two women wept in each other's arms. "It's all right," Elizabeth declared, shaking like she had the palsy, tears mixing with the storm pellets.

The sounds of rifle fire quieted, renewed only by an occasional shot. Jackson had taken off his great coat and tented it over the women, but still they trembled.

Tori found her voice. "We're safe, Elizabeth. I thought you were... I thought it would..."

"I know." Elizabeth composed herself, wiping her face with her hands. "It almost did."

Jackson got them to their feet, and the three of them started a slow progress back to their shelter. There Tori saw Papa coming out of Jessa's tent. A few officers and men were gathered near.

Seeing Tori, Colonel Harding strode forward and fiercely embraced her.

"Jessa?" she blurted.

"Safe in the tent, my dear."

"By God, sir, we drove them off," Jackson said.

Her father turned to him. "Well done. Well done." He nodded at Jackson, their eyes meeting.

Punishing gusts still carried rain and sea foam horizontally across the decking but her father pulled Tori close to him again.

"Oh Papa," she whispered. "I'm so sorry. For everything." Suddenly it was not about sea monsters or the storm, but only about how much she loved him and Jessa, and how insufferably she had behaved, and how little she cared for anything but that her family should be safe.

Long ocean swells rocked the Bridge, a pleasant undulation compared with the frightful storm in which eight men had been lost over the rails. As more flotsam of jungle plants rode by, it was now possible to think of solid land. They would soon reach Bharata.

Still, conversations continually reworked the events of the kraken attack, including the brave rescue of Cora Hamilton by Captain Muir-Smith. When her tent had collapsed under a large wave, the captain had dragged her to safety. Jessa declared herself quit of him, as he oddly had chosen to keep watch over the Hamiltons and not the Hardings, when Tori and Elizabeth had been in so much greater peril. Her attitude cooled toward him, and now other young officers found reason to ride beside her carriage and find her in the evenings.

Tori had taken to riding in the book wagon to read to her prostrate mother, with the filtered light through the tarp giving just enough light to see. Mama was touched by the effort, and soon declared herself well by virtue of her daughter's care. She rode again with her husband in his carriage.

The caravan carried along a full measure of human enterprise and events; two servant women gave birth to lusty boys; a corporal was washed overboard by a freak wave and never seen again; another trade caravan came by bearing ores from the mine at Jhir Ghoda, and Captain Muir-Smith had to shoot his horse when it broke a leg.

As the caravan made its way steadily eastward, Tori became more and more accustomed to gazing out over the ocean, her vision oddly clear. Everything seemed keener than in Shropshire. She was in no wise deflected from her chosen purpose, but with the ocean swells, she felt a new need rise in her that had been submerged before. It had begun with Elizabeth, and might it just end with Muir-Smith?

The caravan had the effect of removing barriers among soldiers and civilians, high and low, ocean and land. But it could not last, for soon their procession would arrive in Bharata. And then her great opportunity would be lost.

Tori gripped the rail to steady her nerves. It was 9:30 p.m. He must come soon, or her absence would be too prolonged and someone would come looking for her. The night, warm and calm, was overflown with stars in breathless numbers.

She had risked a lie to be alone: She was helping with the washer woman's new infant; no one would check on her and risk having to endure a loud and sleepless baby. First Tori had nursed her mother; now she was helping with the infant.

In celebration of the last night of their journey, there was a dance at one of the officers' compounds, with bagpipes and a fiddle. In all, there was just enough commotion to allow freedom of movement and some absences.

But would Muir-Smith come? It was irregular for them to meet alone, and he might well be on duty and unable to attend her or even respond to the note she had sent.

When she saw a figure in a red officer's uniform approaching, her nerve left her all at once. It was impossible. What excuse could she offer now for asking to meet him? Perhaps it was not Muir-Smith at all, but his lieutenant come to say he was occupied.

But no, it was he.

"Good evening." His voice seemed rather too loud, but of course he could not imagine that she wished for secrecy.

"Captain. Thank you. Do you have duties?"

"No. I have my evening. I thought I might join the festivities at the dance." He stepped to the railing and joined her in looking out on the placid sea. "You've found a respite, I see. It's a pleasant sight."

The courtesies having been dispensed with, her stomach churned. "We're almost to the harbor," Tori managed.

"It's been a long journey. You and your sister have held up admirably, if you'll permit me to say so."

"I permit you." She thought she would burst if she did not say what was in her mind. "Captain. May I come to my point—of why I asked you to meet me here? I have little time, and I fear I'll lose my courage if I don't make my purpose plain to you."

He looked at her with some curiosity, frowning slightly. "Of course you may speak freely."

It was all the encouragement she needed. "You must know that I will never marry, Captain. It's a settled matter in my family."

"I don't think…" he began but she interrupted.

"Please don't humor me. I'm at peace. Let me say what I've come to say." Oh, this next part was terribly difficult; best to have done with it. "I will not marry, that is certain. I have a deformity that any suitor would find difficult to overlook. But that has given me the greatest freedom, do you see? Sir Charles raised me to science. All my hopes are there. Natural history will sustain me my whole life, I don't doubt."

He was watching her most carefully. "If this is your resolve, I must believe you are happy with it."

"Believe it, I pray. I wish you to understand that what I'm proposing has nothing to do with marriage."

A look of confusion came over his face.

"Captain, I have never known, nor will I likely ever know, physical intimacy with a man." Their eyes met in astonishment on his part and determination not to falter on hers. "I wish to. Tonight, if possible."

He opened his mouth to speak, but apparently found he could not.

"Please don't turn away from me. Say no if you must, but do so to my face."

He met her eyes, saying very low, "I cannot answer if I do not know the question."

"I propose that we consummate the physical act."

The Bridge lay quiescent on the flat waters as though it held its breath just as Tori did.

"You can't mean to say such a thing."

"Oh, but I do. I have thought carefully about it. I believe I shall never meet a man I trust more, nor who would have the presence of mind to hear me out."

"But…" He shook his head, as though still denying what he was hearing. "Is it your wish that I dishonor you, betray your father…"

"That would only be true if you did it out of passion and cold calculation. What I'm asking is that you do it for *me*." She saw his incredulity. "Yes, for me, because I'm curious to know of sexual matters and I greatly fear that I never *will* know the culminating act. Just once, I would know what it is to be in a man's arms. To know ecstasy, if that is what it offers."

When he didn't answer, she persisted. "Did you think that a woman doesn't feel the heat of a man's presence and long for what men commonly feel and do? Surely you are not one of those men who thinks women only submit to the embraces of their husbands?" Actually, she herself had thought so until meeting Elizabeth.

He looked at her more calmly now. "That is a remarkable speech, Miss Harding. I would have thought it impossible if I had not some acquaintance of you. I don't know what to say."

"Do you think me entirely reprehensible? I hardly have the experience to know how this may end, or if you can at all understand my reasoning. Can you?"

His look grew even more confused, given that he must either acquiesce or criticize her. He murmured, "I think I see your reasoning, God help me."

Her heartbeat quickened. "I even have a place. We must be discreet of course. That's why it must be tonight, when everyone is in a festive mood and the routines are disrupted."

"The place?"

"Yes, to guard our privacy. The book wagon." They stood right beside it.

He looked nothing so much like a man facing an adversary with a loaded gun. Finally he said, "Miss Harding. That you would trust me so far... I am astonished."

"No, do not be. Be amenable, I beg you, Edmond. May I call you Edmond? I will never bring it up to you again. It'll be as if it hadn't happened."

"But even if... I mean, you must be aware, there are *consequences*."

"Consequences? Oh! You mean pregnancy." She raised her hand, showing a small packet. "I have a preventative."

"How..."

"It is most efficacious. A tincture of zinc sulfate. Ladies know these things." She trusted that Elizabeth would not miss the small amount she had removed from her portmanteau. Taking it must be preferable to embroiling her friend in a matter by no means sure of a respectable outcome.

If he had hoped that a small barrier would be enough to dissuade her, he must now realize that it was solely up to him. She had thought through every aspect. She hoped that, in addition to her arguments, the prospect of sex would sufficiently arouse him to be disposed to agree. Elizabeth had said that she was not unattractive. And of course she would keep her shoes on.

He put his hand over hers where it rested on the railing. "Miss Harding—"

"Oh, cannot you call me Astoria?"

"Miss Harding, I cannot do as you request."

"You can," she whispered. "If you would." Fear and humiliation seeped into her. She wished very much to rush away but held her stance. "You don't find me appealing. I understand that. But I thought, for the sake of friendship, you might bring yourself to overlook..."

He shook his head, as though to trying on phrases and casting them off again. "Any man would be capable of desiring you. Please understand that's not my motive."

He went on, "If this were discovered, it would ruin us both. You would never have a place in polite society, not even in science."

"And you would lose all," she found herself saying, but wishing it did not seem so damning.

"Miss Harding, I would be the most reprehensible of men to act upon this. A nineteen year old girl—"

"—Young *woman*."

He shook his head. "This conversation cannot serve either of us very well. I fear I must offend you no matter what I say."

She dared to put her hand on his arm. "Captain, these are impossible questions. Cannot we put them aside, just for tonight?"

He stepped back, his face gathered once again into that galling reserve. "You deserve better than this."

"You are saying no, I believe. Are you?" She must give him a last chance, but it seemed it would be just one more humiliation.

"Yes. I must say no." He looked at her with great intensity—most unguardedly. She almost thought he would change his mind.

"You'll be grateful to me someday."

"So much more so had you said yes." She did not care how craven it sounded, but she could not be brought to agree with his decision.

"I... I pray you will forgive me." A horrid pause. Then he took her hand and she allowed him to bring it to his lips.

She watched as he wound his way back among the carriages and carts. Resentment warred with acute embarrassment.

Then, turning her gaze upon the book wagon, she could not help but imagine a quite different outcome.

11

An old man pressed a flower into Mahindra's hand. "Your blessing, holy one." Mahindra placed his hands together in front of his face and bowed. Seeing this, others in the crowd surged forward, tugging at his robe to partake of holiness. Among the gathered citizens of Poondras he spied local *sadhus* frowning at this show. They wore ochre paint on their skin and their uncut hair reached to their buttocks. He knew how the Anglic patricians turned empty stares upon these practitioners; it was the famous Anglic gaze in which you were kept in place, disregarded.

Mahindra turned away from the crowd, resolutely facing forward, following the baggage train. He did not wish to earn the *sadhus'* envy, for they must eventually come under the Lotus Banner. One land, one people. He had learned much of nation-building in Anglic schools: greatness and power could not come from a collection of tribes, provinces or warring princes. Yes, the *sahibs* had taught him well: All under one.

They passed through the great Poondras bazaar, with the Temple of Sita on one side, its priests gathered like honey bees in the meager shade of its portals. Down the alleyways off the square, people were still pouring into the bazaar, some beating on drums suspended from shoulder straps. People found reasons to celebrate; even the arrival of four thousand armed foreign soldiers was a holiday to them. The carts drawn by bullocks led the way across the Sita Bridge crowded with yet more humanity standing on the short walls above the muddy Ralawindi River. Mahindra could now see the walls of the cantonment, the reinforced remnants of an ancient citadel. Soldiers stood at attention on the thirty-foot ramparts, Bharati sepoys in their green and orange striped turbans. They had been seduced by Anglic honors and income, cherishing their tin medals.

Mahindra passed through the main gate. He had not been in the cantonment for twenty years. He knew its features well: the barracks, pickets, governor's residency, bungalows, St. Mary's church and the schools. One of those schools had been his.

Now more Anglic faces appeared among the dark. Under ruffled parasols, *memsahibs* in their heavy dresses murmured to each other, their words clear by their expressions: *savages, illiterates, blackamoors.* There had been a time when he had taken revenge on the foreigners. He had even killed his share. Those were the days when he was young and believed that revolution could grow like a tide pulled by the moon. But he would not allow himself to think about the losses from that tide, losses beyond bearing.

Here, just inside the cantonment gate was the highest point of the Anglic fortification. From this point the land sloped down to the finest harbor in south Bharata, crowded with junques, supply boats and skiffs and a few three-masted naval ships. In the shimmering heat of the day, he could just make out the great road west, thrusting out into the sea, already groaning with wagons of timber and cotton headed for Anglica. The wharves were piled high with bales and crates, all destined for the west. And what came east, in return? Money. Soldiers. Teachers. It was not a proper exchange.

Reaching the parade grounds, servants offloaded the baggage carts and laden elephants. Mahindra watched as they took down the carpet that would be the *rana's* gift to the new governor. "Take care!" Mahindra shouted as the rolled carpet nearly fell from the elephant's back. Over there, the *ranee* had been dozing in her *howdah.* She was not happy to be awakened, he saw. At her husband's command she had taken no opium today and looked cross to have to face the day—and foreigners—without it. Her women helped her down the ladder and whisked her into the waiting tent.

Mahindra worried. It must all be perfect: the durbar, the gifts, the *ranee.* No piece must fall from its place. To earn this perfection, Mahindra had walked barefoot all the way from Kathore in the dust. The *ranee* was fragile. However, she must only last the day and then she could slip into her dreams.

He looked about him carefully. Would the girl Astoria be on the parade grounds, perhaps strolling under a parasol, talking with her sister? No, it was best that they not meet. At the durbar he would be a fly riding an elephant's ear. He did not crave prominence. Only justice.

∾

Sweat poured from Edmond's face under his pith helmet. The Anglic regiment faced west on the parade grounds, into what seemed a never-ending sunset. Drawn up before the reviewing stand were the companies of soldiers from Poondras and Kathore, red and white vying with Uttam's sky blue. Two richly painted elephants stood in line with the Kathores, their mahouts small and dull perched upon such magnificence. It was all colorful and fine, but Edmond's mind was hopelessly on other things.

Standing next to Edmond, Kathore's political officer Lieutenant Conolly leaned in to say, "That sword's worth a lord's ransom, right there." A servant had just brought forward a ceremonial curved *tulwar*, the hilt studded with gems. Conolly's face was annoyingly dry, the man having weathered four years in Bharata to Edmond's service last year of five months.

At the reviewing stand, between Colonel Harding and Sir John Beaumont, sat Prince Uttam, sumptuously attired in a three-quarter length *achkan*, embellished with gold embroidery. A white plume adorned his turban, fixed in place by a yellow diamond the size of a walnut.

Another gift from the Prince of Nanpura came forward, a carpet borne by three slaves. They unrolled it with a snap, displaying its dark wine hues.

"An Amritsar, you can be sure," Conolly said. "The old man will put it in his study. They all do."

Presently it came to the riflery contest, and still the sun would not set. Edmond barely listened as Conolly discussed the contestants, some Anglics, some Bharatis of his acquaintance, members of the Prince Uttam's guard in their blue *achkans* and tight trousers.

Edmond tried most diligently to listen, but his mind was all on Astoria Harding. Damn, but she was a surprising woman. Well, he surprised himself. After his initial shock at her... request, he had been amazed and even sympathetic to her situation. Also, all unlooked-for, he felt oddly flattered that she could have brought herself to ask *him*.

". . . can't hit the broad side of a Punjabi elephant, that one," Conolly was saying.

Edmond still remembered the way she had said, *I wish to know physical intimacy with a man. Tonight...* Not that he would for a moment have considered her proposal. She didn't realize how much she risked. It was very clear to him, however. Yet he couldn't forget how she argued with such force and logic for an act that she did not in the least believe was shameful. *We must be discreet. I have a place.* The wagon. They stood right next to the place she imagined he would ravish her.

A few of the officers had gone into town last night to find their comfort, but he had kept to his room, thinking of the young woman with the uneven gait, and the dark, challenging eyes. By God, against all odds she had a grip on him. He almost felt he had permission to think of her smooth body under his own, but it was coarse to take advantage, even in his thoughts. He would not.

"That *yuvraj* Sahaj is usually drunk. He's the last up. Ten quid says he misses."

Edmond struggled to recall what the lieutenant was on about.

Conolly cocked his head. "In for ten quid?"

"Oh. Yes, I'm in." The young prince wore pale blue voluminous trousers, tight fitting achkan and a flowing white shirt.

"He's got himself a couple white tigers," Conolly said. "They eat from his hand. I've seen it. He'll be a corker if he gets the succession." He watched the prince take aim. "*Miss*, you black bastard."

Astoria had said she would never speak of the matter again. But they must eventually face each other. She could only hold him in contempt, if for nothing more than what she had suggested to him.

The young prince hit a bull's eye. The crowd cheered as his father nodded to him. Edmond noted the old prince, dying they said, but he looked hale enough.

"Well, I owe you, old man," Conolly said.

Edmond muttered, "Yes, well." He was profoundly thankful that he had turned her down. She didn't realize that it was for her own protection that gentlemen did not make such advances.

But he was being inattentive. He should be pumping the political officer for all he knew. "Uttam could well sign the trade agreements right here," Edmond said. "All the players in one place. Save me a trip to Kathore."

Conolly smiled out of one side of his mouth. "Doesn't work that way. You'll have to pay your respects. And he wants you to see his fortress, to reinforce his position. He wants at least forty percent off Jhir Ghoda."

"Forty, by God? He won't get it. The Crown likes that revenue. He'll take fifteen."

Conolly shrugged. "I hear the *ranee's* got a necklace with rubies the size of robin's eggs. He needs forty percent. You're not married, Captain?" When

Edmond shook his head, Conolly said, "They want what they want. Our job is to give it to them or there's hell to pay."

But not what they want before marriage, Edmond thought. Or *instead* of marriage.

The parade grounds emptied as shadows at last lengthened across the square. The regiment would train at Fort Poondras, then units would disperse to troubled provinces, making a show of force in the hotbed hill villages where traitorous holy men preached against Anglica. Whitehall wouldn't have given Harding a true fighting post, Edmond had to admit, as much as he loved the old man. Poondras was an easy post.

The ranks marched off the field, headed toward quarters. Edmond felt uneasy about seeing Astoria at the dance. Should their paths cross, he had no idea what to say.

⌒◗

That evening Tori positioned herself at the doorway to the patio so that she would not be obliged to walk far to take the patio air. The night was frightfully hot, with an occasional breeze puffing through the open doors and windows, bringing the exotic scent of jasmine and orange blossoms.

Across the room, Tori noted Prince Uttam, imposing in his brocades and surrounded by advisors and high ranking Anglic officers. Near him, the young prince, Sahaj, handsome in his way, but growing more voluble as the champagne flowed. Tori scanned the room, hoping to see the *ranee*. But Lieutenant Conolly had said that the *Ranee* Kavya would not be seen in mixed company.

The strains of a waltz sparkled through the room, and the dancers took their places. Tori had to admit that the officers looked very handsome in full dress uniform with the brocade at the cuffs and collar. Jessa's color was high, with no lack of dance partners including Edmond Muir-Smith. Now that the Hamilton family had announced that Cora and Mrs. Hamilton would return to Anglica with the next caravan, Jessa's fortunes had risen. Poor Cora had never recovered from her fright on the Bridge, suffering nervous palpitations which had kept her abed.

Though Lieutenant Ned Conolly had explained to the family just before the dance that white women were not to speak to the Bharati men under any circumstances, there had been a moment when Tori had almost broken that rule. An hour ago, when she had strolled for a moment into the gardens, a Bharati man in a simple white achkan and trousers had looked directly into her eyes. They passed each other on the stairs to the ornamental fountain, she going up, and he down. He was middle aged and very thin, and by his manner, someone of importance, though oddly he was bare-footed. He inclined his head toward her in a most startling Anglic manner. She had just managed a partial curtsy when Mama found her and drew her back to the party, not even noticing him.

Nearby, Elizabeth Platt waved at her. She had been dancing capably, keeping company with her fellow-teachers who did not have her ease in society. Twice she danced with her cousin. Once Edmond had caught Tori's gaze and nodded to her, but then Colonel Harding had him in tow, directing him to Uttam's contingent, those advisors and attendants that he must cultivate on assignment at Kathore. Even in that brief moment she discerned that Edmond was disconcerted to see her. She still very much regretted the captain's supposed gallantry.

"My dear, if you don't mind." Mrs. Harding was at her side. "It's the *ranee.* Most extraordinary, but she has asked to meet you."

Lieutenant Conolly waited a few steps away. Short and wiry of build, the lieutenant seemed very young to hold the position of political officer in the province.

"The *Ranee* Kavya?" Tori was astonished that she was to have this opportunity.

"Yes. She and her attendants are on the bay porch. I can't imagine why she would ask for you. Lieutenant Conolly thinks that she's lonely for her daughters. Isn't that what you said, Lieutenant?"

"Yes, ma'am. The *ranee* hates to travel, and of course her daughters couldn't come."

Mrs. Harding turned back to Tori. "Lieutenant Conolly will escort you. It's around the other side. Easier to go the back way than across the dance floor." She tucked a strand of Tori's hair into her up-do. "Unless I should come with you?" She looked to Conolly.

"It would be best to respect the *ranee's* specific invitation, Mrs. Harding."

"Oh. Well, I didn't want to miss the fireworks. They are about to begin."

Tori tried not to show blatant relief. Her heart was beating hard. An audience with the *ranee!*

Lieutenant Conolly walked with Tori into the deep dusk of the walkway. Colored lanterns sat upon the enclosing half-wall at intervals, shadowed now and then by bats diving for insects.

"The *ranee* is quite traditional," Conolly said, briefing her as they walked.

"Don't shake her hand or touch her person. If there are platters of food, you must not eat."

"What shall I call her?"

"Highness." In the distance came the chittering of a mongoose, the screech of hyenas, the night more filled with creatures than the day.

"Have you met the *ranee*, Lieutenant?" Tori asked. She wondered if the lady would be intimidating and if her own halting language skills would be adequate to a social exchange.

The lieutenant shook his head. "No. She and her daughters keep to the *zenana.*"

"Then we're lucky that she chose to come to the durbar." They approached the porch, brightly lit and surrounded by turbaned guards.

"Well, she didn't chose. The prince commanded."

"Oh, it's married slavery, even here?"

He stopped at a good distance from the porch steps. "No one would mistake the *ranee* for a slave." He urged her forward, and she walked as straight as she could, past immobile, very alert guards.

At the top of the stairs, a servant girl met her and gestured her toward the *ranee*, ensconced in an enormous rattan chair draped in silk. A servant moved a *punkah* back and forth over the *ranee's* head, but not a hair rippled in her coconut-oiled chignon. Her red sari was shot through with threads of gold. Tori approached and fell into such a curtsy as she could manage.

"Ah, then it is Astoria, is it?" the *ranee* said in heavily accented Anglic.

"*Ek ucch samman,*" Tori said. A great honor.

The *ranee* gave a small, surprised look, her face plump and ageless. "Please be sitting. It will please us to do."

A chair appeared and Tori sat. "*Sukriya, Raniji.*" Thank you, Highness.

The *ranee* paused, lifting an eyebrow at this Bharati exchange. "*Bahut accha.*" Very good. The *ranee* continued in Bharati, "Shall we converse in my language, then?"

Tori smiled, and said, also in Bharati, "Please, Highness, it would be a great pleasure. But my skill is imperfect."

"We must leave perfection to the gods," the *ranee* said. "Is your sister occupied?"

"Oh, forgive me, Highness, we didn't know that she was invited."

"You have only one sibling. This is so?"

"I treasure my sister. She is my only one."

"I have two sons, Sahaj, the *yuvraj* and Jai, whom we protect as best we can.

Your father has no sons." The *ranee* shook her head as though mentioning a dread disease. "This I have heard, that Anglic women do not produce many children. Is it so?"

"Sometimes, it is, Highness. My family's hopes must be with its girls."

The *ranee* brightened. "I have a daughter upon whom my hopes rest."

Tori had heard that she had three daughters, but didn't want to contradict. "What is her name, if I may ask, Highness?"

"Navya, she is called."

"Oh, beautiful," Tori exclaimed.

The porch had gone very quiet. Across the courtyard, the mongoose again, chittering against the faint background of the band.

"Your grandsire once came to visit Kathore."

"Yes, Highness, Sir Charles Littlewood. He studied plants, and loved your country very much."

The *ranee's* attention drifted as she gazed past Tori, into the dark garden, looking perhaps for the noisy mongoose, or Navya. She murmured, "Yes, the Gangadhar Mahal. He studied very much of growing things."

Now was Tori's chance, forward or not, protocol or not. "Highness, he told me so much about the Gangadhar. It's a sight I would love to see for his sake."

"The monkeys have it now," the *ranee* murmured. "They chatter of the old days. Yes, the monkeys remember."

They sat in silence for a few moments. The band soldiered on, as the strains of *If Music Be the Food of Love* drifted through the garden.

Then a whump of a gun came from across the grounds. Everyone on the porch turned to see a golden cascade of fire fall from the sky. The fireworks display had begun.

The servants gathered the *ranee* up and brought her to the railing. Graciously, she turned to Tori, beckoning her forward. Standing by Tori's side, the *ranee* revealed herself as a full head shorter than Tori.

Cheers came from the distant officer's mess as a grand red flower bloomed in the sky and fell earthward in fragments of stars.

The assembly on the porch watched in rapt attention as the display continued, the launch guns barking, the sky lit with streamers of green, silver and red.

"My people also have a show of color," the *ranee* said.

There was a pause in the fireworks, like a gathering breath. Then a glowing fountain rushed upward from the parade grounds. Coalescing in the sky, it resolved into the head of a golden jaguar. A lovely feat, which Tori assumed—

by the claps from around the *ranee*—was the work of Kathore.

Then there was something less lovely about the picture. Was that a frown on the great cat's face? Yes—and now, its eyes slanting deeply into a frown. Hovering overhead, looking down upon them, it held a most unpleasant aspect. Then it began to change even more. The jaguar's mouth exploded into a gaping hole of crimson-drenched teeth. Tori stepped backward, hand on her throat, guessing what came next. And then it did: out of the bloody maw came a roar that shook the garden.

From the dance came a woman's scream. Then laughter. It was only a display.

The phantom crumbled to fragments, leaving a trace of the mouth. At last, even this, in a drooping grimace, fell to splinters.

The *ranee* turned toward her guest, looking serene and if Tori did not impute more than she should, satisfied. "It was only a jaguar."

"If that is what they look like, I hope I may not see a real one."

"The holy men know little of entertainment. Perhaps they go too far."

"Oh, no, Highness," Tori hastened to say. "It was magnificent."

The *ranee* nodded. "Truly, you must come to Kathore. It is not far."

Tori's heart clutched at the remarkable statement. Her very opening!

"My daughters need a distraction."

"Oh, Highness," Tori said, stumbling momentarily and then sallying forth: "I would love to come. It would mean everything to me."

"Then it is settled." The *ranee* flicked a glance at an attendant who was instantly at Tori's side, to guide her to the stairs. "Thank you for visiting, Astoria. I have enjoyed you very much. We shall be friends, do you not think?" Her smile was now dazzling, and Tori felt a warm bond.

"Oh, yes, madam… Highness! Thank you." She had not quite turned away when the *ranee's* servants took their mistress in tow, leading her to the end of the porch, to a chaise lounge. Tori hoped she was well, that she would not fall ill and cancel the invitation. The invitation! To Gangadhar. *Oh, Grandpapa*, she almost spoke aloud.

Her head spun as she came into the garden to find her escort waiting.

"How did it go, Miss, if I may ask?"

"Yeh ek dum sahi tha."

Conolly, who had the language, said, "Perfect," was it?

Tori brought herself back to Anglic. "Oh yes. Perfect!"

〜◦

Light spilled from the second story windows of the governor's residence where the women were preparing for bed, but the deep porch was in shadow except for the red tips of the men's cigars. Ned Conolly puffed happily on his, an excellent Scottish leaf. Sir John Beaumont didn't indulge, content with his sherry and the best rattan chair, courtesy of the new governor, who chose to stand.

Colonel Harding had declared the durbar a splendid success, and Ned had made sure to endorse that viewpoint despite the appearance of the unfortunate growling phantasm. In fact Ned and Sir John were pleased with the dust-up, as it served as a reminder to Harding that local politics wasn't all clear sailing; Bharatis still needed winning over. And that included acceptance of the *ranee's* invitation of a visit by Harding's daughter. The problem was, Mrs. Harding was dead set against it.

"Uttam was furious at the damn jaguar," Sir John was saying. "He had a couple bush priests whipped. Of course that could be just for our benefit. Ask me, he ordered it, just to shake us up a trifle."

As Harding drew on the cigar, his face was a point of light in the darkness. "Is he for us or not? I thought he was dependable."

Sir John gestured at Ned, giving him license to answer.

"He's our man. Shrewd and corrupt, in the best possible ways. He needs us for Jhir Ghoda if nothing else; he's got a decent fighting force, but Anglic fire power is what keeps him in diamonds."

"Religious?"

"That's the thing. They all are. The more gods, the more they like it. They've got no consistency in their beliefs, and in 6,000 years of dynasty they've thrown nothing away. I mean nothing. How they keep it all straight, damned if I know. But when it comes down to diamonds and politics, you can count on Uttam."

"And still he puts a growl into the fireworks." Harding gazed into the dark in front of the residency, his dress jacket open a few buttons. He was relaxed and satisfied, just the mood they'd hoped he'd be in to make an agreeable decision about Astoria.

Sir John shrugged. "He can't appear too docile in front of the bush priests."

"Well, he's made it deucedly hard to appease Mrs. Harding. She was frightened tonight. She won't hear of Astoria's going."

Sir John sipped his sherry, murmuring, "Makes for an awkward moment then, turning the *ranee* down. The prince dotes on her."

Ned piped up. "Your daughter seems to like the prospect."

"I dare say she would. But Kathore's a long slog into the hills. Mrs. Harding wouldn't be up for it. She had a hard crossing, and the heat grinds her down."

Ned exchanged a surreptitious glance with Sir John. The wife was not to go along, they must make sure of that. Mrs. Harding would constantly fuss over her daughter at Kathore, and Astoria must have the maximum freedom to roam. She'd be looking for the lotus. They all hoped she'd find it.

"Well," Sir John said, "that teacher is going along. Astoria would have some company. Uttam's proud of the provincial schools, and with reason."

Harding blew a stream of blue smoke. "But he won't allow a school at Kathore."

Sir John glanced at Ned, pushing him into the topic.

"Sir, the way these people think, everything is negotiable. The prince is holding a few things back. Muir-Smith will find out what when he wrangles out the trade agreement. He comes back to Poondras with a new treaty, your daughter comes back with a few nice saris and Bharati stories, and the neighboring *rajas* get a glimpse of how we treat our allies. Nice little package there."

Harding raised an eyebrow. "Maybe I should let *you* convince Mrs. Harding."

As the conversation lapsed, Sir John prompted Ned as planned. "What's behind this invitation, Lieutenant? Any ideas?"

"Well, the *ranee's* devoted to those girls of hers, so she's always interested in family and children. That's for starters. At the same time she's lonely for the one that got married off last year. My bet is that Astoria reminds her of the girl."

In the distance, from the civilian side of the cantonment, a musket went off amid loud cheers. Harding looked sharply in that direction.

"The celebrations go on," Sir John said soothingly.

Ned thought of the opium-infested *Ranee* Kavya, feeling a qualm of disloyalty in painting her as a mother-figure. But he had his orders; the mission, a top secret priority from the Foreign Office.

Astoria thought she knew all about what Sir Charles had called *Nelumbo aureus*. With her head stuffed full of theories from her grandfather, she thought the plant bestowed scientific insights. No doubt she also believed it was Sir Charles who had discovered this particular lotus.

However, Whitehall had been interested in the flower for a hundred years, given the rumors that it possessed a set of most astonishing and useful attributes that Ned's political minders were determined to put to good use in Bharata. Damned if they'd ever seen a living specimen, but they hoped that was about to change. The *ranee's* invitation, perfectly timed, would set all that in motion. The *Ranee* Kavya might not be the best chaperone for Astoria, but Ned would be there at Kathore to protect her. He'd be right behind her every moment.

Smoking in companionable silence, Ned and Sir John let Harding stew for a while. Lights began to wink out in the upper story. The younger daughter's evening had been a great success, with several young officers vying for her dances. The *ranee's* invitation capped off a perfect evening, all according to plan. Ned had put the suggestion to Uttam. Inviting the daughter, he'd told the *rana*, would be considered a friendly gesture; it would ingratiate him to the governor and loosen up the trade talks. All nonsense, but the *rana* must have fallen for it. And the *ranee* did what she was told.

Even so, Harding couldn't actually be *ordered* to send his daughter to Kathore.

Ned stood up and stretched, making an appearance of weariness. Time to push Harding to a decision. He strolled to the stairs and leaned against the porch column. In the distance, down the hill, lay the harbor where a few lanterns marked the positions of ships. In the moonless night the Bridge was quite invisible. But it was all about the Bridge, that thread that connected a resource-poor Anglica with the vastly rich Bharata, the treasury that had kept Anglica in prosperity for three hundred years. But with the *sadhus* getting notions of autonomy, the ocean road might find itself empty.

The lotus would put the rabble-rousers in their place. And they'd be happier for it.

As Ned had predicted, a little silence brought results. Harding said, "I suppose she could go for five or six days. In Muir-Smith's delegation."

Ned tried not to look triumphant. "And I'll be at Kathore, so she won't be alone."

Sir John set down his glass. "It's settled, then. The right decision, Colonel. But I don't envy your bringing your good wife around to it." He exchanged a satisfied look with Ned.

On that note, Ned's thoughts turned to Leela, waiting for him at his bungalow. A most agreeable finale to the evening. He stubbed out his cigar and shook hands with Harding. "Congratulations, sir. A total success."

Harding quirked his mouth. "Well, it's not *your* daughter setting out into the bush."

Sir John turned on the stairs. "She'll be back in a week with stories of palaces and elephants. You'll see. Our young ladies love the exotic locales."

12

In the parade grounds Colonel Harding watched as the fort gates swung open for the departing band of soldiers and the passenger wagon. Muir-Smith would watch over her, and had damn well be firm, if Tori should get it in her head to plead for more time away. Two weeks only, and even at that his wife was barely speaking to him.

But Tori had to go. He was not able to say what she would learn in Kathore, but she wanted to walk in Sir Charles's footsteps at least for a few days, wanted to know the Gangadhar, though she'd been well warned it was a ruin. Even more than that, she needed to be in the presence of spiritualist practices. To observe that mode of power so that she might ascertain for herself what practical utility it might have. If he was any judge, she would soon learn that for every benefit, the price was a priest who must suffer. Thus, even should there be a scientific application—and he didn't believe for one moment that magical practices *could* enlighten the world—it could not be countenanced for compassion's sake. Damn Sir Charles anyway, for snaring her in this futile aspiration!

Nearby, Mrs. Harding stood with Jessa, faces shadowed by their parasols. They knew Tori wanted to see the Gangadhar. But for her part, Mrs. Harding had no notion of what it meant to her daughter.

But Colonel Harding knew. When he'd embraced Tori in farewell, he was unable to express his foremost thoughts: I wish you weren't going. This is the hardest thing I've ever done, though I've met the enemy in battle. Just to let you do this thing and suffer its disappointments, to leave your hopes behind. It's more than I can bear for you to suffer. But I must let you be.

Instead, he'd said, "Write us, my dear, and tell us how you fare."

If he did not mistake her, her eyes were bright with tears. "Oh, I shall, Papa. I hope you won't worry. Please do not."

"Nothing of the sort. Muir-Smith and Conolly will watch over you or I'll have their stripes."

Her smile came readily. "Then for their sakes I shall have to behave."

"We cannot expect so much, my dear. Just find... your peace."

She had looked at him curiously. "Peace? Shall I be pleased with myself for little reason?"

"I am pleased with you for every reason." It was true. She needed to be nothing more in his mind. But it was what was in *hers* that mattered.

In the hardwood forest, the soldiers mounted their ostriches as the column got underway again. Tori and Elizabeth were the only civilians attached to the unit, since the other teachers who had crossed to Bharata were soon to leave Poondras for their posts in different provinces.

Elizabeth, with a fretful stomach from a meal that did not agree with her, waited in the wagon, with its yellow canopy and blessed shade.

Tori quickly snipped a specimen of *Plumeria alba*. Hurrying back to the wagon and clambering in, she thrust a sprig under Elizabeth's nose. "They're usually red, so the white is a great pleasure to see."

"Oh! So fragrant."

"Frangipani. And the bees love it. See how they swarm."

They were in thicker canopy now, shading them from the sweltering sun. The soldiers' ostrich-mounts—*Struthio camelus maximus*—lifted their remnant wings a little as though airing themselves out, and resumed the march, striding with grace.

Tori wanted to ride an ostrich. That way she could stop to examine plants along the way, but Edmond would not allow it. She was working on that, but since he avoided her at every possible moment, she had not had much chance.

The palm trees of the lowlands had given way to teak, rosewood and cotton trees hugging a rumpled geography leading into the foothills. Epiphytes, primarily *Orchidaceae*, hugged many tree trunks. Tori recorded as many specimens as she could recognize from Sir Charles's herbarium books and quickly sketched some unknown ones.

Oh, to be traveling to Kathore and through the miracle of this forest! This was the very land of *Nelumbo aureus*. She seemed to have outwitted every effort to forestall her bid to pursue Sir Charles's thesis. Certainly the *ranee's* invitation had been a wholly unexpected turn of good fortune. But it would have been unlikely that Sir Charles's connection to the city of Kathore would have been overlooked by the prince's family—nor Tori's command of the language. Nevertheless, finding evidence of *Nelumbo aureus* would be extraordinarily difficult; but if the Gangadhar held another remnant of the flower, she would certainly put its resins to the test. If the lotus vouchsafed her a vision of its location, would she have enough clues to discern how to get there? And would the prince indulge a young lady's desire to travel into the upland forests of Kathore? But she would not be stopped by such doubts, now that she was miraculously on her way.

Lieutenant Conolly came up on his ostrich-mount, matching the pace of their bullock-driven wagon. "How are you today, Miss Platt, Miss Harding?"

Elizabeth pronounced herself well indeed. She had already claimed to never have been sick, and thus she could hardly let the *dal*—spiced lentils—challenge her digestion. "How do you like riding an ostrich, Lieutenant?"

"I'm used to it, Miss Platt. You must teach them who's in charge, though. Ill-tempered beasts."

"Oh," Elizabeth said, "I can't believe that. Their great eyes look so soulful."

"Even in Bharata, ostriches do not have souls, Miss Platt." Charmingly, he gave her a jaunty salute, and flicked the reins. His mount loped forward. Tori marveled that one so young—she judged him not five years her senior—could be so highly regarded as a local expert. He had no family; the army was his family he had said.

They passed through a small village.

Here the sun crushed down upon them, delivering up a stew of odors, mixing manure, dust and chapattis frying. Though beneath her bonnet Tori's face and neck were soaked, the village folk took no notice of the heat. By the central well, pariah dogs tore at a carcass, while in clusters the villagers stared at the caravan trooping through.

Elizabeth clucked her tongue. "The squalor of it," she murmured, shaking her head. "Look how the children run naked, and so thin!"

Squalor was not Tori's first impression. Instead, she drank in the exotic women's dress: their bright colors of vermillion and saffron, and the brass ornaments on the arms of even the poorest. They had their own beauty, spare and bright.

The caravan stopped as Edmond rode up to the *tahsildar*, village headman, for a brief conversation translated by Lieutenant Conolly. Meanwhile a small boy approached the cart, and Elizabeth handed down her frangipani flower into grimy fingers, bringing a stunning smile from the child.

"Oh," Elizabeth exclaimed, "I can hardly wait for my school!"

They camped in a field of pampas grass, giving them a clear view of the Rangnow Mountains ahead, crouching massifs gouged in places into serrated teeth. Kathore was in the foothills of that range, wreathed in evening fog.

The women's tent was pitched in the middle of the camp, with their escort of fifteen Anglic soldiers and sepoys ringed round about. Small fires dotted the perimeter in case of jackals and leopards. Elizabeth retired early, excusing Tori from reading out loud, which the women had undertaken as a custom.

The day had been long, but Tori did not want it to end. She stood by the tent, noting a wheeling gyre of birds overhead. The chatter of a jungle-cock just over there drew her attention, and she headed toward it, aware that the soldiers watched her ungainly walk. Ahead was a great stand of pampas grass, its silver panicles waving in the breeze, from which depths her approach flushed a covey of sand grouse. They sped away in their own swaying gait. She wrote down this observation in the notebook she kept in a pouch threaded through a belt at her waist.

A sound behind caused her to swirl around.

"Oh, Edmond! I thought it was a leopard."

"I'm glad it's not one. You've walked far from camp, Astoria."

She looked back at the perimeter fires. "I have. I know you promised my father that no leopard will feast on me."

"Indeed," Edmond said, "losing you to a leopard would be considered a gross failure of duty." He produced the first easy smile she'd seen from him since the Bridge.

"Well, don't herd me back to the tent just yet. See, there are vultures." She pointed to the circling birds, drifting closer now, their wingspan the largest she had ever seen.

"Searching for a kill," Edmond murmured.

They stood watching the birds, their conversation exhausted. Finally Tori turned to the captain. The gathering dusk planed his face with shadow, giving him a softer aspect than in the heat of day in the hot colors of his uniform.

"Edmond—"

"Astoria—" he said, as they both spoke at once.

"I beg your pardon." He waited for her to resume.

She plunged in. "Since the Bridge... well, you must think me lacking in all civility. I cherish your good opinion of me, and fear I have lost it. Pray do forgive me."

He kept his eyes on the vultures, as he murmured, "I said I had forgotten it. But I have not."

"Is there anything I can do..."

"No," he said, anticipating her request. "There is nothing."

"But Edmond, it was only a moment's lapse." Well, it had been more than that. She had planned to ambush him for days.

He finally turned to her. "I don't think of it as a lapse."

Did he mean that he saw her as liable to break convention at every turn? Surely that was a harsh judgment. It surprised her very much to hear it from him.

"I mean," Edmond said, "that I do not have a poor opinion of you. Quite the opposite. You are courageous and of a remarkable temperament."

At this very nice speech, she felt a relief that surprised her. "Then our friendship is not diminished?"

"It is not, not in the least."

"I'm gratified to hear it." He still seemed distressed, however. "But what..."

He blurted out, "I would speak to your father."

She stared at him. "He doesn't need to know what occurred, surely?"

He reached for her hand, took it. His grip was firm, but seemed ready to release her at a moment's frown. "Astoria. Do you feel anything for me?"

Now it was her turn to be shocked by *his* words. Feel for him? Of course she did not. He was Jessa's. Was he not?

He pulled her a little closer to him, searching her face. "I've been thinking about you ever since we looked through the book on amphibians, ever since the night of the storm at Glyndehill. God help me, but I think of you constantly."

Oh, she had been thinking of him, too, she knew it for the truth.

Whether she moved or he did, she was in his arms, her face pressed against the wool of his jacket, her heart skittering, her body afire. She held onto him, now afraid to look into his face. Jessa's, he was Jessa's...

Placing his hands on her shoulders, he pushed her back just enough to kiss her. His hand was in the small of her back and he half lifted her toward him as he bent, kissing her, and not gently. All thought fled. The taste of him was lovely and shockingly personal.

At last he released her, and in a moment she began to recover her senses. She gasped, "Edmond. I…"

Words fell away as they gazed helplessly at each other. She wanted to say something sensible, something to stop what was happening, and could not happen now that Jessa had forgiven him for his preference on the Bridge for Cora Hamilton… but she could not think of it, not in the least.

When he reached for her again, she rushed to meet him. He pushed his hands into her loosely knotted hair, bringing it down, bending her backward in the thrust of his advance. She covered his face with kisses, as he caressed her through her dress in a thrillingly uncivil liberty.

She was half-enclosed in the stand of pampas grass. They went to their knees, with his hands still moving over her.

"Edmond," she whispered, "I don't know what to do. Whatever it is you would do, pray do it." She would not think of the consequences—oh, there were so many—but she could not bear to think, at all. Desperate to remove her underclothes to provide him an easy passage, she pulled away and began dragging up the hem of her dress.

He groaned as though that were not quite the right thing. She stopped. "You must show me what to do."

Somehow they were lying on the ground, he above her. He brought his arms around her in a close embrace, burying his head into her neck, preventing her from the moves she felt inspired to undertake. She felt his manhood pressing against her through the good wool of his uniform and the heavy muslin of her skirts.

She managed to reach down and touch him. His hand enveloped her wrist and pulled her away. "Astoria, stop."

Stop? They were well hidden in the grass, though it was not entirely private, it was true, but stop? She could not.

Apparently he could. He held her firmly, just far enough away for them look into each other's eyes. "Astoria, I can't love you here. I can't love you at all."

Her heart fell fathoms. What were they about then? What had been his purpose in this display of erotic affection?

Then he said the thing that he had said before, and the understanding dawned.

"I will speak to Colonel Harding. If you let me."

Oh, oh—he was speaking of marriage. She stared at him. "You can't… we can't." It was too far a leap. It was impossible. "You know how I am."

He shook his head, "Don't say it's how you walk."

"But I do say it!"

"I'm far beyond that, Astoria."

Far beyond? How had he gotten past her lurching gait and her hopeless social presence? She tried to imagine them together, she with her limping self next to his perfect grace. She could not, she *would* not, not for a state of dependence, of..."

"I don't care about that," he whispered. "You must believe me."

This must stop, and stop now. She gathered to herself a better frame of mind. "What you find appealing in me would dull over the years, and you'd be left with a woman who can hardly be seen in nice company, who must remain seated. It would not suit you. Oh, Edmond, it would all pale."

"You could not pale. But you don't love me. If you do, say so now. Don't keep me in suspense."

They had risen from their nest, brushing duff and brambles from each other. Her mind churning, she thought of all the married women whom she knew, not one of them happy, not as happy as she had been with her grandfather in the greenhouse cottage.

Sweetly, he was pulling straw from her hair, rearranging her to be presentable. She played for time by finding her combs and managing her hair back into its simple twisted knot at her neck.

She wanted him quite desperately at this moment but she was not at all sure she wanted him as a husband. And he was not a male partner to be merely used, not now that he had declared his heart. Her gaze reluctantly met his. "I will not marry, Edmond."

His steadiness as he gazed at her was so completely admirable and handsome that she almost gave way. His voice went very low. "May I hope?"

She turned away, stepping clear of the stand of grass, backing away from him so as not to be devoured by his vision of marriage, of this fantastical pairing, that would only be, as Grandfather had said, married slavery.

"You must find a woman who is... normal."

"I do not want a normal woman."

"Not now. But you will."

If he looked at her like that even a moment longer, she would lose all resolve. She continued backing up. When she was far enough away from his power, she turned and walked away in her rolling, uneven gait, more loathsome now than ever. Worse was how she had just treated Edmond.

Marriage. Why did it have to be about marriage?

The next afternoon, Ned spied Astoria under the shade of a banyan tree, and joined her there. Across the village square the ostriches were scooping up water from a trough at the village well. Elizabeth was surrounded by children at the book wagon, where she was handing out treats.

"Are you enjoying the trip so far?" Ned asked.

Astoria looked a bit dazed from the heat, but responded quickly. "Oh yes. My sketch book is nearly full already."

Ned knew this business with Muir-Smith had to stop. He'd been amazed when they went at each other in the tall grass last night. He'd keep a closer watch on the two of them from now on. It wouldn't do for Muir-Smith to become over-protective from a suitor point of view. The sooner they could be separated from each other, the better. He plucked a blade of grass and sucked on it. "Your sister must be wishing she was here."

"Jessa? I think not, Lieutenant. She greatly prefers her comforts."

"Well, she prefers Captain Muir-Smith, too."

Astoria looked surprised, but said nothing.

"It isn't my place to figure such things out, but I happened upon them in the garden the night of the durbar. They didn't see me, and just as well."

She frowned. "Mrs. Harding would never have allowed her out alone."

"That's what I wondered, where were her chaperones?"

After a pause Astoria said, "Something improper?"

Just what he was counting on her to say. Good people just couldn't imagine that others could twist their minds. Hurt them. Thank God for good people. "Well, he talks about her, as men do. I assumed he had some permissions."

Astoria stood up, brushing herself off. "Permissions, sir?"

Amusing that her propriety was offended by Muir-Smith and her sister and not the captain practically doing her in the pampas grass last night. "Oh, sorry. That wasn't my place to say. None of my business. Keep it to myself, you can be sure."

He stood up and faced her anger, which she could hardly direct at him, but which she was anyway. Delightful.

"They kissed? Did it go so far?"

"That and then some. But as I say, none of my business. Just thought you might want to speak to your sister, private like. Bharata's a place where emotions can run amok. All that incense." He shrugged and watched her boil.

Oh, this was grand. A little jealousy among the sisters was just the thing, even if he had to make it all up.

In his long practice of being aware of six things at once, he noticed that Elizabeth Platt wasn't merely passing around candy. She was giving out picture books. Time to rein her in before a village elder threw her down the well. Merciful Christ, women on a political junket. It was going to take all his finesse.

Excusing himself from Astoria, he made it to the book wagon just as the village *tahsildar* strode up to bark at the children and confiscate the books. The old rascal didn't want the children educated, nor women either, come to that. Edmond converged with Ned at the book wagon and together they managed to impress upon the school marm that you don't hand out books unless Prince Uttam says you do, and where.

Elizabeth, never one to be counseled by others, huffed, "No illiterate society can be truly civilized." And with that fine pronouncement they got under way again, with no one happier for the rest stop but Ned.

After the close woods, they suddenly sprang free of all vegetation. The sun pounded down on a valley of reddish mud spread out before them. It was devoid of trees, except for stumps. The column descended into this blasted landscape.

Elizabeth looked out in dismay at the horrid prospect.

"This was all logged four years ago," Conolly said.

"But has nothing claimed the land?" Tori asked.

"Once the trees were gone, the bushes didn't like it, I suppose."

Elizabeth took note of a few abandoned logs. "Mahogany, Lieutenant?"

"Yes, same as the forest we just came through. That's next." Elizabeth noticed that Tori, who had been noticeably quiet all day, turned a dark frown on the muddy valley.

Elizabeth tapped her parasol to the wagon driver, signaling she must step down. It was most embarrassing, but her bowels were still loose from the bad lentils. The soldiers and sepoys turned their backs, as Elizabeth crouched behind a stump. Thank God they would be in Kathore by nightfall, where a bath...

A shadow passed over her. A fast moving cloud, a huge flying thing—she could not get the right of it.

Shouts rang out, and the report of gunfire cracked through the air.

Elizabeth had barely time to straighten her small clothes when a sepoy officer, the *jemadar* Maruti tackled her, pinning her to the muddy ground.

"Monster birds, *sahiba*. Lie quietly."

In the little gully she had chosen for privacy, she could not see the road, but a great fusillade of rifle fire issued from that direction. "Fall back to the woods!" someone shouted—it must have been Edmond.

"They come once more," Maruti said, still protecting her with his body.

In the distance she could just see the creatures swooping in again. They were enormous, the size of kraken, their beaks studded with pointed teeth as long as her black board pointer.

A great squawk erupted a few feet away. It was an ostrich escaped from the column. Thrashing its head to and fro in terror, it raced into the gully, almost stepping on Maruti and Elizabeth before loping onto the denuded plain. The creature ran about two hundred yards and flopped down, as unmoving as death.

"Still remain quiet," Maruti whispered, covering Elizabeth's body with his own.

The fight went on around them, with shouts, gunfire, and hideous screams from the birds. Elizabeth craned her head very far to try to see something, and for her effort was rewarded with an underside view of one of the creatures, possessed of quite enormous bat-like wings and trailing long legs. Maruti pressed her harder into the mud.

"Get off me," she choked at him, indignant now.

"No *sahiba*, that I cannot do."

A scrabble of noise just over the gully top, and Lieutenant Conolly slithered down the side to join them. The three of them lay flat, barely breathing.

"How many?" Maruti asked.

"Four. But what the hell are they?"

The rifle volley quieted to sporadic fire. "*Pishachas*," Maruti said, climbing off Elizabeth. Conolly helped her to her feet. In the distance, she could just make out the birds disappearing into the distance.

"Monsters," Conolly mused. "I never saw their like. Bush priests sent 'em, then."

"I fear so, *sahib*."

Glancing at the road, Elizabeth noted that Tori was unharmed in their wagon, but staring fixedly at the retreating birds. Elizabeth ventured, "If they're monsters, does that mean they're not real?" She spat out dust that had fouled her face.

"They're real enough," Conolly said.

Distressingly, Elizabeth saw that one of the monsters had in its talons an ostrich, its long neck twisting frantically as it was borne upside down. It was the creature that had run down the valley, for it was no longer lying there.

"Oh! I thought that ostrich had died of fright right in front of us."

Conolly shook his head. "When they're scared, they flop down."

"The poor creature."

"I sent it out there." Conolly was still squinting into the sky. "Figured the birds might be satisfied with an ostrich rather than one of you ladies."

Elizabeth didn't like his attitude. She responded stiffly, "Then you are a hero, Lieutenant."

He nodded agreeably. "My job."

13

In the deep night, Dulal stood by the garden hole, a gouged socket where once his marigolds held sway. All day he had watched as the workers had mortared the hole in the garden, smoothing its deep sides with fine, wet clay. Its purpose was no longer a mystery. Mahindra had told him that fish would swim here. In their submerged realm they would remind the devout that our world is illusion.

But if the hole was for such a purpose, why need it be so large, one-quarter the size of the garden? From the construction work around him, it was obvious that it would be walled off from the rest of the garden, and thus how were worshippers to derive benefit from the contemplation of fish?

He turned and walked out into the great square. Only the occasional guard kept watch along the walls. In the southeast corner, the Anglic soldiers slept in the guest barracks, no doubt keeping their own watch. The palace servants were much amazed to have foreign soldiers at Kathore; some did not like it and spat in the dishes served them. They had all heard of the great regiment assembled now at Poondras, and they did not like that, either. So this stroll did not calm his anxiety. Something had changed since his visit with Mahindra to the Gangadhar Mahal that day: soldiers as guests, the garden hole, Mahindra's new austerities. And the Littlewood girl. She called herself Harding, but she was Littlewood. Would she remain silent about the holy petal? Did she even know it had been in her grandsire's care? Was her presence hopeful or calamitous? But Dulal was no sage, to see great events or understand great matters. He should sleep, but he could not.

In one of the windows of the *zenana,* candlelight flickered. Sleep eluded someone else this night.

∽

Tori rose from her cushion next to the low writing desk and went to the window. Though it looked out on the enormous central plaza of the fortress, her view was restricted by the fretted wood cross-hatching the opening. This was the *zenana,* the women's quarters. Even in this day and age, no one beyond family must casually see the royal women of the palace.

Along the inner walls, torches sputtered in their niches, and the shadows of guards occasionally passed in front of them. With their turbans and mustaches, hand-made *jezail* long arms and swords called *tulwars,* they looked altogether war-like. She had to admit she would have liked to see more evidence of Anglic soldiers, but they were bivouacked in the farthest corner, out of sight.

Dipping her quill for a letter to her father, she began:

July 15, 1857
Colonel Torrence Harding
Governor's Residency
Military Road
Poondras
Dearest Papa,
We have arrived safely in Kathore. I am in a state of very great excitation to see so many wonders. As I have only been here two days, I hardly have had time to absorb even the least instances of amazement presented to me by Kathore.

We arrived at here in deep dusk, with the sun striking only the tallest dome of the Gangadhar like a flame.

She decided not to recount the attack of the *pishachas.* They had done little harm, and besides, she didn't doubt that Edmond would report it in exhausting detail.

The oxen were parched and exhausted after the climb through the foothills, and Elizabeth and I were covered in dust. When we asked for a bath, which turned out to be a spacious pool adorned with intricate tiles, torches were lit and we swam for our bath, our hair trailing cobwebs, brambles and bits of mud.

Kathore is a fortified city perched on a steep rise and not really a city at all but rather a compound surrounded by fortress walls. The shape is not square or oblong but dips in and out until you think that you cannot describe its shape at all. Some of the walls were once separate structures but now the whole is a complex puzzle of buildings connected by walls. The Gangadhar is one such (very massive) segment. Then there is the rana's *palace, where every room is twenty times bigger than it need be.*

In some ways it is as though I have stepped from a world which was sepia toned, to one comprised entirely of flagrant color. The fabrics, the birds, the flowers—the very walls—are possessed of the most extraordinary colors of mustard, chartreuse, indigo and hot crimsons. The women wear the most astonishing saris, *vying in splendor. Everywhere the vines and bushes are in flower, making every breeze the messenger of lemon and honeysuckle.*

She wished Papa could be here to see this place and its splendor. She missed him. It surprised her how much, especially now that she had been so misused by Edmond.

On the first day the ranee *kindly invited me to join her in her apartments. When I arrived she told me some lovely stories (very long!) The* ranee's *daughters, Bhakti and Rashmika, speak only their native language, and they have already begun helping my pronunciation. The third daughter has been gone a year, having married a prince in a northern province, which the* ranee *cannot bear to talk about, so desperately does she miss her. Elizabeth does not speak the language of course; but, undaunted, she offered to teach the daughters a little Anglic, at which suggestion a most chilling mood came upon the room. The* ranee *does not seem so interested in me as she did before but she seems not to be entirely well.*

To my delight, I find my apartment looks out over the central square to the very front of the Gangadhar, which they call the Gangadhar Mahal, *meaning palace. It used to be the old palace, as you will remember from Grandpapa's stories of its splendid history. The roof is especially ornate. A long dead* raja *had shrines built on top of the Gangadhar to be closer to the gods!*

Elizabeth will stay with me for a few more days before setting out for Chidiwal. The food with its spices is not agreeable to her though I have begged the cooks for some stewed fruit and plain bread.

Edmond would be accompanying Elizabeth. He could not be gone soon enough to suit her. Marriage indeed! He was liberal with his affections, a failing that was hard to credit in so formal a man. Oh, to think he had trifled with both sisters! But as Elizabeth had said, men have many partners and do not bestow their regard on women who allow intimacies. She did not so much care for her own sake, since she would not accept him in any case—but for Jessa's. There was a firm distinction, she felt sure, between that night on the Bridge with her straight-forward proposal of physical union with the man, and his pretenses to be courting two women. She must warn Jessa of his character as soon as she got home, but how could she do so without admitting her own part in the affair?

Oh, but she must attend to the letter:

The oldest son, Sahaj, whom you met, walks about with two white tigers as though they were pet dogs! We are in no danger, for they obey him in all things, and besides we are not to meet Sahaj in any casual way. Generally we must stay in the women's quarters, but it is like a palace unto itself. The younger son Jai has the bleeding sickness, but shows no disadvantage because of it. Jai knows all about the Gangadhar, having made a study of it, and the ranee *assures us we may have our tour tomorrow.*

Be assured that we are being treated most graciously, and that Lieutenant Conolly is showing himself to be most vigilant and solicitous for my welfare. Captain Muir-Smith is often closeted with Prince Uttam, attended by Lieutenant Conolly for translation. I cannot guess how it goes, but his frowns may portend some difficulties. For my own part, dearest Papa, I am forever grateful that you vouchsafed me this opportunity. I am about to visit a great museum of the world and can hardly contain my enthusiasm! I cannot help but imagine that a few wonders yet lay hidden in its precincts.

Please greet Mama and Jessa for me.

Your loving daughter,

Tori

She sealed the envelope and addressed it, keenly feeling her duplicity. The fortress was quite intimidating for all its sprawling beauty; the *Ranee* Kavya was lethargic from a now obvious indulgence in opium and hardly cared to speak with her. And she still hoped that the *rana* would allow her some forays into the forest. To sketch, she would aver. Once Edmond was gone, it might be possible to do it, and in this design she thought to enlist the *rana's* scientifically-minded son Jai.

Bats fluttered just outside the shuttered window. She imagined the Gangadhar nearby, that emblem of all that Sir Charles had stood for: science, adventure, discovery, collection, classificatory order.

It lay just across the plaza, dim in the torchlight.

"Now I see why it is called the Night Pavilion," Tori whispered.

Though the morning was spectacularly bright, the antechamber of the Gangadhar was dark as a moonless night. She stood with Elizabeth and the *ranee's* son, who was their guide.

"Now watch," Jai said, "I will light a candle."

She could just make out that he withdrew a strikeable from a pocket. After scratching it upon the floor, he ignited a small candle.

Elizabeth gasped. "Oh!" The hall flickered light from every wall and crevice and from the reaches of the high, vaulted ceiling. It was not true light, but a ghostly simulation, like sun through dust.

"It is all tiny mirrors," Jai said. "They reflect the light from the candle, and then again from each other, and yet again until past counting."

The women were dumbfounded. In an eerie light as from some distant world, Tori saw her companions perfectly: the slim and handsome Jai in his white *achkan* jacket with pearl buttons, Elizabeth in her tan shirt-waist—but as for the pavilion, it was lost in a glow that confused the eye.

Jai went on, "It is an infinite progression of light, like the lives of men and women, returning to the world again and again."

"Imagine the labor to affix tiny mirrors thus," Elizabeth breathed.

"Work given to the gods is not labor," Jai said in his gentle manner.

Tori had never been religious, but she found herself approving Jai's obvious devotion.

Emerging from the Night Pavilion—the first room beyond the Elephant Gate—Jai extinguished the candle. Light poured into a hallway from a farther room.

The hall led to the source of light, a marble bath chamber tiled in blue and white with high windows for privacy. The bath basin was littered with leaves and dust. A flash of gray at the window, and a small black face peered in. A langur monkey.

Jai noted the women's gaze. "They live in the overgrown courtyard garden just out there. They thrive in its confines since no great cat can disturb them."

Another passageway took them at last into the museum proper.

They paused on the threshold. Oh, it was all as Grandpapa had said: the white marble, the doors mantled with exquisite mosaics, the windows on both sides, forming an alley of light. Tori squinted fiercely to keep her eyes dry.

Elizabeth put a hand on her arm. "So we are here. The world has wonders, and this is one." Tori could not speak.

The prospect before them was of a very long gallery divided by periodic arches. Wooden display cabinets marched down the middle, some caved in and lying in pieces. An enormous vine curled in from a window and hugged the juncture of wall and ceiling, shaking now and then from the movement of an unseen traveler.

Tori touched the nearest cabinet, slipping open the top drawer. It was empty and surprisingly clean. Jai and Elizabeth let her proceed for a time by herself, walking down the cabinet row, opening drawers. She could not get enough of opening drawers, as though she had waited her whole life to open one and there find the great thing she sought: a key, a clue, a reason to be. But it was singular that no drawer held even one decayed specimen.

Behind her, Jai answered her question. "They were all removed before they could rot."

All gone, even the remains? Tori had not expected that. How could a *rana* who cared so little for the museum as to let it flounder also have it cleaned in so particular a manner? "It is curious not to see the remnants."

"Oh yes. The old *rana* was going to have the cabinets removed too, but that task was soon forgotten."

From upstairs came the scrabbling of something running and then a piercing scream. Monkeys. She had heard they ruled the upper realms.

Elizabeth piped up, "Perhaps the museum can be renewed someday. It would take only a little repair."

Jai inclined his head slightly. "May the gods make it so. But in the heat, the plants wilt and decay. It took five *sadhus* to cast the healing prayers upon the museum, stopping the natural decline of the samples. I have often wished they had remained. So much lost!"

Tori traded glances with him. It was her very thought.

Passing through the first archway, they entered a room like a shrine, with carved figures on the walls and images that Tori recognized as Shiva and other gods.

"All these were once the apartments of the women," Jai said. "As you see, the windows look inward to the garden," he said pointing to the right, "and then to the world," pointing to the left.

Given that the museum also occupied the second floor, Tori knew it would take many days to open every drawer. Even now that Jai claimed that the drawers had all been vacated, she was determined to see for herself.

"And how do we get to the roof?"

"The roof?" Jai looked doubtful. "It is too dangerous. Caved in, in places, and some of the parapet has fallen."

"Oh, but I would be so disappointed not to see it, Jai! We will be most careful, I promise." The shrine of Ganesh was up there. She must enter it.

Before Jai could respond, Elizabeth hailed them, beckoning them to a wall she was examining. "Here are very bold etchings!"

Tori could see that they were actually sculptures slightly raised from the surrounding stone surface. The figures were engaged in a most remarkable variety of sexual activities, stooped and bent, legs lifted and crooked, and male figures finding ways to enter the females despite the puzzle of limbs.

"The occupants of the *zenana* had no modesty," Elizabeth said approvingly.

"Why would they?" Jai asked. "Sex is worship."

Elizabeth turned to him. "Extraordinary."

"Do you not pursue enlightenment when you abandon the self to sexual annihilation?"

"Well, not in Cornwall!" she laughed.

Tori found herself heated by what she saw. Did Anglic men know this variety? How remarkable that here in Bharata even religious people celebrated such performances in art. That Jai was standing so near—and his royal mien and carriage so appealing—caused her to blush.

Elizabeth drew her aside, saying, "I trust you needed no such inspiration when you and Edmond used the zinc sulfate."

Oh, she knew! Tori was abashed, hastening to explain. "I feared to ask you for it as I reasoned you should be free of complicity in what I had planned. Pray forgive me, but I did not wish you to have any blame."

Elizabeth smiled. "Oh, it was the very reason I told you of it! I hope your intention was successful?"

"It was not a propitious time."

"Well! There will be more opportunities. Here, we can hope to be free of conformity. You have two weeks!" Her face fell into doubt. "But he leaves with me for Chidiwal tomorrow. I have it! Welcome him back in a week with a viewing of these sculptures!"

Tori had little doubt such scenes would stimulate him to bold action, but she would sooner hug one of the white tigers. Oh, she had been such a poor judge of character!

They moved down the hall, accompanied by the punctuated clump of Tori's uneven feet, the chittering of monkeys and the sliding of drawers, with Elizabeth aiding her now, opening the drawers on the opposite side. All empty.

It was by chance that Tori glanced out a window into the quadrangle. There, purposively striding across the square toward the Gangadhar, was Edmond.

He would not approve her going to the roof. "Jai, I am keen to see the roof. I hope you'll take us up if only for a minute or two. The shrines there are famous, to me, at least."

She prevailed on him, and they moved through the remaining gallery on that side of the museum, and thence around to the next side of the gallery facing across the square to the palace. Here was the most sumptuous chamber of all, with a vaulted, gilded ceiling, now flaking away. Broad stairs curved up to the second floor. The outward-looking windows were deep and framed with tiled pilasters like columns, pitted where semi-precious stones had been removed from the inlays. Festooned from the remains of wooden fretwork hung the long basket-like nests of weaver birds. A yellow head protruded from one, indignant at the disturbance.

Determined not to let Edmond overtake them, Tori rushed up the stairs. From above came the sound of scrabbling on the marble floor. Tori wondered how many monkeys lived here. Coming to the second story she saw yet another trove of cabinets, some of which sat on a brown carpet. The carpet moved. It was a mass of cockroaches. The sight was arresting, but she must push on. At the top of the stairs she pushed open a door that sagged almost off its hinges.

Jai and Elizabeth caught up with her as she looked out on the top of the Gangadhar. An astonishing heat fell upon the roof. Hot pink stone surrounded them on every side, elaborately carved.

Her first impression was that it was a city. Roofed cottages crowded one another, their cascade of roofs boasting turrets, domes, roofs with decorative finials and even miniature balconies. Sir Charles had said that each monument was dedicated to a separate god, of which Bharata had too many to name.

"Oh, are they tombs?" Elizabeth asked.

"Shrines," Jai responded. "Do not enter them lest they shelter spiders, Miss."

"The one for the god Ganesh," Tori said. "My grandfather loved the place. Do you know the shrine?"

He did, and led her through narrow alleys between the monuments to a shrine with a conical roof like a pagoda. He was careful not to touch her or offer her his hand, his behavior all as Conolly had predicted.

Now close to the parapet, they could look out over the entire fortress, which Jai and Elizabeth did for a few moments, giving Tori her chance to enter the shrine alone.

A smell of rotting deadfall met her. Wasting no time, she bent before the god's altar and searched for a cranny such as Sir Charles had described; the one where he stored his field notebook. Tori did not know why Sir Charles would have left the notebook here, except that he had expected to come back. The notes might not tell her more than Sir Charles had already conveyed to her, but she was very eager to comb through it. Grandpapa might easily have neglected to offer his surmise on the whereabouts of *Nelumbo aureus*. What use to Tori, who would never come to Bharata, much less to the great museum?

There were several indentations beneath the altar, cubbyholes filled with twigs and spider webs. She searched them again and again. But there was no notebook. Hearing Jai and Elizabeth, approaching, she stood up just as Jai ducked in.

"Your grandsire was a devotee of Ganesh?" Jai's body was just a black silhouette against the grinding sunlight.

"I don't know. There is so much I wish I knew about Sir Charles's stay here."

"Perhaps Dulal can tell you."

"Dulal?"

"Oh, yes. He was a young man when your grandsire served my great-grandsire. Dulal serves us still, but he is old."

Her mind settled upon a lovely hope. "Can I meet him?"

Jai would arrange it, if Dulal could be spared from his duties at the shrine of Vishnu. Tori began to think that Jai could be the most providential ally. Already she liked him very much.

Here in the darkness of the altar of Ganesh, Tori felt emboldened to ask, "Have you ever heard of a lotus, Jai, said to be golden in color, and very large? It was one thing Sir Charles spoke of."

"Of course. A famous legend."

"But mightn't it be real?"

"You mistake it, I am sorry. This is a holy concept of the creation of the world. That makes it real enough for a believer."

Just as Elizabeth's curiosity overcame her and she joined Tori inside, they heard a distant shout from below. Edmond was looking for them.

Making them promise not to move, Jai hurried off to guide the captain up.

Tori did not feel cast down by Jai's pronouncement. Everyone thought the golden lotus was a legend. Knowledge of it was missing from the world, this Tori had already known. Ganesh gazed down from the carved frontage of the altar, his elephant face looking almost ready to speak, to tell her secrets. She had come a thousand miles to hear his deep nasal voice.

Elizabeth turned upon Edmond's arrival. "Oh, Edmond, here you are! Do not upbraid us for being here. As you can see, there are no gaping holes."

"There's one the size of a water buffalo not twenty feet from here," he said.

Elizabeth danced past him. "Well then, we did well to avoid it, cousin." No doubt seeing a chance for matchmaking, she commandeered Jai, asking to see the cave-in.

"Pray come out," Edmond said, standing aside for Tori.

Without apology for being on the roof, she moved past him into the breathtaking heat. She did not think she should suffer any upbraid from him, but she *was* in his charge until at least tomorrow. It was very hard to be in his presence, with his courteous demeanor so at odds with what she had learned of his character.

He followed her to the parapet where they surveyed the fortress of Kathore, sweeping before them like a city-keep worthy of the Picts. The square below thronged with the thousand servants and courtier relatives of the royal household, variously drawing well water, airing washing and for some reason, even dancing to the horns of a small group of players.

"Did you make good progress with the prince today?" Tori asked, to deflect their conversation from the personal.

Edmond shook his head. "Indeed not. He was in no mood for concessions. We shall not see a single new school built in the province this year." He cut a glance at her, but she would not meet his gaze.

"Perhaps they wish to keep Nanpura as it was. They might deem it better so." Her own statement surprised her. It could hardly be denied that Bharata needed schools to secure the benefits of science for a population greatly in need of equality and progress.

As they looked out, it seemed that Kathore floated above the forest canopy. Green hills humped up to the bare massifs of the Rangnow mountains.

"Oh, it is beautiful," Tori whispered. She took off her bonnet, letting the breeze cool her sweating brow.

"You are quite taken with Bharata, I think, Astoria. I pray you will be careful while I'm gone."

Well, she had been undoubtedly in more peril of a misstep when he had embraced her in the shelter of the tall grass! She didn't know whether it was for her own sake or Jessa's that she so bristled at the memory. Oh, but to her shame, she did know. It was for her own sake.

Tossing off these difficult thoughts, she made haste to answer, "Of course, Edmond. I promised my father I would be vigilant."

As Elizabeth and Jai approached, she turned to them. "To think that I am standing on the roof of the Gangadhar, a thing that would have seemed impossible three months ago."

Elizabeth exclaimed, "Now we are free to do everything fine and grand!"

Tori took her friend's hand. "Everything fine and grand," she repeated. They turned to the vista, looking out at the mountains, breathing in the heat and dust and almond blossoms.

$$14$$

Sitar music mixed with the rhythmic beat of the *tabla*. The sun had long since set, but the banquet hall was no cooler.

Uttam presided over the meal in honor of the Anglic visitors. Ropes of pearls cascaded down his ample frame and his embroidered coat. Above the *rana's* jeweled collar, his face looked drained and blotched. Uttam noted Edmond's gaze and nodded. At the *rana's* side, slathering up mango pulp with wedges of chapattis, his son Sahaj.

Lieutenant Conolly leaned in to Edmond. "The son and the father put on a show. But no love lost there."

"Perhaps," Edmond said, "the *yuvraj* prince will be easier to deal with."

"Let's hope we don't have to put it to the test soon."

Some two dozen courtiers and the Anglic guests partook of the dishes, using right hands only. Tori sat next to Edmond, and on her other side, Jai.

Edmond surveyed the heaps of rice cooked in *ghee*, lamb curries, vegetables fragrant from garlic, mint, cloves and nutmeg as well as stacks of chapattis and melon ices. He well remembered his experience of Bharati meals from his last assignment, when he had first discovered a culture that had never heard of bread and butter.

Further down the low table where they sat, Elizabeth looked completely out of place in her dark flowered muslin dress. Tori, however wore a borrowed sari of inky turquoise shot through with silver. It took his breath away, looking at her. She had tucked her feet to the side of the silk cushion upon which she sat, and her black shoes peeked out beneath the sari's hem, evidence of her conviction that they could not be together. A greater barrier was that she did not have feelings for him. He had hoped… but she had grown colder to him during their journey out.

He was leaving in the morning for Chidiwal. The reception at Kathore had not been fruitful on political subjects. The *rana* had urged him to observe the improvements at the Chidiwal school, as though that would answer Whitehall's demands for concessions. One school did not make for a compromise. It was a delaying tactic, Conolly believed. The *rana* would send them on wild goose chases, asking for more time, more information, until exhausted from curry and the dazzling sun, one officer after another would give up, go home, and brief the next poor sod.

"Miss Harding." It was Sahaj speaking. "Tell us how you think of the Gangadhar. My father and I feel curious to know."

The room quieted. A frown appeared in the *rana's* forehead. It had not been Sahaj's place to speak first.

"Oh, sir," Tori said. "It is a grand place, full of history and old learning. I am entranced. We have nothing like it in Anglica."

Elizabeth asked Jai what they were saying, for they spoke in Bharati, and received his whispered translations. She then leaned forward, saying in Anglic, "A shame the specimens are all gone, though. How great a repository it must once have been!"

As a vizier translated this for Sahaj, he raised his dark eyebrows in exaggerated surprise. "It took high magic to stop the decay of the plant collection. Does a school teacher approve of magic, then?"

Conolly jumped in, also in Bharati: "To be fair, it is not her area of expertise, Your Highness."

Sahaj waved his hand on the way to the lamb kafir. "We have heard that science is Miss Harding's specialty. What does the daughter of the great Colonel *sahib* think?"

Tori did not hesitate "Sir, I believe each discipline has its special place… and that perhaps we could combine the best of both for more understanding."

Now the *rana* himself raised a hand, saying with finality, "Well said. I shall report to Colonel Harding that you bring grace to a discussion."

But it was too late, for Elizabeth was bristling to say her piece, and out it came. "The rules of science are adamant. How comforting it is to know that scientific reasoning always produces a consistent result. Though of course magic as a cultural practice must have its smaller role."

When this had been translated for the *rana*, his face darkened. "A smaller role? Is this what your schools teach?"

Edmond rushed in, using what vocabulary he could muster. "No, Your Highness. We have no judgments as to magic. We have little experience of that subject. Miss Platt does not speak for the Crown."

This satisfied neither the *rana*, the *yuvraj* prince nor Elizabeth, and the conversation lapsed, as the diners turned pointed attention to the curries. Soon they noted Uttam and Sahaj having hot words, and the young man was made to adjourn the room.

Conolly dipped his hands into the brass pot of lime water provided at each setting. "Couldn't you muzzle your cousin?"

No, Edmond was sure he could not. Neither of the women under his protection were much inclined to persuasion.

Once Uttam retired for the evening, the group repaired to the verandah. Tori turned her face into a puff of a breeze, greatly refreshed by it. Jai accompanied her while Edmond and Lieutenant Conolly were detained by the prince's chamberlain.

The Gangadhar shone white under a waxing moon and a bluish haze of aloe wood incense layered across the balcony.

"How do you live with such beauty, Jai, and not feel overwhelmed?"

His voice was melodious. "I might rather ask, how do you live without it?"

"I... I do not know. It is a fair question."

"Perhaps that is why your people have come so far with industry and mechanicals. They have devoted themselves to that, and we to beauty."

"Must it be one or the other then, do you think?"

A voice came from behind them, speaking in lilting Anglic. "We are not one thing or the other, but many things at once." A thin man wearing only a white *dhoti* around his hips stood before them. His head was shaven. A *sadhu*. Jai made namaste to him. "*Baba*."

Tori turned to face the newcomer. Jai murmured, "This is Mahindra, my father's *sadhu*, and our spiritual guide."

The *sadhu* went on. "You answered my prince very well tonight. I congratulate you."

"I hope I did..." Tori paused, uncertain what to call him.

The *sadhu* smiled. "You may call me *baba*. Magic need not contend with science."

"Oh! My grandfather would have said so," Tori replied. It seemed very strange to be speaking with a man who could hardly be considered to be fully dressed. And yet no one else on the verandah took any notice. As she looked closer at his face, she realized she had seen him before: on the steps of the garden at the durbar.

Mahindra went on, "But magic is a capability that must be earned."

"Not discovered?" Tori felt emboldened to ask.

"It is our nation's power, my daughter. Do you propose to take that from us as you have all else?"

"Oh, I hope we do not take more than we give in Bharata!"

Jai stepped closer. "*Babaji*, my father has after all invited the Anglics to help us. We have full granaries from their scientific practices."

"Oh yes, and trains running on time. For all this they deserve respect." The *sadhu* turned piercing eyes upon Tori. "Pardon a lowly bush priest if he does not agree, as you say, one hundred percent."

Tori felt his comment like a slap. He was so calm and yet his words cut most keenly. How could scientific discovery be considered a theft—if indeed that was what the *sadhu* meant? She could not pretend of course, that she did not plan to take something. The cutting. It had never before seemed to her that an act of collecting would diminish others.

"Then you cannot have approved my words to the prince."

The *sadhu* bowed slightly. "I approved your honesty, my daughter. There is little enough of that in the world."

It was a gracious speech but it did not reduce the sting of his criticism. Glancing up, she noted that Edmond stood at the doors to the banquet room, searching her out.

The *sadhu* went on, "If you find aught of magic here, my daughter, you are welcome to talk to me. I strive to know, as do you. *Namaste.*" He left them, threading into the crowd, where the finely dressed Bharatis bowed to him, hands pressed to foreheads.

Edmond joined her and Jai. "So you have met Mahindra. Lieutenant Conolly says that he was educated in Anglic schools here. Have I the right of it, Prince Jai?"

Jai watched as Mahindra left the balcony. "He has no need of mathematics and mechanical knowledge. His wisdom is of the gods."

"One can only be improved by education," Edmond protested.

A slight bow met this pronouncement. "Perhaps it depends on one's path."

Tori thought it graceful of Jai to avoid argument. His poise and open manner recommended him to her very greatly. He was always asking her about Anglic things, as though trying to fairly judge one continent against the other. Perhaps she was doing the same.

Out on the plaza, a blur of white caught her attention. There was the *sadhu* crossing the courtyard to the Vishnu temple, his white *dhoti* soaked in moonlight, making him visible all the way to the arched gate of the shrine.

"Look, Astoria, here are more ways of love." Bhakti stretched out on the grass, her plump hand tracing the erotic drawings. Neither she nor her sister thought it uncomfortable that Jai was present. He was not considered a full man because his mother had declared him too delicate. So deeply mortifying for Jai, yet he seemed to accept his ambiguous position.

Nearby, a fountain bubbled, lending a cooling breath to the *zenana* bower where they sheltered under a pipal tree. Elizabeth and Edmond had left two days ago for Chidiwal, along with a unit of soldiers. She would miss Elizabeth, but she was most anxious to shed the captain's watchful eye. Although she thought herself completely safe, she was not insensible to the undercurrents of resentment against Anglica. Certainly, the *sadhu* had stated them clearly.

Bhakti's sister Rashmika leaned in to peer with kohl-rimmed eyes at yet another pose of love. All through their luncheon, the *ranee's* daughters had been discussing this book in the most direct way, not excluding their brother from the conversation.

"When I marry, my prince will know all the ways to pleasure me," Bhakti said.

Rashmika, the dark beauty of the family, pushed at her sister. "Yes, because he will have practiced upon so many virgins!"

"Yes, of course. So he will not fumble with *me*."

Jai chided his sister. "I think you will accuse him, nevertheless, Bhakti. No man can perform so much as you hope!"

Bhakti shrugged. "Well, a man must rest between exertions, it is true."

So then, more than one performance a night? Tori kept a neutral face, not wishing to show her ignorance.

Jai turned to Tori. "How do your bridegrooms learn all they must? From what you have said, Anglics do not favor such instruction."

"Oh—" She hardly knew what she would say, but ventured, "Our brides are not so demanding."

As Bhakti traded shocked looks with her sister, Jai said, "Then a groom might do the least to reach his pleasure, leaving his lady unmoved."

Another intriguing thesis to augment Tori's growing store. She must ask Elizabeth about it upon her return.

"Who could endure such a man?" Bhakti cried.

Jai intervened. "Perhaps love inspires, with no need of texts."

"Oh!" Tori loved this conclusion. "You may have it, Jai." He gave a most startlingly handsome smile. Even though this remarkable conversation would be considered highly distasteful in Shropshire, she found herself flushed with excitement. How singular it was that she was taking sexual instruction from a Bharati prince!

Tori rose, begging for a solitary walk. Though the women squealed their protest, she wanted to be alone to absorb the morning's lessons. She managed to break away and left the shade of the bower for the walkway, edged with rose bushes. High outer walls flanked the *zenana* garden on one side and two-story verandahs enclosed the remaining sides, creating an oasis of privacy. How extraordinary Bharata was. It kept its women of quality out of sight, yet they enjoyed freedoms and pleasures beyond even Elizabeth's liberal notions. When Tori thought of herself partaking of these freedoms it seemed in her mind's eye to be a doorway out of a shadowy room, one that had never seemed dark before.

On the hot stone pathway rose petals released their intoxicating perfume. Grandpapa had disliked roses, for they were too cultivated, but she wondered how Bharata had worked upon his imagination. Was it all about classificatory order? In her present state of wonder at roses and a lover's wish to please, she doubted for the first time whether it was all about science. Did close understanding remove the patina of delight? Well, surely not. She should be in the Gangadhar now pursuing her work, but she could not in courtesy spend every minute there. Jai had already taken her to the museum for two or three hours both today and yesterday, even opening drawers in a helpful way, not admonishing her that they would all be empty, and accepting her explanation that a scientist is always looking for discoveries.

She stepped off the path. The shade deepened under a long arbor of bougainvillea, with vines completely covering an old trellis. Blossoms the color of raspberries lit up in the filtered sun, drawing her into the flowered tunnel. Traceries of shadow confused her eye. Leaves fluttered on the vines like butterflies struggling to fly. And then a green shank of cloth appeared, blowing out and flowing in mid-air.

She stopped, heart thudding. And there, reaching from the dimness ahead, hair blowing; very long hair. And no breeze. Curiosity fought with an instinct to retreat, but she inched forward to see more. Her stomach clenched as she now saw before her a woman in a green sari facing away. Streaming out from the woman's head, her long hair was writhing in an impossible way, as though alive. The sight both sickened and fascinated her. The woman walked slowly away in a disconcerting gliding motion. Afraid yet intrigued, Tori followed. Ahead the arbor ended in searing light.

Peering out, Tori saw the woman by the garden wall.

"Come, *beti*," the woman whispered, though the whisper was in Tori's ear, not fifteen yards away.

Tori approached. The woman's long hair was shot with gray, her face deeply lined.

They stood regarding one another. Slowly, and to Tori's relief, the long hair came to rest around the woman's shoulders. It seemed to Tori that the frantic hair warned of discontent, and must put Tori on warning that the apparition could do violence. Suddenly, alarming noises issued from behind the zenana wall—squealing almost at the limits of hearing. Filaments of the woman's hair rose again.

Tori backed up.

"They cannot hurt you, or even see you, *beti*." The voice was a breath in Tori's ear, but the woman's lips were not moving. She should race back to Jai and his sisters, but she did not move.

"Why are you trying to scare me?" she managed to say, her voice gone pinched and high. The squealing behind the door grew louder. At that, the woman slammed a fist against the wooden door, all but shattering Tori's resolve to stay.

The noise stopped.

"They do not wish for me to be long gone." Bits of dust fell off the door. The woman's voice came to her: "You have lost your friends to Chidiwal, yes. Now you have only my son Jai."

Her son Jai? But this was not Kavya... She looked down to find that the woman's feet were not actually touching the ground. Merciful God. Tori could not move, nor swallow, nor keep from staring.

The whisper again: "Jai will be showing you where to go. You should be trusting only him, *beti*."

The squealing resumed, louder now. The woman placed her hand on the latch of the door, and as she did so, her hair swept in that direction.

Tori did not want to see what was through that door. The unearthly squealing could not be anything natural.

As the latch clicked down, Tori turned to run, only to bump heavily into someone right behind her. She cried out.

It was an old man in a simple tunic. Backing up, she raised her arms to defend herself.

The man was staring behind her. Now, beset from two sides, Tori spun halfway around to locate the woman in green. All that remained of her was a shred of forest-colored sari sliding through a crack in the door.

"I heard voices," the old man said.

As Tori collected herself, she could only stare at him.

"I am Dulal."

The name made no sense. Tori mumbled, "Did you see the... that woman?"

He nodded.

"*Was* it a woman?"

He nodded again. "A sari in the old style. I have not seen that kind for many years."

Tori's main concern was to find Jai again. Now that the woman had disappeared, she felt a fresh wave of fright wash over her. Her legs were in motion before she had even decided to flee. Not wanting to go through the arbor again, she lurched around it, heading back toward Jai and his sisters.

The old man fell in at her side. *Dulal*, he had said. She remembered now. She had asked to see him.

She glanced at him to be sure he was not fantastical. He was short, with wispy hair surrounding a face wrinkled like a dried grape. He said, "I did not want to see you, but for Jai's sake I came."

They passed a low wall that surrounded an empty pond. She sat down heavily, suddenly needing to be off her feet. "Dulal. Please pardon me. I am quite unnerved."

Standing before her, he glanced back the way they had come. "A spirit woman. It is hard for them to come among us. She used the gate in the wall."

Tori glanced at the stone wall. "Does a spirit need a door?"

"It can help. Long ago there was an outside door to the *zenana* garden. It was a secret door, for a lover to come to the young wife of a prince. I have always thought this door only a story. Why is the spirit coming to such as you?"

A spirit, he said. Were they talking of ghosts in so matter of fact a manner? But yes. This was Bharata. It was not going to be what she had expected, not in any way. Spirit, he said. The thought came, might it be the same one that in different form had followed her across the Bridge?

They kept silent for a few minutes. Her breathing settled, and soon the impropriety of not having a conversation impelled her to say, "You knew my grandfather, Sir Charles?"

"Littlewood *Sahib*," Dulal murmured.

"When he came here, you helped him in the museum? That's what Jai told me."

Dulal's chin barely moved.

She recalled then, what she had planned to say to Dulal if she could speak with him. "Do you have anything of Sir Charles's? I would like to have anything of his. There is one thing in particular. His notebook."

"Does your grandsire yet live?"

"No, I am sorry to say."

"Had he given to *you* anything that once belonged here?"

"He had a specimen, a petal. You know about it, don't you?" Before he could merely nod, she said, "Please tell me."

He paused, then came over and sat a few feet away from her. "The *sahib* came here, wishing to see the Gangadhar, which the *rana* allowed. But he did not tell us that he wished to find the flower, the flower that is to us holy. It is from such deceit that all bad things follow."

Deceit? Tori waited in some apprehension.

"It happened that the *rana* had many enemies, and these nipped at him like jackals, here and there, with the *rana's* soldiers beating them back, only to find them at another door. Thus my master had need of his holy men for creating the fire spears that would drive them away, and the *pishachas* that would be swooping down upon the invaders. And so the *rana* took the holy men from the Gangadhar. The *sahib* knew it would be falling into decay. That was when he stole it."

"The *rana* stole it?"

"The *sahib* stole it."

Her voice went thin and high. "Stole?"

Tears pearled his eyelids. "We had found the lotus petal. For so long it lay unregarded in the collection. The *sahib* said it was nothing. Then one night he packed his belongings and made his way into the forest, along tracks he knew well. He had taken the petal. I followed him, certain that it was the golden petal, for otherwise why would it be so precious to the *sahib*? But I could not find him. He was gone forever."

Tears found the ruts in his face.

"Oh Dulal, I am so sorry." *Stolen.* She would not have believed it, except here was an aged, weeping man telling her it was so.

"If my master had known it was a piece of the holy flower, he certainly would have saved the Gangadhar. And the sacred petal."

"You know the place in the Gangadhar where it had lain?" Oh, just to see the cabinet, the drawer, the very place where it all began. In a museum of ghosts, even emptiness had a meaning.

He glanced sidelong at her, shaking his head. "Do not ask. I will not lead another Anglic to its empty shrine. And truly, what need have you to see the drawer? You surely have the petal now."

"No. My family burned it. They were ashamed of it. People thought Sir Charles was lying about the flower being magical. They accused him of trying to combine magic with science. It disgraced him."

Dulal whispered, "So bad things came to us all." He looked at Tori. "I am not glad for his disgrace. I have my own sins and would not add to them." His voice went even lower. "I cannot keep away what is coming."

In the midst of this dreadful afternoon, she could hardly credit that things could be even worse. "What? What is coming?"

"My punishment." He stood up. Bhakti and Rashmika had come looking for her, anklets jangling. They waved, approaching.

Tori whispered, "Would the gods punish you for an unintended thing?"

"It has already begun. The hole," he whispered. "The *sadhu's* hole."

"Astoria!" Bhakti cried from down the path. "You are alone with a man, for shame! Oh, but it is only Dulal, so never mind!" The daughters laughed, drawing her close and waving Dulal away.

At a little distance, Jai waited on the path, watching Tori with a keen gaze.

15

July 20, 1857
Astoria Harding
Royal Seat of Kathore
Nanpura Province
My Dearest Friend Tori,

I am up before dawn, writing by lantern light. If I do not write now, there will be no time at all, for here at the school we are frightfully busy! (The jungle-cocks have set up a great chatter and now they are answered by the barks of pariah dogs, so one might as well write, as there can be no sleep.) Mr. Ramanath has vacated this bungalow for me (adjacent to the school), though he has more need of it with his wife and five children. However, there is no arguing with him, for he is determined I shall have my position. He is now quartered in the small hut across the way. I have a small bedroom and a sitting room overlooking the main road and some shrine in a most persistent yellow and pink. The kitchen is in back, where my cook sleeps next to the stove, even in this heat. This is how matters are conducted here, and they do not wish to have advice, or rather they listen politely and then do as before.

I said goodbye to Edmond after two days of repair on the school at which he gallantly set his efforts. The roof was not repaired as Mr. Ramanath had said, or rather, it was repaired and then blew off again in a hailstorm if the tale can be believed. Elephants were said to have eaten the first roof. There are so many fantastic things here, one hardly can distinguish between what is made up and what is real.

Any case, Edmond is off to inspect the roads between here and Sirinshwari all the while taking a reading of the villages and their grain stores for the season and the mood of the Jhir Ghoda workers who must be kept healthy and content with their work. There are rumors of the tahsildar taking a cut of workers' salaries, which to our ears is shocking, but is considered no more than a local "tax." Before Edmond passes through Chidiwal once more I hope to have matters set quite straight here.

What needs setting straight makes for a longer story than I can set down this morning, but suffice it to say that I had the greatest joy in conducting a class on my second day here. Thirty-one students from the ages of six to twelve, all neatly washed and wearing clean shirts and trousers. They paid me the strictest attention, at which I was gratified, only to learn that they understood not a word of what I said! So all the claims for learning Anglic are quite out the window. (Though Mr. Ramanath spoke truly, that they can recite the provinces of Anglica, in a dreadful sing-song rhyme which they shriek very loudly and joyfully.) Today we shall begin with letters of the alphabet, which Mr. Ramanath thinks too confusing for the youngest, but of course you cannot jump over the basics, nor does recitation suffice for understanding.

The other distressing thing is that the school's allowance from Poondras has not been invested in desks and paper as was Mr. Ramanath's clear direction. There are no funds left in reserve, so it is good that I brought practice paper with me. Called to account for the missing funds, Mr. Ramanath explained that the children expect a mid-day meal at the school, and he has spent the money on chapattis, otherwise the only students here would be his own children. Indeed, some of the boys leave in mid-afternoon, and cannot be persuaded to stay to receive their homework. I believe that the students do not yet perceive the benefits of schooling beyond luncheon! Well, they are not so different than Cornwall youngsters, I suppose, but I confess I had looked for more enthusiasm and perhaps a few more students as well.

Well, I had not meant to complain, but I see that so far I have not had much good to say. Nor does my letter so far tell of the odious Mr. Gupil.

Oh, the dogs! I must send cook out to disperse them. I see they have found a bird and are driving each other mad by pulling the poor bird's wings off, devouring it a piece at a time.

That done, and now… oh yes, Mr. Gupil. He is the village headman (how appointed, one must not ask, you may be sure it is not democratic). Yesterday he was sitting in the middle of the classroom at dawn (on top of a desk!), waiting for me. Thence began a harangue that the children are needed at the mines, and how the villagers cannot feed themselves without the income, of which the husband's share will not suffice. Needless to say I saw through this fiction. The truth is that Mr. Gupil will have less to steal from the families if the children do not work. Edmond has warned me not to make an issue of this. "We cannot change the whole culture at once," was his warning, but it is very hard to endure, to think of all the poverty here and Mr. Gupil doing very little himself except to steal from his neighbors. In any case, he has complaints (from whom, he is quite vague) that a large force of arms now swells the small cantonment at Poondras. Why, he demanded, are soldiers come among us? I responded with some indignation that these same soldiers are the ones that support his prince and protect the diamond mines from their covetous neighbors. Leaving that aside, he went on to say that we are teaching against religion and culture. I explained that this is not true. We simply teach scientific things and people can draw their own conclusions about their superstitions. This did not satisfy him and he left with imperious instructions that I urge the children to go to temple (which I certainly shall not) and dissuade the boys from adopting customs such as shaking hands and using foreign expressions like "bloody" and "jolly well." I assured him that I would not condone such language it if I heard them, but clearly all Anglic vulgarisms are now laid at my feet.

I pray I am strong enough to play my role. I so wish you were here with me. It would make the days pass more easily if I had someone to talk to. Although Mr. Ramanath is most cordial, he is no substitute for a confidante.

The cook is creating a terrible stink. I am grateful that she brings me breakfast, but though I have begged for plain rice and boiled milk, here I have a curry stew and tea ruined with spices.

The day begins! I shall count each student as he passes through the door. Great things are begun with small steps.

Oh! And I have (shockingly, you will think) cut my hair. It is impossible not to sweat most dreadfully, and one must not stand on ceremony when in the field. I am my own counselor, maid and parson. The freedom I have always dreamed of finding. And here it is, in Chidiwal.

Yours most affectionately,

Elizabeth Platt

PS: If you have written to me, I have not received anything since the problems at the bridge over the river. When things can get through, I expect I shall receive all my letters at once!

Elizabeth lay down her pen and capped the inkwell. The letter to Tori went atop the missives she had penned to the Educational Authority in Londinium, all awaiting the repair of the bridge which separated Chidiwal from the main post road. The report of the downed bridge was sketchy, nor was there any explanation of how that sturdy bridge could indeed suffer so heavy a damage as to prevent delivery of the mail. Mr. Ramanath declared himself worried, and had undertaken to walk the eight miles to the river to see for himself, so now she would have no help with translating her lessons.

Bansi, the young cook, came to clear the breakfast tray, and frowned that so little had disappeared.

"*Sada khana, krpaya, Bansi,*" Elizabeth said. Plain food, please.

Bansi bowed her head submissively, taking the tray.

"But of course nothing will change," Elizabeth muttered.

Bansi stopped, cutting a glance at her. "It will be changing."

The woman spoke Anglic. Oh dear, here she had been muttering at Bansi for four days, never knowing she was delivering insult. And just why had Bansi allowed her to struggle with Bharati the better part of the week? It was strange how small things cut the most. She could endure a leaky roof and lack of desks—indeed, she thrived on the challenge to handle adversity—but the insolence of servants and curry at breakfast made her pine for home.

Elizabeth shooed Bansi out of her sitting room and entered the school. The chairs lined up bravely in their rows, each with a pencil and a slate with paper. The picture of King Albert graced the wall behind her desk. His eyes bespoke a serene confidence in Anglic civilization enlightening the world, but this morning Elizabeth found it annoying.

He had no bloody idea how far the world had to go.

Tori scratched a strikeable on the marble floor, lighting a small lantern.

The Night Pavilion sprang into view with its nether light, but it was not just in this anteroom that she would need her lantern. It was past sunset, and she had come alone to the Gangadhar.

In the three days since she had seen the ghost, she had come round to thinking that between the spiritual and the magical lay a quite porous boundary. Indeed, Anglics had long called Bharata the spiritual continent. Still, nomenclature explained little. She yearned to know more, but wondered if, as Jai had claimed in the case of the *sadhu* Mahindra, the scientific approach did not suit spiritual apprehension. And if it did not, what must she do to move beyond it? For was it not a danger that one would understand *Nulembo aureus* only so far as a specific property, and not its totality?

Emerging from the Night Pavilion and passing the long corridor of the baths, she entered the museum proper with its linked rooms. The stone halls amplified her footfalls, that relentless iambic gait. Already she was known by the people here as the woman with the crescent-moon foot; a foot that curled in a c-shape. It wasn't a bad name. But she would rather be known for something other than her foot.

Despite a gibbous moon, the palace was in profound shadow. Her small lantern made the further reaches seem even blacker, and she forbade thoughts of stalking cats or worse. At one side the inner courtyard emitted the chittering, clucking, flapping sounds of a miniature jungle. She pressed on.

Here was the audience chamber with its paired staircases. She must decide whether to continue her drawer-search on the first floor or go on to the second. The second, she decided. She ascended the stairs, turning at the top into the right side of the gallery, the opposite side of the area she had already searched downstairs.

Out of sight around the corner, came a scrabbling sound. Monkeys ruled here. She imagined their sentries endlessly marching around the quadrangle, protecting Bharata's secrets.

Stepping up to the nearest cabinet, she began opening drawers, but this time she placed her hand in each empty place to absorb any fleeting essence.

For what if the resins from the lotus had seeped into the wood and she might garner a vision, however small and faded, leading her to know the habitation of the complete plant? She had not thought of this approach before her meeting with Dulal, nor would it have been an action to let Jai observe, since she would have been called upon to explain herself. It was now clear that she was indeed Sir Charles's student: she had come to steal. It might be essence or plant sample, but it remained as the *sadhu* had said, as Dulal had said: theft.

Jai, the spirit had said. *Jai will take you there.* But she didn't know how to ask Jai for something that Bharatis saw as their sole property. It greatly encouraged her, however, that the spirit being might be trying to aid her.

At a scraping sound, she pivoted around. Just beyond the halo of light, a monkey stood on hind legs. To her surprise, it walked forward a few steps, but when she held her lantern aloft, it fell to all fours and slipped away. Amid its blue fur, a whitish face looked almost human. She hoped the rest of the troop would not take advantage of her coming here alone.

Pulling open the next drawer, she placed her hand within, pressing her fingers down. The herbarium page containing Sir Charles's specimen had long given up its oils, exposed to air, travel and the press. But here in the Gangadhar, the petal had lain in a drawer for years, perhaps hundreds of years, kept vital by the *rand*'s magical practitioners. Therefore, in what she knew might be a desperate measure, she lay her hand in each empty space, moving down the line of cabinets, some of which had many drawers. But she had all night. And tomorrow night she would come back. *No gloves*, Grandpapa had said. *I allowed its resins to come into me. I saw truths.*

As she proceeded down the row, a squadron of insects hovered around the light, casting fleeing shadows on her work, settling sometimes on her hands. She had just turned the corner to move down the third side of the Gangadhar, when a movement caught her attention. She raised the lantern.

Twenty feet off was a rag tied to a cabinet. There was no old woman, but it was her signature: a gossamer strip of green sari. Flapping.

⌇

The blue monkey stared as the girl approached the flowing cloth. She was not even afraid of such manifest power, but walked up to it, murmuring, "This is the one, then."

Far down the hall, he saw a movement. It was a woman in green. She could be mistaken for nothing but a spirit. The spirit strove to hide herself from him, weaving herself into the fabric of the walls and floor. But he could see her. A *pitri*, an ancestor spirit, her form fading, fading. And now gone.

It startled Mahindra so much that he almost lost his monkey form.

As he returned his gaze to the girl, he saw that she was reaching into the drawer, rubbing her hands inside. But why? She closed the drawer. Then she did a most extraordinary thing. She licked her hands. He completely lost his concentration, and could no longer hold his disguise.

He stepped out of the shadows. "Are you hurt?"

The girl jumped, staggering back.

"Pardon me, but you are hurt, my daughter?"

"Who… oh! I thought it was a monkey." She realized her insult and gasped. "Pray excuse me! I mean that I had feared seeing the monkeys…"

The aspect of the monkey still clung to him, but since he had spoken, she would see only his human form. She was not practiced in seeing more than one thing at a time.

"I saw a light in the Gangadhar," he said, "and came to investigate. And here I find you licking yourself like a wounded jaguar."

"I have been bitten by insects."

"You must let me care for your hands. I am a healer, among other things."

The hands went behind her back. "No, please do not trouble yourself. I have ointments. In the Anglic way." They gazed at each other, judging which lies might be believed. "Perhaps you could lead me out, *baba*."

He swept a hand in the direction of the old servants' quarters, farther along this side of the museum.

She hesitated. "Should we not return the way I came?"

"I know the back ways."

She nodded, looking sickly. How great could her power be if she feared him? But, truly, she had been his to dispose of since the moment she had come through the gates of Kathore. Neither Uttam nor Sahaj would object if she fell into the deep, empty pool of the Gangadhar baths. But they must be patient. Though she clearly did not know where the lotus was, she was abetted by a *pitri*. Why this should be the case, he was most curious to know.

"This way." He walked, and she followed, the bubble of light just behind him. His monkey eyes needed no light, but he stayed close to her, pretending otherwise.

"I came here when I couldn't sleep," she said as he opened the door to the kitchen stairs, steep and dark.

"You came here to find your grandsire, Astoria." He proceeded down.

She stopped at the head of the stairs. "Yes," she whispered.

"I understand. Lost things exert their pull. Do not fear me, *beti*. I also look for lost things."

"Do you?"

"Oh yes." They walked down, the stairway growing cold here where the sun never touched. "You will have understood me from the first, that I want the old Bharata. When magic was wholly ours and *we* were wholly ours." They had reached the lower hallway, with its smell of rot and stagnant water.

"This is the backside of the Gangadhar, where the servants of the *zenana* lived, and before them the *zamindars* of the army. You knew that this was the first palace of Kathore? It has worn many garments, but it remains ever the same." In her odd, heeled shoes, she clip-clopped along. She could so easily fall down. *The monkeys rushed her, she foolishly ran. The baths, alas.*

They stood outside the bath hall. The tiled room suddenly erupted in squeals and shadows. "Bats," he said. "They did not expect a lantern."

Murder. A fall in the baths. He was surprised at the strength of his feelings. It came from years of indignities, decades of scorn. She came among them as though it was her right to touch their relics and take what she liked. He and Uttam counted on that for now; but still, her arrogance inflamed his heart.

He led the way into the Night Pavilion. She stopped in the fey light of the mirrored hall.

"*Baba*, how are you diminished if we learn about magic?"

And straight to the point. He paused, gathering an argument he thought she might understand. "Suppose I came to Shropshire and attracted a great following of people who wished to give up science and the support of aristocrats? Would you feel diminished to lose your engineering and social order?"

"Perhaps we would. But it wouldn't be wrong of you to express your beliefs. Each person must choose the way he prefers."

He well remembered how Anglics could justify themselves. It came naturally to a people who could not imagine themselves in the wrong. "Is it a choice when the stronger seduces the weaker? Surely it is incumbent upon one with great power not to abuse the innocent." The candle in her lantern flickered, guttering. "Does your Elizabeth not seduce our children?"

"Oh, sir," she exclaimed, "such things are far from her purpose!"

He watched as new thoughts flickered around her face like moths seeking entrance. "If we become like Anglica, will we still be Bharata? And if we become like Anglica, will we always be despised imitators of a greater society?"

"Sir, I don't know. But I know what it is to imitate those who do not wish to acknowledge me."

He knew what she desired, but it intrigued him to know what she would say. "Who do you seek to imitate, *beti*?"

"In my country, there is a certain society. A closed circle of men who are free to study natural history. Magic is the key to that circle. I would learn of it. Is this wrong?"

An unlooked-for confidence. She was an innocent in some things. "It depends, my daughter, on what you must destroy to get it." He saw that she did not like hearing the truth, but she had the grace not to defend herself.

He led her out of the Night Pavilion and through the Elephant Gate into the plaza, silvered with moonlight. He bid her goodnight.

So. She wished to penetrate a closed circle of men who would never accept her. It was a vain hope. He well remembered a similar one from his days at the Anglic school.

A moment of compassion pricked at him before he brushed it aside. These soft thoughts would not do. It would not be long before he must completely harden his heart toward her.

She had brought it upon herself, she and her grandsire.

16

Tori finished reading Elizabeth's letter from Chidiwal. She blew out the candle, and opened the fretwork screen to look out on the great plaza, punctuated here and there by the braziers of mendicants. Despite a few setbacks, she felt sure Elizabeth would prevail. Her friend was single-minded. But as for herself, she was not so sure.

Eight days had passed since her arrival in Kathore. And still her goals eluded her. Her most pressing dilemma was whether to trust Jai with her plans. The spirit woman had urged her to do so, but with Jai's religious devotion, she could not believe he would condone her purpose. He had not asked her what Dulal and she had discussed. They maintained a formality with each other that was not entirely to her liking. She wanted to trust this cast-off prince of Nanpura. And truly, she had little choice. Edmond would return for her in six days.

Amidst all this she had the blue monkey to worry about. What forces were in play that she seemed constantly to be watched? For watched, she had been. The albatross, the owl... who was working this magic? And if it was Mahindra—as seemed quite possible—why?

Jai was very surprised that his mother showed such interest in the Anglic girl. Yet again she had summoned Astoria to her side, in a show of kindness that he had thought her no longer capable of.

Outside his mother's apartments, he and Astoria found one of his mother's *sadhus* performing his mortifications near her door. He had thrust both legs over the back of his neck. To summon the *ranee's* fire dream, the *sadhu* had for days bent his body into this impossible position. He had renounced the world and its pain and might thus achieve liberation, but it did not make it right. Austerities should be devotional. Scripture forbade causing the body harm.

"Jai," Astoria said, "the priest suffers. You must do something."

He saw that she was upset, but nothing could be done. "It would not be respectful to interrupt him."

"Let us tell your mother and beg for her intervention."

Jai tried to see the matter from Astoria's viewpoint, but failed. The *sadhu* was honored to be asked for his devotions. Jai had long prided himself in understanding the scientific point of view, the Anglic view. But truly, it was difficult.

"Jai." Astoria had paused, eyeing the *sadhu*, hesitating to enter the *ranee's* apartment.

He expected her to still protest about the *sadhu*. But she said, "I saw a vision."

Intrigued, he urged her out of the hearing of the guards at his mother's door.

"The vision spoke of you," she said.

"A dream?"

"No, a manifestation. It was an old woman. Her long hair hung loose around her shoulders. I've seen her twice. Each time she was wearing a dark green sari. Dulal saw her too."

"But who could this be?"

She frowned. "You don't know?"

Truly, he did not. "Did she look natural or monstrous?"

"Well, natural, I suppose. Except her hair stood straight out from her head, blowing all the time."

He greatly wondered at this. "It may be a *pitri*. An ancestor spirit. If a *sadhu* created her, she would not have a very good human face. Her skin would be some color like purple or red."

"Or blue?"

"Yes, or blue. Blue is a good magic color." How extraordinary it was that a *pitri* would appear to an Anglic woman. Yet in some way he could not quite define, it did not surprise him. From the start, she had been nothing like what he had expected.

"The vision said something about you. She said that... that you would help me."

He was astonished by her words. "Help you in what matter?"

After a long pause, she said, "The spirit said you would show me where to go."

"What does this mean, Astoria?"

"I don't know. I thought you might."

But they must not keep his royal mother waiting. He gestured toward the door, but again Astoria hesitated.

"Jai. Does Mahindra have... a hole?"

After a moment's thought, he answered, "Do you mean the hole they are digging in the garden of Vishnu?" He shrugged. "It is a fish pond."

"Should I fear Mahindra, Jai?"

"He is a holy man. Does he make you feel unwelcome?"

"Yes, a little." She nodded in the direction of the *ranee's* apartment, and the guards opened the doors to let them pass through.

The muslin curtains had been pulled wide, letting the morning sun stream onto intricate wall tiles. Silver stands burned sandalwood incense.

"My children," his mother said, beckoning them forward. A lone servant was massaging her bare shoulders with jasmine oil. Jai bowed from the waist. He had long since accustomed himself to the *zenana*. The palace considered him unmanly, but Mahindra had taught him to endure this as a spiritual test, even so far as the taunts of Sahaj.

As they approached her settee, his mother set aside the hookah. She regarded him with heavy-lidded eyes. "Jai, my prince." She nodded to Astoria, "And lovely Astoria. Sit beside me."

Astoria sat on the silk cushions next to her, as commanded. "Highness," Astoria said, "It is lovely to see you."

"Yes, but why do you wear those dark colors?" The *ranee* picked at the folds of Astoria's deep blue dress. "You must have a sari from Rashmika; something to attract the eye." The masseuse worked her shoulders, causing the *ranee* to sigh.

"I can't wear something so fancy for every day, Highness."

His mother partook of a slice of mango from a tray. "Nonsense. Take off your shoes. You shall have my servant rub your feet."

Jai felt a pang of annoyance. "Mother, it is not her custom."

The *ranee* irritably pulled away from the servant's ministrations. "Astoria, let Mishka pour oils on the foot. The foot that the gods have made differently."

Astoria paused, then nodded her assent. Jai looked away as Mishka undid the shoe.

Once done, and with Mishka kneeling at Astoria's feet, his mother said, "We must love all of creation, not only what is common. This is something your house does not know." She toyed with the strings of pearls around her neck. "A god may have the head of an elephant, after all."

Languidly, his mother pulled Astoria's skirt to her knee, exposing her legs. Jai found himself stirred, and he moved to a place where he could see nothing.

Mishka poured jasmine oil and began her work. To Jai's surprise, Astoria closed her eyes as though to savor the girl's ministrations.

Satisfied that the massage was going well, the *ranee* reclined and drew long on the hookah. "Child, we all desire what we cannot have. It is how things go. Do not be ashamed. I long for my sweet Navya, so far away. I pray for Jai, that the gods will keep him with us forever." She closed her eyes, occasionally drawing on the pipe. "Did you know that the night Jai was born, a spirit appeared to me?" She went on without looking for an answer. "By this I knew that Jai was blest. Yes, even though he bleeds."

Mishka poured more oil, and Jai heard it dripping into the pan under Astoria's foot.

"I will tell you a story, my children. Once, the god Rama sought through the world to find things without fault. He lay with beautiful women, collected fabulous paintings and found poems of great brilliance. But the women grew old, the paintings rotted and the poems grew tiresome with repetition. He then retreated to his home on Mount Mahameru. From this holy place he decided that should a thousand perfect things ever be found, the world would end. Therefore to preserve the world, Rama declared that every manifested thing should have a flaw."

When Jai looked again at Astoria, he saw a tear trailing down her cheek. He wanted to wipe it away with his hand. She opened her eyes then, looking straight at him. He was startled to be caught in the net of that gaze. He would have looked away, but he thought that she would do so first. She did not, and as they looked at each other, she with her naked feet, and he, trembling on the settee opposite, he felt her invitation.

Mishka dried Astoria's foot. Looking up, she received a nod as to replacing the long stocking and then the shoe. Mishka puzzled over the laces, but managed to arrange all satisfactorily.

The hookah dropped from the *ranee's* hand, and she slept.

Jai led Astoria from the *ranee's* apartment into the marble hall. They walked in silence. They might be moving to the garden, but they both knew they were not.

Jai stopped suddenly. From a side corridor came a rustle of courtiers, and then his father entered with attendants. Jai bowed as Astoria made such a curtsy as she was able.

His father passed by, paying them no heed. Then, a shocking sight: Sahaj came just behind with his entourage, including his tigers. Forbidden by his mother, the white tigers were never to enter the palace, yet now Sahaj flagrantly disobeyed.

Jai pulled Astoria back behind a pillar so that they need not bow to such a brother. He wondered what the presence of the great cats implied, for nothing happened in his father's presence that did not carry some larger meaning. He greatly wondered if Sahaj had found his way back into their father's favor. But for now his mind was very much on other things.

Still behind the pillar with her, Jai said very low, "The shrine of Ganesh."

He longed for her gaze to penetrate him again. And then she looked at him. She nodded.

At that moment he knew what the *pitri* had meant. He would show her where to go. He would take her to that place she longed for. Her own body.

"Go," he whispered, and watched her make her way through the palace hall.

Always, in her imagination, Tori had imagined love-making to occur at night, in the dark, or by candlelight. Now it would be brilliant daylight, with no one braving the great square in the molten bright, no one thinking that the roof of the Gangadhar could house such a union.

She came at the shrine from behind, steering well clear of the gaping hole which guarded the rear approach. Her nerves were so taut she thought she would scream if she saw the least stirrings of a monkey or bird. Already she was soaked in sweat from just having crossed the roof. And she had brought no water! Slipping into the empty stone shrine, she leaned against the wall, heart thudding, thoughts spinning away the more she tried to gather them. Oh, but it was not about thinking, that she knew quite well. But what was it about, then—and why oh why was everyone in Anglica silent on the topic of pleasure!

It was not love. For that, she might have sought Edmond Muir-Smith, if he had been faithful, if she had not ruined his estimation of her, if he had once abandoned himself to her and whispered, *The shrine of Ganesh*, the most laden words she had ever heard.

With her back to the door, she saw a slab of light on the floor, barely illuminating the windowless room. As her eyes grew accustomed to the dark, she gradually came to see the carving of Ganesh with his elephant head, and only one tusk—the other broken off?—and his headdress of lapis lazuli. She felt certain it all meant something, for everything in Bharata held a story, a history, a larger import. With skittering thoughts, she began to fear that Jai would not come. The stone shrine held the heat of the day, pressing the light out of it, making the air thick.

A shadow at the door. She instantly feared that it was someone come to apprehend her before she could contravene every known social stricture. But it was Jai.

He stood deeply silhouetted, a black shape, so filled with power to her eyes that she gasped. Blind from entering the dark room, he reached out for her. She took his hands, leading him into the nest of darkness. That was as much as she knew to do.

To her consternation he pulled off his achkan. Was it to be so blatant, that they must first discard all their coverings? But he only laid his garment on the floor, as wide as it could spread. Gently, he brought her to her knees, and sitting behind her, he wrapped his arms around her, cradling her against him. Gradually her trembling stopped and she began to think well of the enterprise again.

"You see Lord Ganesh?" he softly said. She turned her head to look up at the statue. Jai murmured, "He will bless us if we give ourselves to the gods."

"But shall I not give myself to *you*?"

"Oh do, my lady." He put his face into her neck. "I beg you." Drawing away again, he said, "But there is no difference. It is all one." He began to unknot her hair, slowly removing pins and putting them within reach on the altar. "What is this?" he asked, seeing at last the vial with the tincture of zinc sulfate.

She told him, and to her surprise he laughed, low and melodious. "Then I need not hold back."

"Oh," she smiled, "please do not."

From behind, he combed out her hair with his fingers. It took such a very long time, and the longer it took, the more aware she became of him and his fingers untangling her. She wished that he would move where she could see him, but he remained behind.

"Buttons," Jai said, as though he thought them a great hindrance.

"They come undone."

"Ah." He began to take them apart. She felt embarrassed to have said they could be undone, for of course he knew that. He knew everything that was required. She wished that he would begin to do everything very soon.

Her dress fell from her shoulders. Then with great efficiency, he pulled the whole thing quietly over her head, folding it and putting it down as a pillow. Each garment came away, peeling from her skin, freeing her at last from encumbrances.

By the sound behind her, he was shedding his own clothes, and she turned to watch him. She had found her sight in the darkness of the shrine, saw him move like a panther in the woods, like a god through dreams. The room was very hot, stripping her of every inhibition. A shadow passed across the door, but it was only a monkey loping by.

She heard a cup fill with liquid, and Jai brought it to her lips. She took a sip, thankful that he had remembered they would need water. As he faced the light of the doorway, she gazed on him, so very beautiful, his lean and muscled limbs glistening with sweat, his manhood filled and ready. She had, of course, never seen an unclothed man, and never one filled with passion. It was intoxicating to think that he would share such wonders with her, and it was then that she thought she knew what *he* must feel, seeing her thus naked.

He knelt before her. His touch began under her throat and moved down her body with a shuddering sweetness. She felt herself swell to him, lean to him. It did not seem possible to know such delight as this and they had just begun.

At last he put a hand in the small of her back and brought her prone. He whispered, "Do you know who the Lord Ganesh is?"

"A god," she whispered, but to her, Jai was the holy one.

"Yes. The god of opening doors."

And at last, and none too soon, he entered her.

She opened. Through a stab of pain, she felt an urgent desire. It was a delirium, intimate beyond boundaries. Oh, what was this territory? She whispered to Jai, Take me there, and he moaned an answer, presumably yes, for he grew more inspired, and withdrawing from her, placed her in another position, which continued their dance in ways that now swept her along in hungry gasps. She straddled him, and then he did the same to her, opening her.

At last he brought a cup of water. They rested, and then he opened her again. She thought how many hundreds of poses there were, and wished that the day were longer.

When he took her to the last place, he gently placed his hand over her mouth. Somehow, she was crying out.

At last stopping, and with scientific rigor, they applied the zinc sulfate. Lifting her hips onto the pillow of his achkan, he held her in his arms.

~⌒◦

She told him, as they waited for the preventative to seep in, all about why she had come to Kathore. It rushed from her like a confession—which it rather was—but also like the release of dammed waters. She did not care about the consequences. Well, she did. But she could not believe that he would repudiate her now.

What he said next greatly shocked her.

"I know why you came among us."

Then unfolded Jai's story, even more startling than her own. Sahaj knew her purpose and had commanded Jai to spy on her to lead him to the flower. Jai had resolved not to betray her, and would have had said nothing to his brother had she found anything of interest. Jai begged her pardon, but he did not believe a holy flower belonged in the world of men, nor would be found in a museum, so he thought Sahaj's orders harmless.

Despite Jai's nonchalance, it alarmed Tori that Sahaj *knew*. Did Prince Uttam know? And Mahindra?

"Why does Sahaj wish to find the lotus?" she asked. "He is not scientific, nor yet religious, is he?"

"He is neither of those things. And if I asked him why, he would not tell me, I am sure."

He helped her to dress and bind her hair. It all seemed a bit ordinary after the passion of the hours preceding. Already she wished that she could repeat what had just occurred. But they both knew, she felt sure, it was an afternoon they would never have together again.

"Astoria, if you found the golden lotus would you undergo austerities? Do you wish to become a renunciate, to attract uncommon powers?"

She adjusted the pins in her hair, feeling sad that they were re-entering the normal world—the world of science, it shocked her to realize. "I cannot be a renunciate. But what if magical knowledge could be gleaned by... other means?"

"I have not heard of these other means. Perhaps you wish for it to be easier than it is."

"Oh yes. I do. I admit it." She paused, remembering Mahindra's challenges. "Jai, is it wrong for our two countries to become more similar? Do you think it wrong?"

"How could it be wrong?"

"Well, might you lose yourself if you change? And if I am curious about magic, and learn about its properties, is this wrong? Does magic belong to Bharata, or to us all?"

Now that they were dressed, he took her into his arms. "There is enough to share," he whispered into her hair.

"The longer I'm here, the more I am swallowed by your world. I love your world."

"I think our world loves *you.*"

It might be so. Already she dreaded having to go back to Poondras where she would be, to all purposes, back in Anglica.

He led her to the door. "You must return to the *zenana.* I will wait an hour, then follow."

And just like that they separated, without promises or complexity or social expectations.

Oh, surely *this* was the world she had been made for.

17

Ned Conolly quietly closed the screen of his apartment window. He'd almost been able to see into the little shrine with his spy glass, but not quite. Obviously, though, they'd been at it like jackals for well over two hours; and in the light of day, no less. Even for a heathen prince, the audacity surprised him. And as for Astoria Harding, well, human nature never failed to trump its own values. He would give his left ball to know what they'd talked about. The post-romp confidences and all.

There was a part of him that regretted the affair for Muir-Smith's sake. Poor bloke was besotted with her. Of course he'd done the captain no favors by mucking up his reputation with the girl.

But it was for the Crown. They needed Bharata. He'd spent a decade carrying out nefarious activities for the sake of God and country. You didn't let personal things get in the way. But still, damn shame for Muir-Smith. Best not to tell him. She could still keep it secret if she was discreet. God knew, Uttam would simply unman the prince if he knew. Unless Uttam ordered him to do it.

He put it on his list to find out.

In her apartment, Tori held in her hands a package wrapped in a white cloth. It had been waiting for her on the bed when she returned.

She fancied it might be a gift from Jai. But truly, she hoped it was not. What had happened between them was not a romantic interlude. It could not continue. And no one must know. Falling backward onto her pillows, she clutched the package against her breast, her thoughts filled with the shrine on the roof and the god of opening doors. Scenes of their intimacy assailed her every moment, and she relived them in a fugue of rekindled desire.

She could not have chosen a better lover to show her the way, nor would marriage be a word either of them could utter. It was perfect.

That it had also been lascivious gave her great satisfaction. It had been, she was sure, so very un-Anglic. Her delight in this aspect made her aware that in some ways she had harbored a great bitterness toward her own society. She had not even known that she had felt it, but now assuredly she had been stripped clean of anger or self-pity. In its place was something wholly unexpected: laughter. She held the package and gently laughed.

Oh, Papa, she suddenly thought. I hope you've known such pleasure with Mama. How wonderful it was to think that her own life might have started with such joy.

She still held the package.

Sitting back up, she pulled the twine away and opened the cloth. It was a book with a worn leather cover. "Dulal," she whispered.

Carefully, she opened the cover, revealing handwriting in Anglic.

"Oh, Dulal had it after all," she said, smiling.

⁓

June 15, 1808

Rain again. The monsoons have driven us all to our apartments, a welcome banishment in my present state. The dreams linger. The servants think I have malaria and sent for the palace doctor, but I managed to show myself well enough and he went away.

It can only be from having touched the petal. I was careful to wash my hands, but traces must have an effect. At first I thought that I was losing my reason. Thus the old priest at Gwalior had told me, that one must never touch the holy flower, for its excrescence would by degrees render one mad. But despite all precautions I have absorbed the vital fluid. The petal is now enshrined in a herbarium page—two in fact, so large it is—but still, I reap the reward of a careless touch.

Here it comes upon me again, in a wave.

She read hungrily, hearing in her imagination her grandpapa's voice. Here were the events that he had hesitated to reveal, the things he thought the world would revile him for. It was all here, written in his lovely script that she knew so well. In mounting excitement, she returned to her reading.

A glass of quinine water and the juice of a lime brings me around.

A fearsome noise issues from the great square outside the palace, a commotion in unison with my thoughts.

My mind is all cacophony and scenes of imagination. I labor to record these scenes, hardly knowing whether they be mad dreams or some altered knowing:

A high palisade of weathered rock, riven with holes where boulders once crouched now lies vacant, as though the eyes of the mountain had been gouged out.

Through one of these dark passages, I come into a maze of rock pathways. Darkness surrounds, but a brilliant darkness, wherein one sees in shades of red what must be invisible to the normal eye.

Flickers of real light. I feel I am about to have revealed some great hiding place where fires are lit and people dance in frantic adulations.

But not so. The room that I enter is empty of human form. There is only the great, phantasmical lotus. Ah, the golden flower. As I knew it must look. The rock chamber is flooded by the light of the flower. I fall to my knees, stupefied. It is as large as the oak by the well in Shropshire. Not as high, but as wide. . .

Dulal wakens me. I pull the covers over the notebook, fearful lest he see what I have written. But he cannot read even his own language, much less mine.

I realize, my mind now clearing, that I have been vouchsafed a vision of the habitat of the golden lotus—which I will call Nelumbo aureus. *Why I should be privy to such a vision, I cannot think. Unless my incessant attention to the plant's habitat directed my faculties, under the tropes of the lotus's resins, to know the answer. I must persuade Dulal to take me to the caves. For there are caves nearby, no more than a few miles. We hunted there, the* rana *and I. I saw those palisades.*

Tori stared at the notebook entry, reading it again. So these were his visions. Of the habitat of the flower! If the visions were true… she read on:

Dulal is at the window, pointing. The rana *is mustering his troops for an action in Sirinshwari, unheard of in the monsoons. I cannot think why Dulal is nattering on.*

It is the Gangadhar, he says. The patient sadhus *are all gone. The* rana *attaches them to the army, for fire weapons. I have trouble focusing on his problem.*

Then it comes to me. The museum is being deserted. Can the rana *mean to abandon his high purpose, the great collections? I try to calm Dulal. All will be well. He does not believe me. Nor am I sanguine about the effects of war upon the great repository. Dulal's anguish matches my own. If the practitioners of magic end their watch, the collections will decay.*

But I do not tell Dulal that one specimen has been vouchsafed its redemption. It is sequestered already, preserved in a herbarium sheet. The world must not lose this singular discovery.

If the rana *will not safeguard what God has given into his royal care, then I must.*

Laying the notebook in her lap for a moment, Tori tried to absorb this confession—and its casual justification. She did not want to condemn her grandfather, but she would have liked to have seen a shade of misgiving or regret. If he had doubted his actions or if they troubled him, the notebook gave no hint.

Dulal leaves, still agitated. Outside, shouts of the soldiers and mahouts. A war elephant trumpets. I peer out into the steaming courtyard. They are proceeding to the main gates.

And I shall leave in their wake, mixing into the great press of villagers bidding the soldiers farewell.

But I will make a last trip to the Gangadhar, to say goodbye. Oh, holy place!

And then he had hidden his field notebook there. The notes were in his head, he did not need them on his person, where they might be confiscated if he were apprehended. And he had always hoped to return.

"Stop hovering, Jeffreys."

Lying on a cot in his office, Colonel Harding tried to rise up on one elbow. Despite Harding trying to shake him off, his orderly helped him sit up, propping a pillow behind him. The room, smelling of medicinals and dung, was stifling despite all windows thrown wide.

"Christ, leave off." Sitting up, Harding's vision cleared. He'd been determined this morning to attend to duties, but this malaria was hitting rather hard. He waved a hand to receive the mail packet, lying on the table by the office window.

Jeffreys crossed the lush Amritsar carpet, so thick it showed every footprint.

Reading out the correspondents' names, Jeffreys got a nod as to reading Muir-Smith's report out loud.

Sirinshwari, Nanpura
July 22/57

Sir: *A tour of the central delta of the Darband River leaves me with the distinct impression of a disgruntled populace. Persistent demands are for higher wages at Jhir Ghoda. Also widespread, rumors that the villagers will be forced to learn Anglic science in place of magical practices. The headmen deny their people are agitated, but I do not trust their veracity. It is significant to note that all are appointed, or approved by, Prince Uttam. In Sirinshwari I visited the local jail where six youths are detained for destroying government property. It was no more than broken windows at the rail station, but in an interview they admitted it was retaliation for the refreshment of the regiment at Poondras. They have also heard of a white woman (Miss Platt) brought in to replace a Bharati teacher at Chidawal school, another grievance. I find the situation less supportive of our interests than we had been led to believe. In Kathore, the prince had assured me that local support was strong. This is not the case, at least north from Sirinshwari to Lakka. Advise a reassessment of Chidiwal school. Cannot guarantee security for the students and Miss Platt. I will leave for Chidiwal immediately to await your orders. Under circumstances, advise that Miss Harding at Kathore return with me to Poondras soonest.*

E. Muir-Smith, Cpt.

Colonel Harding felt a stab of unease. It wasn't like Edmond to overreact. If he thought the situation unstable, likely it was. He trusted him a damn sight more than Conolly, who'd practically guaranteed Tori's safety with a cavalier unconcern that Harding now viewed as rash.

He swung his feet to the floor, none too steadily. His first bout with malaria was giving him a bit of a go.

Jeffreys steadied him as he attempted to rise. "Sir, you're not..."

"Damn it. Astoria's out there." He shook off the helping hand, but found himself on his knees. "Get Major Kemp in here," he rasped as Jeffreys got him sitting on the cot again. Kemp would have to carry on, but he wanted a company of dragoons down at Kathore...

"Major Kemp is in infirmary, Sir."

Infirmary? A dark malaise stole Harding's strength, pulling him down. He sprawled onto the cot.

A strange dream came to him. Tori was on a barge on a river, wearing a blue-green sari, rippling in the wind. There was a panoply in back of her, the shelter of some person of distinction. He seemed to be standing on the bank of the river. Tori lifted her hand to him, but was she greeting him or saying farewell? Which way was the river flowing? Oh Tori...

When he opened his eyes, his physician, Captain Reed, was sitting beside him. Mrs. Harding was there too, standing just behind Reed.

His skin burned with fever. "Quinine," He whispered.

"You should stay out of the room, Mrs. Harding," the doctor said.

"I certainly will not."

With this damned blurred vision, he couldn't see her well. "Olivia, do as the doctor says. Just a... touch of... malaria, my dear." She always worried so.

"Colonel," Captain Reed said. "It's more serious than that."

"Well... out with it," he rasped.

"I'm afraid it's smallpox, sir."

The room spun, by turns hot and frigid.

"Dear God," he heard Mrs. Harding whisper.

18

Tori strained against the fretted sandalwood screen to observe the plaza in the gathering dusk. Her view was constricted by elaborate curlicues, making it difficult to see Jai's signal when it came, if it came.

Then, the brief flare of fire: Jai's strikeable from a portico in the Gangadhar.

He had seen Mahindra enter the palace, likely for evening prayers with Uttam. Which meant that Dulal was alone at the Shrine of Vishnu.

She found him by the side of a large pool. Surrounding it, new plantings of young Neem trees and a cane brake. The scent of ketaki flowers almost masked that of the freshly turned soil.

"This is the hole you spoke of," Tori said.

Dulal didn't turn around. "Yes. Here are fish, too." His voice was flat, as though the presence of fish weighed down his heart.

She stood where she could still look over the half-wall of the shrine to see any signal from Jai that Mahindra was returning. "Thank you for Sir Charles's field notes."

"The *pitri* guards you. Maybe you are sent by the gods."

"Oh, no. I'm sure I'm not." But Dulal was not the only one who wondered why the spirit had come to her. Some days she thought the woman could have malign purpose. Sir Charles had not blindly trusted magic. He knew it could go both ways.

Her mind spun with the afternoon's reading of the field notebook. It had all been there, a record of Sir Charles's entire Bharata journey. But it was the last few pages that she had read a dozen times. It was incredible if Sir Charles had been vouchsafed a view of where *Nelumbo aureus* grew! The cave, the palisades… But he did not want to say so outright, not before he had a vital specimen as proof. But what were those visions—glimpses of scientific reality, or wish fulfillment? For, she had to admit, it had always been a possibility that the lotus offered no more than a drug. Sir Charles had admitted this. It needed proof.

She had come here to ask Dulal about the caves, but first she needed to know something. "Has anyone else seen this notebook?"

The old man shook his head. "It has been hidden these fifty years. No one has seen it, not even I, for I do not have the skill of reading. You must not let anyone read it, if it contains forbidden things." Dulal got to his feet, turning his sad eyes upon her. "He is following you. You must not let him."

"Who?"

"Mahindra," he whispered. "You must know, for you waited to come here until he had gone. Have you seen a blue monkey in the old *mahal?*" Indeed she had. "Mahindra is following you, hoping that you know where the holy plant resides. Your grandsire knew. *You* know. But do not speak of it! Keep it secret. Otherwise…" he stopped as he contemplated the pool. "Otherwise we will see it here; uprooted, defiled." He nodded at her puzzled expression. "Oh yes. My master is wishing to have it in this holy shrine. But it will not make us more holy. It will damn us. The golden flower is of the gods. Now do you see why I fear the hole?"

Surely Dulal could not be right. How many golden lotuses were there? Surely their numbers were small since they had never been recorded except in symbolic drawings. To pick one, even to transplant one—especially given its massive size—this could not be scientifically approved.

Amidst all this, now she had proof that Mahindra meant to exploit her.

She kept her gaze firmly fixed on the ground floor of the Gangadhar, for Jai's signal.

"Dulal…" she began, seeing how it weighed on him that he had set this cascade of events in motion. "Dulal, this was not your fault."

He turned an anguished face to her. "But I serve him! I love him. I tend his garden. And I could have sent all the *rana's* army to pursue your grandsire. I kept silent." He waved his hands at her suddenly, and she staggered backward, down from the planting mound on which she stood. Her left foot gave way beneath her and she went to her knees.

"Go now. Go!" Dulal looked over her head toward the plaza, waving at her frantically. She lurched back to her feet.

"Leave Bharata," he said, "and take your knowledge with you. Leave this pond to the carp. We are holy enough."

She backed away, unnerved by Dulal's distress. "I'm sorry," she whispered. But he had already rushed into the shrine, covering his ears, terrified to hear what she knew. But of course, she knew nothing.

That was not what Mahindra thought, though.

She passed out of the shrine's gate, now more than ever concerned lest Mahindra find her in the precincts.

Someone coughed. She spun around. To her vast relief, it was Lieutenant Conolly.

"Lieutenant!" she blurted.

"Miss Harding. It's not a good idea to be out here at night. Why are you, by the way?"

No plausible lie came to hand. "I needed to thank Dulal for something." As he waited, she went on, "He had something, a small notebook that belonged to Sir Charles."

"Extraordinary."

"Yes. He was Sir Charles's servant during his expedition here."

"Well, it was good of the old chap to admit he had the notebook." He saw that her hands were empty. "Did he give it up, or just show it to you?"

"Oh, I have it. Back at the palace."

They began walking across the plaza. "Not too safe, this plaza at night."

"I'm the *rana's* guest. I'm sure no one would disturb me." She tried to sound offhand, to make believable that she would enter a dark shrine at night just to say thank you.

"Not so sure about that." He nodded at the Gangadhar. "Did you know that the *rana's* younger son was lurking around, watching you? He's not been forward, has he?"

"Certainly not. What an idea." But now she wondered that Conolly would even mention such a thing. But by his attitude, he knew nothing. Deflecting the conversation from Jai, she said, "Lieutenant, do you know of any caves around here?"

"Caves? There are some. About four miles north." He gestured over the top of the Shrine of Vishnu. "You'd need a map of them to come out alive. Caves of Kathore. If you get an urge to see them, I'm sure I could get up a party for a hunt. Take you along."

Coming across the plaza directly toward them were three figures. They were approaching too rapidly to present a casual encounter, and Conolly stopped her, putting her behind him.

"Your Highness," Conolly said, in Bharati, addressing someone. "Please put the tigers on leash. I have a lady with me who may become alarmed."

The cats were free? With a shiver, Tori took a step away to see.

Thirty feet off was Sahaj, in a white achkan and pajamas, reins empty in his hand. One tiger was at his side and the other had advanced some ten paces in front of Sahaj.

"These are only pets, Lieutenant. I often take them out loose at night."

"Not when young women are present. Stop them now." To Tori's alarm, he drew his pistol.

"If you kill one tiger, the other will be on you in a heartbeat. They are sisters."

"The closer they get, the better my aim."

Sahaj smiled genially. "They are just curious about the young miss. Let them have a look."

"Surely you can give them one of your harem girls, instead?" As one of the cats moved languidly forward, Conolly cocked the hammer, drawing down.

Sahaj made a snicking sound and the cat turned back, coming to his side. He attached a leash to it. "Not very *sporting* of you, Lieutenant," he said, using the Anglic term.

Tori wanted to see the animals at close range. She came from behind to stand at Conolly's side, receiving his firm grip on her arm.

Sahaj looked at her with bright eyes, not so much acknowledging her as studying her.

Conolly's aim followed the other cat as she returned to receive a leash on her gold collar. Satisfied, he holstered the gun. "For sport, my men pride themselves on their aim. Perhaps Your Excellency would do us the honor of joining us for target practice at the barracks."

"We might arrange something of the sort."

One of the tigers yawned, teeth finely displayed. As grand as the animals' silver and black faces were, Tori was most taken with the size of their paws, looking softly padded, heavy as cudgels.

"*Namaste*, Excellency." Bowing as though it had been a pleasant interlude, Conolly steered Tori off at an angle back to the palace, keeping between her and the tigers.

Once under the overhang of the gallery, Tori said, "I think he didn't like you drawing your gun on his pets."

Conolly led her past the guards into the reception hall. "Sahaj would have been disappointed if I hadn't. He intended to provoke us."

"His guests?"

"Just flexing his brown muscles. He wouldn't have set the animals on you. These people like to flaunt their power." He smiled in genuine pleasure. "So do we."

They parted ways at the women's quarters, and the women guards at the carved doors to the *zenana* opened them for her. Once inside, Tori leaned against a stone pillar, feeling the need of its cool solidity against her back. She must get it all straight. What it all *meant*.

Mahindra had been following her. He was the blue monkey! And was it possible, he had also taken owl form in the sycamore tree, and that of a blue albatross on the Bridge? Was it not very likely that she had been lured to Kathore? Mahindra wished to find *Nelumbo aureus* for his spiritual ambition. Surely they were not all in collusion, for what advantage would it be to Prince Uttam to have a rare flower growing in the Shrine of Vishnu?

In the Shrine of Ganesh, there had been a shadow in the doorway. One of the monkey troop, she had thought, but likely it was not. Oh, so much for secrets! Mahindra certainly knew about her and Jai. She began to see that she had quite misunderstood things. That her desires were known and not only that, manipulated. She began to worry exceedingly about who knew what and when.

Angry at the palace and at her herself, she vowed that she would never lead Mahindra to the flower. But there did not seem much danger of that.

She had only three days left.

⌒

Jai threw his weight against the door in the garden wall. With a final heave, he burst it open, and they were through.

It was miraculous. He and Astoria were on the other side of the fortress wall. Under a bright moon, the slope fell away in jumbled, strewn boulders.

They gazed out at the mountain peaks in the distance, disrobed of snow this time of year and just visible in the moonlight. Above them, the wall towered thirty feet, a prodigious defense. They had little space to stand, for along the outer wall was just enough flat ground for a hyena to walk.

"This is where the pitri went," Astoria said. "When she left me."

Watching her, he waited for her to say her reason for coming here. How exquisite she was! But he could not make a match with an Anglic woman. Neither of their fathers could consider such a thing. Not only that, but though he had been well for weeks, he was a man who could not live long. He would die of bleeding, this he had always known and accepted. She was completely beyond his reach, and yet here she stood next to him, with scents of their lovemaking still upon her, or still in his imagination.

"We cannot stay here, Astoria. You cannot be gone so long from your rooms." She had been most insistent that they speak immediately, this night. He could not imagine what might be the subject, but felt sure it had to do with Dulal.

"I have a favor to ask you," she said. "A very great one." She put a hand to his lips, causing him almost to swoon at her touch. "It isn't because of what we shared this afternoon. This is separate. You owe me nothing." Her hand came away. He was hopelessly in her power.

"Only ask me."

"My grandfather saw the golden lotus."

His incredulity must have shown even in the night shadows. "It is of the gods."

"Yes, perhaps. But it is also on the earth. Sir Charles saw a vision. He touched the petal, and it showed him something real. Where the flower resides. It is in the Caves of Kathore."

"This you read in the book which Dulal presented to you?" He saw that it was so. And then he knew what she was going to ask, and his chest filled with a terrible pain. The thing she wanted from him was something he must never do. It would be a sacrilege. He backed against the wall and sank down, staring at the distant peaks, feeling cloven in two.

"Oh, Jai," she said, kneeling next to him. "You do not have to do it."

But when your lady asks you for her heart's desire, do you not say yes? They sat for several minutes as he fought with his own impulses. There was no way out.

"Isn't it possible," she whispered, "that the spiritual stories have attached themselves to *Nelumbo aureus*, but that the gods do not favor one flower over another?"

"You do not know us, Astoria. The golden lotus, if it is present in the world—it is holy. The gods have warned never to touch it." He looked at her beautiful, moonlit face. "And, besides, it does not grow upon the earth. Your grandsire is wrong."

"Then let me know that at last! We will go, and it will not be there. And then I will know."

"The caves are miles away. And where will we find mounts to carry us, and how to find our way in the caves—and all this without my father knowing?"

"I don't know yet. But we have all night to plan."

And just like that he knew he would help her. It was only sacrilege if they found the flower. Certainly, they would not.

She was still trying to persuade him. "It's my only hope. To bring home a cutting. To find a new way of knowing. If I can't make a great discovery, I will never have a life."

"You have a life."

She shoved away from the wall, distressed. "If it could be for science, then yes. But I can't bear to be shut away in a... a *zenana*!"

After a long pause, Jai said, "Your grandsire taught you to love things only a man can do."

Hearing this, she shook her head. "Even you do not understand me."

"I understand you." He touched her cheek. "You are a caged thing. Leashed just as my brother's tigers are."

Her voice trembled. "Yes." She felt the collar around her neck, a golden cirque.

His arm came around her, and she rested her head against his chest. "Yes," she whispered. "And when I break free, they will shoot me."

"We will not let that happen. But I will take you to the caves."

"Oh Jai. Shall you indeed?" She pulled back, crouching before him, holding his hands. He did not flinch from what he had said.

"Only, I must tell you," she went on. "Dulal told me that Mahindra also seeks the flower."

She said this so simply. He stared at her with incredulity.

"He wants it for his spiritual ambition, to have the mythical flower in his pond at the shrine. That he must not do. It is true that I will take a cutting of a plant that is at the least very rare. But his plan to uproot it is wrong."

Was it so, that Mahindra thought the flower dwelled among men, that it could be touched and seen and... uprooted? Jai now began to be very afraid. He desperately hoped that Mahindra and Sir Charles Littlewood were wrong.

But he had already told Astoria he would help her.

19

Elizabeth lay on her bed, her sweat soaking the sheets. A fever had come upon her during the night, and now she had slept until the sun came blasting into her room. Where was her servant? If she would just close the shutters her stomach would not rise so.

"Bansi!" she called.

From the back room came the repulsive smell of cooking, with its vile cardamom and ghee. The sun and spices combined in a hellish concoction.

She reached for her cup of water, but it crashed to the floor.

"Bansi…"

Her stomach roiled, threatening to erupt. Oh, she must get to the bucket in the corner. Managing to rise, she staggered to the bucket and kneeled before it. Her stomach clenched in a fearful spasm, forcing its hot contents up and out. Again and again her gut heaved, finally producing only bile.

She sat back, wiping her mouth, desperate for water.

Bansi must help her clean up. Staggering into the schoolroom, she found some of the students already at their seats. They stared at her. She realized how she looked: hair frayed, her nightdress fouled. How late was it? Why had Bansi not called her nor come to help? Furious at the woman, Elizabeth rushed into the back room.

Bansi was at the little stove. She did not even look up, but stood cooking chapattis, adding yet another to a stack.

"Bansi. I'm sick."

The woman glanced at her. "The children are wanting their lunch."

Lunch? Why was she cooking, of all things? "Leave off, Bansi. Help me to dress."

"You should go back to bed, Miss. Your nightshirt is soiled."

Such insolence left Elizabeth speechless for a moment. "You will come now and help me. I have purged. Take the bucket away and help me dress." It felt like every word was an effort. The slow-minded servant seemed hardly to comprehend.

Bansi flipped another chapatti onto the platter. "We have been hearing you purge. Please shut the door. It distresses the children."

The stench of the room, the heat of the stove was unbearable. Elizabeth leaned a hand against the wall to keep from pitching over. "Bansi. Help me."

Infuriatingly, the woman ignored her.

Elizabeth grabbed a long-handled ladle from the stove and struck Bansi on the shoulders. "You foolish cow! Leave the chapattis!" She drove Bansi back from the stove, her fury mounting. Bansi cried out as the blows fell on her. As she fled out the back door, Elizabeth followed, beating her on the head and shoulders, enraged that she dared to run.

They stood in the cart path behind the school. Villagers stopped to gape at the scene, as Elizabeth pummeled Bansi with the ladle, trying to beat sense into her. At last Bansi managed to snatch the ladle from Elizabeth's hands, throwing it aside. People gathered around, women in bright saris, men leaning on staffs, staring with gap-toothed astonishment at the white woman in her night dress. The school children poured outside, peeking now from around the adults' legs. Some were laughing.

Elizabeth turned to seek refuge in the school, but instead her knees buckled and the ground came up to meet her.

She awoke, emptying her stomach into the dirt. All that came up was a ghastly yellow gruel, smelling of curry and cardamom. Villagers crowded around, making her degradation complete.

Bansi crouched next to her, smirking. The hatred in the woman's eyes was clear.

Poison. Bansi had poisoned her. Elizabeth swooned again, her face falling into the vomit and dust of the path.

❧

"My beauty," Prince Uttam said. He scratched vigorously with his crop at a spot on Iravatha's neck, as the elephant raised her chin to receive the scrape of bristles against her hide.

Mahindra watched as his old friend doted upon the war elephant. Amid the pungent odors of manure and the breath of his elephant, Uttam was happy, even when the tumor sent swords of pain through his gut. Uttam called these pangs the ghosts of war wounds. Uttam's war days were long over.

Uttam waved the *mahout* away, clearing a space for privacy. "Where is the banner you promised, *babaji?* We have waited many days for the girl to show us. Perhaps there is no holy golden flower."

"She searches for it. She knows it is real. Soon it will reside in our shrine of Vishnu."

"Ah yes, she searches. Looking in the drawers, day after day." Uttam took a handful of sweet grass from the bin, holding it as Iravatha made a soft curl in his trunk to take it. "Yet nothing."

"The *pitri* bides its time. But it leads her, Highness. I have cut myself, begging the spirit for haste."

"I have not forbid you yet, *babaji.* But I do not favor spilling your blood."

Uttam no longer believed in suffering. Mahindra bowed, daring to say, "Just a little blood, old friend."

Another tuft of grass went into the gnarl of the trunk. The prince murmured, "Perhaps the scarf was always there, and blew in a gust."

"Forgive me, Highness, but as your majesty knows elephants, I know magic. The spirit tests her. When she is deemed worthy of her task, knowledge will be given her."

Another voice: "Perhaps she knows already."

Mahindra turned to find Sahaj making a bow to his father. He had abandoned his usual adornments and came dressed in simple trousers and a fine but plain shirt, girt with tooled leather.

When he got a nod from his father, Sahaj went on. "We must force her to tell."

Mahindra caught his sovereign's eye. It had not been their plan to share the truths of the lotus with the impetuous Sahaj. Secrecy was vital, until they were ready. Now it appeared Uttam had revealed all.

Uttam noted Mahindra's reaction. "It is time to bring him into our counsels."

Mahindra looked with dismay at Uttam. Perhaps his friend knew he was dying. If so, Sahaj must be made ready to lead. He appraised the *yuvraj* prince anew. His eyes had flint and he looked more the prince than ever he had in brocades and sashes.

"My prince," Mahindra said to Sahaj, "it could be as you say. Yet we may learn more by following where she leads."

"She evades us, wasting time. The hills men know the pox has weakened the fort. They are eager. A sword sheathed too long goes to rust, *babaji*."

"You are right, my son, it is almost time. But first the banner. Without it, we shall have war without a purpose. And worse, we will only draw the full might of Anglica upon us, when they cross the Bridge to avenge Poondras."

"I do not need a banner, father," Sahaj said to Uttam. "They will follow me, for your sake. They love us, and they do not love the Anglics."

Uttam pursed his lips. "Here is a truth. My people have always gone to war at my command."

Mahindra kept his face passive. Neither father nor son grasped what a fight against Anglica would mean. Their purpose could not be merely to slaughter the cantonment. The banner of the holy lotus would bring every province under Nanpura. The princely states would have a true ruler for the first time, from ocean to ocean. Only unity could bestow authority on Bharata. It had only been by subverting each prince one at a time that Anglica had ever conquered them. If such an ambition could not light a fire within the father, Mahindra would have to kindle it in the son.

He regarded Sahaj. Time to begin his education.

Sahaj went on. "In the hills, they smolder over the army at Poondras. There are rumors the Anglics will force us to give up the gods, to learn their tongue. My spies say the villages are ready to drive the regiment into the sea. They have already destroyed the bridge over the Darband."

Now Uttam frowned. "At my word, Sahaj. They are ready then. Not before."

Sahaj bowed, his jaw stiffened.

Turning to Mahindra, Uttam said. "One more day. Then bring her to pain." He turned a sharp eye on Sahaj. "Nothing must alert the cantonment until then. Do not spend yourself early, my son. This is war, not pillow matters." He patted Iravatha and walked away to join his retinue waiting just outside.

Sahaj rose from his bow, eyes slashes of black. He murmured, watching his father depart, "He has grown old." He faced Mahindra. "We must attack before the fort is laid waste by the pox. The people wish to strike at living flesh."

"My prince," Mahindra said, "the smallpox began with our gift of the Amritsar rug. But it has not had time to spread. I have seen it with the orange eyes of a circling bird. They are yet strong."

The *yuvraj* prince shook his head in wonderment. "I marvel that you do not thirst for this as I do. I had thought you would strike for your sons' sake.

For their memory."

The stable was silent except for Iravatha's soft munching. Gathering all his discipline, Mahindra turned a pleasant expression on the young prince. "I do not speak of those days."

"Yes, you speak of patience and who is easy to fight. The Anglics killed them in the glory of their young lives. But you have no heat for your revenge."

Against Mahindra's will, the image of that day came to him, the skull of his youngest, shattered, as he lay bleeding in his father's arms. His brother beside him, dead of a musket ball in the chest. It was the image for which he cut himself every day.

It had been a minor uprising, quickly put down by the Anglics. But his two sons had died for it, fourteen and fifteen years in age. It was their first skirmish. Mahindra stared at Iravatha's stall, looking far beyond it. Some memories were carved in flesh and felt as ripe. But in one thing Sahaj was wrong: It was not about revenge. He would not allow himself pleasure at the ground soaked in Anglic blood.

But he would not look away, either.

In the stall nearby, Dulal crouched with his head in his hands, rocking, rocking, and trying to banish what he had heard. Oh, that he had ever told the *sadhu* the tale of the white man's theft. Oh, that he had never set these things in motion. A storm was coming. Call it mutiny or call it revenge, it meant war.

A sprinkling of rain drove Rashmika and Bhakti from the garden, Tori trailing behind them. It was maddening to act naturally in their presence, with her night-time escape just hours away.

A distant thunder rolled over the countryside. Rain could ruin her plans.

How could the ostriches manage the miles-long trek in the rain? And could Jai acquire the supplies that they would need? Edmond would surely be back in the morning, and then she would not have another chance.

Pleading a headache, she went to her room. There she found Lieutenant Conolly rifling her trunk. Seeing her, he didn't stop, but continued throwing out the contents.

She closed the door behind her. "Perhaps you should ask me for what you're looking for." How had he even made his way into the *zenana*?

He abandoned his dig through her trunk and stood to face her, not the least discomforted. "I'll have that notebook, Miss Harding."

Conolly was trying to find Sir Charles's notes. She didn't know why he wanted the notebook, but she was delighted to foil him. Fortunately, she had been careful to hide it. "Kindly leave. I shall report this behavior, you may be sure."

He closed the trunk and sat on it, looking too relaxed by far for a young man caught in a woman's bedroom. "It's time we had a bit of a talk."

She waited. He was silhouetted against the arched window, his face in shadow.

"We know the botanical specimen is in the Caves of Kathore."

"What specimen?"

"*Nelumbo aureus.* That's what you call it, isn't it? The great lotus … the golden lotus. We want it."

He was pursuing the lotus! Oh, but why? And she realized with dismay that she shouldn't have asked him where the caves were, walking back from visiting Dulal.

Conolly went on. "The question is, where in the caves? We could spend weeks thrashing around there, and I'm afraid we don't have that much time."

Yes, he might well thrash around in the caves. But she didn't intend to be so hampered. Her great advantage was that the *pitri* was guiding her.

Conolly stared at her impudently.

"When my father hears of this—"

"—Let's be clear, Miss Harding. I don't work for the Colonel. I work for his superiors. Whitehall, in fact. And they want the damned flower. It's my job to get it."

Her face must have shown her confusion.

He nodded. "Yes, I'm afraid this goes a bit beyond your hope to publish a paper on magic."

She'd heard this kind of condescension before and it never failed to infuriate her. "Get out. Get out of my room." She went to the door to throw it open.

He was a step behind her, grabbing her arm, turning her to face him. "We're not playing at science now. Please control yourself. Listen to me." He took her to the trunk and made clear she was to sit. She obeyed, her temper high. But she was now in fact curious about what he had to say.

"Whitehall has reason to believe the golden lotus exists. They believe it may have properties of value."

Tori stared at him in astonishment. "You mean they think Sir Charles was right?"

He sighed. "No, the old man was daft, of course. His majesty's government is looking for... more practical benefits."

"Such as?"

He smirked. "Don't you know? A woman of science? Well. You don't need to know. But you do need to tell us what Sir Charles knew about the caves. Which cave, and so forth. It's rather important, so I hope there won't be unpleasantness between us."

She stiffened at his implied threats. "I don't know where in the caves."

"Well I bloody well don't believe you."

Since he already knew about the caves, there was nothing more the notebook could tell him. "See for yourself. The notebook is in the shrine of Ganesh on the museum roof."

Conolly's face darkened. He went to the window, looking out as rain began pelting into the courtyard, sounding like distant gunfire. "I'll have a look. But if you're telling the truth, then that's a damn shame. There are miles of caves up there."

He was so sure of himself and of his privileges. But this was *her* privilege, this time. The golden lotus was the gift of her grandfather; it was her only legacy, and Conolly was not going to usurp it.

"We don't have time," he murmured. "No damn time." He turned back to face her. "It's best that you don't mention this meeting to Colonel Harding. I know the foreign office can depend on your discretion. A matter of national welfare. Your father's career, you see? By the way, I've called off your little expedition. You didn't think I'd let you go charging off into the jungle, did you? I've spoken with Jai."

He saw her startled reaction. "Spies in the villages. It costs plenty to keep them on my side. They told me that one of Jai's servants had hired ostriches and a few guides. I agreed not to tell Uttam, and he agreed to stick close to his mother's skirts until you're gone." He shook his head. "Spoiled little bitch. You want to be Sir Charles, do you? I suppose your paper on magic was your only hope. Unless fucking the prince's invalid son is a consolation prize."

She charged at him, raising her hand to strike him. He easily caught her wrist. "Also, you should know that we have a few problems. Smallpox has broken out at Poondras. In the cantonment."

Tori must have blanched, because he nodded soberly, releasing her arm.

"And more bad news, the bridge over the river at Chidiwal has been destroyed. A rather nasty slap in the face of our mission here. Could be the start of something larger."

Alarm raced through her. "Edmond..."

"Yes. Wish he wasn't late. Don't pretend that you give a damn for him." His face held a full measure of contempt. "Poor sod. He was head over heels for you, you know."

She shook her head. "Head over heels for several women, you mean."

He laughed, a short snort of derision. "That business about your sister? I was wrong about that. Muir-Smith never laid a hand on her."

She felt the breath go out of her. "You lied..."

He stepped closer, his face florid. "Oh, I'm a liar. I'm a fucking spy for His Majesty's government, so lying's my craft, my duty. I don't take pleasure in steering enemies over the cliff, even if they are cheating, backward and vicious. But you? You don't give a damn for anything larger than yourself. Your little expedition wasn't to be for science, but for yourself. Getting naked with the son of an ally prince was nothing to you but a chance to get laid. You make me sick."

How dare he say these things to her? But even if there was a wisp of truth in what Conolly said, the *pitri* believed in her. It was from the spiritual world, and it was by God *helping* her.

He stalked away from her, then paused at the door. "I want you to pack and be ready to leave in the morning. Time to get you back to Poondras before the natives decide it would be fun to take you one at a time in that hot little shrine on the roof. I'd have a go at you myself, but I owe the captain a bit of loyalty."

Then he slipped out of the room.

20

Rain lashed at Tori as she hurried across the empty courtyard. It thundered down on the stones of the great square driving away the servants, functionaries and beggars. She was alone in the courtyard as she held a shawl over her head, certain that eyes watched her from behind fretted screens, pillared verandahs.

She had been watched all this time. Not only by Mahindra, but by Conolly. It had all been politics from the very beginning, and she had stepped into it thinking herself clever to have arranged a visit to Kathore. How stupid she'd been, and how many mistakes she'd made! But was her tryst with Jai one of them? She didn't owe Edmond fidelity. And though he wasn't courting her sister, he must surely have had numerous sexual experiences. Why should it be different for her? And why, indeed, did any of this matter, since she had already spurned his marriage proposal? Amidst all this, smallpox at the fort. *Oh, Papa,* she thought. And her mother and Jessa. But Papa would know what to do.

At the archway to the shrine, she ducked into the garden. A flash of lightning blinded her for a moment, while thunder roared from near the Elephant Gate. Fat rain drops hammered the pond, still empty, but awaiting its trophy.

She hurried to the shrine entrance, her dress clinging to her like seaweed. Conolly wanted her gone tomorrow. But she would not go, not quite yet. There was still a way to prevail and that was through Mahindra. He wanted the lotus. Well, so did she. It was time to parley.

An acolyte wearing an ochre robe appeared in a passageway, making *namaste.*

"*Mahindrā, krpayā,*" she said. Mahindra, please.

He bowed and disappeared into the darkness.

More thunder, this time from the distant hills, as though warning of downed bridges and disease.

Mahindra now stood at the end of the corridor, beckoning her. She followed him. He led her into a side hall with a raised platform toward the back, draped with woven cloths. He gestured for her to sit on a muslin cushion.

"I am glad you have come," he said in Anglic. Today he wore a shawl over his thin shoulders, a *dhoti* around his lower body. His face was unlined, ageless. He might have been forty or sixty. She realized that he had once been handsome, but now he was thin, the soft parts stripped away.

She sat down as he stoked a fire in the brazier. "I've been avoiding you," she said.

He blew on the coals, which flared to flame. "Yes, *beti*. But soon I would have come to you."

As a man or a monkey? She wanted to ask. Looking into the *sadhu's* eyes, she felt that she saw the eyes of the dusky owl in the sycamore tree. Was he one and the same?

She tried to keep her voice steady. "I've come to ask your help; even though I'm not welcome here. We're none of us welcome here. I finally see that."

He sat on the cushion opposite her. "It would be meritorious if you understood *why.*"

"I do. We've been treating your land as though it were ours. It's not." And where had that come from? Had she known this from the start, but ignored it because of what she wanted from Bharata? And what she still wanted? But there was a difference from taking a country and sampling a plant just to prove it existed.

Mahindra fed little cakes of dung into the brazier. The heat and pungent stench drifted over her, warming her. "You have begun to see."

"*Baba,* I'm worried about my friends at Chidiwal. The bridge over the Darband has been destroyed. I think Miss Elizabeth and Captain Muir-Smith may be in danger."

"The people are angry, yes. You are right to fear for your friends."

"Can you help them? *Will* you help them, for my sake?" She wanted to add, *for the lotus,* but wasn't quite ready to say it. What she knew of the lotus was her only leverage.

"What would you have me do, daughter?"

"Send word to let my friends pass. Let us go home."

"Ah. Calm the villagers." Another brick of dung went in, turning the coals blacker as the temperature dropped. His gentle voice held no outright rancor as he said, "Do you think that my people are in need of restraint?"

But hadn't Prince Uttam asked for Anglic presence? Hadn't he championed the cause of Anglic schooling? "Some are innocent," she said. "Elizabeth means only well."

Mahindra murmured, "Sometimes the innocent die. Sometimes they are caught up in larger things."

She stared at him. He was talking of death. So the bridge at Chidiwal *was* the beginning of some larger violence. The cold stone shrine began to feel like a prison from which she must flee.

"I will do what I can for Miss Platt," he said. "But Captain Muir-Smith is a soldier." He held her gaze. She understood.

In the panic of the moment, she blurted, "We didn't know that you hated us."

"Am I to love my enemy?" He was taunting her with her own religion, teachings that even Anglics did not obey. Rising to his feet, he said, "You use love when it suits you. And guns when it does not."

"If not love, *baba*, then compassion." She stood up also. "And one thing more." It was time to say where the lotus was. So that he could take it. And give her a cutting. It was a terrible compromise. He would uproot it... but she would have her discovery. Silence pressed down on them while she hesitated to broach the topic.

She wandered over to the raised platform. Amid brass stands with burned out cakes of incense, were remnants of offerings: wilted flowers, pieces of fruit. And there were brownish-red stains on the platform. Dried blood. Pointed skewers lay on a tray, wiped clean, but their purpose was clear.

Mahindra was beside her. "Sometimes life comes to pain. I have learned to endure it. But I think, *beti*, you would not find it a spiritual experience."

These words sank in slowly, growing more horrific with every moment.

"I cannot restrain Sahaj," he murmured. "He will come for you. Unless you give us what is ours, after all."

Sahaj? The thought chilled her. "What... what is it that you want?"

"Your grandsire had knowledge of the golden lotus. It belongs to us, does it not?" He shook his head in evident regret. "You are unclear what is yours and what is not. I am sorry for you, *beti*. Anglica has not given you a proper education. Sahaj will come for you, it grieves me to say."

Her mind slowed, crawling with fear. Why did Sahaj care about the lotus?

He was no *sadhu*, intent on spiritual peace. How could this be happening? What had begun so innocently… But had it ever been innocent? Hadn't they all, every last one of them, concealed things?

Hoping to bluff, she summoned a calm she did not feel. "I would help you if I could. I admit that I came here to seek the lotus. But I have found nothing. So if Sahaj comes for me, it will be a terrible mistake. I can tell him nothing."

"Not even about the *pitri?*"

So they knew about that. "The *pitri* brought me to a drawer in the museum. But it was empty. I know nothing. Nothing."

Mahindra looked at her with an expression of admiration mixed with sadness. *"Shabash, beti,"* he said. Well done. He bowed, his hands pressed together, touching his forehead.

The interview was over. Sahaj was coming for her. She backed away from Mahindra, unsure whether he was holy man or demon. Reaching the door, she turned from him and rushed away.

The rain had stopped, but since evening was coming on, it grew no lighter. Tori had changed dresses and dried her hair, but she was shivering in the deep shade of the Elephant Gate leading into the Gangadhar.

This was the meeting place she and Jai had settled upon. Disguised, they were to have slipped out the nearby main gate and gone down to the hamlet in the valley. They met amid the ruins of their plans. The expedition could not matter anymore; things were far beyond that now.

Jai listened in disbelief as Tori recounted her conversation with Mahindra. "They shall not hurt you," he swore. "I will go to my father."

Tori was not sure that would be good thing. If confronted, the prince might reveal himself as approving; it could force his hand.

Outside, the courtyard was filling with people again, even as distant thunder promised more storms. In the direction of the barracks, they heard the sounds of rifle practice, broken up by the screeches of monkeys from inside the Gangadhar. Every noise shattered her nerves. Even Jai started at the chaotic sounds.

He paced back and forth in front of the great arch, going from muted light to deep shadow and back again. "When Muir-Smith *sahib* arrives, he will make my brother pay."

"The captain isn't coming back." Tori knew they would never let Edmond enter Kathore. She hoped he wouldn't try. They could pick him and his soldiers off one by one as they climbed the switchbacks.

She went on. "And they won't let Lieutenant Conolly leave, either."

"How do they dare!" Jai whispered. "Your father will come with all his troops and obliterate them."

"He is not coming." Dulal stood in the arched opening.

Startled, Tori and Jai turned to him.

"Dulal!" Tori cried. "What do you know?"

"Colonel *sahib's sepoys* will turn on him, if they have not already." He entered the portico, looking behind, scanning the plaza, glistening from the rain.

Jai moved to Tori's side as though to protect her against him. But Dulal was no threat. With a sinking stomach, she knew that he bore some dread message, and she would rather flee into the Gangadhar than hear it. But her feet would not move.

"Tell us."

Dulal's face bore all his years. She had never seen him happy but here was the face of exquisite pain. The old man's voice was flat as he pronounced, "They will be slaughtering the troops at Poondras."

Oh, she did not want to hear! But he was not done talking.

"Sahaj is eager to do so, however Prince Uttam wishes to wait. But it is coming." Dulal looked balefully at Tori. "As soon as you tell them where is the holy flower."

"But why would they wait for the holy lotus?" Jai blurted. "This is not sensible." He was about to dismiss Dulal, but Tori put a hand on his arm.

"Dulal, why do they want the flower?"

"For war!" he cried. "For the sake of a holy symbol that proves the gods bless the uprising. To give Prince Uttam the power of all the princely states. So they can be striking as one."

Jai shook his head. "You are wrong. The garrison is ten thousand strong. They have cannon and good muskets. They cannot be defeated."

Dulal's voice was very small, but no less assured. "They sickened the cantonment with the terrible pox. And when it is thick upon them, the *sepoys* will strike and open the gates. This is why they are wanting the lotus."

Tori felt the truth of it like a blow. Oh, this was the truth, at last. Mutiny.

They would come for her. And she would tell them, eventually. And then the uprising would ignite. She thought of her family, her mother, Jessa, all the proud soldiers by whose side she had crossed the Bridge. "Papa," she whispered. "Papa…"

"Has my father allowed this?" Jai asked. "Or is it only Sahaj?" Dulal had already answered that, but Jai couldn't accept it.

"The *rana* wishes it. Prince Sahaj is over-eager, but eventually, the *rana* will call for war."

Tori's mind raced, clutching first at one plan, then another. "I have to get to the barracks. To tell them." She turned to Jai. "And we must send warning to the cantonment. Do you have anyone to send?"

Jai looked at her starkly. "No one will go against my father."

"Someone must." Conolly would find a way.

Leaving them, Tori rushed with barely controlled panic into the courtyard.

Turning down the lane where a small bazaar was always spread out, Tori dashed toward the soldiers' billet at the far end of the fortress. She prayed that Conolly would be there.

When she came out of the narrow street onto the reviewing grounds, she froze in stunned alarm. Anglic soldiers lay in pools of blood. Among them milled the prince's soldiers in their blue and white, kicking at the corpses. Gun powder crept up her nostrils. Oh, this—*this*—had been the source of the rifle shots she'd heard.

And then, from a side street opposite her, Prince Uttam came with his retinue. He stopped to survey the carnage, then strode toward the barracks. There could be no doubt, Uttam had not authorized this. His demeanor bespoke barely contained fury.

His son emerged from the barracks door, *tulwar* drawn and bloody.

Uttam's voice carried. "Take him."

Sahaj stepped forward, unafraid. "You are old, my father, to cringe at death! And you are blind, as well, not to know your own enemy."

"You dare speak to me so!"

"Yes, and you are sick." Sahaj looked around at the gathered soldiers. "They know you will be soon dead."

"Take him, I say," Uttam snarled at his guards, but to Tori's astonishment, the guards did not move. They backed away from Uttam as Sahaj came forward.

He stood toe to toe with his father. "You have not listened to me."

The *rana* sneered, "Why should I listen to a youth without hair in his armpits?"

"Because of this." Swift as a boar, he thrust the *tulwar* into Uttam's stomach.

Uttam fell to his knees, clutching his belly.

"No!" came a cry from somewhere. And then Mahindra was rushing across the reviewing grounds. Mahindra caught Uttam as he fell forward. The *sadhu* sank to the ground with him, cradling him, holding the *rana's* head in his lap. Blood covered Mahindra's white *dhoti.*

No one moved.

Except one person, wearing green. A woman walked amid the bodies. She seemed to glide among them.

"Jai," she said, her voice blowing into Tori's ears. "Jai, do not fear. Now a son must replace the father. It shall be you."

Tori turned around to see Jai standing in mute horror, surveying the scene.

The *pitri* walked through the bodies, past the anguished Mahindra holding Uttam, toward Jai. "It is time for a new *rana,*" she whispered. The *pitri* glanced at Tori. "And you shall help him."

No one paid the least attention to the *pitri*, no one except Tori, and now Jai. He backed away from the *pitri*, dismayed, overwhelmed.

The *pitri* passed him by, her long hair streaming out behind her. "Follow me."

They did. Jai walked as one entranced.

Sahaj watched them leave, his dark eyes promising them he would attend to them later. For now, he was too overwhelmed by his victory to care.

They walked behind the pitri, seized by her command to follow her, stunned by events. There was nothing to do but follow. Jai had lost his father. Tori was about to lose everything.

It had begun. The mutiny. The slaughter.

21

In late afternoon, a bedraggled squad of Anglic soldiers rode slowly into Chidiwal. With Edmond Muir-Smith at their head, they had ridden hard from Sirinshwari and only slowed at the outskirts of the village for an orderly entrance. The exhausted ostrich mounts now and then flicked their wings, shivering themselves free of mud.

Riding next to Edmond, the *jemadar* Maruti spoke softly. "Captain *sahib*."

"I see it, Maruti." The village looked crabbed and deserted, pervaded by a smell of doused fire. At a doorway, a mother wrapped her skirts around a toddler and pulled him inside. A few men lounging at the well turned to watch the line of soldiers approach. It was a far different Chidiwal than the city Edmond had left only ten days ago.

Heavy clouds lumbered overhead, bringing an early dusk. At the turn in the road, Edmond saw the school. Burned to the ground.

He drew his pistol. "Sergeant, cover us from the granary."

"Sir." Sergeant Fisk took three men off to the mud-walled storage shed as Maruti and Edmond approached the school with the remaining seven men of the unit. Along with the school, the fire had consumed the great pipal tree next to it, and its blacked skeleton stood in relief against the lush rice field beyond. A few desks stood resolutely upright in their places. A cook stove squatted in one corner of the ruins. The rest was gone.

At the sound of a door opening, Edmond turned in his saddle to see Mr.

Ramanath standing in the doorway of his hut across the road.

"She is here." He swept his hand toward the inside.

"I will go, *sahib*," Maruti said, frowning at the quiet and the mood of the place.

"No. Wait for me." Edmond holstered his gun. It would not do to enter the house with weapon drawn.

In the dim interior Edmond saw Elizabeth lying on a bed in the corner. He went to her side. Ramanath's wife huddled in the corner with three small children.

"She is sick of poisoning," Ramanath said.

Elizabeth didn't stir when he put his hand on her face. She was cool to the touch, and sweating profusely. "Has she wakened?"

"Only she is asking for water, but then not keeping it."

Edmond stood up to face him. "Who did this, Mr. Ramanath?"

The man was terrified as was his wife. Here was a white woman near death in the home of a Bharati. "Bansi," he said very low. "She is gone now, knowing you would return."

"And the school?"

Ramanath stood ramrod still, flicking his eyes in the direction of the outside. Then, almost at a whisper, he said. "The *sahiba* beat Bansi with a dipper. Everyone saw. Then they ran to the school and were throwing the books into a pile. And the picture of the King." He locked glances with Edmond, as though to say that if one were an emperor one should do better than burning.

Edmond went to the door, telling Maruti to find a wagon. They would take Elizabeth immediately, and no time to lose with daylight fading. Maruti would pay for the wagon or not. He would know what to do. The villagers must be made to feel shame at this act of treachery.

Within twenty minutes they had made as comfortable a bed for Elizabeth as possible in a rickety cart and commandeered a bullock to pull it. Three soldiers rode the wagon facing backward, Enfield rifles casually riding on their thighs, their mounts tied to the wagon sides.

Edmond nodded to Ramanath as he stood in the doorway, watching the loading. "You should come with us." Ramanath would be a target now.

"This is my home."

"I will report your act of bravery."

"Please do not."

It drove home how tenuous the situation was, where a Bharati in Anglic employ found it better to refuse its honors. Leaving Ramanath at the hut, the squad set out with pariah dogs following the cart for some distance. They dashed away when the mud clods started landing.

Young men had crept out from cane brakes and were pelting the column with rocks and dung. Maruti turned in his saddle and fired his rifle into the air, then lowered it, pointing it toward the clusters of men, who hesitated.

"Hold fire," Maruti said as the soldiers in the wagon kneeled to aim.

The soldiers frowned at being denied a few shots at Elizabeth Platt's tormentors, and they crouched, ready for Edmond to countermand the order, but he did not. He rode at the head of the column, showing the village his back, these cowards armed with dung. He was much more concerned with how widespread these inflammatory incidents were, and how the tale of the beating of the servant with the ladle would travel—and grow in the telling. Add to all this, Ramanath had told him as he'd left that the bridge at the Darband River was destroyed. To get to Kathore, they had to ford the river. And do so at night.

After a silent ride through the darkening forest, Corporal Brockie rode up from his forward position to report that the river was just over the rise. He couldn't tell if the bridge was down, but Edmond had no cause to doubt Ramanath.

They would not risk cresting the rise to present a bulky target for anyone waiting on the other side. Edmond sent Brockie and another corporal into the brush to find a path to the river. Now they would have to leave the cart behind.

While they waited for the scouts, Maruti fashioned a sling-carrier out of blankets for Elizabeth, and Edmond's thoughts went to Tori. Pray God she was safe at Kathore. The only question was what role Uttam played in the unrest, and whether he was in fact behind it or at least prepared to exploit it. Uttam's intelligence of his own villages was appallingly lax; either that or he had deliberately misled Edmond. If the latter, he must have confidence that he would suffer no penalty for the treason. Might he have lured Tori to Kathore in order to have her as a hostage in a conflict with Poondras? The idea was stunning in its audacity, its perfidy. Edmond had left Tori a fortnight ago, ostensibly in the care of Uttam and his doting wife and daughters. If this had been an elaborate conspiracy, he had ridden away from Tori, leaving her in the hands of a ruthless enemy. That he had done so with such confidence galled him exceedingly.

He had much rather be angry than worried. Uttam would answer for this.

Edmond could not arrive at Kathore soon enough and they would travel all night to get there, Elizabeth's precarious condition notwithstanding. Left alone in that fortress was the woman he loved. And the daughter of the regimental commander, by God.

But the river lay in his path.

Now came word that a way could be found down the embankment. They hid the wagon in the brush and began a single file descent into a ravine stuffed with pampas grass. A trace of the day remained, extending their sight as far as nine or ten yards. Wind whipped the grass stalks into their faces but also served to disguise their passage, since twelve men could hardly walk through tall grass without announcing their trail.

When Elizabeth began to moan in her sling, they were forced to fashion a gag for her. She quieted. Brockie led them to the riverbank where they must test the depth of the water. A soldier was sent in with his mount, heavily bridled lest the bird screech as ostriches did in fording.

Fortunately they found the river slow moving and shallow enough for a man to walk. But just as the lead ostrich climbed out the other side, a ragged volley erupted from the farther shore, taking down the soldier and his mount. More reports followed as the troops scattered to what shelter they could find behind rocks and bigger clumps of grass.

He spied a man in the middle of the river, standing, he could now see, on the ruins of the bridge. He had good cover amid the beams of the old structure, and spurts of water erupted as bullets fell. Edmond's men pulled Elizabeth back into a stand of willows, leaving her wrapped in her blankets.

The squad returned fire toward the bridge ruin, receiving furious volleys in return. Ostriches managed to scream through their bridles and went down thrashing. Edmond didn't know whether he was wet from the river or from blood. But they couldn't remain pinned down. They must take the center of the river.

Maruti crept close to Edmond. "They are on the other side. And in the middle."

"Take half the men and wade out to the bridge," Edmond said. "When it's ours, circle around and we'll get them between us."

"I will take Levens, Doers and Manley."

"No, take half."

"*Sahib*, that is half."

They had lost four already. As Maruti crept away, Edmond took a tally of who remained. It was Sergeant Fisk, Corporal Brockie and Private Tait. Leaving

Brockie and Tait behind to guard Elizabeth, he pointed at a prominent boulder just visible in the shallows, and he and Fisk waded down to it. The two of them reloaded and began a furious salvo against positions they had marked on the river's far side by the eruptions of smoke from hand-made *jezails*. Under this relentless fire, Edmond thought that the enemy reports grew less frequent. In the heavy dark they could no longer see the bridge, but heard distant fire and knew that Maruti had engaged with the occupiers. As soon as Maruti crossed over, Edmond must meet him to complete the trap, but not too soon or he and Sergeant Fisk would face their entrenched position alone.

The sergeant said, "It's quiet. I think they're done." But whether Maruti had taken the ruined bridge or was done for, Edmond could not assess.

"We cross," Edmond said.

They waded in, counting on the dark to cloak them, but immediately, an intense fire broke out. Fisk screamed, falling back into the water. Edmond lunged in that direction to haul him out, but immediately lost sight of him. He scrambled for shore, holding his rifle high and his pistol as well.

Once on shore, a figure came at him out of the brush, wielding a musket like a cudgel. Edmond had only time to slam his pistol into the man's skull. Then he stepped back, took careful aim with his pistol and fired into the man's chest. Around him erupted the sounds of close fighting. He threw down his rifle, switching his pistol to his left hand and drawing his sword, stabbing and hacking at whoever came close.

An eternity later, Edmond still had not left the narrow shore, as around him lay men writhing from wounds. A hulking figure appeared from the trees: Maruti. He rushed down the slope to finish off the wounded with his sword.

By the time it was done, they were down to four men, but they were across.

Tori and Jai entered the Gangadhar *Mahal* at the Elephant Gate. The *pitri* led them into the Night Pavilion and thence inside: the old quarters, the baths, the gallery.

In the first gallery, the *pitri* turned to face them. Jai went to his knees, bringing his hands up to his forehead in *namaste*.

"It's the vision, Jai," Tori said. "It is she."

He didn't speak. It looked as though he couldn't.

"Who are you?" Tori's voice wobbled, but whether from confronting a ghost, or from the scene of the barracks massacre, she didn't know.

"Yes, you are wondering," the *pitri* said. "I am no one anymore. I lived too long ago to matter. But my name was Draupadi." She turned to Jai. "Are you trusting me, *beta*?"

He looked up at her in mute wonder.

The *pitri* advanced on him, her facial features sucking in toward her skull in horrid aspect. "Are you?" The monkeys in the inner garden screamed like demons, filling the hall with their wails.

"Answer me!" Her voice echoed around them.

A langur monkey crouched on one of the arched window sills leading to the garden. "Answer me!" it growled in deep baritone. The *pitri* sliced an impatient hand, silencing it.

Tori began to shake uncontrollably. It was a scene of madness. The pitri had been bad enough before, but now her very face was hideously out of proportion, the size of a melon.

"I... I do not know," Jai gasped.

The langurs now mobbed the garden railings, prancing and screeching. To Tori's horror, a flattened, inhuman face rested its chin on the sill, its worm-like back disappearing into the garden well. She staggered backward until the *pitri's* angry glance stopped her short.

The *pitri's* face plumped back, her look turning tender. "You had a grandmother once. A hundred years ago. That was the woman I used to be: Draupadi. She had a son like you, who bled and could not live. But she healed him. I can be telling you how. Shall I?"

"Yes, tell us," Tori rasped. They must keep her talking. This Draupadi was the only thing that kept the garden monsters in check.

"I died," she explained. "I died to save you, sweet Jai, to save my son so much like you, who was bleeding from every small cut. I swore to do *tapas*, and renounced food, finally giving up all. And the gods were listening. My son became a great *rana*. Oh, the glory of his reign!"

The flattened face on the garden ledge extruded a long tongue. It flopped down the wall into the gallery, lolling next to a cockroach. The cockroach started crawling up the tongue toward the demon's mouth.

Draupadi watched this, her hair drooping around her shoulders, snapping but listless. "My companions are not liking me long gone. Each moment emboldens them." Hearing something, she jerked her head up toward the entrance. "They are coming, yes. My companions wait for Sahaj. He will be sweet to play with. But his time is not yet."

She disappeared. From the direction of the Night Pavilion, soldiers' voices barked. Jai and Tori stood to meet them. The garden settled into intermittent monkeys screams. When the soldiers laid hands on Tori it was almost a relief to see humans again.

It had taken Ned Conolly almost an hour to make his way around to the hidden door in the *zenana* garden wall. Back at the barracks, the black bastards had started firing all at once, and he'd barely had time to slit the throat of the stable boy and exchange clothes with him. He'd managed to slip out the gate just in time. State of war. He saw that now. He'd been too damned focused on his mission and hadn't seen the signs of mutiny.

He was amazed his network of spies was still hanging together. The dependable Parvesh was to bring Edmond up from the village, where the captain had come straggling in this afternoon, wounded and exhausted. Parvesh would know his way in the dark.

Jai had brought Astoria here. Handy little door to know about.

A tortured purple sunset threw the Rangnow Mountains into jagged relief. It couldn't be dark soon enough for him. He and Edmond and whatever was left of the company would have to secure the *zenana* and grab the Harding girl. He'd worry later about how to persuade Edmond to get to the caves.

The girl knew where the lotus was. At Vishnu's shrine, he'd overheard her tell the *sadhu* that she had a spirit guide. Preposterous. But *someone* was guiding her, or Mahindra was completely fooled. The bush priest was an old political operative, too shrewd to go by mere claims. After this little revelation, Ned had planned to grab the girl and get her out of the fortress immediately. But he'd waited too long.

He scanned the slope, cracked and rutted with ridges, watching for Parvesh's turban, hoping the sentries on the wall above were joining in the general mayhem in the fortress and not watching. Sounds of rifles going off and happy shouts came distantly to his ears. Damn the mutinous coolies to hell.

A cascade of falling rock signaled someone approaching. Ned drew his pistol and aimed into the dusk.

It was Parvesh. Behind him, Edmond came, his shoulder wadded up in a bad bandage. But where were the other men?

Ned stood, nodding at Parvesh. The old loyalist knew he could count on remuneration, eventually. Right now, Ned had nothing.

"Captain," he said. "How bad is it?" He nodded at the wounded shoulder.

"I can still shoot two-handed," Edmond said. They shook hands.

"Where are the rest?"

Edmond looked back down the ravine. "I left three men with Miss Platt."

Three? The fighting had been worse at the river than he'd thought. Ned nodded, dismissing Parvesh. As the man slipped back down the slope, Ned thought about picking him off, just for general assurances, but he couldn't risk the noise.

He filled Edmond in on the ramp up to the skirmish at the barracks. He left out Astoria's assignation with Jai. The poor bastard had other things to worry about. As the rain started up again, they huddled in the doorway.

"How'd you fare at the Darband crossing? Resistance there?"

Edmond smirked. "They were waiting for us. We lost six, but got across. They wouldn't stand against our volley."

"How close was it at Sirinshwari?"

"All quiet there. But at Chidiwal, Miss Platt beat a servant and the village went to arms. The servant had been poisoning her, but Platt took leave of herself and badly beat the woman in the public square with a ladle. The villagers fell on her. Then they took the school apart. It spread from there."

"She'll live?"

Edmond nodded. "A few broken ribs. But the poison's taken its toll." He looked up at the wall of the fortress. "What do we know about the layout of the *zenana?*"

"I know the layout." Ned didn't bother answering Edmond's quirked eyebrow. "Maybe it's best there's only two of us."

"One of us."

"How do you mean?"

"Ned, I want you to find your way back to Poondras, alone. Warn the cantonment that there may be traitors among the *sepoys.* Keep the gates shut and shore up the defenses. It gives us two chances to warn them. I'll take Miss Harding and Miss Platt around the south fork of the Ralawindi."

"Sir, if I may say so, that's a bad plan. You don't know your way in there. The colonel will have your balls on a skewer if you don't bring her out."

Edmond locked him in a dark gaze. "I'll bring her out."

Ned hated this kind of heroics. It was why he'd gone into political service: nobody tried to pretend their shit didn't reek. But, "Sir," Ned said, nodding agreement.

A high shriek pierced their ears. Overhead, an enormous form drifted over the fortress, wings silently lifting, the deep scalloped edges silhouetted against the sky. The leathery neck twisted to and fro, scanning for movement. Silently, it plunged down the hillside as he and Edmond pressed against the ramparts. In the far distance, another one, just visible against the dark mountains.

"Calling out their *pishachas*," Edmond said, as they stepped forward to watch the creature's descent to the valley.

Ned nodded. "The bush priests are having a little hunting fun. And we're their quarry."

"They're not spirits. We saw one grab an ostrich, so they're real enough."

"Right. These fanatics can bring the inanimate to life. They did the same thing with the water spout in Londinium." He spat. "With the *pishachas*, they just sew whatever pieces of animals together and get 'em moving. Bat, crocodile, vulture." It was a nice skill, but you had to be a savage. God gave Anglics the power of reason, and Bharatis the power of magic. Right now, it was a toss-up which one would take the thrashing.

Rain pelted down again. He and Edmond knelt to scratch the *zenana* layout onto the muddy ground. Ned pointed along the route to the Harding girl's room where, if the mutineers had any decency, they'd keep their hostage in comfort.

"Good luck," Ned said as they prepared to go their separate ways.

He wanted like hell to tell him that she'd been screwing Prince Jai. It would take the sting out of her death, if that's what happened. But looking into Edmond's face, he couldn't do it. Some men, they need to believe in things. It kept them going.

And what kept *him* going? No family, no big ambition, a middling army career. All he had was the great game: outwitting whoever Whitehall set him up against, and that included Astoria Harding. Thing was, she'd led him a merry chase, and he'd got nothing for it, except to maybe see her die at the hands of a Bharati prince.

Some days the game wasn't worth the coin.

∽

July 23, 1857
Miss Astoria Harding
Royal Seat of Kathore
Nanpura Province

My Dear Sister,

Please forgive me for writing in such haste and with such alarming news. I am not supposed to send letters from the fort! The post is not to leave the cantonment because we are in most desperate straits and it must not be known outside how hard it goes with us. Oh, Tori, a contagion—they say it is smallpox—has swept most unmercifully through the civil and military lines, taking four hundred and sixty souls in the regiment. Worst of all, our dear Papa is gravely ill, among the first to succumb. I am desperate for you to come home and watch with us by his side. We are all dreadfully afraid—but they will not even let me in the same room with him! I pray God for His mercy. My maid has a brother who must travel toward Kathore, and I have entrusted this missive to his care to be given only you. I pray that Mama will forgive me my disobedience, but I felt I should not be able to face you had I remained silent and the worst happen. Tomorrow a company of dragoons will set out to bring you safely home, but they cannot travel as fast as my courier, and I do hope that, receiving this missive, you will have Lieutenant Conolly escort you to Poondras at once, and thus you shall meet the dragoons upon the way. Every hour is of the essence. Dear Tori, pray come to us in all haste!

Your devoted sister,

Jessa

Setting the letter in the grate, Mahindra watched the paper blacken and flare. Four hundred and sixty dead. A terrible way to die, but it was war, and they had brought it upon themselves.

He watched the letter burn. A company of dragoons. Astoria's sister was better than any spy. He would send word to stop them in the narrow defile of the Kopol valley.

Shuffling feet outside his cell reminded him that people had flocked to the shrine. Even this late in the night, the fortress gates were open as the hills men trickled in, looking to fight or perhaps to mourn their prince. Anger and sorrow were so perfectly wed; they leaned on each other. This Mahindra knew well. For now, it was all sorrow, as he thought of Uttam, dying upon the ground before the barracks. The wound to his gut had been profound, spilling entrails. His last words were, "That smell, *babaji*, is it me?" Mahindra hung his head, hearing his friend's voice, over and over again. Meanwhile Sahaj reveled in his new role, striding through the grounds, receiving the bows due a *rana*, but unable to tell the difference between respect and fear.

Beyond the doorway, people shuffled by in a long line for prayers at the shrine. He rose and went to the darkened archway, watching the worshippers who smelled of dank skin, of human imperfection. Many of these would die in the coming storm. Although compassion for the girl had snaked into his thoughts earlier, now his pity was all for his own people. The Anglics would mow them down and never think them fathers, brothers, sons.

At dawn Mahindra would lead Sahaj to the girl's prison cell. He hoped the girl with the crescent-moon foot would not be brave.

22

Following Conolly's advice, Edmond made his way through the empty *zenana* gardens and waited for his chance to enter the only unguarded access to Tori's room: the *Ranee* Kavya's apartments.

Her female guards left her door now and then to look over the balcony into the square, with its milling crowds and atmosphere of panicked celebration. During one such lapse of the guards, Edmond ducked through the apartment doors, opening them just enough to slip by.

The *ranee* lay on her couch asleep or passed out. A hookah sat on her bed stand, more evidence of things they had ignored. It was not a dalliance with opium, it was a compulsion. He paused, considering and then rejecting the idea of tying and gagging her.

Her bed lay directly in the path to the window from whence he planned to make his way along the balcony toward Tori's apartment. He hadn't asked how Conolly knew the *zenana* so well. The political officer had his fingers in plots and spies aplenty, but not enough to have foreseen this disaster.

He greatly feared that the uprisings at Chidiwal and Kathore weren't isolated, that once word spread of the beating of the cook at Chidiwal and the burning of the school, that malcontents would take arms and run amok throughout the region. Even with local telegraph lines down—and he had seen much evidence of this—word would travel with uncanny speed through the villages. If they converged on Poondras and if the *sepoys* mutinied, the regiment might not prevail. Not an hour was to be lost in warning them.

But first, Tori. He dreaded what he would find when he got to her room. It would give the devils special joy to murder an Anglic woman. And he had not been here to protect her. He was now desperate to put that to rights.

Kavya sprawled naked across her bed, snoring lightly. How easily they had trusted this household: Uttam's command of the fractious villagers, the patricidal Sahaj!

Something grabbed at his jodhpurs as he passed the bed. Looking down in alarm, he saw that he had snagged the hookah tube where it dangled from the bedside table. He disengaged from it, creeping silently past.

Moving onto the porch, he looked down on the immense courtyard, crowded with soldiers, mahouts and cooking fires. Though the balcony was not well lit, he immediately saw how perilous was his strategy of bringing Tori over from the four foot gap separating the two balconies. They might so easily be seen, if Tori could even manage the crossing.

He returned to Kavya's room and picked up a discarded sari which he knotted into a rope. In his left hand, he carried away betel nuts from a platter near her divan.

Once outside, he threw one at Tori's window screen. He prayed it was Tori's window, that it was not the one on the other side of the *ranee's* apartments. He threw another, pinging it against the sandalwood fretwork.

A shadow behind the screen. Someone moved there, but it wasn't Tori, the person was too tall. Edmond plastered himself against the palace facade, but a moment later he heard a woman's voice: Tori.

It took a moment before she was able to unhook the wooden fret work enough to see him. Behind Tori stood Jai. Edmond breathed with relief.

"Edmond!" she cried.

As loud as he felt he could, he said, "Tori. Dear God, Tori." He found his throat constricted with emotion. "Stay inside. I'm going to get a rope across to the next balcony."

"Edmond, they killed Uttam. Sahaj did. They mean to attack the cantonment!"

"I know, Conolly told me everything. Put out the lights."

"Elizabeth, she's with you?"

"Yes." He secured the rope to the railing next to him.

There was a low murmur, presumably she and Jai talking. The lights went out, and he heard them remove the screen. Tori crept onto the balcony.

"Edmond," she said, her voice closer now. "I'm so sorry. I've made a mess of everything, and I only meant to have a life, but it's all gone to ruin. I'm so sorry."

He was crouched down, looking through the balustrades at her form, dim in the shadows. "Tori, I've been frantic for you. But you mustn't blame yourself. We'll make it through. I promise. Can you and Jai fasten the other end of the cloth? You must use it to come across. I'll reach for you."

"It won't work, Edmond."

"It will, Jai will help you from that side, and me from this side."

"No," her voice came to him. "I'm not coming."

Shouts came from below, but it was the general mayhem, no hue and cry.

She could not be saying this. "You have only to reach out for me, and I will bring you over." His shoulder might be out of action. But somehow he would do it.

"You have to warn my father."

"I've sent word already. You must come now."

"The bush is full of Sahaj's soldiers! Whoever is sent might not make it. You must go and tell them, and if I'm with you, you'll never make it."

Dear God, she was serious. "I'll stay on this balcony until dawn, but I'm not leaving you."

Gunfire erupted from the Gangadhar. Revelers were up on the roof there. It was a perfect time for her make the move across.

"If they find me gone, they'll hunt for me, track us down. You must get to the fort, quickly. You'll have to go alone."

His heart plummeted. Leaning into the balustrade he tried to see her, to persuade her through some force of will.

"Go, Edmond!" she urged.

"Tori. Don't ask it of me." He would force her to go. But she was four feet away, locked away from him. His helplessness made him sick.

Her voice was very calm. "When you see my father, tell him that Bharata belongs to Bharata. We never should have built the Bridge. We never should have crossed it. Whatever happens, beg him for my sake not to retaliate. Be safe, I pray, Edmond."

"*You* be safe."

"I shall."

He thought her voice choked. That she wanted to say more.

"Now go, Edmond."

To his horror, she was climbing back into the apartment. He called to her once more. "Tori, take this."

In another moment, her hand reached through the railing. He saw her pale arm in the fires from the plaza below. He stretched to his utmost, and placed his pistol into her hand. Then she withdrew, clambering back through the window.

Bitterly, Edmond sat on the stone balcony, planning how he would force her to come with him. One plan after another arose and fell away.

After a few minutes, he stood up and walked through the *ranee's* bedroom, hardly caring if she wakened, almost hoping that she would cry out, bring the guards in, let him share Tori's fate. But Tori had reminded him of his duty, and despite a heart now turned to stone, he would do it. He doubted that she knew how to use a pistol, but he was sure Jai did. Jai would know when to use it.

Each step took him further from the thing his heart told him to do: bring this woman with him. But she held all the power. This foolish, stubborn woman. Who owned his heart.

You be safe, she had said. He held the words close. It was all he had.

In a warm drizzle of rain, Sergeant Major Garuda Patil looked out from the blockhouse at Fort Poondras, watching the muddy Ralawindi, swollen with the early monsoon. Beyond the river, in the heart of the city, was the Temple of Sita where from the roof he would see the heliograph signal.

The signal to open the gates.

He nodded to his men standing guard, formerly loyal members of the Nanpura Native Infantry. They chafed uneasily in their green and white uniforms, eager to cast aside these badges of Anglic service. Garuda knew they had been offered a share of the plunder, and was proud that they disdained it. Few of them wished to see a united Bharata or could even imagine what that meant, but they *had* heard of the white teacher in Chidiwal who beat her servant to death with a ladle smeared with cow blood. These men were as eager to avenge the sacrilege as was Garuda. With more than eight hundred Anglics dead or lying sick, vengeance would sweep the cantonment once the tribesmen converged from the villages, outnumbering fit Anglics fifty-to-one. Even the Colonel *sahib* was laid low, not dead yet, so they could not take satisfaction yet in that.

His men would begin with the *memsahibs* who carried themselves like great ladies but were nothing but foreign wombs bearing little soldiers, teachers, engineers.

Garuda looked down on the parade grounds inside the fortress walls. This morning a company of the 22nd Dragoons had set out for Kathore to accompany the Harding daughter home. The contingent might be allowed to enter Kathore, but would never depart, much less with the girl in custody. The departure of the Dragoons proved that they had no suspicion of the coming battle. They had no reason to suspect their Indian brigades of discontent. But if they tried to disarm the *sepoys*, Garuda was to commandeer the main cannon and train it upon the parade grounds.

But no general muster had been called. There were no *memsahibs* rushing to the ships with their ruffled parasols, followed by dark-skinned *ayahs* carrying their baggage. The wives of the officers huddled in the guest bungalows on the furthest edge of the cantonment, down Artillery Road, waiting for the contagion to ease.

But if they had only known, that was the least of their problems. Garuda watched the Temple of Sita. No signal yet.

But it was coming.

Jai sat at the window, staring into the night at the cooking fires in the plaza. Tori wanted to comfort him for his loss, but he was too stunned to grieve just yet. His brother had committed patricide; monsters stalked him, not the least of which was a woman who claimed to be his ancestor. Nor had the *pitri's* words at all soothed him: to think that he must be the new *rana*—how could that be?

The noise from the great courtyard had receded to occasional shouts and the squawks of war ostriches.

It was all coming unraveled. Everything had changed, dashing her hopes. Even Anglica's: for it was clear that the colony of Bharata was also unwinding. Mahindra's words came to her: *You are unclear what is yours and what is not.* Mahindra was her enemy, but he was not wrong. It was all coming undone now, Anglic claims to Bharata, the slow trickle of Anglic education, the rich temptations of Anglic trade. Without putting all the pieces together, she was still sure that the message she sent home with Edmond was right. Bharata belongs to Bharata. How bitter it was to think of her family's peril, and to believe they had brought it upon themselves!

She did not often pray, but she did so now, imploring the deity—whichever one looked out for soldiers—to protect Edmond, that he might be safe and that he might warn the cantonment. And then she prayed for herself. Sahaj was coming for her.

Jai turned to her. "What is happening to us, Astoria?"

"It's all changing. Only a day past, we were happy. And now..."

"How can Sahaj be so lost? We never loved each other, but he has murdered our father. Murdered. I saw him die in the square. Sahaj is a calamity."

She went to him, sitting on the floor by his side. "Oh Jai, I'm sorry."

He stared into the room, more calm than she would have been had it been her father.

"The golden lotus does not exist on this earth. It is of the gods. But is this why war is coming, because they thought you knew its secrets?"

Dear God, she hadn't thought of it. Had they risen up because of her, because they thought Sir Charles had known of great magic, and told her? Surely, surely, it was larger than her. And it was all a misunderstanding, because she knew nothing.

He turned to her. "I am sorry that you are blamed for things. Astoria, on my life, I am sorry for my people's actions, and my brother's. If he comes to this room ..."

Tori put her hand out in the darkness to touch the pistol. She staggered to her feet to find a way to lash it to her leg. If they took her away, they might not search her. She lit a candle and began lurching about the room searching for something to tie it with. Finding nothing suitable, she thought of tearing the linen sheets on her bed.

Something touched her ear. Batting at it, thinking it a moth, she found her hand entwined with strands of something. She cried out, pushing it away. Groping, spider-like hairs streamed at her. A glimpse of green. The *pitri*. Tori staggered back, crashing into the window frame.

Jai was already prostrate on the floor.

"You do not wish to be *rana*?" the *pitri* spat at Jai. She turned, keeping Tori and Jai both in view. "Every man wishes to be a king." Her hair snapped about her, buzzing.

Oh, the ghost was back.

Her voice was in Tori's ear, but filled the room. "Sahaj is not a good man. You have seen the spell he is casting on the great cats? They do not like him, oh no, and they are calling to us for mayhem." She smiled in a way that no one could call happy.

Tori wildly looked around for any sign of demons. But there was only this spirit being who called herself Draupadi.

"Stand up, my prince," Draupadi said, advancing on Jai. As she moved past Tori there came a faint whiff of rot from the folds of her sari.

Jai obeyed, reaching out for Tori, drawing her into the shelter of his arm.

Tori didn't know whether it was Jai or she who was shaking. She still held the pistol, unsure whether she would need it against the ghost, or demons or Bharatis.

Draupadi went on, her voice turning wistful. "It is so hard to do good in the world. I died of it, yes. But now is my chance. You shall be following the path of my dear one who was healed by the holy lotus. You shall be sleeping in the shadow of the lotus. Then you will arise in strength and never fear a blade. You will cut yourself and find that you bleed only in good measure. And when the people see you thus healed, they will know the gods are touching you. And you will be *rana*. I see Sahaj falling from a great height, yes. But all these things depend on *her*."

She pointed at Tori with a half-crazed stare. "You came among us, an unbeliever, but a desiring woman, a woman of heart. I stayed near, waiting for a sign. And—oh how I rejoiced to see it—you loved each other. Then it was that I knew you would help him. Now, I need your hands. Are you willing to tie him to the lotus?"

The lotus. The *pitri* might think it was holy—Jai might think it was—but all Tori could hear was the part about sleeping in the shadow of the lotus. That it *had* a shadow. And they would be in it.

"Are you willing to tie him to the lotus?"

Jai put his hand on Tori's arm, murmuring. "It cannot come into the world. It cannot be... ."

"Where is the lotus?" Tori whispered.

"Ah, you are wondering. And wanting a piece from it! I shudder at your ignorance. But you are an unbeliever, so one may overlook. My child, I am waiting to hear."

"What shall I say?"

Draupadi closed her eyes. "Say yes."

Tori did not hesitate. "Yes." Next to her, she heard Jai moan.

The *pitri* turned and walked to the bed. There she pulled back the covers to reveal two people, lying perfectly still. Tori stared in shock to see a young Anglic woman with dark hair—herself—lying there, and beside her, a slight young man in a white achkan. Perfectly formed, the two lay as though asleep, as though alive. Then Tori understood. The false bodies might gain time for them to escape.

Draupadi lay the coverlet over them. When she turned back, her hair sparked in excitement. "Now we are walking to the caves."

∾

"What is that noise?" Elizabeth moaned. It was like a low muttering in her ears. It was pitch dark. How had it become dark so fast?

"It is the river, *sahiba*."

"My books, we must keep them dry…" She had been sleeping. Dreams trailed. From close by came the noises of the bush: the hooting of owls, the shrill croaks of monkeys. The room smelled of mud and grass. Why was she lying on straw?

She tried to rise up, but her stomach heaved when she moved. Leaning over, she retched onto the ground, her stomach clenching with brute spasms.

Hands helped her to lie again. A wet cloth came to her mouth, cleaning her. "Bansi? Is it you?"

"Your cook is gone, *sahiba*. Maruti cares for you now." Hands pulled a scratchy blanket over her.

She pushed the hands away. Memory flickered at the edges. Bansi, that horrid, impudent woman, cooking while her mistress was in distress. She had taken ill during the night with sinking fits. No, it had been day light. The school room hot. The children waiting. Bansi stirring her pot. And then, oh then… the assault in the road. They beat her, struck her with blinding pain. Bansi laughing.

Elizabeth came fully awake. Moonlight revealed that she lay in a tent, a very sorry one, with only three sides. In the distance, jackals howled. Edmond slept heavily on the other side, a bloodied bandage wrapping his shoulder. Oh, he had been shot, she remembered.

"How does his wound?" she asked the *jemadar* Maruti, who sat between her and Edmond.

"It has stopped bleeding, praise the gods."

Maruti's face was streaked with filth, his eyes dark and hostile. Bansi, she remembered now, Bansi had poisoned her. Oh, the woman had tried to kill her! The memory of that hour now came to her with intolerable clarity: The villagers beating her with staves, kicking her, being all against her, despite all she had done in their behalf.

A cup came to her mouth. Maruti was offering her water. Her eyes met the *jemadar's* and she hesitated to drink. Was it poison? Perhaps he hated her. They all hated

her and her school. Even the children had not loved the school, but only came for chapattis. They laughed, watching her beaten in the road. Christ God above, the indignity of it. And the sadness, now breaking open a chasm in her heart.

She turned away from the proffered cup of water.

Maruti said, "It is pure, *sahiba*." But she ignored him.

The jungle enveloped the tent with chittering and screeching. Elizabeth imagined monkeys hanging from branches, bats flapping, hyenas foraging and snarling. A revulsion came upon her, a nausea of all the disorder of the natural world. What was needed was to proscribe, to bring order where none existed, to impose decency and the civilizing disciplines upon the ungoverned.

Maruti was staring out of the tent, frozen in place. He turned to her, placing his finger to his lips. Oh merciful Christ. The soldiers had found them.

He did not waken Edmond, but kept his position, watching the jungle. Elizabeth hardly dared breathe. Why had he not taken up his pistol? Edmond's saber lay within reach and Elizabeth stretched out a hand for it. She would not be weaponless when the barbarians fell upon them. But Maruti noticed her movement and slowly shook his head. All was unnaturally quiet. No chittering, no rustling branches.

Then, in the small clearing in front of their tent she saw a movement.

A long tubular form, whitish yellow, came into view along the ground. Perhaps two hand spans across, its outline was irregular. Elizabeth thought it would slither into the tent, but it turned away, rising partway up, very like a snake. The topmost portion twisted, as though trying to sense their presence. Then it lay back down and wound its way into the bushes, still trailing its uncanny length.

At last it disappeared.

Maruti turned back to her. "The questing smoke," he whispered. "Prince Sahaj sends it to find us."

"Will it come back?" She was still staring out of the tent, watching for tell-tale yellow.

"It cannot see us. We are protected." He raised his hand to his forehead, where now she could see mud smeared in semi-circle.

She touched her forehead. There was dried mud there, too. Magic. He had put a spell on her. Grabbing the blanket, she started to wipe her face clean, but Maruti stopped her with a hand on her arm.

"Miss, leave it. Otherwise you are clear to the yellow snake, and it will call to its masters. We must all be brave."

Brave! How dare he tell her to be brave! Hadn't she traveled from Cornwall to Chidiwal, crossing the great Bridge, staring down sea monsters, and then

Mr. Gupil and the elephants and the villagers crowding round her, striking, breaking her bones.

"How dare you," she snarled.

"I dare much. And so shall you, *sahiba*."

Abashed, Elizabeth took in a breath of fetid jungle air. They were fleeing into the bush, wounded, poisoned, and exhausted. Maruti's magic might in fact protect them. Edmond lay over there, mud on his forehead, whether he knew it or not.

Nothing was simple anymore. And had not Astoria said that both magic and science had their place? She would suffer the mud. For now.

When Maruti offered her the cup of water again, she drank. If the questing snake found her, at least she would not die thirsty.

23

Jai set foot on the rope bridge, a swaying gossamer thread spanning the gorge. He felt himself to be in a dream. The ancestor spirit led them, perhaps into another realm.

In the moonlight, he looked down the thousand foot drop. Draupadi danced across the rope bridge without hesitation. To her there was no up and down, and she had no fear of death.

Jai put out a hand for Tori, to steady her. The bridge moved to the slightest touch. Tori waved his hand away, placing her hands along the rope railing. From the gorge came the scrabble, cries, and chittering of the inhabitants. They lived in the ravine's rocky vertical surface as in some towering *mahal*. When they died, Jai imagined them dropping away, letting the river take them. There was beauty in such an end. Draupadi, most assuredly, had no such peace. Why was she still concerned with the world of men? Were her descendants to blame because they had not performed devotions to ease her way from *Pitru-loka* to unity with God?

They crossed the defile, following the glow of Draupadi's path.

"You are still bleeding," Astoria said. "I should bind the wound again." His fall two hours ago had been only a slight misstep, but a broken bamboo stalk had pierced the skin on his temple.

A pale moon burned through the clouds, showing Astoria disheveled and grimy. She had gathered up her skirts, fastening them with liana vines so that she would not trip.

"I will do it." He was determined not to be an invalid. But in addition, he did not want Astoria to touch him. It had to do with Draupadi. Astoria did not respect the ancestor spirit, not as a spiritual manifestation. She did not believe. And to his chagrin, that disturbed him.

Down his face blood washed, thinned with the shadow rain of the canopy. Sitting on the cold roots of a banyan tree, he tore another strip from his achkan and dressed the wound.

Draupadi's voice came into his ears. "There is one who follows us."

Jai turned in alarm. Astoria had heard Draupadi's voice, as well. She lifted her skirts, fumbling with a wrapping that kept the pistol next to her stomach.

"Give it to me," Jai whispered. It was his place, not hers, to use force. If it was Sahaj, would he kill his own brother? The enormity of the thought made him quail. But Sahaj must not have the holy lotus.

Astoria aimed the pistol in the direction they had come. He had shown her how the pistol worked and she had paid attention.

Backing up, they found themselves crowded by a thorn thicket, barbs prickling their backs. The night was alive with insects chittering, distant monkeys cooing alarms.

In a few minutes they heard a tread upon sodden ground. And then a man emerged from the shadows, dressed in a *dhoti* and cape.

Jai stood up. "Do not come closer. Do not run. We will shoot you."

The man stopped, raising his hands in a gesture of innocence. In heavily accented Bharati, he said, "Don't get worked up. You don't want to fire that thing and bring your enemies here." He spread his hands in a gesture of reason. "I'm only one man."

"You!" came Astoria's astonished voice.

Jai saw that it was Lieutenant Conolly, dressed most strangely.

Astoria used two hands to keep the pistol directed at him. "You never went to Poondras."

"No, obviously. Put the gun away. If you fire… all hear it." Jai's Anglic was imperfect and he strained to hear.

"I don't think they will," Astoria said. "It's a long way back to the fortress. And speak Bharati, please."

"Whose side are you on?" the lieutenant said, still in Anglic. "They sent the pox… *sepoys* open the gates." Jai missed some of this.

Astoria responded in Bharati. "Whose side are *you* on? Edmond sent you to Poondras. Yet here you are."

Finally in Bharati the lieutenant responded, "I'm supposed to protect you. You're not making it easy." He came a step closer.

Astoria cocked the gun.

He stopped. "They gave Elizabeth a beating in the road, did you hear? So much for your happy Bharatis."

"It's you who thought them happy. They have no love for us."

He coughed a laugh. "We knew they didn't *love* us. It's to keep them from slitting our throats that we need the lotus."

This was indeed news to Jai. Anglica wanted the golden lotus? The thought sickened him.

"Sit down," Astoria said.

The lieutenant didn't move.

"Sit down, Lieutenant, or I'll shoot you in the leg."

She came forward a step and aimed the pistol at the man's groin. He sat.

"Jai, take the strips and bind his hands and feet." She jerked her head at the length of material she had just unwound from the pistol. To the lieutenant she said, "Put your hands behind you."

Jai stooped to gather the torn lengths of cloth. He saw that her hands were shaking with the tension of holding the pistol out.

"If you tie me up," the lieutenant said, "I'm a dead man. Hyenas would find me before long. Maybe worse."

Astoria motioned Jai forward. "Don't try to grab him. I'm aiming for your leg, but anything might happen."

Jai wrapped the cloth around the man's wrists. The lieutenant submitted to the tying, but Jai could feel his muscles tensing, ready for a surge if Astoria's aim faltered. He wiped the blood out of his eyes, thinking her a tiger of a woman. A flash of the old feeling for her returned.

The lieutenant said, "How do you know which cave, by the way? The notebook said nothing on that score."

Astoria didn't bother to answer. "We'll come back for you in few hours."

"And if the hyenas find me before then?"

She hesitated. "Bad *karma*."

"*Karma*. You've become quite the little Bharati, haven't you?"

As Jai cinched the knot tight, the lieutenant switched to Anglic again. "The golden lotus…"

"Speak Bharati," she snapped.

He complied. "The plant will save Anglic lives, think of that. Sahaj's army won't stop until they drive us into the sea. We can take the lotus and give them pieces of it. It makes you giddy with spiritual emanations, the kind of thing these people love. It'll keep them in religious ecstasy."

"*That's* why you want it? *That's* it?"

"It's perfect for their temperament. They want visions, let them be lulled by them."

The plan was as evil as Jai could imagine. Could the great king in Anglica have approved this? He began to hope that the lieutenant would make a run for it and that her aim would be good.

Astoria's voice dropped low. "The lotus... doesn't give... religious visions."

"You prefer your grandfather's version? Magical kinds of knowledge? That's all blather. You'll see."

Jai took another length of cloth to bind his ankles. High overhead, a kite screamed, rousing the jungle to a brief crescendo.

The lieutenant went on, "His Majesty wants peace in Bharata. There's only one way to get it."

"No." Her voice had grown strangely harsh. "There are two ways."

Jai finished his binding and backed away from the lieutenant. Truly, she should kill this man. When he approached Astoria, he thought by her expression that she just might.

"The other way is to leave."

The lieutenant bowed his head for a moment. Finally he looked up. "And you'll bring home the lotus. You think Whitehall is going to let you talk about it? Much less *keep* any of it?"

"And do *you* think we're going to let you uproot it?"

"We know it's rare. We'll take seeds. Cultivate it."

Jai couldn't believe what he was hearing. They were talking about the golden lotus as though it were a mere plant, a thing to be controlled and abused.

Astoria approached, kneeling in front of the lieutenant, the pistol still cocked. "You should have gone to Poondras."

"Get a hold of yourself," the lieutenant said, his eyes showing fear for the first time.

"You should have warned Colonel Harding. Alerted the cantonment. What if the *sepoys* there turn on us?" She raised the pistol to his forehead. "And yet here you are."

"You're not going to kill me. A nice performance, but I don't think so."

Jai watched in fascination as Astoria crouched unmoving, eyes locked on the man, the gun in her now steady hands.

"When you come back for me," the lieutenant said, "I'll just forget this conversation. We'll start over again, all right? I've been harsh with you, harsher than I should have been. I'm just a soldier. Remember that."

Jai held his breath as Astoria remained crouched in front of the lieutenant, perhaps forgetting that the pistol was still cocked.

∽

Edmond called a stop. Brockie and Tait carefully lay Elizabeth on the ground. They had been carrying her on a wool blanket sling since dawn.

At their left, the Ralawindi charged by, swollen and furious, masking the sound of their clumsy progress, but also making them deaf to any pursuers. Fragmented clouds scudded overhead.

"Maruti," Edmond said. "You did not ask permission for the mud." He had woken this morning with a daub of mud on his forehead. They all had.

"No, *sahib*. I request it now."

"What is the price of it? Not cutting."

"No, Captain." He paused as Edmond waited. "I have given up food."

Good God. Maruti was his best fighter, and now he hadn't eaten? It would not do. Not under Edmond's command. "How long?"

"Three days. When I saw that the province was heading to mutiny."

"Back in Sirinshwari?" He got a nod. Maruti must be weak by now, after all their exertions. Edmond looked around at his small group. All five of them had a slash of mud on the forehead.

"I think we've left the questing smoke behind," Edmond said, planning to give him the last of the rations.

"No, *sahib*. Can you not tell it is near?" Maruti lifted his head, taking in a smell that eluded Edmond.

"Let me do the fasting, then," Edmond said.

Maruti frowned, perhaps at whether an Anglic could work magic, or if it would be proper. "The longer I fast, the stronger my protection."

Yes, there was the damn price of magic. But why the Bharati gods wished people to suffer, Edmond did not know.

Maruti seemed to catch Edmond's thoughts. "Renunciation makes us pure. It is good for its own sake. But it also gives us good mud." He glanced at Edmond's forehead. If it were only the men under his command, Edmond would not allow it. But for Elizabeth's sake... He nodded at Maruti, and that was the end of the matter.

Turning, he saw that Elizabeth had risen and taken a few faltering steps.

"I can walk," she announced.

Brockie, the youngest of them at twenty-two years, looked hopeful at this pronouncement. It had been a hard slog carrying the litter.

"No. You'll slow us down." Edmond smiled at her. "Your weight is easy for us, Elizabeth. Don't fret."

"I'm not fretting," she rasped. "But I shall walk."

Well, if she were able, it would go faster this way. "Keep with her, Tait." Her bodice was grimed with vomit and her short hair clung to her temples. But he thought she just might live after all.

Brockie cut open mangoes he had found and they made a meal of it, while Maruti stood guard.

Edmond had no doubt that the villagers had reported them to Sahaj. So it was not just yellow smoke they must watch for, but scouts who knew this geography intimately. It was impossible to say how organized the revolt was, how widespread. But with Uttam murdered, Edmond thought Sahaj had felt emboldened by the prospect of a mutiny in full swing.

In hindsight, it was easy to see Nanpura province as having been a tinder box ready to ignite. Despite Uttam's efforts to placate his Anglic masters, the bush priests had been preaching against the Crown for years. The more Uttam cooperated, the more tenuous his hold on the native population had become. Whitehall, Sir John Beaumont, even Ned Conolly had all underestimated Sahaj. He had the pulse of the tribesman of Kathore, and perhaps that of the province and beyond.

And then the water spout in Londinium. Had that been merely the work of fanatic *sadhus* out of control, or had it been sanctioned by Uttam and Sahaj? As Edmond thought about the cascade of events, he wondered whether the arrival of the regiment at Poondras was also carefully orchestrated by their Bharati enemies, precisely to inflame local passions. And Mahindra had doubtless been standing close at hand, urging the princes on, perhaps even masterminding receiving Tori as a hostage.

They must waste no time in getting to Poondras to warn the cantonment. Once Nanpura rose up, it was five-hundred to one.

If only Tori had been within his reach on the balcony. It did no good to think how it should have gone. But his thoughts were always with her, as though by such attention he could somehow protect her from whatever was happening. How was he to tell Colonel Harding that he had left his daughter behind?

They set out again, with Maruti taking the lead, finding a path and hacking away the vines when the way was clogged. Through the canopy, patches of sunlight fell upon the group, showing the dirt and blood on their clothes. Edmond knew that they owed their lives to Maruti. They would not have got so far without him, without his magics. So for all that Bharata had thrown at them of misery and betrayal, it had also given them loyalty and care.

But he did not know how much longer the *jemadar's* strength could hold out.

Tori dared not look down. Her only purchase on the side of the palisade was a goat path barely the width of her shoulders. Up, up she and Jai trudged into the realm of the caves that Sir Charles had described in his notes.

Jai was far ahead. Favoring her good right foot, Tori's progress was slow. Add to that impediment, at Draupadi's insistence she carried in her bunched skirt a load of papyrus reeds, *Cyperus rotundus*, which she and Jai had collected. All part of the ritual that somehow would, Draupadi claimed, make Jai a worthy *rana*, and a healthy one.

A view of the fortress was now exposed above the treetops. It crouched on its distant precipice, stony and baleful. Had Sahaj's soldiers abandoned it already, rushing to Poondras? Or were they streaming into the jungle after *her*?

If the latter were the case, Conolly had no chance.

She hadn't been able to kill him, of course. But his horrid purpose! Conolly and his army masters wanted to subdue the continent with a terrible potion. While she didn't believe the lotus possessed such properties, she couldn't be sure. Without scientific experiment, it was all conjecture—even the *pitri's* claim that it would heal Jai. Were the dead always right?

Jai and Draupadi had rounded a bulge in the hillside. Fashioning her disheveled hair into a long braid, she tied it off with a strip of petticoat and continued the climb.

In the last few hours Jai had grown distant from her. She wished their bond to be more in evidence, but when he saw the *pitri*, his aspect had changed. She must remember, however, that he had lost blood and must be weakened.

When she rounded the corner, she saw the two of them waiting for her on a ledge. Jai sat cross legged, head slumped. His achkan was shockingly red.

Joining them, she noted that they stood before a jagged opening in the hillside. Beyond it lay stolid blackness. Draupadi declared that before entering the cave Jai must be blindfolded. She instructed Tori to tear into her underskirt and create one. Jai must not look upon the sacred flower, the very reason

Draupadi needed Tori, an unbeliever—to lead him.

She knelt in front of Jai. He smiled at her, but looked ghastly pale. It was inconceivable to turn back, but Jai needed a doctor's care. Perhaps, however, they would be safer hidden inside; perhaps she could wait there with her great discovery until the mutiny had passed, then make her way to Poondras with her cutting... if anything was left at Poondras. She pushed this thought away. It was too dreadful to dwell upon, and the lotus beckoned. It did, despite everything.

"Are you strong enough?" she asked Jai. "Shall we rest?"

Draupadi barked, "The longer the rest, the more blood. Come."

Tori looked up at the ghost. She had been doubting the *pitri* during their long trek through the bush. How could a flower grow in a cave? And what were the chances that a lotus seed could have taken root there? But these were narrow thoughts; here, it was best to let magic have its sway. And as for religion, it threaded into the world in ways she had never imagined. She felt Bharata claiming her more and more. One could choose to be blind to things unproven, as Sir Charles had said. She would not be one of those.

The *pitri* pointed in the direction of the entrance. Tori tied the cloth snuggly around Jai's eyes.

It was time. Draupadi walked straight into the cave opening without bothering to duck down. Tori watched in consternation as Draupadi's head and shoulders passed through the solid rock. Though it should not have been a surprise, it was unnerving to behold.

Gathering up the reeds once more, Tori placed Jai's hand on her elbow and walked toward the cave.

"Bend low," she said, helping him pass under.

The light from outdoors immediately fell off, surrounding them with a cool, musty darkness diluted by Draupadi's nimbus of light. They were in a passageway of jagged rock. In the cold, sweat congealed on her neck and arms.

Jai held onto Tori's arm and adopted her cadence of walk, her little lurch. Already the *pitri* was twenty feet ahead, her hair waving as in some water current. The tunnel turned, and again, into the ponderous geology of the cliff. From time to time Jai stumbled, blind and weak as he was. Soon there appeared openings to alternate passageways. Draupadi led into one, unhesitating.

In this maze they would never find their way out if the *pitri* abandoned them. Tori picked up a rock and scratched an x into the wall showing which way to turn on the journey out. The gesture might be futile. They had not brought any strikables to light a torch, nor anything except the papyrus reeds to burn.

"Astoria." Jai's voice was loud, amplified by the stony throat of the place.

"What is here?"

"A tunnel. Many tunnels."

Draupadi's light disappeared. Darkness fell thickly around them. Tori stopped.

"What it is?" Jai asked.

How utterly black it was. Now as blind as Jai, Tori turned, listened, trying to eke out a sensibility from her ears. She stepped forward, trailing one hand along the wall, her other aching with the effort of holding the reeds.

"Draupadi?" she whispered, fighting panic.

In the growing light, Conolly was now able to lope along the trail left by Tori and Jai. They hadn't even thought about covering their tracks.

Thoughtfully, they had let him keep his weapon, not that a pistol would have helped him much against a jaguar or *pishacha*. But now he'd be able to dispatch Jai quickly. With all that the boy had heard of the Bharata pacification program, his death was essential. He rubbed his chafed wrists as he ran. It hadn't been much of a knot.

They'd had two hours' head start, what with his having to wait for dawn to follow them. He only hoped that Astoria's club foot would have slowed them enough to give him a fighting chance. He needed to get them in view before they disappeared into the caves.

When he broke out of the undergrowth, he bent over gasping for breath, his sides stitched with pain. He looked up at a palisade of hardened yellow mud.

They were nowhere in sight. Gone. Gone, already, into the maze.

Sloughed off rocks formed a wide base beneath the hillside. He wondered how she had managed to stagger across. The cripple and the bleeder. It was hard to accept that they had escaped him. Hard to swallow that she had threatened him with a pistol. He keenly felt that ugly moment in the bush when she had pointed her weapon in his face, holding his gaze. How he had hungered to slap her into her place.

How had they known which cave to enter? Perhaps it was magic. Maybe Jai was a secret practitioner, not a bleeder at all, but one who practiced *tapas* for powers. Conolly would have bet a month's wages that Jai didn't have it in him, but...

Then he saw it. A flicker of light.

From the hole just up there. Yes, unmistakably, a light shone in one of the dark entrances.

Just in time. If he hurried, he'd be just in time to follow them. He sprang into action, finding his footholds on the talus slope, falling once, cutting his hands. Undaunted, he raced across the slope and watched for a path. Found it.

And there, footprints. Christ God, this was luck.

He drew his pistol and climbed.

In the tunnel, the *pitri's* light had found them again, though Draupadi must have been several turns ahead of them. Tori and Jai shuffled forward. She stopped to mark the walls at every turn where there was more than one choice. In the faint light, however, Tori could not be completely sure her marks were clear enough to see by torchlight. But the process of scratching on the walls eased her mind. They *would* be returning.

They rounded a last corner, and a great room opened suddenly before them, profoundly glowing. It was a giant cavern some eighty feet across.

Against the far wall lay a large pool of water. And, oh, upon its surface…

Tori put her hand to her throat, feeling the wild beat of her pulse.

Resting upon the surface of this pond was a single, yellow, flowering mass. It shimmered with light. But there was no source of light. The water, the cave walls, the ground reflected the flower's glow, like the Night Pavilion of the Gangadhar lit by a torch. The blossom must have been six feet across, its circular leaf below, far larger.

It glowed from within. Impossibly, from within.

Tori knew what this was but did not dare give it a name yet.

The papyrus reeds fell as she let go of her bunched skirts. She clasped her hands in front, trying to still a sudden shaking. Jai still grasped her arm, and she led him forward to the edge of the pond where she bent down, plunging a hand into the water. A ripple fanned out, the ridges catching the flower's light in arcs of fire. The pond was real.

"What is it?" Jai whispered.

Now closer to the pool's lone bloom, she saw how the flower petals curved upwards in a perfect bowl-shape. The petals—some as long as four feet, others smaller—ranged from creamy white through burnished yellow to deep amber. Between the petals she glimpsed the conical seed pod, so defining of this genus.

Now that the biology was noted, she felt herself sink to her knees. Arrayed in rotary fashion around the flower's center, dozens of amber petals were streaming with light, sometimes hot, sometimes pale. At her side, Jai's skin was wreathed in light like everything in this room.

Grandpapa, I'm here. I've found it. Sir Charles was almost palpably near. By all that was right and proper, at such a moment he *should* be here.

If he were, she knew he would first wish to know by what mechanism the plant glowed in so prodigious a manner. It must be magical. She had assumed the flower's essence conveyed magical powers; but she had entirely missed the idea that the plant itself would not be a natural phenomenon, but magical in itself.

"What is that perfume?" Jai asked, his grip on her arm vise-like. She smelled it too, a profound sweet scent like attar of rose.

"A pond," Tori stammered. As she gazed at *Nelumbo aureus*, she summoned the courage to say: "And the lotus."

Jai fell to his knees beside her. They might have been in a church, for all that they were both in a state of awe and, yes—grace.

"Jai," she whispered, "it is wonderful. In the center is a giant lotus flower. It appears to be glowing from within. I don't know if it's real, but... I think it is." Whatever it was, this blossom was easily the most beautiful thing she had ever seen.

She noticed a skiff resting against the cavern wall. Draupadi, who had been missing from the cavern until now, was back, beckoning her over to the boat.

"Jai," she said. "I'm going to bring a boat for you. All right?"

He didn't answer, but made *namaste* in the direction of the light.

As Draupadi's hair snapped impatiently, Tori hurried over to where the boat lay. Woven and clumped rushes comprised a little canoe no longer than a man was tall. It was stiff with age, and some creature had gnawed a hole in the bottom. Now she knew why Draupadi made them carry the papyrus reeds.

Urged on by Draupadi, Tori dragged the skiff to the water's edge. With Draupadi commanding her, she balled the reeds into a plug. This she jammed into the hole in the boat, caking it with mud.

The *pitri* looked down at her. "It was the *rana's* bed, yes."

Tori had figured out that much.

Draupadi went on, "He built it with his own hands. That is why it did not go according to plan."

Tori stopped her work, looking up.

"Oh yes, he became healed. But he did not wear a cloth around his eyes and he looked upon what no believer may see. Then he came to distrust me and though I saved him he did not love me. He it was who ordered my death."

"You said you died of *tapas*, of privations!"

"Yes, I died." Draupadi looked over Tori's head toward something.

"He killed you!" She wondered what kind of healing this was.

"Because he looked upon the lotus. That is why you are here. You see?"

Tori went back to her work, disturbed. As she continued stuffing the reeds into the hole, they began moving. Like Draupadi's hair, the rushes took on a writhing life. They wove themselves into the existing structure, lacing all together into a tight mat.

During this repair, Tori's mind had retreated from the stunning presence of *Nelumbo aureus*. But when she looked at it again, it staggered her. It cast a blaze of light onto her hands. She looked over at Jai. His face was bronzed with the impossible light.

Oh, Grandpapa. Look. It is here. It is real.

A groan behind her made her yelp in startlement.

A demon had appeared at a hole in the cavern wall. It had many arms, with a face like an armadillo, pointed and armored. It made little gargling noises.

Draupadi listened, frowning, her face sucking in, revealing that there was no skull there. "Put him in the boat!" she shouted.

Tori jumped at this outburst, heart thudding.

"You are taking him into the pond!"

"What is it?" Jai wailed.

Tori crawled over to him. "The boat, into the boat." She needed to follow Draupadi's orders, because now the demon was walking toward them. Oh, merciful God, and more demons besides.

"Jai, hurry!" She helped him scramble into the little boat, now half launched in the water. He had a knife tied into his waist sash, but it would do little against these beings.

"Take him to the flower," the *pitri* cried. "Tie him to the flower. He sleeps there! One night!"

Tori was waist deep in the water. How deep was it? She couldn't swim. But she pulled the boat out, shrinking from the demons who now grabbed hold of Draupadi and led her away to the hole from which they had issued. Draupadi looked back, making sure that Tori obeyed.

Then Tori realized that she had nothing with which to tie Jai up. She brought the skiff closer to the shore and, finding a place to stand, yanked at her petticoat to create more strips.

"Nooo," moaned Draupadi. "Go, go."

"I need to tie him!" Tori shouted in frustration. She yanked at her shredded underskirt, but it was no use, the cloth would never be long enough. Something snapped at her hand. She yelped in fear. A rope had twined together from the boat's reeds. It coiled in the bottom of the boat next to Jai, who now crouched in the bottom of the boat in a child's pose, hands stretched out in front of him.

The reeds were alive. The reeds were magic. Tori was losing her mind.

One of the demons, a fat one with a sagging gut and enormous gonads hanging between its legs began lurching toward the water.

With a great shove, Tori launched the boat into the middle of the pond, holding on to its bow. She coughed as she swallowed brackish water. She kicked furiously into the center of the pond.

24

Sahaj tore back the silken covers of Astoria's bed as Mahindra looked on. With the covers stripped off, they saw that Jai lay beside the girl. Both were fully clothed. But neither of them stirred.

"Poison," Sahaj growled. "They are dead."

Unable to deflect his purpose, he drew his knife and lunged across Jai's form to grab the Harding girl. But her body was limp. To waken her, Sahaj drew his knife down the side of her face, a small cut to begin with.

The wound did not show red beneath, but closed up without a scar. The soldiers at Sahaj's side could not contain their amazement.

"What is this?" Sahaj whispered.

Mahindra walked to Astoria's body and opened her hand that was curled like a baby's. The palms were blue. At his touch, her wrist darkened, and soon her true color traveled over her skin, up her neck and across her cheeks.

"False people, likenesses only," Mahindra said. "They have escaped."

At this terrible pronouncement, Sahaj began stabbing at the sleepers, plunging his knife into neck, bodice, arms, and bellies. But it was no use, Mahindra knew. These forms were insensible.

Shouting for the *zenana* guards to be brought in, Sahaj turned in circles, looking for hiding places, for something living to strike at.

The women guards were hauled in and made to kneel before him.

Mahindra saw that their lives were forfeit. He stepped in front of them.

"No." He turned to the nearest guard. "Send them to wait in the hall."

The guard pulled the women into the corridor, while Sahaj watched in consternation. The knife remained in his hand, still thirsty. But the boy-*rana* did not realize that the guards still loved his father; or if they had not loved Uttam, they revered Mahindra. If the *sadhu* spoke quietly and with assurance, he would be obeyed. For a few days yet, before Sahaj seemed to all like a prince, the people would follow the one with authentic power. Mahindra.

"This is not the guards' fault," Mahindra said. "The *pitri* is helping them."

Rage and fear rumpled Sahaj's face. "*Pitri, pitri*, who cares for a ghost?" Then, eyeing his guards and seeing their discomfort that he had spoken against an ancestor spirit, he added, "Who has seen this *pitri*? Who knows but that it may be a *daitya* or a *pishacha* created by our enemies?"

A commotion from the hallway. In came a soldier with an old man in tow, dressed in the brown turban of the hill tribes. The hills man had information about the Harding *sahiba*, news that lightened Mahindra's heart. They now knew where Astoria was, or likely was, as a white woman had been seen near the Banda gorge.

"They say there is a *yaksha* with her," the old man said.

Mahindra exchanged glances with Sahaj. Mahindra could not blame the hills man for not knowing the difference between an ancestor spirit and a spirit goddess.

"She does not believe," Sahaj muttered. "She has done no devotions. She is Anglic. Why, therefore does it help her?"

An excellent question. How strange that the *pitri* would have come to a *sahiba* and not a *sadhu*. A cold doubt drilled down into Mahindra. What if the *pitri* did not support his ambition for the lotus?

They abandoned the *zenana*, with Sahaj now issuing orders for the search and taking a good Anglic rifle from one of his men.

As they hurried into the courtyard, Sahaj jabbed a glance at Mahindra. "My soldiers wish for a taste of blood, *baba*. They must slake their needs. It was very foolish to spare the two guards."

Mahindra snapped, "Shall we turn on our own?" He thought of Uttam.

"If required."

A shouting throng gathered round them, soldiers, tribesmen, villagers, itinerants, courtiers and even boys, each carrying a weapon, of army, village or barracks.

Mahindra looked about him in growing alarm. These people wanted a taste of blood; they were growing too strong to be restrained. If they did not find the lotus, then they would still demand a fight. Sahaj could not contain them. Nor a *sadhu.*

Sahaj cried out. "In the forest are two that must be found, my brother Jai and the Anglic woman. The girl is a thief, having come to the Gangadhar to steal holy things. My brother, forgetting all piety, helps her. Bring them alive to my hands, but bring them. Show me your valor in this, no matter if there are demons who confront you!" He raised his rifle, shaking it overhead. "Show me your valor! After that, Poondras!"

A great roar went up. *Tulwars* and muskets rattled at the sky.

In the wake of that great roar, Mahindra's heart contracted. It might yet be a great mission. But for the first time he felt afraid.

As they dragged open the gate of Kathore, the crowd began streaming toward it. Stable boys brought ostriches for the local chiefs and for their new *rana.* The birds were tall and black, wearing their tack fiercely, their gums punctuated by serrated teeth, whipping their long necks in agitation. Sahaj mounted the largest of them, sitting his mount with ease.

"They must be brought to us alive!" Sahaj shouted, and urged his mount forward.

Mahindra was helped up to a howdah on an elephant's back and the beast set out amid the mass of soldiers.

They surged through the gates of Kathore. Streaming from the fortress, they bore long and short knives, *tulwars, jezails,* muskets, Anglic lances, pistols, clubs and staves.

An impressive force they were, but suddenly there was more.

To Mahindra's surprise, at the very head of the army he saw a twisting form of ghostly ochre arise from the ground. Threads of questing smoke slithered from every direction feeding the phantasm, braiding into a column. A head formed upon it, the monstrous head of a kraken, with baleful, round eyes and teeth as long as daggers. Formed of yellow fog, it glowed turquoise from within. It quickly reared high above the mob, swaying as though for balance. Then it craned its vast head toward the sky and bellowed with a guttural, hill-shaking roar.

The army cried out in joy, raising their weapons in salute.

The giant kraken began to move, whiskers bristling and eyes questing for the enemy. It led the delirious army down the hillside.

Mahindra looked around him for evidence of *sadhus* at work. And found it. In the rear, a wagon covered with bright cloths was setting out, pulled by oxen. Power emanated from it.

So. Sahaj had turned to other practitioners to inspire his army. Perhaps Sahaj did not wish Mahindra to suffer for the sake of a phantasm. But the lesson was not lost on Mahindra, that Sahaj had more than one source of magical power.

Ten minutes into the tunnel Ned stopped. Sweat congealed on his skin in the cold underground, colder than he would have guessed. Damned shame he wasn't in uniform.

The light still glowed ahead of him just enough that he could make his way, following them. Pausing like this was no good. He'd have to keep going or they'd soon be too far ahead of him, and if the tunnel branched, he'd have lost them.

Then too, he might get lost himself.

Behind him, the blasting light of day shone like a faint star. He could still make his way back, now. He could fashion a torch, maybe even get a fire going. But by then his quarry would be gone.

As he stood in the narrow, bony tunnel, every sense was alive to the cave and the dark. The world felt somehow larger than before, an unexplored realm. It was opening out before him, seemingly endless, like the pathways of his own mind.

He was not often so fanciful. It was the blackness. One's thoughts played out upon it.

He shook off this notion and walked forward, following the torch that Jai and Astoria carried. Something about the light troubled him. It stopped when he did. Perhaps they wanted to lure him in. He drew his pistol.

How did they plan to find their way back out? Jai must have a map. Another issue was how long their torch would last, especially if they had misjudged how deep the cave went. Ned turned back to assure himself that he could still see the light from the cave entrance, but it was lost in the last turn of the passage. Now was the time to think carefully about whether he needed to go farther. He knew which cave entrance it was. He could come back here with an expedition fitted out with ropes and gear. True, as the maze continued it would be hard for a research team to eliminate dead ends and false tunnels, but in time it could be done.

The longer he thought on this plan, the better it seemed.

Now with another plan to weigh, he began to give more credence to his doubts. How likely was it that a species of flower lived deep underground? It might be a confounded golden lotus, but it was only a type of lotus, and as such it needed the sun—unless what lay within the cave was not the plant at all but a cache of seeds, hidden away by some ancient monk…

That would be a treasure, indeed.

His imagination played out this notion. He pictured himself in the Foreign Office opening a carved wooden box, the officers and civilian fancies gathering round for a close look. The seeds of the golden lotus, perfectly preserved. He wanted that moment. It was a fitting peak to his nine year career in bloody Bharata. Something to show for it, for all the grubby posts, hill stations, and mosquito-infested forests…

He kept walking. Finding his way back would be no problem. His sense of direction had always been superb.

They were alone on the pond. Jai collapsed in the prow, Tori huddling in the middle. The demons were gone, having pulled Draupadi into a hole in the cavern wall.

A ping of water clanged onto the pond. Looking up, Tori saw stalactites glistening with water. Sounds were magnified here; light mirrored; color deepened. In tides of color, buttery yellows and nectar-dark ambers surged through the lotus. Underneath, the peltate leaves formed a round floating base for the blossom, slightly raised out of the water on its peduncle, a five-inch thick stalk. But it seemed inadequate to describe *Nulembo aureus* thus. Could it be a magical creation, only pretending to the forms of nature?

The lotus was so near. Its light flared over her face. She could reach out and touch its nearest petal. But no, not yet.

Jai lay on his back, in an exhausted sleep, blindfold in place, and his achkan splattered with blood.

In her hurried launch from shore, she hadn't thought how to get back to the pond's edge. The thirty feet might as well have been one hundred to one who had never swum, had never even waded. Leaning over the side of the skiff, she peered into the murky water.

At last she talked herself into testing the depth. Retrieving Jai's knife and sash, she cut a length from the cloth for later use and tucked it away. Then she made a belt to secure the blade. Gathering her resolve, she lowered herself over the side of the boat, keeping a grip on the edge. The skiff lurched wildly as she scrambled over, plunging down, skirts puffing around her. The shock of the cold water brought a gasp to her lips. Then her feet touched bottom, though she had to keep her head lifted high to keep her nose out of the water.

Still holding to the side of the skiff, she picked up the vine rope anchored in the bottom like an umbilical cord. Now she must tie the boat off.

She turned her attention to the lotus. The lowest spiral of petals lay deeply open, pointing at an angle toward her. However, the tough floating leaf of the plant kept her too far away to secure the rope at the petal's base. Leaning her weight on the pad, she inched forward, extending her arms to the utmost, reaching for the petal. She touched it. Its surface was soft as a dove's breast, and as warm.

She pulled the vine around the petal as low as she could, hoping it would prove strong enough to hold the rope. Lying upon the lotus pad, she finished the tying off.

Then, still balancing upon the pad, she withdrew the knife from the sash at her waist.

From the moment that Draupadi had said she would lead Jai to sleep by the lotus, Tori had known what she would do. There was a great risk. But she would not hesitate now. Up until this moment she had stood outside of things in life. It was as though she had been looking through a window at a room full of people dancing and working and striving and falling in love. She knew them intimately, but she was an observer.

It was time to experience things in full.

Using the knife, she sliced the edge of the petal where it gave way like a rime of ice—not without resistance, but with a soothing tear. A scallop the size of a plum fell into her hand. She sliced it in half. And put one segment in her mouth.

It crumbled against her tongue like a wafer of the Church. The taste: bland as a stranger's regard but warm with yellow phloem. It filled her mouth with a pulsing glow.

She swallowed.

Now, then...

Having wrapped the other half of her sample in the cloth she had reserved, she tucked it into her bosom. As she waded back to shore, her skirts ballooned out around her like the wings of a swan, the water slowing her progress yet lifting her aloft with each stride.

At the edge of the pond, she sat grasping her knees to her chest. Her stomach had begun rumbling.

Ingestion of the cutting was rash. But who would not have done the same, if they cared for knowledge, and knew the lotus might never be found again?

It was what Sir Charles would have done. She knew this with a calming certainty, a giddy sense of having reached out to him in spite of distance and death. He believed that there were modes of knowing. Magic was one of them. He had touched a lotus petal, had seen the vision of this cave. He had been here, in his imagination. Perhaps even now he was here.

She waited. The skiff lay still upon the water. The lotus surged and ebbed, by turns tranquil and fiery. She was alone, without *pitri* or demons.

Oh Grandpapa. If you could only be here. It is the golden lotus, more beautiful than we knew!

The cave had grown warm. It seemed necessary to discard her clothing. Her dress and slips, stockings and shoes lay in a heap. She was at the edge of the pond, one foot already sinking into the water. It would be lovely to swim. Her father had taught her to swim—the one environment where she would move as well anyone. Those days at the seaside, learning the many strokes. At the same time, she doubted he had ever taught her.

But she stepped in to her knees, to her belly.

Filling her lungs with air, and lying upon the surface, she kicked off and plunged down. With sure and easy kicks, she passed through pockets of water stained vibrant green, glowing apricot, peaceful blue. The roots of the lotus ribboned around her, brushing her with their tentacles. Up to the surface to breathe, and down again, to this hidden world where she was all grace, her hair curling around her, reveling in its freedom. Above her, the great pads of the lotus spread out like a floating world. Who was this swimming woman? There were large questions, but she pushed them away. If she was not herself, then perhaps it was better to be this person. She came to the surface again and again, growing tired, but reluctant to leave the womb of the lotus.

She swam up to the skiff looking over the side. Here was Jai sleeping with a cloth over his eyes. She swam to the other side, frolicking under the boat. When she shook the water from her face, a woman was sitting in the boat with Jai. Reclining on brocaded cushions, the two of them were dressed in sumptuous garb, he in gold, and she in turquoise. But it was no stranger sitting there with Jai. It was herself. He handed her a slice of mango, and she ate it from his fingertips. Sugars broke open in her mouth, sheer joy. The Tori in the boat said teasingly, "A *rana* does not serve his wife." Jai smiled at this, shaking his head, offering her another slice.

She lay on her back upon her pile of clothes, staring at the roof of the place where she was. Where exactly was it?

Oh, it was the book wagon. Children's books stacked on either side of her, framing her with stories. And Edmond was removing his coat, unbuttoning his shirt, inflaming her. He lay down beside her. Tori was both looking at the scene and a part of it. It was not quite right, but it was only a dream after all. "Are you sure?" he said. "I will leave if you say no."

"I say yes... to everything."

He smiled down at her. "That is much to have. Everything!"

She laughed. "Everything you want."

"And what do *you* want?"

"You, Edmond."

"And then we speak to your father."

"Yes, then we do." She doubted she should have said that. She doubted that she *did* say it.

She grew cold and found dry clothes. A maid helped her dress. The shoes were most elegant, with curving silver tips. The left shoe was built higher to even out her stance, but it was still beautiful. When her servant opened the double doors, Tori found herself looking into a grand audience hall.

Crimson walls topped by massive crown moldings were lined with bookcases and punctuated here and there by arched doorways leading to further reaches of a great civic building. At the far end of the room, a slightly raised stage and a lectern. Next to the lectern an elaborately carved wooden table held a potted palm and a handsome, oversized portfolio displayed on a stand.

Men in top hats and women in fur-trimmed gowns were clapping. Many had turned around in their chairs, watching a woman make her way forward. Tori watched herself standing in the center aisle. She was both watcher and participant.

Allen Goodwin beckoned her to the stage. From in front, Sir Charles stood up, clapping and nodding to her. This was, she somehow knew, in the upstairs meeting room of the Royal Society. She walked, the other Tori walked forward, her excitement mounting.

She passed a woman wearing a hat shaped like a sailing ship. How strange. In the tall windows at the front, the sky was a most brilliant shade of green. Was that quite the thing? A green sky?

Allen Goodwin had just said—the words did not seem so outrageous when he uttered them a moment before—that Astoria Harding had been voted a member of the Royal Society for her contributions to botany.

She stood next to Goodwin on the stage. The portfolio displayed on the table was her book, *Flora Anglica*.

Sir Charles sat in the front row, his eyes shining with vitality and pride.

"I thought you were dead." She looked at him uncomprehendingly. "But you must get dressed."

Dressed? Was she not?

Jai crouched next to her. "Astoria, you are shivering. Are you well?"

At the edge of the pond, Jai's skiff lay pulled up on the shore. *Nelumbo aureus* had cooled to a faint yellow-green.

Her mind felt like a wobbling top, about to fall. "Jai. How?"

How had he got the boat to the edge?

"Your blindfold!"

It was gone.

"I am not looking behind me," he said. "I awoke, and you would not come. It has been many hours." It was night, or what passed for night in this grotto. The cold air seeped into her bones. Jai fumbled with her dress, trying to help her put it on. The cloth was heavy and chill against her skin.

Thus close to Jai she saw that his face was clean of blood. There was no trace of the wound.

He sat upon his feet, allowing her to examine him. "I am healed," he whispered.

She nodded, remembering why Jai had come here. Behind him, the flower was rapidly dimming.

"Astoria. You touched the lotus. Did you receive knowledge?"

"I don't know. I saw strange things. I did things I cannot do. Things happened that did not happen."

"Dreams, then."

"No." She thought they were not, for they were too vivid.

He put out his hand to help her up, but she ignored it. "Jai. Shall we ever marry, do you think?"

His forehead wrinkled in concern. He knelt in front of her, holding her hands. "Astoria. It can never be. Our two peoples would never accept it."

"Perhaps as a concubine?"

"Never. You must know this." He looked at her in distress, thinking that she wished to marry him. Truly, she did not.

But once upon a time, Tori did marry him. It made no sense. But the moment she thought it, she felt it was right.

It took forever to dress in the damp clothes. Jai helped her as best he could, never looking behind him. It seemed very sad that he was not to see the lotus, but he was still obeying Draupadi. And where was she?

"We are finished here," Jai said. He led her toward the gaping tunnel. He walked erect and proud. He had come into his strength.

"You are healed," she murmured at his side.

Now she knew what the lotus was for. For healing. That was a great wonder. Perhaps the greatest wonder of all.

"You see," Jai said, "the gods are real."

They stood before the tunnel, and as they peered into its inky length, they saw just ahead a fluttering green scarf infused with light.

Tori turned for a last look at the golden lotus. Oh, its petals were closing up. She stared as they formed into a tight bud. Then the shield-like pad upon which the flower rested subsided into the water, slowly and relentlessly.

"Oh, Jai! I should have harvested seeds! If the lotus heals, it can change the world." Her thoughts had been so sluggish, she had not even used common sense.

But Jai shook his head. "Only the gods can heal."

As the lotus sank, light drained from the room. At last all that was left was an ember glowing just beneath the surface of the pond.

Perhaps the lotus would bloom again. But who would it bloom for and why?

They followed Draupadi into the darkness. Jai was very quiet, but her own thoughts were chaotic.

"I saw us married in Bharata," she whispered.

"Never in this world," Jai said, gently taking her hand, as though she were a child needing comfort.

Draupadi's voice whispered in her ear. "There are existing more worlds than this."

"So I did marry him."

"Once, long ago."

PART III: FOREST OF THE CRESCENT MOON

25

"When I am *rana*, I will have no jewels." Jai supported Tori as she walked. Now she was the weak one, sick to her stomach and half-demented, though she couldn't admit why to him.

Since he had washed his shirt in a jungle pool, now it was pink in color instead of blood red. He wanted to be presentable when he accepted the allegiance of his people.

Draupadi had disappeared. She had created her *rana*. Perhaps now she could be dead.

Tori staggered along, sick to her stomach, aching in every bone and ligament. She had taken too much of the lotus; its effects walked with her every step through the jungle, giving her visions of things she knew, or almost knew. An hour ago at a pool where she'd drunk, came an acute waking dream of Poondras under attack. In horrid color, she saw the slaughter, her father fighting with desperate bravery. She must try to avoid water, for it worsened the visions.

"I will give my diamonds to the poor," Jai said. "We shall have village schools—Bharati schools—and shall teach botany and religion all together." He was reveling in a new vigor. Marching toward a confrontation with his brother, he rehearsed his plans for his reign.

She dreaded the meeting with Sahaj. "Sahaj will kill you before he'll give up power."

"He will try. But when the people see that I am healed, they will know the gods have blessed me. Draupadi has created princes before."

They made their way along a path to the gorge, ultimately to reach Kathore. She would not go so far with him, but hoped to find succor in one of the hill towns. Perhaps by now there was an Anglic presence in the area.

Along the path Jai found the bindings they'd used on Lieutenant Conolly. "He will not get far once I send my soldiers for him."

Tori stared at the dirty cloth strips. Had Conolly followed them to the caves? If so, she could only hope that the lotus would sink very deep, giving no sign of its presence.

She could go no farther. "Jai," she pleaded. "Wait." Sinking to her knees, she rubbed her legs, bunching with spasms.

He knelt beside her, his face filled with concern. "Touching the holy flower has made you sick."

"It ... it has." She thought he would not like it if he knew she'd eaten some of it.

"Lean your head against me," he urged. "Rest a few minutes." She did so. As she gazed into the foliage, a blue-green butterfly flickered among the blossoms of elephant creeper.

She wished Draupadi had stayed. She had more questions. *More worlds,* Draupadi had said. There are more than this. If true, then what Tori had seen— what she was still seeing from time to time—were not revelations of useful knowledge.

The crowded lecture hall of the Royal Society was not a right and sensible place; how could the sky be green, how could the fashion be that a lady would wear a hat like a ship? What if it was a world very like our own, but altered?

She said as much to Jai, but he shook his head. "Why would there be places like ours but also unlike? Would it not be wasteful of the gods to create so much to so little purpose?"

"But you heard Draupadi say so."

"She speaks in parables. We must ask a holy man."

"But, Jai, what if in the byways of the mind are many present moments, each different by a degree or two?"

"Then it is a dream, if indeed it is only in your own mind."

"But what if the worlds truly exist?" Might the things she had seen in the cave, might the things that Sir Charles had seen, be other versions of now?

"I think it more likely that what you saw was a spiritual teaching. Your reward for helping Draupadi."

"But I am not instructed, Jai. What do I learn by seeing that in some unreachable world one has the desired thing?"

For whatever place Astoria Harding was actually a member of the Royal Society, *this* Astoria was less likely than ever to achieve it. She had no great discovery to bring home. Of course, the lotus and the magical path of knowledge had always been a thesis awaiting proof. She had known that—and yet, how bitter it was to think she had traveled this far to find only the ashes of her grandfather's surmise. She wished she had never come here. Whatever the gods were trying to teach her, she did not care.

Exhausted, Tori felt herself dragged down into sleep.

Jai cradled her in his arms. What was he to make of this woman? Here they had shared a supreme spiritual experience, and she had understood little, still chained to ideas of physical worlds that her worship of science must suggest to her.

He watched her as she slept, his emotions warring. Would he ever understand her? It could not matter, for soon they would be separated, he to rule and she to return to her people. But when, back in the cave of the lotus, she had spoken of marriage, his heart had lifted in amazement. He had told her it was impossible, but was it? Deep in his core he thought they were destined to be together, to share a great journey. But a *rana* is not free to do what he likes. Nor had Draupadi instructed them to marry.

This talk of other worlds was greatly disturbing. Truly it seemed likely that she would always range too far for him, never perceiving things in a spiritual sense, but always looking for a logic that he must find irreverent.

He pushed a strand of sweat-matted hair from her forehead. For all the tenderness he felt, he could not love her, would not woo her. She had walked into the presence of the gods and seen nothing. He knew himself to be moving away from her, warmth giving way to a cool detachment that in the previous days he would not have thought possible. It was how he must be. But he did not wish it.

When Tori awoke, she felt able to go on. Her feet ached, but she limped on, the ingested lotus spinning out its versions of the world. At times she saw Jai dressed royally, with a brocaded coat and ceremonial sword.

She thought of how the Crown had pursued the lotus, believing it gave dreams of wish-fulfillment. Whatever rumors they had heard, they were as false as those Sir Charles had believed. How astounded they would all be to know that the flower was a spiritual manifestation, not a naturally occurring botanical specimen. She could come to no other conclusion, thinking of how the giant flower grew without sun and glowed from within. She thought that even Sir Charles would have had to agree.

"Jai," she said, touching his arm, making him pause. "Is everything all right?"

He refused to meet her gaze. "You should not have touched the lotus. I think you should not have seen it."

She felt his words like a slap.

"Come, we must find Sahaj before things come to harm."

They found a stream. Despite her vow to avoid water, she drank and drank, not caring if it activated the lotus.

It did.

The door was a familiar one: the entrance to the greenhouse study. She put her hand on the doorknob. At the same time she lay sprawled on her back in a nest of vines, staring into a sun cut up by black branches. Giving herself over to the vision, she crossed the threshold.

Sir Charles was leaning over his work table, writing, wearing his morning suit with gray silk cravat.

He looked up. "Ah, there you are *piari!*"

Her lips parted to greet him, but nothing came out. He had a specimen under the glass of a newer, better microscope than she had ever seen. The Remington typewriting machine lay in the corner, covered with folders and dust.

"Piari, you must tell me your adventures! I dare say the old *rana* was still mad about the lotus petal wasn't he? You see how I had no choice, though! They would have allowed the collections to rot. They didn't know the treasures they had in the Gangadhar, to them it was a hobby, a showcase for the native flora. But there was no science in it. Not even a catalog!"

He took another look through his microscope and jotted a comment in his notes. "And now we find that the theory didn't quite hold up." He shook his head as though distressed at the passing of an acquaintance. "That is a shame, but take heart, my dear, theories are meant for testing. You can't investigate if you don't know what you're looking for. First the theory, then put it to the test, that's the way of science."

"I know. I'm the one who tested it." The new Astoria spoke, but it was much the same as Tori herself would have uttered.

"Yes. Well, don't be downcast. We must go on. That's the main thing. I have another idea or two that I'm writing up. I've got an assistant, did I tell you? He's a young chap recommended by Goodwin. Done some interesting fieldwork in mycology. We'll jointly publish a little abstract, see where it goes."

It bothered her very much that Sir Charles was not looking at her. "I could have helped with that."

"What? Helped? Well, you had your own work. You were typing up the *Nelumbo aureus* manuscript. Er, no, you finished that, didn't you? It's here somewhere." He rose and began rummaging with the files on the typewriter.

"It's all right. It didn't work out."

He turned to her, finally looking her in the eyes. "I had great hopes of it. But no."

"Did you have hopes for me?"

"For you?"

"Yes."

"You were indispensable, always."

"For your lotus theory. I helped prepare the manuscript. I urged it on Allen Goodwin."

"Yes, the sod. Jealous and narrow. You did the best you could."

"I think he gave a poor report of me to the Royal Society. It wasn't my place to be so forward."

"Nonsense, that's—"

"—Did you ever think how I might find a place in the world?"

"*Piari.*" He looked down at his microscope, at his notes, as though he might find a clue there of how he could have given some thought to her welfare. "If I had succeeded, you would have benefited. The family name…"

"I wanted to be you," she whispered. "I loved you."

"Ah, *piari.* That wasn't love. That was ambition."

They stared at each other, struggling to deal with the things that had been said, the things that had been done.

Sir Charles walked slump-shouldered to his seat and sank down. "They do not have open minds, for a woman in science. Had *aureus* proven efficacious, it might have been different." His gaze drifted to his microscope. He would have liked to get on with whatever he had been doing.

She saw herself look at the map on the wall. It wasn't quite her childhood map. It was bigger and more finely drawn. Perhaps he had had it recast, or perhaps, in his world, there had been no child who worshipped her grandfather. But it was still full of pins.

She took a new pin, a large one with a pearl head. A good one for *Nulembo aureus*. The golden lotus hadn't been what they'd all thought, it had been greater than that. In the end, it hadn't been a plant at all, but a doorway to the self. She was still digesting it, and didn't know what would come of it. But she still wanted the pin in the map. She pushed the pin into the map of Bharata, in the province of Nanpura, in the Rangnow foothills.

At the door she turned back to look at her grandfather. "Magic is no shortcut after all."

Writing another observation in his notebook, he murmured. "No. I suppose we must do it the long way now."

He bent over the microscope, fine tuning the view. She slipped unnoticed out of the room.

Tori looked down from the rope bridge at the river, curling white over the boulders. Behind her on the bank, Jai stood watching her. She would be safer on the other side, he said, because he planned to wait here for his brother, and Sahaj's soldiers would be unpredictable.

She stopped after twenty or thirty paces and turned back to him.

"I'm not going home."

He watched her with something like the old regard. They were parting, but they had not admitted it.

"Jai. Let me stay." In the side of the gorge, a flock of green and yellow parrots bunched on an overhang, cawing. It was so typical of the casual, ripe beauty of the place that no one remarked on such miracles. "There is nothing at home for me. And I love Bharata. I love it." It was true. This was a land that had accepted her, even her enemies. She had been part of their schemes and hopes and passions. They had allowed her into their circle. "Let me stay."

She began walking back to him.

He came onto the bridge a few strides to meet her. He touched her face, but only just barely. "Your father will come for you, with a thousand troops."

"I will refuse."

"Yes, but then he will take you."

"Not if a *rana* pleads for me."

"I cannot. We are at war. You don't hear the screams of battle, but we are deep in the forest." He pointed toward Poondras. "Out there, it has already begun."

She looked over the canopy of the trees, where a mist had gathered, hovering until the sun would burn it away. She could not stay. She could not live in a *zenana*. Nothing about the plan was sensible.

Her urge was to go into his arms, but she could see that he needed to have a formality at this time. He was no longer her lover, but a king.

"When we meet again, it must be different between us," he whispered.

"Yes. I know." This reserve between them was difficult to bear. But if he could muster a royal demeanor, certainly she could call forth an Anglic deportment.

For a moment it seemed he would say more, but she saw in his eyes that he would not.

"Tell Sahaj," she said, "that my father would rather deal with you. I'm sure that he would."

Jai smiled. "I will tell my brother that I have your endorsement."

She had never heard Jai use irony before. It became him.

"Do." She smiled fully back at him. Then she turned and crossed the swaying bridge.

⌒

From the howdah atop the elephant, Mahindra watched as the two brothers faced each other across the gorge.

It was not the confrontation either Mahindra or Sahaj had envisioned. Jai stood alone on a rock outcropping, with the expanse of the Banda gorge separating him and Sahaj. Eerily still, he neither acknowledged his brother nor shied from the spectacle of the army ranged along the opposite cliff. There was no sign of the Harding girl.

The tribesmen looked to Sahaj for orders, but he only stared across the gorge in confusion. The way Jai stood—so close to the edge of the chasm—had transfixed them all.

If the *pitri* had led Jai to the holy flower, and it was on the other side of this gulf, how would they ever transport it back to Kathore? They would have to build a road and go miles north to the log bridge. Mahindra would persuade Sahaj to it, he must. But had Jai found the lotus? Mahindra leaned forward, straining to see the boy more clearly, to try to divine what had brought him to stand on the precipice in the mid-day sun.

The yellow snake phantasm that had been leading the army into the bush had gradually subsided. Sahaj's holy men must save their blood. For now. Mahindra did not mention this show of magic, but it lay between him and Sahaj as a barrier.

Sahaj approached and looked up at Mahindra. "If we cross the bridge, he will jump."

Mahindra thought he might. He stood like one possessed.

"What does he want?" Sahaj demanded.

"He wishes for us to see him."

"Yes, but why?"

"Let us watch and discover."

Sahaj looked at the thousand men crowding the banks of the gorge and frowned at their helplessness. "I have no time to watch and wait." He lifted his rifle. "I could kill him now. An easy target."

"Your brother is not a target for a bullet. Do not show to your army how easy it is to kill a prince." But of course Sahaj had already shown his army that.

A loud murmur came from the men. Looking across the ravine, Mahindra saw that Jai was holding something up, pointing it at the sky. Sun glinted off a blade.

Sahaj snorted. "Let the fool kill himself then." But even he was fascinated if he was to watch a suicide. He walked over to the cliff edge.

Jai removed his achkan, letting it fall at his side. Then, with a swift pass of the blade, he made a deep cut across his chest. Then another cut, just as fast. Blood welled, trickling down to his waist.

Oh beti, Mahindra thought, why? Why do this? He loved Jai, had seen him born and grow up, seen him suffer and accept his lot. Jai had his own bravery, though his father had never acknowledged it. He was glad that Uttam was not here to see this.

From across the gorge, came Jai's words, distant but clear: "I will mend! I am a whole man. Healed by the gods!" He tucked the knife into his belt. Sitting on the rock outcropping, he used his shirt to wipe away the blood.

Mahindra leaned forward. These were terrible cuts for one such as Jai. What could it mean, that he displayed himself and his wounds thus before them? A growing excitement pushed through him. Had Jai come into the presence of holiness, with this result? If Jai sat on that rock and his bleeding soon stopped, then it would be a certain miracle.

Soldiers turned to Mahindra, watching his reaction. Was it holiness or illusion?

"What is this trickery?" Sahaj shouted across to Jai. "Slit your throat then, show us how you live with that!" He looked around him, noting that his soldiers were muttering and uncertain. Stepping closer to the edge, Sahaj shouted again. "We don't need your magic! The *sahib*, Colonel Harding, is dead of the small pox. Poondras is ripe for the taking! We will win a great victory without you. So use the knife little brother. Finish it!"

Mahindra held his breath. Oh yes, now Sahaj urges him to finish it. He does not wish to see a miraculous healing. Perhaps Sahaj does not believe what Jai claims. But Mahindra knew that the gods had ordered the world and made life and death and white tigers and pipal trees and that they could heal a man's bleeding if it pleased them.

After a few minutes, though Jai's chest was smeared red, even Sahaj could not deny that the bleeding had stopped. The welling blood had ceased in a way that was not possible for Jai or perhaps for any man. The voices of the tribesmen rose, some understanding what they were seeing, and some denying it. A few went to their knees.

Mahindra must act. He must interpret this moment. Was Jai now a worthy successor to Uttam? Did this healing signify the arrival of a great prince among them, one who must cast down an unworthy rival? Sahaj looked at Mahindra and his eyes held fear that his primacy was at an end. But did the people need a man of holiness or a man of the sword?

"Baba!" a soldier cried out to Mahindra, his face full of dread, "what do the gods wish us to do?"

And Mahindra did not know. Would Jai with his love of the Anglic woman accept the foreign yoke as had Uttam? Or would he bring holy power to their cause? He did not know.

Sahaj tore his gaze from Mahindra and walked to the bridge. Mahindra saw Jai do the same. They would meet in the middle. What could Sahaj say to him, except *Your Highness?*

And then Mahindra knew what he would say. He knew Sahaj. He had always known what he was. Urgently, he signaled the mahout to bring the elephant to its knees. A dozen hands helped him to the ground. Through the press of men he couldn't see what was happening. Everyone was staring at the bridge and no one noticed that Mahindra was rushing forward, fighting through soldiers and spears and muskets to reach the bridge. Someone punched him viciously in the side. He went down, but no one noticed, so intent was the crowd on the events on the bridge. With the breath knocked out of him, he could not stand, but crawled, clawing his way forward through the forest of legs.

Then, for a moment, an opening in the path of soldiers. He saw the bridge swaying under the tread of the two men, now meeting in the middle.

Sahaj walked like one entranced, and Jai like a king. The younger brother held his hands in the air, showing that he had no need to hold onto the side ropes. His gait was even and graceful, and his chest did not bleed. Seeing Jai approach, Sahaj knelt before him in obeisance.

Mahindra's heart lifted. This is not what he had imagined.

The murmuring of the soldiers fell to silence.

Sahaj bowed down until his head rested upon the bridge planks.

His brother called out to the assembled tribesmen, "I do not bleed! The gods are with me!"

The army shouted back, "Jai! Jai!"

In a gracious gesture, Jai walked forward to Sahaj and pulled him to his feet.

Watching Sahaj take hold of Jai, Mahindra knew a terrible thing was about to happen.

He thrust himself into bird form, into a great hawk. Beating his wings in desperate exertion, he rushed toward Sahaj who seemed about to kiss Jai, but instead he pushed Jai savagely against the ropes on one side.

The bridge careened wildly as Mahindra stooped toward Sahaj, talons outstretched. But it was too late.

With a great shove, Sahaj pushed Jai over the side, clearing his feet of the ropes, sending him plummeting into the gorge. Mahindra dove with him, desperate to break his fall, but as a hawk, he could do nothing.

Jai reached out to him, somehow knowing that the hawk was not a hawk. A great, crying screech came from Mahindra's throat as he looked into the boy's eyes and knew his terror.

Just before the rocks, Mahindra swerved, sprayed with water from the rapids, arcing up, but leaving his heart behind.

Oh my son. Oh Jai. You were mine to protect. I have a way of bringing death to young men. As he flew up to the rope bridge for a moment he saw a woman standing upon it, her green sari blowing in the wind, her hair whipping as she leaned over the rope railing. Her wail was awful to hear.

Mahindra flew into a knot of soldiers, his hawk-presence unnoticed, as Sahaj held up his arms, calling for his troops to cheer. And they did, roaring their approval. But what else could they do? He was the *rana*.

And he was evil.

Tori watched as Mahindra's elephant tramped back along the way it had come, followed by most of the soldiers. She had been hiding within a stone's throw of the massed warriors as they watched Jai's drama play out before them.

In the thick cane brake, she buried her face in the fallen bamboo leaves. Jai was dead. That ghastly fall, seeing him plummet. Oh, Jai. Where had Draupadi been, where were her powers? The *pitri* had reached out to hold onto Jai, but her hands had passed through him. Her wail, the worst sound in the world.

But that was not why Tori could not lift her face from the ground.

Her father was dead.

"No, no, no," she whispered into the moist earth. Let it be wrong. Let him live. Dead of small pox.... She had thought he would be always there, he *should* always be there. It must be so. She shut her eyes against this pain... and saw her father lying on the surgeon's table. The doctors had done all that they could. A *sepoy's* tulwar had pierced him, and though the battle still raged, the hospital staff could not keep Tori from his side.

"Papa," she whispered. She took his hand. "I'm here."

His voice was a soft rasp. "No place for you. In a field hospital."

"They can't make me leave." She told herself she would not cry, not make it harder for him. Her face swelled up with the tears waiting to get out.

He smiled. "No, I don't suppose they can." He gripped her hand. "Never should have brought you here. Forgive me."

"Oh, yes you should have. The garrison will win, and push them back, and we'll have peace again. You must not worry, Papa. I won't let them defeat us."

"You are the Crown's best weapon, then, Tori." He tried to smile, but a groan came out.

One of the doctors came forward to take her arm, but she glared him away. "I will stay with him." To the end.

"You'll be a support to your mother? Promise me."

"Oh, I do promise. I will be the best daughter that ever was. I will..." The tears flowed. She could not see Papa's face. Furiously, she wiped at her eyes.

"You already are... the best daughter. Always remember that."

"And you, the best father."

"I hope you will forgive me that I didn't let you go... to Kathore. Too dangerous. Couldn't bear to put you at risk."

A volley of rifle fire in the distance was followed by the shouts of officers on the parapet. A boom of cannon. It was coming apart: the fort, their lives.

"I didn't need to go. I needed to be here with you." To say goodbye. Thank God almighty that she had been here at the end.

"And now," her father whispered, "they come to our very gates. I'm sorry, my dear. I love you, but it's never enough." As though giving evidence, his grip on her hand fell away.

"It was enough." She leaned over him and kissed his forehead. Pulling back, she looked down at his beloved face. "More than ever enough, Papa."

"You must be happy," came his weakened voice. "All worth it… if you are happy."

She thought she could never be happy again. "I promise," she whispered.

His eyes closed and his head fell gently to the side.

"Not yet," she whispered. But he had slipped away, taking with him the world of his love, his presence. The world as it should it be.

Rifle fire in the distance. Soldiers shouting on the parapets.

And then a rustle at the door.

Mama stood there. Oh, she had let Tori have his last words. If that wasn't love, what was? She went to her mother and took her in her arms.

26

Three packing chests lay open in Jessa's bedroom. Over there, a dress spilled out, the one she had worn to the durbar. All so long ago now, though only three weeks.

Jessa had dismissed her maid, deciding to attend to the packing herself. It had been unbearable to sit with the officer's wives in the candlelit drawing room drinking tea and trying to be brave. As the governor's wife, Mrs. Harding must set an example, but the subdued talk and avoidance of any discussion of her father or the smallpox—much less the talk of Lady Morton's lemon cakes and Mrs. Lowe's biscuits—made her wish to scream.

Jessa recalled how the reverend had said that God welcomed each person in his time into the eternal embrace. But somehow that did not comfort. And she missed Papa and dreaded life without him. How could her mother be the head of a household? It was all upside down: Tori off in the middle of the jungle and Edmond on a dangerous mission at Sirinshwari. This was not how she imagined it would be at the cantonment, not what the *durbar* had promised, with its orchestra and lovely gardens with everyone dressed in their finest, and the graceful military protocols. They were to have come home with husbands after a season in Bharata. And now here they were packing and Tori still gone...

In her hands were the yellow slippers that her sister had selected for her the day she first met Edmond. She stared at them, her heart swelling, making her chest ache.

224

She heard strange noises through the wall.

Who was mother talking to in the next room? Perhaps Mrs. Lowe had come up with her. But the noises did not sound like people talking.

Jessa walked down the hall to the open door of her mother's room.

There she spied her mother lying on the bed, sobbing most dreadfully into a pillow. Nor was the crying of a sort Jessa had ever seen before; no demure sobbing, but a loud, braying and choking wail. Her mother rolled back and forth, as though assailed by unbearable pains. Jessa started to go to her, then stopped on the threshold. Mama must cry. This was better than sitting on the divan pouring tea for Lady Morton and calmly thanking the maid for a fresh plate of sandwiches.

Oh, let her mother cry.

Jessa wandered back into the hallway, and leaned against the wall. She still held the yellow shoes. She cradled them against her chest, clinging to things past.

"There ain't a one of 'em alive, sir," Brockie whispered. "Not a one." Crouching at the tree line, Elizabeth also surveyed the carnage, her face set hard.

Fifty or sixty Anglic soldiers lay slaughtered in the valley. Edmond looked through his spyglass, but there was no movement on the silent battlefield. These were the 22nd Dragoons, by their dark blue jackets, and were likely the detachment that Harding had sent to escort Tori home.

Uttam's soldiers had done this; a stunning treachery.

Before them lay the Kopol Valley, the same clear-cut valley they had gone through on the way to Kathore. Among the troops, a few ostriches lay dead; the rest, no doubt taken by the *rana's* men. They could offer no assistance to any soldiers who might still be alive, since the battlefield might be watched. Edmond didn't believe anyone would have been spared. He could only hope someone had escaped to report back to the garrison. Or that Conolly might have gotten through.

This rout of Anglic troops was a bitter blow. Gone was Edmond's plan of intercepting the detachment out of Poondras, the one he had urged Harding to send for Tori. This company had marched into the Kopol ignorant of the overwhelming force that might be waiting for them.

"Not a one," Brockie whispered again.

"Steady now," Edmond said. Brockie's only career action had been at the Darband River, and that had been at night. In broad daylight, slaughter hit a man differently.

Maruti crawled up beside them. "The nullah is passable, sir. Very low water."

That was a bit of luck. They'd have some cover by walking in the watercourse that crossed the basin.

Private Tait supported Elizabeth as they made their way toward the gully. Edmond scanned the sky for shadows. Vultures circled, not alighting. Did they see an ambush behind the hillocks? He walked with weapon drawn.

They entered the riverbed. By crouching as they walked, they could keep their heads below the level of the bank. They proceeded slowly, tickling the water with careful tread, while around them the valley lay unnaturally silent. He didn't like it. But they couldn't delay their arrival at Poondras. With any luck, the *sepoys* at the fort would remain loyal, refusing to join the revolt. Maruti doubted that the 53rd Nanpura NI, the main Native Infantry at Poondras, would break, but thought they could be subverted if the town itself joined in a siege.

They had seen only one appearance of the questing smoke today. Maruti had renewed the mud upon each of their foreheads, with Tait and Brockie objecting, saying that magic was against the Church. "Not in Bharata, it isn't," Edmond had pronounced. "And not when we have Miss Platt to protect." They seemed to accept this, not that they had a choice.

As they crept through the ravine, Edmond occasionally sent Brockie to crawl up the embankment to watch for ambush. They would pass within two hundred yards of the nearest bodies.

Edmond's thoughts veered again to Tori. He wanted to believe that Sahaj wouldn't kill her, given her value as a hostage. He told himself that. Why else go to so much trouble to bring her to Kathore? He thought of the night on the balcony, reaching for her through the balustrade, just touching her hand. It was in that moment that he understood how powerless he was in the most important things in life. As a soldier, as an officer, he had always thought that by his wits or bravery he could carry off the things he must do, but this wasn't so. Nor was it just that she was physically out of reach. Beyond her present danger, she remained unattainable for him. She did not love him.

"Oh Christ God." Brockie was peering over the embankment.

Maruti steered Elizabeth to an overhang in the gully, urging her in, swinging his rifle into position at whatever was coming at them.

Edmond scrambled up to join Brockie where he lay hugging the slope.

"They're eating 'em..."

Two *pishachas* had landed on the battlefield. They were slowly flapping their wings as their beaks pulled meat from the bodies beneath them.

Brockie brought his rifle up, taking aim, but Edmond snapped, "Hold your fire."

"It ain't right, it ain't right," Brockie pleaded. "We can't just let 'em *eat* our fellas."

"Corporal, stand down. Go below."

Brockie didn't move. Mouth agape, he gripped his rifle with bloodless hands.

Edmond kept his voice steady, casual. "Now, Brockie, you don't want to disobey an order. I think in all this noise, you didn't hear me say hold fire. Go below."

Brockie looked at him then, stunned. He was eye to eye with his captain, and he had been given an order he'd ignored, argued with. "Sir," he managed to whisper. Sidling down the bank, he landed on his knees in the trickle of the stream. He bent over and threw up.

Even for Edmond, it took all his resolve not to fire on the monsters and let the noise bring on a fight if it came to that. He crept back down to the gully.

"*Pishachas,*" he said to Maruti's inquiring look. He glanced at Elizabeth, conveying that no more would be said, but Maruti knew immediately. "We'll say nothing in Miss Platt's hearing," he told Brockie who had dragged himself upright.

They resumed their ragged progress down the streambed, cringing every time they heard a triumphant cawing from the field.

Brockie was still shaking. He glanced at Edmond. "I'm sorry, sir. I wasn't myself."

"We won't speak of it. I know I can count on you to do your duty. You proved that at the Darband."

Brockie looked at him with undisguised gratitude. Well, he would not be so grateful if he'd known how close Edmond had been to gutting him with the knife he had had at the ready. Silence might be the only thing keeping them alive.

He didn't think the mud on their foreheads would fend off a *pishacha*.

When at last Tori crawled out of her hiding place, it was late in the day, with the sun coming aslant through the trees. The shouts of the soldiers searching for her had long since retreated into the forest on the other side of the ravine.

She walked to the edge of the cliff and looked down on the river, a frothing ribbon far below. A black kite swooped under the bridge crying shrilly, riding the thermals.

At the edge, someone had laid an orange firecracker flower, *Crossandram infundibuliformis*. As she gazed at it, more flowers appeared: marigolds, sunflowers, orchids. Slowly there grew a small jungle shrine, with a stone marker, and at last a statue of a god with numerous arms. The god pointed in many directions, to all the ways the world might be. Garlands looped around the god's neck. People remembered that a great man had died here. Or at least, in some world, people would remember, and honor him.

It could not matter to Jai, now. But it comforted her to think of all the directions of the world. The gods were promising that it was all complete, somewhere, the things we might have done, the things better left undone, the lessons that might have come in time, the thing whispered that could have set us free.

She bowed in *namaste*.

She must find a village. And go barefoot, because her feet hurt so dreadfully in her tight shoes. Sitting down on a log, she removed the shoe that hurt her the most, the left shoe with the elevated heel, pulling off her stocking as well.

Her foot did not look right. It was changing.

Up ahead was the sound of singing. For hours Ned had seen nothing in the darkness of the cave, heard nothing but his own breathing. Then this angelic sound.

Just when he had reconciled himself to death, he heard the singing. Perhaps he *was* dead. He had always thought that death was black nothingness, but he had not counted on being awake for it. Surely, if he was dead, this was hell—to be thirsty and in blackness, lost in a maze of stone.

He began to follow the sound. Holding one hand out to the side, he walked beside the tunnel wall. Sometimes he passed through chambers, at other times, the passageway became so narrow he had to turn sideways. His great hope was that the singing came from outside the caves, but it would not have stopped him had he known otherwise.

When he saw a glow ahead of him, he rushed forward, rounding one curve and then another, abandoning stealth. He knew it wouldn't be Astoria. She had gone beyond his grasp, denying the Crown its ambition, pushing him to this failure, perhaps an ultimate one.

When at last he stumbled into the enormous cavern, an intense light painfully struck his eyes. A broad sheet of gold lay before him. No, it was a lake lit from within.

A figure occupied the great cave, standing before the lake. By her *sari*, it was a woman, and it was she who had been singing. The words came to him clearly now, of sorrow and loss.

Her voice soothed him, helped him accept that her feet did not touch the ground. In the shadows of the stalactites that formed against the walls he saw shapes moving. He drew his pistol.

"They shall not harm you," came her voice, like a whisper in his ear. "They are less greedy now that I am going home."

The lake was very clear. In the water was the source of the illumination that filled the cave with a gloaming light. It drew him toward the edge, to peer in. Something floated in the depths. It was a gigantic flower, closed up.

The pool steamed here and there, and its vapors began wafting toward him, climbing up his legs and chest. It cooled his mind, draining him of the desperation of the hours just past. He dropped his pistol. He was done with those things now.

"What is this place?" he asked, his voice sounding shredded to his ears.

"The cave of the lotus. Of the gods."

He looked at her. Her face, deeply lined, was wet with tears. Her black hair hung down almost to her waist. Weariness overcame him as he inhaled the vapors of the pond. Almost without intention, he murmured, "When did I die?"

"It happened by degrees."

He looked down at the lotus. Now he knew why they called it golden. Not because of the color but because of its light.

"It's been here all the time," he said. It was too late for it to do him any good. He grew more weary with each passing moment, as though, now that he knew he was dead, he could not hold on to the world.

"It's rather pretty."

She held out her hand and he grasped it. She was cool and smooth as soapstone.

"We will be walking in now, *beti*. I am ready to go back. I have failed in my great effort."

"So did I."

"That is common. But there is no shame."

She led him in. He could not feel the water at his ankles, nor his shins, nor his thighs. He had died by degrees. This was just a formality. To descend into the golden water. He walked into the depths, unafraid.

27

The cascade of water scoured Tori's naked body. Under the small waterfall she used moss to scrub her skin, glorying in the spray of water against her face, her breasts, and her aching legs. She stayed under the stinging water as long as she could, growing colder, cleaner, her hair falling around her shoulders in ropes.

Done at last, she sat on a rock in the sun. She thought she might live. After finding a downed cluster of dates under a palm tree, her stomach now had something in it other than lotus, a very good thing, indeed.

She thought of her father. Of Jessa and her mother now alone at Poondras. With such a weight of sadness, it seemed wrong to love the warm rock, her clean skin, this moment of peace.

She waited for her clothes to dry from the rinsing she had given them. Legs stretched out in front of her, she stared at her feet. She turned her left foot to and fro. There were her toenails, even and in a row, visible from straight down her leg. Gone was that twisted c-shape, wherein her foot always turned in a direction she did not wish to go. She could not get enough of looking at that foot, the one that did not look like her own, but which, miraculously, was. Despite her sorrows, she admitted to a grateful happiness.

The lotus had done it. *Nelumbo aureus* was a cure for wounds, defects and very likely, sickness. Whoever had it in their possession could use it for enormous good or despotic control. Of course, the great flower might not last.

If there was only one, and if it were ultimately consumed by the suffering of the world, then its benefits would be tragically squandered.

What was she to do with this knowledge of the lotus? Truly, she did not know.

She pulled the wrapped piece of it from her bodice, contemplating it, but not allowing its resins to touch her. It didn't matter, the vision came anyway.

Nearby, Jai sat on a divan, dressed in gold-wrought cloth and a turban with diamond aigrette.

The Astoria of this world was seated a little lower, as befitted the guest of a *rana*.

How happy he seemed to see her! By their conversation, Tori understood it had been an absence of several years. They recalled their adventures: how the uprising was aborted by Jai's timely intervention; how nevertheless the new treaty with Anglica now kept Anglics as minor partners in a land where they were only guests.

They talked of Sahaj. How he fell at the Banda gorge. He had chosen to fight, and with Draupadi's help Jai had overcome him. Jai told how it pained him to recall that day. How he made offerings for Sahaj's spirit, allowing himself few luxuries.

"You should not have eaten of the holy flower, Astoria," he said. He chided her gently, acknowledging that she knew no better.

"I did it for science," Astoria said. "I had to know."

"And what did you learn?"

"Nothing." Then she added: "I learned that there is no swift path to knowledge."

He shrugged. "My *sadhus* could have told you that."

"Yet they use magic."

"True. But it is no faster."

She looked around her, aware that in this world, someone was waiting for her. It might be Edmond. The door to the *rana's* apartment was ajar, but she could not see who waited in the hall. She could not linger here. Rising, she made *namaste* to the *rana*, and he, in return.

"Do not be sad, Astoria. The striving is in itself a gift. Do you see? Accomplishments do not matter."

She begged to differ. "Oh, Jai, they do matter! It's just that they take a long time to bring about." She looked down at her feet, trying to remember whether they matched or not.

He sighed. "It is the difference between us."

When she looked up she was alone.

The headman at Pankot surveyed his rice field. The early rains had flooded his field, drowning the shoots. Dinesh had worked all day to divert the water into culverts and still hoped the crop might rally. Nor was this the worst that beset him.

He had lived in Pankot all his life. He was the village headman and his wife was the one to whom all wives came for counsel. But now things fell apart. The young men of the village had left to fight for Kathore. The women of Pankot were grieving their losses already. Dinesh did not believe the old *rana* would have led an army against Poondras. The fort was too strong, and the *rana* was not warlike, except to protect the villages, as he should. Then came word that his own son had killed him, a sword to the stomach. It was the same princeling who loved his white tigers and his wine. It did not seem possible that Prince Uttam was gone, who used to ride to the boar hunt on the back of the great Iravatha and scatter rupees to the villagers.

Now, war. Dinesh knew that the Anglics, whatever they suffered at Poondras, would come into the villages and set fire to the houses and granaries. They would level the shrines and torch the fields. So it could not profit Sahaj to win at Poondras, as more soldiers would come over the Bridge to avenge those who had died. If it was to be believed, Mahindra was said to favor the new *rana*. Dinesh shook his head in wonder. Had not the *sadhu* been raised with Prince Uttam, and had they not been as brothers?

The world was falling apart.

And then, the pox had visited the Anglic fort. Soon it would rage through Poondras itself. Calamity nipped at the heels of calamity.

The sun came slanting through the trees. He shouldered his hoe. It was enough work for one day.

When he reached the road he saw a figure he did not recognize. It was a woman, leaning upon a stick as she walked. Dinesh stepped out into the middle of the road. It was his duty to know who came into his village.

She was dressed in ragged clothing, with dark, tight sleeves and her skirts bunching out to the sides. As she drew nearer, he saw that she was barefoot. Never had anyone so strange come down this road. Her hair was parted in the center and pulled back, though adorned with a twigs and moss. Now he could see that this was surely an Anglic woman. Pale and sunburned, almost staggering. If she had the pox, he would not let her come.

To his astonishment, she addressed him in perfect Bharati: "Sir. Pray tell me where I am. I would be much obliged to you."

"How can you be lost, *beti*? There is only one road."

"I have not been on the road, but came that way from the rope bridge." She pointed north, into the jungle thickness.

"The Banda gorge? Were you with the soldiers who went there?" A great rabble had swarmed through yesterday, but they would not say where they were going or why.

"No, I am not with them. I was a guest of Prince Uttam. But he was killed." She swayed. Alarmed, he peered at her for signs of the pox, but she had no pustules, at least not yet.

Then it came to him that she might be the Anglic woman who was said to have come to Kathore. Rumor said that the *rani* had begged for company and that the prince sent for an Anglic woman who spoke Bharati and could entertain the *rani*. It was also said that she had a curved foot. They had named her the woman of the crescent-moon foot.

But there was another white woman. "You are not the teacher at Chidiwal?" Everyone had heard that she had beaten her servant to death.

"No. My name is Tori. I must get to Poondras." She stopped, as though she had run out of words.

"*Beti*, I will bring you to my wife. She will know what to do."

He led her toward the village. At the door to his house, he paused. "Is it your custom to walk without sandal or slipper?"

"No. I left my shoes in the forest."

He did not wish to discomfort her, but it was his job to know who came to his village and his home. "May I see your feet, *beti*?"

She looked down, sweeping her ragged skirt aside. They were the feet of a normal woman.

"Who are you, *sahiba*?"

"I am… I was a guest at Kathore. Prince Uttam welcomed me, and then I fell from favor."

"The woman of the crescent-moon foot?"

"That's who I was."

In perplexity he asked, "And now?"

"Healed," came her whisper.

He believed her. What this portent meant he did not know, but when a god touches you, you pay attention. He led her inside, telling his wife that a holy woman had come to their village and she must have a chapatti.

After the night's rains, the hot morning sun brought steam from the roofs of the city and the jungle beyond. It looked to Jessa, standing on the sentry walk, as though the world were quietly on fire, emitting smoke from its pores.

She welcomed the sun, although just four days ago they had all been saying how welcome the rains were, as a respite from the heat.

Four days. How greatly her life had altered in that time! She had lost a father, but so had the children of all the soldiers laid to rest in the last week.

From the gaps in the parapet she could view the King's Road passing over the Sita Bridge, past the Sita Temple and, beyond, the bright tents of the bazaar. In the far distance, the last of the storm clouds bunched up against the mountains, rising up the flanks like sheep heading over a hill.

She thought of Tori, surely by now winding her way down from those hills in the company of the 22nd Dragoons. How sad would be their reunion, but how comforting! Mama had rallied of course, but she was remote in her grief, with no thought for Jessa's loss.

It would so gladden her heart if, when the Dragoons arrived, Captain Muir-Smith was among them. His task had not been without danger, and she and mother had found time to worry about him amidst their other cares. There were rumors of disturbances and vandalism in the provinces. A police station had been attacked just north of there, and even in Poondras, crowds gathered every evening at the temple to hear malcontents declaiming. Yesterday Colonel Campbell had sent a company out to disperse them and they fled, for smallpox had not yet entered the city, and they did not wish to face infected troops.

A *sepoy* was watching her. It was impudent, but she daren't report him for she shouldn't be up here at all, having only sneaked onto the sentry walk for a few minutes in the hope of seeing the Dragoons crossing the bridge. The *sepoy* carried a rifle, proud to have such a nice one, unlike the plain muskets of most of the native soldiers. His superior officer spoke to him, and he turned away.

She turned for a moment to the vista in the other direction, toward the sea. It was a brave view, with the military lines sloping down to the west wall of the fort and the Bridge jutting into the vast ocean. But she had much rather watch the road. Against the blistering sun, she unfurled her parasol, but that was a mistake.

How tiresome, but Major Nicholson, Campbell's adjutant, had just spotted her. He had been walking across the parade grounds, and now made his way in her direction. Just as she was about to descend the stairs to spare him the discomfort of escorting her, she spied movement on the road.

Oh, but it was only a knot of people, not the Dragoons mounted with their colors. But she spied a red uniform.

She rushed forward to lean out the parapet. There were soldiers. Anglic soldiers, but not bravely seated on ponies and ostriches, but walking, carrying a litter. Horrifyingly, they were surrounded by angry-sounding townspeople. It wasn't the Dragoons. The awful thought came that this might be a remnant, battling its way through unfriendly crowds. She was about to warn someone, but the lookouts had already taken notice. From the yard came a commotion. She found herself flattened against battlements as soldiers ran past.

Below, the gates of the fort groaned open.

Edmond's bedraggled and exhausted men walked into the outskirts of Poondras in the high heat of the day. Elizabeth had collapsed again and was borne along by Brockie and Tait on a makeshift litter.

Native women brought them gourds of fresh water, tasting like nectar. Edmond cut a glance at Maruti, but the *jemadar* would take nothing, still protecting them, though magic had not come against them for several hours. It was only another mile to the cantonment.

They were now deep into the city, surrounded by those who might be against them. Did the monk riding past in the horse-drawn tonga rudely avert his eyes? And those women washing clothes at a stone tank, did their lips press together in contempt? He watched. Maruti watched. No one came to their aid after the water gourds.

"Look smart," Edmond urged Tait, whose shoulders were slumping. They must still have the bearing of Anglic soldiers.

Ahead he saw the single turret of the Sita Temple marking the crossing of the river near the fort's gates. Silence and stares met them as they continued their march, now entering the bazaar. On cloths presided over by merchants, piles of grain lay in small pyramids alongside stacks of pomegranates, garlic, almonds and mangoes. They must walk a gauntlet of food stalls with perfumes of ginger, mint and nutmeg hitting them, and bearers and ghari-cart drivers eating chapattis slathered in ghee.

Anger kept them going. The slaughter in the valley, Kathore's mutiny, the peril of the Colonel's daughter, all combined to fuel their steps. But to

Edmond's surprise, he began to have doubts. How could the Crown hold a land of so many millions? And if they could, should they? It was a treasonous thought, he was well aware. And it had been given utterance by the young woman he had grown to love. A full-blown mutiny, if this is what it was, might change her mind. Opinions were all very well, until one saw young men hacked to death with *tulwars*. When it came to a fight, he knew what he must do. But he did not relish answering Tori's challenges. Although he had always thought political issues were more properly the topics for Whitehall and the King's Privy Council, he knew that at some point he must look Tori in the eyes and say whether or not they should have built the Bridge.

Now within sight of the fort, a group of young Bharati men dogged their steps. A couple of them pushed to the fore, taunting Brockie and Tait and leering at Elizabeth. Some were hardly more than school boys, but they were going to cause trouble. Maruti unslung his rifle, carrying it casually but ready.

Edmond thought if they could just make it to the Sita Bridge, they would be spotted from the fort and have their reinforcements. But no sooner had the road narrowed over the Ralawindi than the press of townspeople thickened, turning oppressive. The smell of the swollen river mixed with the sweat of the rabble, and Edmond shot a glance at the sentry walk thinking how lax was their watch, that they had not yet been seen.

In the now nearly impenetrable crowd, Maruti was forced to use his rifle butt to clear their path. One youth took the shoving amiss and struck back. Edmond dared not leave Elizabeth's side, but drew his pistol as Maruti swung a fist, felling his attacker. At this, the crowd erupted into shoving and shouts.

Dropping his end of the litter, Tait went down, bleeding from the side of the head. Maruti fired into the air, clearing a few feet around them and giving Edmond time to haul Elizabeth to her feet. Brockie grabbed Tait, supporting him, and they staggered forward. "Easy, hold fire..." Edmond ordered, not wishing to incite a greater riot, which the first blood from the natives would be sure to provoke.

As they dragged themselves forward, Maruti plowed their path, hurling invectives in Bharati and presenting a formidable display of authority and violence.

Then knives appeared, glinting. Two youths rushed Maruti, thrusting, catching him on the arms as he swung to meet them. Edmond dragged Elizabeth between Tait and Brockie, backing up to her and firing into the crowd. They were besieged from all sides. A scream from behind him caused him to turn. To his astonishment, Elizabeth had a sword in her hand.

She lunged past Brockie at a boy who was charging them with a musket. The boy fumbled his aim, shooting into the bridge wall, and Elizabeth rushed forward, driving the sword into his stomach before he could reload.

At this, the crowd howled outrage and surged toward her. Edmond tossed his empty pistol and hacked his sword at the nearest of them, driving them off. Out of the corner of his eye he saw troops sprinting onto the bridge. The mob gave way, but the soldiers, seeing Elizabeth spattered with blood, began firing into the throng.

Elizabeth stood on the bridge in a widening circle, supported by Edmond.

She stared at the youngster lying dead in the road. He could not have been older than ten. Her arm fell to her side. The sword clattered to the stones of the bridge. Turning away, she pushed forward into the mass of the newly arrived soldiers, shaking off Edmond's help, walking slowly toward the gate, moving like one in a dream.

But it was a nightmare. The commanding officer called a retreat, and the soldiers fell back in an organized withdrawal, firing in volleys. They had little effect on the masses who swarmed after them. One of the gates opened a shoulder's width.

As Edmond's party slipped in, they slammed shut the gate.

It was not far to Kathore. Before dawn Tori and the headman Dinesh set out, followed by a few villagers who had seen her foot and felt it would not do for her to go unescorted to the fortress. They had taken to calling her *mataji*, as though she were a holy woman. It was perhaps wrong to let them think so, but she still had things she wanted to accomplish.

After a few hours' sleep and a bowl of rice, she was thinking clearly again. The confusion of the last two days had vanished as the lotus passed through her body. She was learning how to walk again. She no longer needed her habitual sway from side to side, but now she must learn to stride forward as most people did. The walking stick helped. Dinesh's wife had insisted she wear sandals made of hemp. With these, and a good supply of water that Dinesh carried in a gourd, she thought she could walk forever.

Along the dirt path to Kathore tribesmen streamed past their little group, heading to the fortress. Tori and Dinesh stood out of the way, letting them pass, and the armed men took no notice of her, with her head now covered by a scarf against the sun.

Dinesh walked in front. She watched him, copying his gait. He walked like Edmond did, with a muscular grace.

Every time she thought of Edmond she expected that she would see a vision of him, teasing her with how things might be. But the lotus had made its passage, had relinquished its stories. She didn't think she could bear it if Edmond had not gotten safely to Poondras. She prayed he might live, with a fervor that surprised her.

Her thoughts returned again and again to the lotus. How had it come to dominate her life? Her grandfather had set his sights upon it. The great thesis of his life had passed from him to her, like a spirit abandoning one body and inhabiting the next. It would not have broken him to be wrong. As her vision had shown her, he would likely have gone on to the next thing. Nor would it break her. He had taught her more than classification and the hunger for discovery. He had given her something to love. Science. And, oh, she did. For the things he could not give her, she forgave him.

It was important to be clear about Grandpapa. To put things in order. Because she was going to put herself into harms' way. It might not turn out well.

She must get to Mahindra. If they would let her pass, if they would let her get so far. For no matter how much power the *rana* had, it was the spiritual leader who could persuade the people best. Surely by now Mahindra must see that Sahaj would bring ruin to Bharata. It was her mission to drive the point home. Mahindra must be brought to see that not all Anglics were thieves, that they must leave, but not at sword point. Astoria must be the one to make amends. She though she understood how to do that.

They stopped at mid-morning to rest. From their vantage point at the head of a valley, the promontory of Kathore lay before them, swooping up from the plain, the road switching to and fro, climbing to the ancient stone walls.

Along it were lines of warriors, tribesmen with their staves and lances. They crouched or stood on the road, for the fortress was full, its army bulging out of the open gates. Their voices came to Tori's ears like the distant crash of the surf at Hastings. Every now and then they would raise their *jezails* and muskets at a figure who stood on the wall, dressed in sky blue and white, a gleaming sword at his side.

If she squinted, she thought she could see that he held reins in his hands. Below him, hidden behind the fortress walls would be the white tigers. She hoped he would not bring them to war. For they, of all the actors in this drama, were truly innocent.

28

Behind his desk at the regimental headquarters Colonel Campbell steepled his fingers in barely controlled impatience.

"Sir, at least let us inspect their quarters," Edmond said, furious that Campbell had not taken alarm yet. The acting commandant had doubled the watch at the gates but, incredibly, despite the slaughter at Kathore and in the Kopol and Astoria being held prisoner, he did not believe that a full scale mutiny was at hand. For now he was more focused on small pox quarantine and sanitation regulations.

Standing beside Edmond, Maruti wore a crisp new uniform not much spoiled in effect by his arm in a sling, and a meal had done wonders to renew his strength.

"Ah, the inspection," Campbell said. "But if we want the *sepoys* to remain loyal, don't provoke them. They'd take it as an insult. When you've been here longer, you'll see how things work. Saving face is important to these people." A furtive glance in Maruti's direction.

"Pardon sir," Edmond rejoined, "but we've lost quite a bit of *face* with the 22nd Dragoons." Sixty men slaughtered in the valley, food for *pishachas*. Ned Conolly still not heard from…

Campbell drew up. "Yes, quite. We're on alert. What would you have me do, march out to Kathore and snatch the Harding girl, torching villages as we go?"

"No sir. But permission for my *jemadar* to speak? Hear him out, at least."

The colonel waved a hand at Maruti.

"Sir," Maruti said, "last night I walked among the 53rd Nanpura. They were at their ease, you see. Many were saying that at the bridge we should not have fired upon boys so young. They are saying that the colonel should suffer a retribution."

"Do they indeed!" Campbell leaned forward, staring at Maruti with hawk-like intensity. Edmond was glad something got his blood up. Campbell was entirely too sanguine, lulled by Anglica's long history in Bharata, out of touch with how things were changing. He could not imagine not being the master here; could not credit an uprising taking root, much less succeeding.

"Retribution, by God," the colonel said. "Perhaps you agree with them, *jemadar*?"

Maruti stood ramrod still. "No sir, I do not agree. I was on that bridge, and I shot the boys myself. A boy old enough to shoot a gun is old enough to die. But the men use it to goad each other. They exchanged looks. Of what they were not saying."

Campbell rose impatiently from his chair. "Are you a mind reader, *zamidar*? Do you coax snakes from baskets as well?"

Maruti's face darkened. He stared at the floor.

Edmond intervened. "Colonel, the forces at Kathore will come at us—"

Campbell interrupted. "We know that. I have your report."

"With respect sir, when they attack, they will want a way to disarm the cannon, even control the gate from inside. May we put the Grenadiers on the cannon, at least?"

Campbell turned from the window. "No, Captain. We will not demote the 53rd when they have done nothing to deserve it. You don't command loyalty, you earn it. The Nanpura infantry is ours, I'd stake my life on it."

And perhaps you will, Edmond thought.

The interview was over.

Across the parade grounds, down Military Road, the tents of the regiment squatted in empty fields, leaving the barracks for infirmary use. Already the polo fields were dug up for new graves, as the contagion, though easing, wreaked its toll. Jessa and Mrs. Harding had been spared, thank God. But the loss of Colonel Harding had taken the light from their eyes; Edmond felt the loss keenly. Gone at sixty-two, and not even in the coming battle, one that he would have been honored to die in.

Outside the headquarters building, Maruti let a frown take over his face. "I did not expect when we arrived at the garrison we would be offered a bath and a mutton dinner."

"Nor I, Maruti. Are you up for a walk?"

"Captain, *sahib*? You do not mean to the *sepoy* tents."

"No, Maruti. To the fort wall."

The walls of Fort Poondras were the sturdiest of the Anglic fortifications in Bharata. Instead of earthen walls, they were mortared stone and twenty feet high. Loopholes gave a view out to the distance or angled down for close defense. Bastions projecting outward held fifteen large bore cannon firing 100 pound shells from forward emplacements.

It was this impregnable aspect that so assured Colonel Campbell and most worried Edmond. Even if Sahaj's force ranged upwards of 30,000 men, he could not hope to best the garrison here unless the gates were open. Nor could they starve the fort out, with access to the port controlled by the western guns. So why was Sahaj so confident? Edmond didn't like distrusting the Native Infantry.

But it wasn't going to stop him having a look at the watch upon the eastern wall.

As Maruti and he mounted the stairs near the gate, Sergeant Major Patil came to attention. "As you were, Sergeant Major," Edmond said, strolling down the sentry walk. Patil's artillery battalion had a long record of service and had distinguished themselves in the Bengal campaign. But that had been long ago.

"What shall we look for, *sahib*?" Maruti asked.

"For now, the sights." Edmond did not want to give the impression of an inspection. As soon as they looked in a footlocker, the evidence would disappear from other footlockers. The search must come as a surprise.

The two men stood at an embrasure, looking out on the city, now in a state of forced calm. Gatherings of five or more were forbidden even in daytime. The Sita temple was an exception. Unfortunate, since the temple had an exceptionally large compound, and was in addition a rifle shot away from the ramparts. The famous high turret rose over the city, its balcony staring right into the fort. That would be the first place Edmond would have inspected if he were in charge, which Colonel Campbell had made abundantly clear he was not.

They walked on. "Now, Maruti, you stroll forward, around the bastion, and watch for anything farther down the wall."

Maruti continued his walk, entering the bastion with its cannon emplacements, and then walked on, to the straight wall of the fort, where the

53rd NI patrolled.

But Edmond was particularly interested in the cannon. It was these six inch bore artillery that would scatter Sahaj's forces before they could cross the Sita Bridge.

Sergeant Major Patil, seeing that Edmond meant to walk into the battery of cannons, walked over to join him.

It was not the sergeant major's place to speak first, and Edmond ignored him for several minutes as he inspected the cannon. Finally he said, "Sergeant Major, please empty the cannon shot basket."

Patil hesitated. "Yes, sir. All of them?"

"This one." Edmond pointed to the nearest.

Patil ordered a *sepoy* to remove the cannonballs. Edmond watched the man perform this heavy chore, as he lifted each ball and stacked it against the parapet.

He allowed the last shot to remain. Then he pointed to the next basket in line. "Now that one, if you please, Sergeant-Major."

Patil set his jaw but signaled for his man to proceed. Out came three shot. Then the sepoy glanced at his sergeant major, apparently at a loss for how to proceed.

"Is it enough, sir?" Patil asked. "They are all regulation and neatly stored."

At that moment Edmond saw Maruti fifty yards down the wall, waving a length of cloth. Patil was sweating heavily under the golden heat of afternoon, but not only for that reason. The cloth Maruti waved was light blue. The color of Kathore.

Ignoring this for now, Edmond said, "Private, empty out the basket. Turn it upside down."

"Sir," the *sepoy* said. "Please."

Edmond strode forward and yanked the basket away, spilling its contents onto the floor. Out fell a white tunic and length of light blue cloth.

With his gun already drawn, Edmond brought it to full cock and trained it upon Sergeant Major Patil. "Have your men place weapons on the ground, Sergeant Major."

Down the wall, Maruti stood toward the edge of the sentry walk training his own weapon on the *sepoys* there.

"Bring a troop to the wall!" Edmond called below. A startled officer saw him with his gun drawn, and rushed with a unit of men to the stairs. By the time they arrived at the parapet, the 53rd Native Infantry and 6th Artillery had surrendered.

Instead of cannonballs the shot baskets contained the colors the *sepoys* would have changed into when they'd turned the cannon onto the parade grounds and opened the gates. Maruti found forty uniforms hidden in the locked rifle magazines.

The 2nd Grenadier Guards marched the *sepoys* down from the wall. Before Sergeant Major Patil was led away, he cried, "Long live the *Rana* of Nanpura! *Maro! Maro!*" Kill. Edmond had an urge to gag him but thought the measure too harsh for his senior rank.

"The likes of 'im," he heard a man say, "put him in the pox ward till he grows spots."

They led Patil off, and the Grenadiers took charge of the bastion and the wall.

Maruti joined him at the bastion and nodded in the direction of headquarters, where Colonel Campbell had come out with his staff onto the verandah. "He will not like that we held an inspection, Captain *sahib*."

"Did you inspect anything, Maruti? Didn't you see a bit of blue cloth sticking out of the magazine?"

Maruti grinned. "Just a tiny bit."

"Eyes like a falcon, Maruti. There'll be a medal in it for you, damn me if there won't!"

A dust devil spun on the slopes leading to the citadel, stirred up by the mid-day sun. It touched down on groups of soldiers camped along the road, obscuring them in a golden cloud and moving on like the random hand of God.

All the way up the steep road, Dinesh attempted to clear a path through the press of warriors, calling, "Let the *sadhvi* pass!" He did his best, but most did not accept that a white woman could be a renunciate and his efforts provoked scowls.

Tori leaned on her staff, wiping the sweat from her face. Just two more switchbacks, and they would be at the gate. If it had not been for Dinesh, she didn't think that the soldiers would have tolerated her presence, or else they would have taken her under guard. But Dinesh was known to some, and the crowd behind her had swollen to a few dozen, those who had heard she was no longer the woman of the crescent-moon foot and meant to see what she would do next.

And now Sahaj had seen her. It was clear that he watched her from up there on the battlements, perhaps enjoying her struggle to climb to Kathore and pass under the gaze of leering soldiers.

The last time she had been on this road she had been in a wagon, as the oxen lumbered to drag the cart laden with her, Elizabeth and their luggage. It had been at dusk that they had arrived at Kathore that day, with the setting sun falling upon the shrines atop the Gangadhar, gilding them with oriental splendor. Today the fortress's aspect had much changed in her view: dour and massive, bristling with sentries on the battlements, the palace domes with their spires just visible like upraised swords and the roof of the Gangadhar, a cluttered and forgotten ruin. Thinking back to the day that she had first come here, she thought with deep sadness of those who had lately been struck down: Prince Uttam, Jai, and the Anglic soldiers entrusted with her care. She hoped that Elizabeth was safe. Dear Elizabeth, with her dreams of bringing civilization to the villages. How wrong they had all been.

They came to the gates. Inside, the square was unrecognizable. It was crowded with so many soldiers she could not see the extent of them. She looked over a sea of turbans, many of them yellow, the color of valor and mixed in, the pale blue of Kathore. There must be ten thousand men inside the fortress walls, and thousands more on the road. A fearsome display. But they would have to hurl themselves against the stockade at Poondras and would be met by cannon. She gripped her staff to control a shaking that had come upon her.

"To the shrine, if you please, Dinesh." She gestured toward it.

But Dinesh paused. The crowd had parted for a well-dressed chieftain, wearing a light blue turban denoting him as the *rana's* man. He made the smallest movement with his head for Dinesh to stand away.

Barely looking at her, the man said, "You are to come to the palace."

"Thank you, excellency, but my business is with the *sadhu* Mahindra."

He grabbed her arm, and would have forced her, but Dinesh's staff came down on his hand. Outraged, the chieftain's fist swung out and slammed Dinesh to the ground. Other men in blue and white closed in, but not before Dinesh crawled toward her and, astonishingly, hugged her legs through her skirts.

"See," Dinesh cried, pulling her dress away from her feet, "see how the crescent-moon foot is now straight! The gods have touched her! Thus you may not!"

The chieftain kicked at him, but Dinesh took the blows unflinchingly. He began pulling her sandals off, and Tori let him.

An old man had pushed his way forward. He bent low to look at her feet. When he rose up she saw that, by heaven, it was Dulal. "The woman of the

A THOUSAND PERFECT THINGS

crescent-moon foot is now walking like you or I," he pronounced, turning to those around him.

A movement on the palace balcony. Tori saw that Sahaj had come out and was watching.

"How do we know she was ever deformed?" the chieftain said. "Did she not always clothe her feet in leather, thus hiding herself?"

Dulal drew himself up. "The *Ranee* Kavya herself inspected that foot, and her servant Mishka washed that foot, and we heard that it was curled like a slice of melon, with her toes pointing to the center."

The crowd began to mutter, and even Sahaj's men looked doubtful.

"Does this look like such a foot?" Dinesh demanded.

The chieftain looked up to see Sahaj's gesture of permission. She was to be allowed her progression to the shrine.

Now there were many tribesmen following her across the square. The courtyard fell into silence, as soldiers looked on in various postures of surprise and hostility.

Mahindra was waiting for her in the garden.

The pipal tree spread its great arms over the shrine wall and the empty pond. If Mahindra had had his way, the lotus would be there, dangling its roots into the depths of the pool. Now it was empty.

Under the tree sat Mahindra, reading a book. He wore a small pair of wire-framed glasses that she had not seen before.

An acolyte bowed away, taking Dinesh into the shrine and leaving her alone with the *sadhu*.

He looked up at her. "What is this I hear, *beti*, that you have renounced the world?"

"Who told you that?"

"It is everywhere, on all lips." He put the book aside and looked at the pool shimmering with a wobbly sun.

She approached him and sat nearby, leaning her back against a low pipal branch that could not, by its sheer weight, rise to the level of the other branches. The scent of jasmine curled around them. "*Babaji*, I still want the world. I hope I'll be able to have it."

"If that is your desire, you should not have come into the arms of Sahaj."

Mahindra would soon learn why she had come. She glanced at the palace façade across the square. "How does the *ranee*? Such terrible losses. I am sorry for her."

"She left to go to her daughter Navya, in a far province. She could not be consoled for her husband's death. When they lifted her to the howdah she called out curses upon Sahaj and he had her gagged. He forbade his sisters to accompany her; he will make profitable marriages for them, third wives to old monarchs no doubt."

Poor Bhakti, Tori thought, remembering her dreams of a handsome groom. She did not think that Prince Uttam would have been so ruthless with the girls.

"Jai is dead," Tori said. "You saw him fall."

Mahindra bowed his head. "To my sorrow."

She saw by his stricken face that she need not blame him for failing to protect Jai. His own blame would suffice. "The *pitri* foretold that Sahaj would have a long fall," She said. "But on the rope bridge…"

"The dead are not necessarily wise," he said.

"But you, *baba*, I think that you are."

"No. I have been foolish."

Hope surged within her, seeing that her surmise might be correct, that Mahindra had seen Sahaj's true nature, one that made him unworthy to have the lotus banner.

"I also have been foolish," she said. "The golden lotus is a holy thing. As you said."

He nodded. "It heals to a touch." He gestured toward her feet, now hidden by her skirts spread around her. "And you know where it is."

"Yes. I do."

"So, the truth at last." He did not rush to know, but let the conversation unfold. Musket fire came from the square and cheers. She hoped Sahaj was not coming just yet.

"What will you do, my daughter, now that you have your great prize?"

"Nothing," she said. "It's not mine to use. Nor Anglica's."

He watched her carefully. "What, then, of that closed circle of men who guard knowledge? You could be one of them."

"Not this way."

"It was your heart's desire," he murmured.

Spoken so simply, she was made to feel the loss very keenly. But, she whispered, "Some things aren't what we should have."

"And do you say it is the same with me?" His voice rose in some heat. "That my people should forgo the lotus power as well?"

Well, that depended.

"*Babaji*. What I say is that you must stop Sahaj. Sahaj is a bad ruler. I think you see it, too."

Mahindra looked out onto the square with its milling army. "You want me to tell them to go home. Do you think they will listen?"

Perhaps they wouldn't. But the *sadhu* could at least withhold the imprimatur of the golden lotus. "It may be too late. But do not give them more power."

She held his gaze.

He made a slight bow.

And just like that, their agreement was complete.

"*Babaji*, it is in a cave nearby. I'm giving it back to you. I will show you the way. But only you." She trembled, feeling that something momentous had passed her lips.

He stared at her, whispering, "Is it so?"

She nodded.

Slowly he stood and walked to the edge of the pool, gazing at it a long while. When he turned back to her he had tears in his eyes. "I would have hounded you forever for it. Now, it is this easy? A gift."

"A return."

He regarded her a long time. "Does the holy flower confer wisdom as well as healing?"

"In some way, I think it does. It takes the sting from what we can't have. And it gives us things we never thought we *could* have." The healing especially, though how Mahindra would use it or parcel it out, she didn't know.

Mahindra was gazing out over the garden, but he didn't seem to see it. He murmured, "Promise me that you will find someone worthy to know the dwelling place of the golden lotus."

"I think I've found him already."

"No, I am not the one. I am not worthy." Mahindra paused. "I desired the holy flower too much, and you see what has come of it. I have been blinded by this desire, *beti*. You must find a purer soul."

She stood up and joined him at the pool's edge. Amidst all the peril swirling around them, she felt a quiet joy that the fight, at least between the two of them, was over.

He gestured to the plaza. "They are waiting for me, to bless them." He nodded to himself. "That much I can do."

Mahindra turned and began walking to the gate of the shrine. She followed him, keeping pace. "You haven't asked to see my foot."

Out in the square the masses were growing louder.

"I do not need to." He made *namaste* to her, then flicked a glance at his acolyte, who stepped forward to take her arm. "Do not come out, Astoria. My blessing is best without an Anglic by my side."

Tori was surprised by the force of the acolyte's hand on her forearm, but allowed him to lead her into the shade of an almond tree, from where they could see the masses surging forward now in the courtyard.

Mahindra raised his arms, and the army greeted him with a great shout. It was more warlike than Tori wished. Rifles and muskets jutted into the air as people screamed, *Mahindraji, Mahindraji.*

Other acolytes now crowded into the garden from the shrine, leaning over the low wall, watching. Dinesh was among them, and Dulal and others.

Mahindra was helped to stand on the shrine wall where more might see him, and there he raised his arms for quiet. But no sooner had he done so than the report of a rifle came loud across the square. He fell. There was blood. Tori saw those closest to him catch him as he slumped, his head streaming blood, dripping upon his white *dhoti.*

Tori stared in shock, thinking, it is only a flesh wound. He will live, it is only… but when they lay him all the way down on the top of the wall, she saw that the shot had taken away part of his skull. He had been standing on the low wall. The force of the bullet had knocked his glasses off, and they lay on the ground, one lens shattered and spattered with blood.

Dulal battled his way forward through the crowd, managing to clutch at Mahindra's out flung arm, sobbing into it, showering it with kisses.

Everywhere people were shouting. Chaos erupted in the square as tribesmen and soldiers crowded around to see with their own eyes and wail at what they saw.

"*Hatya!*" Murdered, they screamed. "*Hatya!*"

She strained forward to the wall, but the acolyte pulled her toward the inner recesses of the shrine. She was brought to a stone bench, and made to sit. Someone brought her a cup of water and bade her drink though her hands were shaking too hard to hold the cup herself.

She drank, hearing from the courtyard the clamor of shouts and chants. *Hatya, Hatya.*

When she looked up she saw Sahaj standing before her, him and his tigers.

"You killed him." She could not all at once fathom how Mahindra was dead, and how she felt. But she knew that Sahaj had done one more evil thing.

At a slight gesture from the *rana,* the acolytes scattered. "He was weak. Sentimental."

"Was it sentimental for him to have loved Prince Uttam? Your own father! And your brother…"

"Oh yes, very much."

She wondered if he and Mahindra had come to hot words over the deaths.

Sahaj went on, holding the tigers' leashes carelessly, fingering them. "His vision was for a great unity of the land. What need of unity, when each state has its prince? I do not care for these things. Otherwise I would cut off your fingers until you told me where the holy flower is."

"I do not know, in any case."

"I do not care. The warriors are liking you, and I am pleased to give them their trifles. But I am not gullible. I do not believe your claims to holiness. I do not believe that you ever had a crescent-moon foot." He dropped the reins.

The tigers came to her, sniffing, sniffing, and thrusting their great heads into her skirts. Sahaj let them push at her, enjoying what he imagined was her fear. In fact, she was very much afraid.

"Your revolt will fail," she said, trying to keep her voice steady.

"We shall see. It was never the flower that would conquer. It is arms that win, and valor."

"If valor, then you shall never win."

Sahaj had been just turning to go, but now he swung back to her, hand on his sword. He drew it.

"I would see your foot."

Tori hesitated. Her chest contracted in fear. Sahaj raised an eyebrow.

Oh, why had she goaded him? She drew back her skirts, exposing her feet. Here was her left foot, perfect and whole, the mirror of the other one.

The sword point came down between her feet. "Which one do you claim was the curled foot?" he softly asked.

"The... the left."

He placed the sword point on the arch of that foot.

Then one of the tigers stepped forward. With a great paw, he batted the sword point to the side. The paw came across, slicing the blade across her foot, but it was only a superficial cut.

Sahaj frowned, but seeing the acolytes watching him, he gave a forced laugh. Then, picking up the leashes, he pulled the tigers to his side. As the three of them walked out of the shrine, the sun shone brightly on the cats' silver and black fur.

29

Edmond stood in the hall of the governor's residency at dawn, waiting while Mrs. Harding made herself presentable. Jackson had taken some persuading to summon his mistress, but damn it, this wasn't Shropshire, even if the vestibule held potted palms and a table for calling cards.

He'd been on the ramparts, and he hadn't liked what he'd seen.

Villagers were gathering at the Sita temple, ostensibly to pray, but in reality to mutter against the cantonment and the deaths of the young ruffians on the bridge. Colonel Campbell had ordered ammunition given out, and if the group exceeded one hundred, a troop was to be sent out the gates to disperse them. It was the very opposite of what he should do, especially at the temple, where an incident could only provoke tempers.

Campbell's attitude was cavalier in the extreme: the hills men would not come down, or if they did, they would be squeezed to a nice point crossing the bridge, making for a clean target. Furthermore, like every commander before him, he thought Fort Poondras impregnable and the position made him bullheaded. He would not tolerate a breach of his orders that no gatherings should come 800 yards of the gates. This whole area was a tinderbox waiting for a spark. Edmond now feared it would be Campbell that would light it off.

Mrs. Harding came down the stairs. Her hair was pulled back into a soft bun and she wore her black with a startling elegance. He hadn't realized before how like Astoria she looked.

"Captain, pray pardon me for keeping you waiting." She led the way into the parlor, with Jackson stiffly holding the door.

"You will take tea?"

"No, ma'am. I have only a minute and then I must rejoin my company."

He looked to the door, thinking that Jessa might join them, but not at all sure she should hear what he had to say.

Mrs. Harding smiled. "She is rushing to dress."

"I pray she will not on my account, I have only a moment." He sat opposite her as she gestured for him to take the wingback chair. "How does my cousin Elizabeth?"

"Oh, sleeping, bless her, finally sleeping. The doctor gave her a potion, but a light one since her stomach cannot bear more."

Mrs. Harding had taken Elizabeth in and was personally nursing her. He would remember that kindness. "Mrs. Harding, how exceedingly hard this time is for you. I would not have disturbed you but for a matter of some importance." He must be most careful what he said. It could be interpreted by Campbell as insubordination.

She waved Jackson from the room. "Go on, Captain."

"May I ask if you are quite packed to leave? That is, are you ready, would you be, if passage were offered on the *Richmond?*"

"The *Richmond?* But it is a supply ship."

"Yes ma'am. By good fortune it's been delayed in offloading its goods from Calcutta. It makes its way home from here." He lowered his voice. "I feel your late husband would want me to secure passage for you. To encourage you to leave by ship, where you will likely be more comfortable, than by carriage."

A small frown overtook her carefully arranged face. "I don't understand. We were to cross the Bridge with a small contingent from the 81st Regiment on Friday."

"Yes, so I heard." He looked in the direction of headquarters. Then, pointedly at her: "The Bridge is not necessarily safe, ma'am."

"Oh! Not safe?"

"Well. In case of... pursuit." Mrs. Harding could not contain her surprise. "I do not say one would suffer from skirmishes along the way. I do not say that at all. But you will certainly be more comfortable upon the *Richmond.*" He pleaded with her with his eyes.

"You speak, do you, of the unrest in the hills?" Mrs. Harding asked.

"No, I do not. Please understand that under orders from Colonel Campbell, we have prepared adequate defenses against any possible attack. My superior officers have assured us that no matter the numbers brought against us, we are well-defended here."

His meaning began to dawn on Mrs. Harding. She picked at the handkerchief crumpled in her hands. She looked up at him. "Surely we could not leave without Astoria?"

"But it does Astoria no good for you to delay. I will wait for her, I promise you."

Jessa had entered the room. "Wait for Tori?"

Mrs. Harding turned to her. "Captain Muir-Smith suggests that we leave for home a bit early, my dear." She turned back to him. "I think it would not look well for us to abandon the residency. Colonel Campbell has graciously let us stay here. It would be… a statement."

"It must not seem so. If you take care to say that the *Richmond* will be the more conducive mode of travel. You may tell any of the officers' wives that the ship has berths. Such vessels are always eager for the income from private passage." That was not strictly the case, but Maruti had spoken with the skippers, and they understood their duty.

Jessa found a chair near Mrs. Harding. Her hair was charmingly clasped at her neck, and her mourning dress became her. "But why leave so abruptly, Mama, when we were to go by carriage within the week?"

Edmond stood, rather wishing not to be in the room when Mrs. Harding lay her surmises before her daughter. "I must take my leave, ladies. Pray excuse me."

"But, Captain," Jessa continued, "may we not all return to Anglica together?"

"I have my duty station here. It will be some time before my assignment ends, so my leaving is out of the question."

The women rose to see him from the room.

Mrs. Harding found her voice. "How much shall we bring?"

"Only what one maid and Jackson can carry. Space may be a priority on board. There are four ships at anchor. Three should be given over to the sick who will be no help in the defense." He refrained from saying that they must not be left behind if a retreat formed up on the Bridge.

"Mrs. Harding, you might be at an advantage to be quartered on Military Road, in a bungalow near the west wall. In case the *Richmond* must accommodate an early sailing." *Or in case 50,000 hills men cannot easily be pushed back with six cannon*, he thought.

"No," Mrs. Harding said. "We shall be perfectly suited to leave from here." She cocked her head at him. "Once we are seen with our bags, it will be best to proceed directly."

She understood things perfectly.

"Perhaps so." Moving to the front door, Edmond tried to find words that might reassure them while not undermining their resolve. He failed. There was nothing that could make their situation less dire. "When my *jemadar* Maruti comes for you, he will have only minutes to bring you to the quay. He cannot be spared from duty any longer than that."

Before he departed, Jessa leaned on his arm. "Pray... take care, Edmond." Her smile flickered, went away. "I know it is not what a soldier does. Yet I shall pray for your safety."

"Thank you." He wanted to say, *Best pray for Tori*, but felt it would not do to instruct her how to care for her sister.

"Keep watch for Maruti."

"We shall." Jessa's eyes glistened, but she held up. She and Mrs. Harding held hands. He looked at them standing in the calm of the residency and fixed the image in his mind, of peace and calm and the Harding women safely underway. If there could have been three Harding women, it would have eased his heart. She seemed to be in the vestibule then, standing in the early morning shadows by the stairs. Was that a book under her arm? Mabry's *Amphibians*?

He made himself turn away and leave the mansion on the double.

Private Tait sipped at a cup of water proffered by the infirmary assistant. They said he had got himself a concussive, so he had to stay abed. It didn't seem like a proper battle wound, though he had a bloody bandage around his head, at least. It still made him wince to think how he'd dropped his sword, and the school teacher saved the day with it. But still and all, it was better to be alive than trampled by the mob out there. He'd never seen anything so fresh as a line of red uniforms advancing on the devils.

Brockie had been in to see him. He'd looked around, skittery-like and nervous, though now that they were safe, it didn't seem right. Maybe he didn't like being one barracks over from the pox ward. They'd closed the windows in that direction, but no one wanted to be in the infirmary unless ordered. Himself, he'd rather be up on the walls taking out a few heathens. Let them come at the fort. They said the crazy *rana* was coming. Well, let him, and taste Anglic lead, too.

Edmond had just come out of the officer's mess, when a shot rang out near the city gate. He sprinted past the armory and the horse stables to the wall where, amid a commotion he saw a man down. The Grenadiers were aiming through the loopholes of the parapet, and it looked like Major Shaw might give orders to fire. But all held quiet.

A runner pelted down the stairs, making for headquarters, followed by a man known to him, Sergeant Middleton.

Edmond met him by the gate. Middleton saluted smartly. "It's Lieutenant Wellesley, sir," he blurted. "They killed him, a shot straight through the forehead." They could hear cheering from the temple, as the villagers must have guessed the shot told.

Maruti had joined them. He and Edmond exchanged glances.

"How did they approach the gate without being seen?"

"Didn't, sir. They had a man in the turret, eye like an eagle, or a lucky shot."

"It sounded like a rifle."

"That's what it was, sir, an Enfield."

The runner came back, taking the stairs two at a time, reporting to Major Shaw.

And then, to confirm his worst fears, he saw activity in the bastion where the wall bulged out toward the city.

They were priming one of the guns.

Colonel Campbell came out on the headquarters verandah. He was far enough away that Edmond couldn't see his expression, but he was sure it was stern. If a fanatic had hit an enlisted man, it might have been tolerated with a quick slaughter of those gathered in front of the temple. But an officer was a different order of insult, and Wellesley had been a favorite.

Campbell wouldn't be content with firing into the crowd. He was going to make an example of it, and with something much worse than mowing down the rabble. They were going to take down the Sita turret.

The order to fire came. The deafening crash of the gun broke the silence, sending a flock of crows scattering from the walls. The gun could hardly miss at this range, but its crew sent another volley for good measure, thundering against the Sita turret. Though Edmond could not see the tower from where he stood, by the sound of the crashes he was certain the volley had hit home.

"We will have trouble now, *sahib*," Maruti murmured.

Middleton sprinted away to join his company. Down the stairs they bore Wellesley's body, with soldiers staring on in mute anger that some son of perdition should have the temerity to kill an Anglic officer. And with one shot.

It was not to be borne.

Now from the direction of the temple, they heard shouts of a mob approaching. A few stones hit the gates. On the sentry walk, soldiers took aim. As Major Shaw paced behind his men, the order to fire was given, and a volley crackled out. Men screamed as they fell before the withering fire. All this was clear to Edmond, though he could not see the action.

He and Maruti returned to their company of the foot guards on the far side of the parade grounds, forming up the men in readiness, even as the rifle fire at the wall diminished. Evidently the first surge of villagers had not been followed by others foolhardy enough to believe that their gods would protect them when they had fired on the Anglic fort.

It had begun, Edmond and Maruti knew. Word was spreading that the temple had been fired upon, the turret demolished. They might wait until nightfall. Maruti thought so. They would not be allowed to remove their dead until then. It was no example unless the people could see bodies.

"We gave 'em what for, didn't we sir?"

Edmond turned to an excited corporal. His pressed uniform bore a smart-looking cartridge belt and polished buttons. He had probably never seen action before and was happy at the prospect of being in on some.

"Yes, Corporal." *We took out an eight hundred-year old turret at a range of 200 yards, and killed a few dozen worshippers at the neighboring temple. Good start to the day.* "We avenged Lieutenant Wellesley. You may be sure of that."

Toward dusk, a high-sided wagon, covered with colorful tapestries, was towed by four oxen to the far end of the Sita Bridge. The villagers, who looked to be peasants and not soldiers of any army, made no attempt—which would have been stopped—to haul the wagon over the bridge. Instead, they settled it in a grassy field and led the oxen away.

Edmond and Maruti went to the wall to look, but neither they nor anyone else could guess what the wagon contained.

It was just out of range of the rifles, though not of the cannon. For once, Edmond noted with wry satisfaction, Colonel Campbell decided not to shoot at an obvious target.

From the palace balcony Tori searched the plaza, but there was no sign of the tigers, probably resting in a cool niche until evening. The great square of Kathore was empty of people. Long shadows fell, projecting the domes and stupas of the palace roof across the empty grounds, and now inching toward the Gangadhar. No one stirred except, here and there in doorways or windows.

Before he and his armies left yesterday, Sahaj had loosed the tigers in the courtyard. He had never liked to pen them up. Now they could prowl where they wished until he returned from his battle. It kept things quiet in his absence. Soldiers, the few that remained for defense of the citadel, left haunches of meat for the cats in the middle of the square.

So far the tigers had not come for them.

Earlier, a group of acolytes from the shrine had accompanied Tori across the square. They had garbed her in a sari the color of saffron. They told her the color was for holiness. She wasn't sure if this was what they really thought— because of her foot—or an elaborate pretense set in motion by Mahindra himself to assure her survival. But it had its effect. The soldiers did not come down and prevent her from returning to the palace. Several made *namaste* to her from the battlements, but their officers watched her rigidly. The tigers, wherever they were, allowed her to pass. Perhaps they didn't like the sound of the hand cymbals and drums that the acolytes thought prudent to keep them at bay.

It all seemed strange and dreamlike to her: the hot and deserted courtyard, her heeled foot—still asserting its adjustments to her gait—Mahindra's death, and Jai's. To even begin to manage, she placed short term goals in front of herself: must get to the palace… must survive the crossing of the square… underneath all this, the ominous knowledge that Sahaj's massive army was marching on the garrison.

She had said goodbye to Dinesh and the villagers. He went with her blessing—he had insisted—and her thanks, so that before the great gates were slammed shut behind the departing force, he was allowed to return home. He was distressed that he would have to pass the *sadhu's* body lying on the slope of the hill where it had been flung from the wall. By denying him cremation, Sahaj thought to assure that his spirit would not soon be merged with the five elements and his soul purified. So there he lay, disgraced. No doubt Sahaj had expected Mahindra's change of heart. He wasn't to have been given a chance yesterday to urge the soldiers against Sahaj.

After she had seen to Mahindra's burial she would go home. Burial would not have been his preference, but Dulal felt he would permit it in an emergency. So when darkness came, Mahindra would be given respect.

Would she be allowed to leave? Sahaj had no real need for her, and she might even be dangerous for him to keep around, given the miracle of her foot.

She didn't know what instructions he had given his lieutenant—or even who it was who commanded Kathore in the interim.

She went barefoot at all times, just to make sure no one forgot her authority.

As soon as night fell, she and Dulal met at the hidden *zenana* door.

They crept out and began the long trek around to the main gate of the fortress. She wore sandals taken from the *ranee's* apartment, for her feet were bruised, and she could not easily walk over stones. The wound on her foot from Sahaj's sword chafed against the sandal ties, and she had stuffed a rag on top for a cushion.

It was a moonless night, as the two of them stumbled along the edge of the battlements, fingers trailing against the stones so as not to stray outward and lose their footing. Dulal bore a long sheet dyed red, the color, he explained, of those with the capacity to destroy evil.

It took almost an hour to reach the great gate of Kathore where, high above, torches sputtered. Looking down from the place where the sadhu had been hurled, they could see nothing on the hillside. It was utter blackness.

They began to search, passing to and fro on the incline in the hope of stumbling upon the body. But they found nothing. They had not dared to bring a torch, but it would have been their only hope to discover the body amid the bracken- and boulder-strewn slope.

"The gods have taken him," Dulal whispered. But they continued their search.

Tori looked up to the battlements, seeing that a guard had come up next to a torch and stood gazing out. She and Dulal froze in place. They waited through dreadful minutes, scarcely breathing.

Then soft fur brushed against Tori's arm, and she jumped, emitting a low cry.

Something was standing next to her, a dark shadow against the black hillside. In her fear, she forgot about the guard—who had not raised an alarm or moved—and began backing away.

A hand grasped hers. It was warm and leathery.

And there, standing very faintly before her, was a blue monkey. She heard Dulal gasp. As the monkey gripped her more firmly, she felt tears spring to her eyes. "Show me," she breathed.

It led her down the slope.

Mahindra's body had fallen much further than she could have guessed, and it took several minutes for the three of them to descend so far, careful not to dislodge stones and create the slightest noise as they went.

The monkey was now unnaturally vivid to her eyes, blue fur almost glowing.

It watched her with glistening eyes.

"Mahindra," she whispered. "What shall become of the golden lotus?"

But the monkey only led her on. For all his magics, the *sadhu* could not make the spirit creature talk. Nor could he make it last. Just as they found the body wedged against a huge rock, the monkey began to fade. It still grasped Tori's hand, but lightly now. Its form faded to black. And her hand grew empty.

As Dulal wrapped his master in the cloth, Tori considered that Mahindra's last act of renunciation had been to give up his life. He had known they would kill him, had arranged for the acolytes to be sure she did not crowd near when he climbed atop the shrine wall. And forming the blue monkey had used the last of this lingering power.

She and Dulal managed to bind the body into the cloth and carry it between them, struggling up the slope, and along the wall. The guard had moved on, having seen nothing.

They buried him in the zenana garden near the door, as a blessing to any who had desperate need of that passageway. Leaving no marker except several leaves from the pipal tree at the shrine, they sat back and contemplated their work.

She undid a fold in her sari and removed Mahindra's shattered glasses. When she placed them in Dulal's hand she felt a tremor overtake him. Gripping the frail wire frames, he bent his head toward them. There had been a moment in the last few hours when she would have liked to have had the glasses for herself. But then she thought of the legacy of carrying things off from Bharata and decided that if she was allowed to leave the spiritual continent, she would take nothing with her.

"What shall you do now?" Dulal asked her some time later. He glanced at the door. "Slip away?"

"I won't get far on foot." She looked over at him. "I need an ostrich. And I need permission of the *sardar* to leave."

He shook his head slowly. "That is much."

She drew out the rupees that she had been given by her father for her trip. "This is all I have. I would be grateful if you would purchase a mount for me, and a few chapattis. The *sardar*, I will handle myself."

He stared at the rupees. "That is much."

Good, she thought, if it would buy an ostrich.

Tori raised a torch in the Night Pavilion, watching the room explode with light. She thought it was this sight more than any other by which she would remember Bharata. She had been here with Elizabeth, with Jai, Mahindra, and Draupadi. Everyone paused here, offering respect to Bharata's munificent past, and marveling how even dusty mirrors loved the light.

She would not have much time, so she moved quickly on to the galleries. The guards might see light flickering from the museum, and think she was up to some mischief.

It was rash to have crossed the plaza at night. After two hours of indecision, she had finally set out, slinking along the wall and at the last taking a lit torch from its sconce. But she could not leave Kathore without saying goodbye to the Gangadhar. With Grandpapa's notebook under her arm, she made her way through the old museum displays, past the room with the erotic friezes and thence up to the second floor.

She hesitated on the great staircase near the main room at the front. The monkeys were quiet tonight. On one side of her was the massively overgrown inner courtyard, emitting only the soft murmur of crickets and the clucking of birds. Of demons, she saw nothing. Draupadi's entourage had gone home. Turning down the far gallery, she made her way toward the cabinet where she had seen the *pitri's* scarf affixed. She didn't know if this was the drawer where Sir Charles had found the lotus petal, but she believed so. Opening it, she placed his notebook inside.

Sir Charles had been reluctant to divulge, without scientific proof, that he had experienced visions. Very well, then. She closed the drawer as a swirl of bats flapped out of the courtyard, setting up a protest of birds from within.

She felt a lump in her throat as she hurried back the way she'd come. It was very hard to leave, even after all that had happened, the deaths, lies, betrayals. Not all of them had come from Bharatis, of course. She was well aware of her own complicity in the great furor of the golden lotus. But, by heaven, she was grateful for it all, even so.

That was, until she stood face to face with the tigers.

They had come out of the darkness after she had replaced the torch in its socket. As they watched her, it seemed they waited for her to move. But she could not. They looked very fierce in the light from the wall torches. Trying to keep from falling down in terror, she told herself that the tigers had plenty to eat, all that wild boar or whatever it was the guards found for them, and besides, they had had one chance to kill her, when Sahaj had stabbed her foot, and they...

259

One of them came forward.

It growled, very low in its throat. It sounded like a fog horn in the silent square. She nearly crumpled.

After a moment she found that she was walking, very slowly, toward the palace. It would not do to stand confronting the tigers when perhaps all they wished was for her to leave their territory. Her back rippled with foreboding all the way to the arcade in front of the palace. As she opened the door, to her shock a tiger rushed past her knocking her against the door and throwing it fully open. The other tiger was in the square, so whether she shut the door on one or the other, she would still have a tiger.

Leaving the palace door open—the place was deserted she noted hopelessly—she walked through the vestibule and into the great columned hall. One tiger went before. The creature seemed to know the palace byways and did not pause to explore. The second tiger padded steadily behind.

They might have walked forever through the deserted palace. Later, it would seem as though they had. Time slowed. Everything assumed an unnatural clarity: the mosaics, bas-relief carvings, perforated windows, the niches with their statues. They might have stumbled upon Rashmika and Bhakti painting their faces or the *zenana* guards playing at dice or a *sadhu* still folded into an intricate posture, unable to unwind now that the *ranee* no longer required his contortions. But they saw no one. On through the marble halls they went, now headed directly to the *zenana* garden. The cats might have taken the scent of growing things and known it was a better place than palace or courtyard. Or they might have known—in some magic way—that therein lay their freedom.

When she finally realized what she must do—perhaps what they *wanted* her to do—she almost wept with relief. The white tigers were splendid, imbued with awe. But it was an awe she did not care to sustain.

A few torches from the balconies above barely lit her way. The tigers, of course, needed no light, and now both surged ahead of her.

She followed them to the door in the *zenana* wall. It did not swing freely, and she had to put her shoulder into it. Another shove, and it sprang open.

The tigers hurried through in a great tide of sinew and fur, passing close enough to her that she felt them whisk her sari. They disappeared into the night. *God speed.*

She closed the door. "Now we are all free, *babaji*," she said.

All of us but one.

30

During the night, enemy campfires sprang up outside Fort Poondras, across the river. Staged in the greensward along the river and in the bazaar, in the alleyways and courtyards of the town they lit up in the thousands. Sahaj had come.

From the wall, Edmond estimated Sahaj might have fifteen or sixteen thousand, and perhaps many more not visible in the city warrens. Colonel Campbell stood nearby consulting with the headquarters staff and Major Shaw who was commanding the wall. Campbell had taken the precaution of putting the native infantry to posts away from the two gates, the town side and the seaward. Perhaps he doubted loyalties a bit more now that the rumors held that Sahaj had 50,000 fighters. The *sepoys* would fare worse than others in the coming battle and could expect no quarter. But Campbell's move was another blunder. By showing doubt, he only sowed dissatisfaction in the native infantry. So far they were handed out ammunition with the rest, but by their expressions, they knew they were being watched.

One stroke of good fortune was that a ship of the line had come into harbor yesterday, the *Suffolk,* having been summoned from Madras. Its guns now covered the shore, protecting the Bridge and the harbor.

Other than that, Edmond thought they had squandered every advantage. The sick should have been evacuated long before; now the seaward gate must be opened for them to remove to the newly commandeered hospital ships. But Campbell still delayed that move. It would look like he expected the infirmary would be in jeopardy. Edmond and Maruti could only commiserate with each other and hope for the best.

At dawn, the garrison could see the extent of them. The bazaar was a milling mass of warriors, packed like shot in a cannon basket. Their numbers bulged into the many side streets feeding into the bazaar, and down the King's Road as far as they could see. The light blue of Sahaj's army hardly dominated; here were tribesmen from the hills, villages, and even neighboring states. Campbell's face, as he took stock, showed nothing. But he stared out for a long time.

A few thousand warriors had begun to line up along the far bank of the river, where they had the best view of the fort. They stayed on the far side of the river, just out of range of the guns. Ominously, they knew where to stand, so someone had been able to precisely inform them the range of the cannon. But eventually they must come in range.

Soon the guards upon the wall knew why the enemy soldiers wanted a good view. It was to watch the first fire spears appear from heaven.

Powered by whatever holy men could be persuaded to the revolt, a hundred arrows burst from the sky and arced over the river to stream down upon the wall and the parade grounds. Immediately a fire broke out at the stables where fodder had been stacked. Bucket brigades were ready. They had known the local *sadhus* might use fire spears, a favorite weapon in internecine wars among the princes. The flaming lances came in waves, screaming overhead, trailing smoke and burning for a time even when come to ground. A pall of smoke soon drifted across the parade grounds, but little damage had been done.

Watching from the wall with Edmond, Maruti said, "It will exhaust them. They cannot send many more."

Edmond's King's Company had the south wall, but his men were itching to engage at the main gate. "Keep a sharp eye," he urged his sergeant. If they tried encirclement, he'd welcome it, the better to pick them off from a strong position. But Sahaj's forces remained formed up in front. He didn't like it. It was as though they were waiting for something.

The first inkling that the enemy had a plan was when the fire spears did not diminish, but increased their range and worse, sought out wooden structures. They rained upon the bungalows of Artillery Road, driving families out of the wooden structures, and forcing the Prince of Wales Company to set up tents against the seaward wall, presumably out of range. It began to feel as though the ragtag army was inflicting damage, though none of it did tactical harm. And still the army was out of range, and waited, watching, cheering each time a curtain of fire was conjured from the sky.

"Maruti," Edmond began, "how do you think they can keep it up?"

"Many *sadhus*, Captain. They have been collecting. But still, it is only smoke."

"Maybe they need the smoke." He looked down Military Road. The governor's house was not in range so far, but he had made up his mind. "Maruti, when the fort is full of smoke, they will make their move. It's time." He nodded in the direction of the residency. "Take them, Maruti. They can slip out the seaward gate now. Come back if you can, if you can get back through the gate. Otherwise…" He stopped, not sure what to say to the *jemadar*. They would win the day of course. Maruti would have honors, having already earned them several times over. But if it should come to a rout? Surely not. But if so… would Maruti go over the Bridge or stay?

"If it comes to the point," Edmond said, "I will find a place for you." In Anglica, he meant. It seemed best not to say it. But Maruti nodded. Their eyes met, then Maruti saluted briskly, and headed for the stairs.

The main gate became the focus of the conjurations. Edmond couldn't see the number of spears that now studded the gate, but judged it was many by the activity on the wall. The Grenadiers were ready with full cisterns and poured down streams of water, creating what sounded like roars of indignation from spears whose fiery lives were extinguished. Clouds of steam joined the smoke, creating a growing wall of white.

Out of this acrid curtain issued the unmistakable bellow of an elephant.

Then, impossibly, above the parapet appeared the tusks and trunk of a monstrous-sized elephant. It rose upon its hind legs and roared, sending the troops above the gate staggering in terror.

Corporal Brockie was already covered in grime from fire duty. The 3rd Company officer had sent him up to the bucket line at the stables. Half the company stayed at their post at the armory, ready to defend it against he knew not what. Word was, the native infantries would make a rush at it, but from what Brockie could see, the *sepoys* were working harder than anyone and had already taken initiative, as a precaution, to water down the roofs of the infirmary barracks.

Here at the stables he was among the first in his troop to see the monster elephant's head push up above the front gate. No elephant could be twenty feet high, or as broad as this. On the wall he heard yells of surprise and horror.

The soldier next to him dropped his pail of water—getting a shout from the officer—and got back into line. The fire was their job, and buckets got passed down the line, but everyone stared up at the gate. The lieutenant shouted orders to heave more water and faster. The fire was getting on toward gutting the stables and looked like it might jump to the ostrich pickets next. Horses ran loose. Upon seeing the elephant and hearing its thunderous roars, the animals charged off across the parade grounds crashing into units just now running up to support the gate.

"Illusion from the bush priests!" the lieutenant shouted at them, urging them on to fight the fire. "Not real! Swing your buckets!"

Filled with dread, Brockie put muscle into the chore. If the elephant weren't real, how could it trumpet? He knew a thing or two about magic and when a thing like that had teeth. Those poor blokes in the grass at Kopol got eaten sure enough, and by creatures God never made. The scene of that day—the tearing flesh, the limbs streaming blood—went round and round through his mind, even at night, even now.

Then, to their consternation, the elephant was inside. It erupted out of the smoke-charged air and roared fit to bring the walls down. Everyone was shouting, some screaming, as the bull charged anything that moved. It rammed tusks through soldiers on the wall, but left them alive, standing. Call it illusion, but you can still die of fright. Bedlam took over the wall as soldiers fled the gate and the cisterns.

Brockie's unit stayed on the fire line as the lieutenant shouted "Illusion! Hold ground!" and brandished a pistol to put iron in their resolve.

Edmond rushed his troops along the sentry walk into the gap above the gate. Sending his men in, he paused to lean through the embrasure to look at the front gate. Bales of combustibles had been brought forward under cover of smoke and were now blazing against the gates. Heavy though the gates were, they could not burn for hours, and the *sadhu* fire did not douse easily. He saw that the main cistern was abandoned, and he dashed down the wall to take control of it. Abandoned hoses sprayed water uselessly inside the compound.

Major Shaw had by now managed to direct his rifles away from the ghost elephant and had formed up his unit to aim a blizzard of fire through the loopholes against the enemy dragging firewood to the gate.

"Grab the nozzles!" Edmond shouted, as he directed one out a downward-facing loophole. Shaw dashed forward, hauling the water tubes and handing them off to men for directing through the embrasure at the outside of the gate. It was too late.

"Gate breached!" came the yell from below as black smoke gushed up from the inside of the gate.

Edmond saw that a unit of *sepoys* were dragging carts laden with sandbags toward the gate. He relinquished the hose to a Grenadier and was about to rush below to help when an exultant yell burst from the enemy, now thick on the grounds before the fort. Two normal-sized elephants approached, harnessed together and bearing an enormous log between them. A battering ram. He drew a sharp breath.

"King's Company!" he shouted. "Kill the mahouts. Stop them!"

He took careful aim with his rifle and one of the mahouts toppled, only to be replaced by one of a dozen who rode the back of the elephant. He turned to Major Shaw, whose white-blonde hair was begrimed with black powder.

"The cannon, sir," Edmond said. "If the gate goes down…"

"I'm ready to spike them, Captain. Take your men and fall back to the church. It won't burn and makes a good rallying point. Hold it at all cost. Send reinforcements down to the bungalows. Evacuate the women and children to the ships."

"Request to put the order in writing, sir."

"Which one, for Christ's sake?"

"The evacuation." He held out his field notebook and Shaw scrawled the order.

Edmond glanced through the nearest embrasure. Outside, the smoke cleared just enough for a clear view of the decimated Sita turret and covered wagon in the field next to the bridge.

Shaw thrust the scrap of paper into Edmond's hand, and waved him on.

Rushing to the stairs, Edmond called out ten men to follow him. As they ran past the gates, they heard the ram crashing against the wood. A hinge burst like a ripe seed pod. They tore across the parade grounds and past headquarters with its brave flag post and on down the road to the civilian lines.

At the intersection with Artillery and Church Roads, Edmond sent his orderly with the rest of the unit down to the bungalows to evacuate the women and children. Pray God the families were ready to go, but if not, his orderly was to force them to move without delay. Seeing them off, he sprinted across to St. Mary's church, its white-washed walls and tall spire now wreathed in gun smoke.

Tait was never so glad to see anything in his life, as when Captain Muir-Smith strode into the nave. Now they were saved, he felt. The church walls were thick and they had a store of food on the second floor, so the enemy could never starve them out.

The patients had already smashed out the lower panes of the tall windows and manned them with their best rifles, waiting for the onslaught they felt sure was coming. Seeing that he was now the ranking officer, Captain Muir-Smith began reordering the church, with the men who could not stand transferred to the altar, and beds dragged against the windows for better cover. Outside, on Church Road, Tait saw the evacuation of the pox barracks underway, with a sorry troop of bastards hobbling and carried on stretchers by men with faces wrapped against breathing their air.

Muir-Smith walked over to Tait's window, peering out into the compound where for now the shouts of units and the movement of troops had quieted.

"Sir, the gates. Still holding?" Tait asked, voice low, in case the answer was bad.

"I don't know. We'll take them if they come, though, Private."

"Yes sir." He was glad to have a rifle in his hands again, even if, with his head wound, things looked a little blurry. "Pardon sir, but 'av you seen Brockie? He never been the same since the *pishachas*."

The captain looked at him with a terrible frown, just staring, mute-like. He turned away and slapped his thigh with a sharp crack. "Damn me for a blighted fool."

He called for Corporal Bledsoe. "Corporal, go back to the wall. Tell Major Shaw or whoever's in charge to do whatever they must to destroy the covered wagon across the river. It's jammed with *sadhus* and they're going to do worse than that phantom elephant. They've got big magic in mind, I'm sure of it."

"*Sadhus*, sir?"

"Tell him, *sadhus*. They're cutting themselves for power, that's why they wanted to be near the gate. Now run, Corporal."

The corporal dashed off, and Muir-Smith paced, muttering.

Tait retied his head bandage that kept creeping down his forehead. He strained to see out the window, watching for big magic, and wondering what worse the bush priests could do.

Muir-Smith sat down on an unused bed. He looked like he hadn't slept in days. His uniform was streaked with soot, and his eyes peered out of a face dark with grime.

Tait inched over to him and murmured, "Begging your pardon, sir, but I thought you might want to know." Getting a nod, he went on, "We seen the colonel's wife and her daughter going on down the road an hour before. They was with a few others and a *jemadar*. Any luck, they'll be on board a ship by now, sir.

The captain looked up at him and his lip twitched, not quite making a smile. "Thank you. The surgeon said you're to go, now, Private. You can't see to shoot."

"But he don't know, sir! He ain't in my head, is he?" He straightened the bandage around his forehead, trying to put himself in order.

The captain gestured at the long line of evacuees parading by outside. "Go lend a hand with a stretcher, Private."

Tait stood at attention. "Permission to speak, Captain." He got a nod. "Sir, it's true things look wobbly, but I'm a better shot than half this lot in here. So it makes up for it, in a manner of speaking, sir, if you see what I mean. And I promised Brockie I'd wait for 'im, if we fell back to the barracks like we have."

The captain chewed on his lip. "All right, Tait." As Tait slipped gratefully back to his window, Muir-Smith said, "Don't waste ammunition. Right between the eyes or don't shoot."

A tumultuous din of shouting and the sharp crackle of arms fire came from the parade grounds. They were through the gate. They were pouring in. Whatever chance they'd had to take out the wagon was surely lost.

∽◦

Thunderous explosions from the wall came in sequence. And then silence. The cannon, spiked.

Until that moment, Colonel Campbell hadn't believed the invaders could penetrate the wall. He and his staff still occupied the headquarters building, a low building with mud walls and too many windows. But now that it had come to a breach, the soldier in him took hold. By God, they'd make a hole in the bloody mass of insurgents.

His orderly handed him his rifle, and Campbell knocked out a window as turbaned warriors came streaking down on them. In prior days he'd been the best sharpshooter in the brigade. His rounds took their targets down, with his orderly passing him a loaded rifle as fast he could empty one. The verandah was filled with screaming fanatics, throwing themselves at the windows, trying to punch through. Major Lowe knocked against him, shot through the throat, eyes bulging as he suffocated.

Still, he had a better end than the rest of them. The furious scuffling on the roof soon revealed they'd started a fire. Now the doors were barred, and the enemy soldiers stepped back, milling. Campbell started counting his kills: fourteen, twenty-six... His orderly fell dead beside him. When everyone was gone and the building filled with smoke, he drew his pistol and shot himself in the mouth.

He hadn't noticed the shadow that fell across the verandah, nor heard the raucous cry overhead.

∽

Elizabeth faced off with the *Richmond's* captain. "These decks must be cleared for the wounded."

"Don't see any wounded, missus. And it's my cargo. Destined for Plymouth, aye. We've barely got room for you women as it is."

Elizabeth swung around in bewilderment. The holds, the decks, all were stuffed with bales of raw cotton.

She managed to get to Mrs. Harding before she went below decks. "Mrs. Harding! Pray convince Captain Rawls that we must take on the sick. They can at least lie on the deck!"

Mrs. Harding's eyes widened. "With small pox? But they must go on the other ships! And they are not even coming yet." She looked toward the fort, its stacking cloud of smoke now smearing out on the horizon.

"But they shall, now the attack has come."

Mrs. Harding looked unconvinced. Booms thundered in the distance, cannons firing at last? Elizabeth, barely upright, ran to the rail. "Maruti!"

He was just walking down the pier, but he came back at her call.

"Maruti, where are the evacuees from the wards?"

He pointed to the seaward gate, where just now the first of the wounded were sheparded through by hospital assistants and a few soldiers in uniform. They poured onto the beach and headed for the quay.

"Maruti, tell the soldiers to bring some of them to the *Richmond.* There's no time to waste!" Behind her, the captain was cursing and shouting out his own orders to Maruti, who nevertheless strode off to help the evacuees.

The three other ships were already loading patients, but with the river of patients now pouring out of the gates, it was clear they would soon be overwhelmed.

"We can't be a plague ship!" Captain Rawls protested. "They won't let us dock anywhere in Anglica."

Elizabeth rounded on him, suddenly freshened by anger. "And you won't be able to sell cotton with small pox clinging to it, either, will you? Well, since you shall not, then make room on the deck!" She hailed a strong-looking sailor and ordered him to throw a bale of cotton over the side. He looked at her like she was raving. He made no move.

Now Maruti was coming down the pier, leading a line of men, the sick and the wounded. Elizabeth rushed down the gangplank. "You must take command, Maruti. Make him see reason. The fort is burning up, is it not?"

Captain Rawls raised his pistol and, cocking it, trained it upon Maruti. "I'll not be letting a black mutineer tell me how to run my ship."

Down the pier, a half-dozen soldiers kneeled to train their rifle sites on Rawls. The surgeon, Major Ames, covered in blood but still wearing his insignia, said, "Stand aside, sir, or my men will shoot."

Rawls holstered his gun and stood by, glaring, as Elizabeth hurried Maruti up to the deck. There, Maruti heaved over the first bale of cotton. Soldiers from the hospital joined him, crashing crates and bales over the sides and splashing them into the bay.

From farther out in the harbor the *Suffolk's* guns boomed.

"Who are they shooting at?" Elizabeth asked Maruti.

"*Sahiba*, they have no target, but they mean to show they command the harbor."

Elizabeth looked around her. The evacuation was a barely controlled race to the ships. Fire jumped into the sky from the center of fort, showing that the battle was engaged very deep into the garrison. The Bridge lay upon a quiescent ocean, barely rippling, a tether to home.

Maruti worked furiously to rid the deck of its cargo as Mrs. Harding, and now Jessa, rushed to bring water to the sick where they lay on the bare wood deck.

Elizabeth braced herself against a mast and tried to keep her stomach. The nausea passed. When she looked up, the soldiers were marching back up the pier, and Maruti was moving down the gangplank.

She managed to hurry down to him. "Maruti." His clothes were covered in ash so that she could hardly see the brown of his uniform.

"Maruti. We have need of a soldier on board. We cannot be under Captain Rawls, for he is against us. Against the patients. And it is a long trip home."

"You will be in no danger, *sahiba*. The colonel *sahib's* wife will be keeping him in order."

She expelled a frustrated breath. "I'm saying you may come with us, Maruti."

Just then, the seaward gate slammed shut with a distant crack. The few soldiers on the wall had perhaps not liked opening them up at all.

Maruti stared at the gate, his face hardening.

"Please." She put a hand on his arm, acutely aware that she must not. But she left it there. "Come with us."

"That, *sahiba*, I cannot do."

When a man like that said he could not, he could not.

"What, then?"

"This is my home." She had not thought of it in that light. The battle would be won or lost, but this was still his country.

He touched his forehead in a gesture of respect, and walked away.

Mrs. Harding was waiting for her on the deck. "We must get you off your feet."

Before they went below, Elizabeth took a last look at Fort Poondras, and the great Bridge, its span rocking gently on the surf. Her thoughts were of Astoria and Edmond; she could hardly bear to leave them behind, but it was not hers to decide. Her gaze went for the last time to the Bridge. She did not think that she would come back. There were children who needed her in Anglica, she liked to think. And she might have some new lessons for them.

Her thoughts turned to home.

31

Despite the brutal exchange of fire, Brockie peeked over the up-turned wagon and watched, sickened, as the *pishacha* flew low over the parade ground, dragging its awful stick-like legs. It could pick up a soldier and drag him anyway, eating him like he was nothing more than a slab of mutton.

"Illusion," the bloke next to him muttered, but Brockie knew better. Some magic could kill. He hadn't thought to shoot at the bird when it went over, but wished to heaven he had.

"Volley firing!" the lieutenant called. "Ready. Present." A dozen tribesmen fell.

So far enemy fire had done little damage to those behind the barricade 3rd Company had formed in front of the armory. The enemy was firing from behind salvaged bales of fodder, but were coming off the worse for their poor cover. But as they continued to pour into the fort, their ranks seemed inexhaustible.

Across the parade grounds the headquarters building continued to burn itself out. The old man was done for, and the monkeys were already tearing down the flag on the post.

The enemy was still streaming through the gates and the ragged hole in the wall where the guns blew up. Hundreds of invaders lay slaughtered near the bastions. They had been trying to take the cannons and got a surprise when the cannons took *them*.

Five hundred men crowded behind the barricade and inside the armory, where soldiers handed out loaded guns and took back empty ones. It seemed like they could keep fighting until doomsday. But all Brockie could think of was, *the pishacha will come for us.* He didn't want to be a coward. He could face the *tulwars* and the heathens, but those death birds… He wasn't a slab of mutton, was he?

Captain Muir-Smith said he'd proved himself at Chidiwal. Brockie fired again, killing a maddened tribesman trying to rush the barricade. The shot went home. No coward, he exulted. But then he watched the sky for the *pishacha* to return.

⌒⊃

St. Mary's Church was originally built in 1630, and had three features of military consequence. It had thick masonry walls, narrow windows perfect for defense, and a spire with belfry allowing a territorial view. By two o'clock in the afternoon, it was packed with soldiers who had been falling back as the garrison's fortunes worsened.

Major Shaw had come in at noon, miraculously having survived the breeching of the wall. With him, a platoon of men. Word spread briskly then, of a *pishacha* swooping through the garrison, grabbing victims and taking them to the walls to tear apart.

After inspecting Edmond's defensive arrangements, Shaw asked him to climb with him to the belfry. From there they noted the battle at the armory, coming to their ears as a ferocious barrage, but distant, muffled by the trees shading Church Road.

The parade grounds were a mass of shouting warriors, now spreading out into the fort. In the harbor, *The Suffolk* stood out to sea, helpless. *The Richmond* and the other two merchant ships were still at the quay, no doubt prepared to weigh anchor at the first provocation. So far the invaders had not gone around to the shore.

"Edmond," Shaw said, "I'm sending you down to the bungalows. A special assignment." He paused, looking in the direction of Artillery Road. "My wife and Colonel Campbell's wife are still down there."

Edmond shook his head. "We evacuated them two hours ago, sir. I sent my orderly and a unit of men to lead them out."

"God help me," Shaw said. "I didn't think to tell you back on the wall, but I think they might have hidden."

"Hidden, sir?" He felt sure the soldiers would have rousted everyone out.

"There's a storage cellar in the Campbell garden. I told my wife, if things got bad, to go there and take Francine with her—Colonel Campbell's wife. To wait it out." He nodded as understanding dawned on Edmond's face. "They won't have heard the soldiers evacuating. They'll still be there."

"They might be safer in a cellar, Major."

"That's only if we keep the citadel. Edmond, do you think that likely?"

Shaw gazed out on the chaos of the burning fort.

"No sir." It was bitter to admit defeat. Weren't reinforcements coming from Bangalore? But when they came, it would be days too late.

"Best to go alone. And go now."

As they descended the stairs, Shaw stopped and faced him. "One more thing. Once they're out, stay out."

"Begging your pardon, sir. Permission to return."

"Permission denied. Someone needs to survive. To say what happened here."

"Sir. I promised Colonel Harding's wife that I would wait for her daughter."

"Wait for her? Is she going to come walking home through the jungle?" Shaw looked at him, sizing up what *wait for her* might mean. "I'm sorry, Captain. But she's not coming back. Not until that lunatic prince extracts his ransom. When we come back over the Bridge, we'll put things to rights."

At the nave, Edmond saluted. "Good luck, sir."

Shaw returned the salute. "Time for a bit of that, isn't it?"

Next to Brockie, behind a dead horse, Travers took a bullet in the temple. One moment they'd been talking about taking revenge for Colonel Campbell's being burned alive, and the next, Travers was dead.

The *pishacha* watched the armory from a perch over the ruined gate, screeching, laughing at Travers' death, the unholy monster.

Brockie crouched and started to pull Travers away, but the lieutenant said no, from now on the bodies would be piled up to form part of the barricade. That got some bad looks all around. Brockie didn't think he could do it, lean on the body like it was a sack of grain. He was still warm! But the sergeant-major helped him make a stack, and talked him through it, saying how the lads would want to help still, anything to win the day. They'd been fighting since dawn, and now at dusk, everyone was worn out, desperate for water. If they didn't get some soon, it'd be over. Maybe it was over already. The enemy had devised a wagon with a wood wall facing forward, and were advancing, finally able to get close enough and high enough to kill in earnest.

A barrage of fire from the armory made no difference. On came the wagon. The tribesmen were firing through holes in the wood panel, while behind, a dozen of them pushed the cart forward.

From down the line of the barricade, a few of the boys darted out and came around the wagon shooting their pistols at point blank range. They went down, but soon another sortie followed, all mowed down, but not before the wagon was brought to a halt. Brockie was sickened that the men had died just to stop a wagon, but then someone behind him said the wagon was full of explosives and would be touched off as soon as it got near.

The *pishacha* squawked every time an Anglic soldier went down, sometimes flapping its wings in excitement. Then it lifted its wings and floated down to sink its talons in a red uniform.

"It's just magic," someone shouted to keep their spirits up. "Not real!" But Brockie knew the truth. The demon bird needed to feed.

Brockie stood up. A few soldiers looked at him like he was crazy. The barricade wasn't that high, but he went past them, discarding his rifle and drawing his pistol. Calmly—he had never been so calm—he walked to the end of the barricade and went out the gap the sorties had used. Heedless of the musket balls flying about him, he approached the *pishacha* which had just plunged its beak into the breast of a red uniform.

He walked closer, until he could see the phlegm dripping from the creature's round yellow eyes. The *pishacha's* breast was covered in blood, with a length of intestines somehow stuck at its throat.

Brockie strode forward until he could not miss, and as the *pishacha* shifted to note his advance, shot him square in the left eyeball. The demon opened its mouth and shrieked, blasting Brockie with a foul emanation. He sent his next shot straight down the creature's gullet. From the barricade came a spontaneous roar of joy.

The monster shook and lurched. And collapsed into the dust. The astonished enemy horde stared at the dead *pishacha* for a frozen instant.

Then Brockie felt the back of his head come off. It hurt like the very devil. But thankfully someone had shot him from the barricade. He fell forward moments before the mob descended, *tulwars* raised.

Sahaj watched this from the back of his war elephant, where he had just entered the ruined gate. He screamed revenge, and the tribesmen rushed at the wagon, pushing it the last yards to the barricade, lighting the fuses.

When the explosion came, it threw shards of wood and bone in every direction for hundreds of paces, killing his men, but also destroying the barricade and the front doors of the armory.

An exuberant yell burst from the tribesmen, and they rushed the armory.

Edmond lifted the trap door of the cellar a few inches. Though dusk strengthened the garden shadows, he heard tribesmen still shouting to each other in the streets and from second story windows of the bungalows, from which they threw the hated artifacts of Anglica: children's toys, boots, and chamber pots.

Earlier, as Edmond had crept down through the back yards of the civil lines, he'd seen the thoroughly looted bungalows, yards littered with broken furniture, pillows and garments scattered across the marigold beds. It had taken two hours to make his way, hiding as groups of enemy soldiers searched the homes for civilians and weapons.

As Major Shaw had feared, his wife and Mrs. Campbell had not been evacuated earlier in the day, but had taken refuge in the garden cellar. It had taken some persuading to get them to unlock the door to admit him. He judged the residential area too dangerous to leave, and joined them in their hideaway. They begged for news of their husbands, which Edmond relayed, vaguely in the case of Mrs. Shaw, but for Colonel Campbell's wife, he knew the end.

As he spoke, she had put a hand to her stout chest as though to protect her heart.

"Mrs. Campbell, I'm very sorry. Your husband died gallantly at the headquarters building along with all of his staff."

Her voice went pinched and high. "He is gone, Captain? My Lawrence is gone?"

Mrs. Shaw took her arm. "Oh, Francine," she murmured.

With visible effort, Mrs. Campbell held herself together. "He never looked to have the fort," she murmured. "It was to be his last posting. He'd say goodbye to his old brigade... and then Colonel Harding..." She couldn't finish.

"He did his best for us. A very brave man."

They doused their lamp to save fuel. Sitting in the dark for some time, Mrs. Campbell finally whispered, "We shall come back, you know. They cannot prevail against Anglica."

"Yes, ma'am," he murmured. It could not be tolerated, this abject defeat. Over the Bridge would come more armies, better armed. And this time there would be no durbars, or books or exchange of visits. As soon as *The Suffolk* sped home with the news, the Anglic lion would roar. It gave him some satisfaction, he had to admit.

Deep in the night the calls of the soldiers and the crashings from the bungalows subsided. Edmond could not completely trust that no tribesmen roamed in the neighborhood; but from the battle still resounding at the church, he thought they might rather be where the action was.

"Can we not leave now, Captain?" Mrs. Shaw pleaded. In the flicker from the lantern, she looked frail as a fawn. Dressed in an unfortunate cream-colored dress, she would be easy to spot as they crept through the bushes.

"Soon." He would leave the door ajar now and listen.

When, twenty minutes later, he heard a concussive explosion, he greatly wondered. Was it the church? Soon a rush of enemy soldiers streaked down Artillery Road toward the east wall.

Clearly, they could not risk leaving now. He let the door close above him. What had exploded, and at whose hands? He pushed back the spike of hope that reinforcements had arrived. If they had not, it was too cruel to raise the women's hopes, or his own.

They cowered together in the hole, hearing the muffled cries of soldiers in the neighborhood.

∽

When Sahaj heard the explosion, he left off his viewing of the siege of the white shrine. It was becoming tiresome. The cowards fired at will through narrow windows, and only when his men succeeded in hurling a flaming bomb through a gap did his army slay any within. The enemy allowed his men to carry off the dead and wounded within their rifle range. By granting this mercy they flaunted their power, and perhaps hoped they might have mercy in return. That was not his plan.

From the cushioned chair of the howdah, he bid his *mahout* take him to the wall. Eager to move away from the gunfire, his elephant took him placidly past the graveyard, past a garden with an open-sided viewing stand and then among the tidy houses of the *memsahibs* with their verandahs and chairs that went to and fro on bent legs.

He wished very much to meet an Anglic soldier and challenge him to a fight, for he had not yet met a white man in combat. Perhaps it was best that a *rana* did not. But he was restless. When, led by his men, he got to the great wall of the fortress, he saw what the explosion had been. He did not know whether to be angry or rejoice. The Anglics had demolished their own fortress door. Why they would do this, he did not know. Thirty of his guards, posted there after the fort fell, lay dead in the wreck of the door and surrounding wall.

His men picked through the damage, searching for the vandals. They beat through the undergrowth near the wall and spread out toward the foreigners' houses.

"Find them!" Sahaj shouted. They would die slowly, these Anglics who damaged his fort.

A runner came to him, abasing himself. His personal soldiers crowded around and by their faces, he surmised they had already heard some large news.

Sahaj lifted his hand in permission, and the kneeling servant blurted out how, may the *rana's* glory live forever, the body of Mahindra had disappeared from the waste ground at Kathore.

Fury swept him. He managed to keep his face serene. It had always worked well for Mahindra, who commanded respect by never letting one see his true thoughts. "Animals have consumed him," he proclaimed.

The servant looked terrified, and it annoyed him. His voice rose. "Is it not so?""Yes, majesty! Animals! And..." The runner thought better of the utterance. His forehead touched the ground again.

"And? And? What more can be said?"

"Highness, the animals left a length of red cloth under a rock."

Red for holiness. Someone had defied him. Rage filled his chest, banishing logical thought. His men picked up the messenger, brushing him off, crowding around. They looked up in joy at Sahaj thinking that this event blessed their fortunes. When they saw his fury, they closed their faces, but Sahaj knew the damage had been done.

They did not know that Mahindra was against their victory here, that he had intended to preach like a woman, for mercy. Now they would think of the *sadhu* as having been blessed by the gods, who took him up whole, without need of cremation.

"Animals cannot lift rocks," Sahaj said, his voice quaking in anger.

The runner turned to him. It was always best to agree with a king, and he said, "Yes, Highness!" Some of his men raised their muskets in premature celebration.

Sahaj leaned forward. "Someone has stolen the body, you fools! No more talk of cloth! The body is gone. We have enemies among us." Let them spread *that* rumor.

He ordered his *mahout* onward. As he sat, very still and straight, he felt stares raking his back. They loved their gods. Mahindra had always said so. Why had Mahindra turned against him? Had the *sadhu* not urged his princely father on toward bloodshed? He had wanted all of Bharata in one kingdom; denied this foolish dream, he had recklessly decided to forgo all. Sahaj slunk down in his chair, resentful and perplexed.

Being *rana* had more knots and twists than he had thought.

32

The fort smoldered into the night. From the back of her elephant, and high on the hill overlooking Poondras harbor, Tori tried to absorb the calamity of what had happened at the fort. Dulal, acting as her *mahout*, remained silent. During their long journey from Kathore, she had ridden behind him on the elephant's neck, arms wrapped around his waist, her head often dropping onto his shoulder as she fell in and out of sleep. Her rupees had easily paid for the better mount, and Dulal had driven a hard bargain, determined that his mistress would not suffer the indignity of riding an ostrich.

From her viewing point a mile to the south of the fort she could faintly see the lights of ships in the harbor; thank God there were some. From the fort, she heard distant gunfire, and something else: the low gong of a bell.

If she were not imagining it. There were degrees of reality, she knew. She had seen other nows, and they hadn't revealed things useful to the study of natural history. But in his diary, Sir Charles had surmised that the visions might focus on things most present in one's mind. If the worlds were never-ending, then somewhere was just the one that pertained. This made the gift of the lotus a game of chance, as to whether a vision were useful or not. A roll of the dice. It might be so, but she had begun to think that the gods weren't so capricious. Perhaps our very worship of them had bound them to us, so that they must take part in our suffering. Perhaps they wished for us to see our desires and know that what we already have is good enough.

Because sometimes, she knew, it had to be.

Gong, gong, gong. So very faint across the palm tree tops, almost submerged under the constant puffs of guns. And then she knew. It was the church bell. It was the call of retreat. Three rings, a beat, and three again. They were holed up in the church. And any who were not must get to the ships. Gong, gong, gong. Were all the buglers dead? How singular it was, how unbearably sad, to think so.

As though in answer, came the discharge from a warship. A puff of smoke showed where its cannon had fired. Had it a target, or was it saying, *to me, to me, I am waiting?*

"What now, *mataji?*" Dulal asked.

"Can you not call me Astoria?"

He did not look behind, but slowly shook his head.

She sighed. If they were to keep the pretense going, she must be a holy woman. It was not clear to her whether Dulal was in fact pretending. But in any case, if she was to be a *sadhvi*, she would have to work on the role. Her life depended on it. She had begun with renouncing wealth, for, after the purchase of the elephant, they had given away all the rupees left over to villagers along the way. She had had no idea that papa had given her so much money.

"Down to the Bridge, please," she answered him at last. She couldn't see the Bridge, for it blended into the ocean like a tiger in the grass. At the place where it sank its pylons into the shore, she would say goodbye.

"I will not wear a dead man's clothes," the major's wife repeated in the gloaming pre-dawn.

Edmond held a ragged kurta shirt, only slightly stained with blood from the body lying at the foot of the wall. It was black, and would partially hide the cream-colored dress. But she refused.

He muttered, "Then we may all die in our good clothes, Mrs. Shaw."

Crouching by the shattered gates of the fort, Edmond strained to see out to the bay. The thick fog hid the Bridge and the lights of any ships that still waited.

"Once we leave the shadow of the wall we will run," Edmond told them. "No matter what you hear or what happens, we must get to the dock. No matter what. If I fall, you must still run, do you understand?" Could the enemy see well enough to fire from the walls? He hoped that they hadn't bothered to man the walls since the fort was all but theirs. It had been quiet the last hour, with no gunfire coming from the church—not necessarily a good sign.

Mrs. Campbell said, "We shall run, do not doubt, Captain. And you, my dear, shall wear the shirt." In the dark, her voice brooked no dissent. Soon the garment was taken from his hands and Mrs. Shaw blended into the night.

By the time they reached the dock, it might be light enough for the ship crews to see them. Of course, the enemy would see them, too. But at dawn, they would be exposed no matter where they were. It was time to make their dash.

He gathered them on either side of him. The quay was some five hundred yards across the pebbled shore.

Then they were rushing down the sloping beach, Edmond curtailing his stride for Mrs. Shaw, and Mrs. Campbell trotting gamely at his side, soon huffing with the effort of running upon sand and stones.

The world was gray upon gray. Swirling mists united the sea and land in one vast ether. He firmly held the women's elbows, practically dragging them onward. The cold seared their throats, the salt mist blasted their faces. It seemed they made no progress as their feet sank down, pushing against the clattering pebbles.

Now Edmond could see that the dock had no ships. Christ God, had they left? But in another moment amid the blowing fog he saw the winking running lights of a ship. Ships stood off in the harbor. Would their crews see them?

Down went Mrs. Campbell, crashing onto her knees and then her ample bosom.

"Go, go!" Edmond whispered hoarsely at Mrs. Shaw, pushing her toward the quay. "Go to the end of the dock!"

"But…"

"Now, by God!" he snarled. He kneeled by Mrs. Campbell as Mrs. Shaw stumbled away.

Dawn began to color the fog. Its grays went to dull white. Down toward the Bridge, the ocean breeze tattered the fog for an instant, showing the broad road lifting and falling, a life raft upon the sea.

"Can you stand?" he asked Mrs. Campbell.

"My ankle," she moaned, trying and failing to rise.

"Bravely, now. Your hand around my waist." He began hauling her up.

Down the quay, Mrs. Shaw was waving wildly at the ship. And from the Bridge, someone was coming toward them down the beach.

Edmond drew his pistol.

A woman dressed in dull orange was rushing toward them. Her sari was a patch of livid color in the whiteout. The sari came off her head, her hair whipped around her face.

Still, he must get Mrs. Campbell to the dock. "Mrs. Campbell! Can you walk?"

"No, it is broken!"

He looked back at the approaching figure, taking aim. But as the woman in the saffron dress came closer, he drew a breath between clenched teeth. His heart hammered on his ribs. It could not be. It was.

"Tori," he whispered. "Oh God, Tori."

"I'm alive Edmond. I lived! And you!" Tears streamed down her face. "And you."

He abandoned Mrs. Campbell standing on her one good foot, and staggered forward, holstering his gun. They went into each other's arms, Tori sobbing against him for a moment, and he clinging to her with a stunned relief.

Then he held her at arms' length, taking in her face, the beauty of her skin in a saffron color that drained the Anglic from her, making her Bharati in a disturbing and compelling way. She was back. He had not realized until that moment that he secretly feared her dead.

But there was not a moment to lose. He took her arm. "We must get to the ship. They may be watching from the walls." But she stepped away, looking to the fort. He wondered if she had been released to lure them back; if the enemy had some devilish plan for her.

Mrs. Campbell exclaimed from behind. "Heaven above, is this Astoria Harding? You poor girl!"

"Tori, help Mrs. Campbell. She cannot walk."

The dawn came on, relentlessly lighting the shore. Tori said, "I'm not going with you, Edmond. I can't."

He could scarcely breathe. What was she saying? "Your mother and sister are waiting. You must come, Tori."

Was she running from him? The thought struck with lacerating pain. "Even if you don't want me, come with us. Be free, but come to the ship!" He stepped toward her again, this time taking her firmly by the arm. His grip was rather too hard, but he had the sense that she was about to fall away from him forever.

"Edmond. We cannot be together. I don't belong in Anglica. Not anymore, not after all that we have done."

At this, Mrs. Campbell, who had been watching this exchange with astonishment,

said, "That *we* have done! Gather your wits and your pride, girl. What can you be thinking!"

"You can't mean that," Edmond said more gently. "What you've been through would test the ablest soldier, but it will all be well. It will be put right." He looked wildly toward the fort, seeing with relief in the thinning fog that no one was upon the walls.

"I cannot be a soldier's wife. I cannot be a wife at all."

Edmond pulled her closer, whispering, "Then do not marry. I swear I will never ask again." And he would not. She was lost, lost. But yet, she must live.

Mrs. Campbell could bear no more. "She's hysterical, Captain! Do not listen. You must force her to come, or we shall all be murdered on this wretched shore."

"If we had not come to conquer, we would not be dying," Tori said, glancing at her.

Mrs. Campbell sharply drew a breath. "May God forgive you. And for your father's sake!"

Edmond still held Tori's arm. He searched her eyes for some proof that she was not hysterical, that she spoke a truth that he could accept. "Can you mean to say that it is all wrong? Everything that we have done and brought here? Can you believe that?"

She brought her hand to his face, touching his cheek. "You see how it is with me. I have taken off the collar. God help me, Edmond, I choose to be free."

"What collar," he asked. "What collar?"

"The one with the leash."

A dinghy came on toward the quay, furious oars slapping the water. The sun peeked over the tree-lined beach, hitting the Bridge, lighting up its gate, moving down the segments of the great road, showing the path they might have walked.

Tori knew that Edmond must go now. The ships were waiting. She had kept him too long.

"If it were a different life," she said, "I would be yours. If we were free to be together but also apart, to share some things but not others..." She thought of the golden lotus and how his superiors would hound them for what she knew, and how she must lie to him and say she knew nothing. And yet, beyond that, the whole truth was simply that she did not wish to marry. And she did not wish to return.

Edmond still held her but she felt his grip easing.

On the fort wall, a soldier was leaning out an embrasure. They had been seen.

"By Christ, they will kill you," Edmond whispered harshly.

Now there were a dozen soldiers looking out.

"They won't kill me." Pulling her sari aside, she lifted her left foot to show him. "They healed me." She didn't have time to tell him the story, so a simple phrase must do.

At the end of the dock a woman was shouting frantically. The dinghy had tied up to the pier and sailors were taking the woman in hand. Another shot rang out from the wall, falling short again.

At last he released her and put his arm around the injured woman's waist. He still held her gaze. "Has Sahaj released you, then?"

"In a way, yes. And I have friends protecting me."

"Friends," he said, looking bewildered. Then his voice came from deep in his throat. "Shall you be happy, Tori? May I be sure?"

"Yes, I promise. And you too, Edmond, find happiness. I will pray for it."

Edmond tore his gaze from her, and resolutely put his arm around the matron's waist. Bullets flew, but still he hesitated.

Thank God for Mrs. Campbell, Tori thought. He would not have gone if this woman did not require saving.

Then, without meeting Tori's eyes again, he turned, and led the woman away.

In the harbor Tori saw a warship bringing its guns to bear upon the wall. And at the same time, a commotion at the fort's gate, as a large wagon draped with tapestries was dragged into view.

The sunrise cooked away the last of the fog. In the bright morning, Tori saw coming down the beach, an elephant with an old man on his neck. Dulal had not left as he had promised, but had come back for her.

Hundreds of soldiers now crowded along the parapet, all of them watching the elephant. They stopped firing at the dock, for Edmond had joined the women in the boat, now well out of range.

When Dulal was finally close enough to speak to her, he said, "Try to climb up when she is raising her leg. I will help you. It will impress the soldiers."

At his command, the elephant raised a knee, and Tori scrambled onto it, using her healed foot for leverage. As she balanced there, Dulal's hand came down, and he hauled her toward him. With his help, she flattened herself against the elephant's flank and crawled to the top.

A few men on the wall laughed. Someone else cheered—a soldier in the blue and white of Kathore, one who knew her story.

When Sahaj climbed the stairs to the wall, soldiers rushed to make room for him. He had promised them a great display at dawn, and they had been gathering along the wall in expectation.

The Anglic shrine that had withstood them through the previous day and most of the night now lay in ruins, finally brought down by massive stores of gunpowder from the armory. Within, one man survived the assault and stood on a raised platform in the back of the shrine, ready to fight them with a saber. By his uniform, he was a private, crowned with a white bandage around his head.

Standing on the wall now, Sahaj turned to his men who held the man in custody, and nodded his consent. They sent him out the toppled gate. Like a man asleep, he walked down to the shore, still carrying his sword as though the enemy might still like a good fight. The men wanted to reward him for bravery and Sahaj had suppressed his disappointment that the man should not be brought to pain. He was learning that what one's soldiers wanted had some importance. They loved him for this mercy. Still, as he watched the Anglic soldier stagger down to the dock, his hand fingered his rifle.

His gaze traveled to the woman on the elephant. Wearing the colors of renunciation, she was some distance down the shore from the fort, her back to him as her elephant made for the forest. It did not take long guessing to think who this was. His men had seen her, and let her go. He might allow this for now. Where could she go where she would not be under his watch? He could pluck her like a flower whenever he wished. But she was of no consequence now.

Ominously, the big ship had swung around to present its broadside. As he knew it would, it held its fire as note was taken of the last man to leave the fort.

From one of the other ships, a dinghy set out to retrieve the private.

In the time it would take, the *sadhus* must finish their work.

To outward appearance, the Bridge looked the same as yesterday and the day before, but it was not. His renunciates, culled from across Nanpura, had been performing their *tapas* with great rigor. They had begun gathering from the day the regiments arrived at Poondras and the great jaguar appeared in the sky. They had sent *pishachas* to kill the school teacher and the Harding girl on their way to Kathore. Some of these things they should not have done, but his father was not the only one who hated the Anglics. Now these same ascetics were pleased to follow Sahaj's judgment:

Bring down the Bridge. Bring it down across the sea forever. Make it fall at each end and let mother ocean suck it down into herself. Let Bharata and Anglica remain separate, or let travelers suffer a long voyage. And if they come, let them ask permission.

Blood dripped from the floorboards of the wagon.

Soldiers shouted and pointed. The pillars of the eastern gate of the Bridge had begun to lean in toward each other, drooping like trees ready to fall. And then they did fall, crashing forward onto the decking with a resounding crash.

A hush fell upon the ramparts. All was still, on the wall, on the beach, on the Bridge.

Then, with an enormous groan, the first pontoon subsided into the water. It fell into the gentle surf, boiling along the edges, as though it could no longer bear the water. The next segment was already fizzing and crackling—Sahaj could hear it from where he stood—and then the next segment passed the contagion along. Now there were ten or more sections trembling and quaking.

The crew of the dinghy had stopped rowing, staring in consternation.

The great road was dying one segment at a time. It grew in speed, becoming more violent, with pontoons cracking, caving in and buckling, descending into the bay with screams of twisted wood and metal.

Sahaj led his army in a cheer. Muskets and rifles fired into the air, joining the roar of soldiers whose victory was not only complete, but everlasting. This was the Bridge his father had loved, that brought him riches and made him a slave of Anglica. This was the Bridge that Mahindra thought could be controlled by a great prince who would raise the continent to greatness. But what did Sahaj, what did these armies, care for Bharata? Their hopes were all for Nanpura.

It was enough to be *rana* of Nanpura. It was all he had ever wanted. To be rich was to be great. And now he was also safe.

In the harbor the Bridge fell and fell.

In its wake sprang up a great wave with a hump like a mountain.

A hundred feet high, the wave bore down on the ships. The war ship had no time to come around and, struck broadside, heaved and rocked, masts gone horizontal for a breath-taking moment. It righted, heavily damaged. The other ships, including the little dinghy, had fared better, riding out the palisade of water that now rushed upon the shore taking pieces of the pier with it and sending them crashing onto the beach.

The waves swept up the shore. When they had finished, the wide bay was scoured clean. In the far distance, and for many minutes, the Bridge spewed foam and sank into the sea.

33

April 12, 1869

Tori was packing again. She and her assistant Anand were accustomed to being on the move. The village had offered succor to them for the past week, but it would be a burden on them to have guests longer. And she was anxious, besides, to reach her destination and honor an old duty. It had been placed upon her eleven years ago, and now there was not much time left to discharge it.

As dawn approached, their host brought chapattis to her and Anand in the small garden, giving them privacy to break their fast. It was best to be underway at first light. Tori was forbidden to be in the province, but she had many friends in Nanpura and they assisted in hiding her. In the first years she and Dulal had moved at night from village to village to evade Sahaj, who had let it be known that on his boar hunts he wouldn't mind spearing an Anglic woman. His hold on the hill tribes was not as strong as his father's had been. He hadn't dared come between the villages and their *Ardha Chandra mahila,* who liberally shared her knowledge and stocks of medicinal plants—as pale as their effects might be compared to things still hidden in the caves of Kathore.

Dulal had been with her for a long time, but when his time had drawn near, he had trained Anand to take his place, a young man who wished to know *prakrtika itihasa.* Natural history. She had been teaching him as Sir Charles had done, a role that gave her the utmost pleasure. He was not only a gifted student, however. He was, she thought, the one worthy of Mahindra's gift.

Anand carried the last of their things to the cart—a few clothes and a teak chest with her medicinals. As he did so, Tori took out the letter folded within her *sari* and by the flickering lantern light read it once more.

February 3, 1869
Astoria Harding
Ardha Chandra Mahila
Nanpura Province
Bharata

My Dearest Tori,

May this letter find you well. If this letter finds you at all, I shall count it a miracle, but one I expect to be fulfilled! I am in such a great hurry, I hardly know what I shall say, except that I am coming to Bharata. Not a moment is to be lost, for there is a packet ship leaving this very afternoon, and my letter shall be upon it, and thus you will have some warning of my arrival before I embark on the Clifford *in a fortnight. (Our packet service has suffered the most grievous losses from kraken predations, so they hardly go; thus my eagerness to send this today.)*

Oh Tori, I am relieved beyond measure to learn that you are still upon the earth, and thriving! My dear friend, your mother has just had the most welcome news of her military contacts in Bharata, whence stories have reached her about an Anglic woman who travels in the bush as a healer. Such rumors have trickled out of that continent before, but a few days ago, a name surfaced in that regard, wherein Mrs. Harding was given to know that the woman was sometimes called Ardha Chandra. *This we found can be translated as crescent moon woman! She knew at once that it was the name you had been given in your stay at Kathore (you are the subject of a great deal of speculation my dear, and we have not been sanguine about tracking down every wisp of information that might improve our understanding of your situation.)*

To come to the point, it is thus: I have the family's commission to be their emissary to you, both undertaking the journey, and acting as your advocate in any arrangements that may be made for your future welfare. Glyndehill Manor still awaits its heiress; it provides an income sufficient for you to pursue your studies. My own inheritance could not be better spent than in modernizing the Greenhouse cottage, if you should be of the opinion that improvements would be to the point. I even can imagine a teaching function may come about, and have already made inquiries for you at Cambridge where lectures for ladies are gaining approval! But

I move ahead of myself.

I must first, of course, persuade you to come home.

I wish for you to think of me as your most devoted supporter. I am, and shall always be. And as for the strictures of marriage, which I know you must regard with the highest suspicion, I believe we can safely lay the matter aside. You would never have to marry. I have not, and no one dares to fault me.

Pray do not set yourself against my proposition just yet. If you are reading this letter, I am already on my way on the Clifford, *which will bring me to Poondras by April 20. Let me see you, dearest Tori. I make no demands. As well, I wish to see Bharata a last time that I may pay my respects. I have unfinished business, too, dear Tori.*

I will be on the bridge at Ralawindi before the gates of Fort Poondras. Look for me there!

Yours with the greatest affection,

Elizabeth Platt

She tucked the letter back into her *sari* and joined Anand in the cart path. It would take all day to reach the caves, and they must not tarry.

Now that she had made her decision, she was in the greatest hurry to put it into effect. What a risk it had been, all these years, to be the only one with the knowledge of the location of *Nelumbo aureus!* When she had finally spoken to Anand a few days ago about the golden lotus, his understanding and enthusiasm had been a profound relief. Mahindra had said that she must find someone who was worthy to know about the holy flower. She believed it to be Anand. He it was who could do the right thing with this knowledge. Even a great thing.

They set out down the road toward the Banda gorge.

Tori lay a branch of *Caesalpinia pulcherrima*, the peacock flower, with its red-orange flowers, among the other offerings at the edge of the Banda gorge.

It had been her custom to bring flowers every year to the little stone shrine at the gorge, but a few years ago, Sahaj had ordered it cast over the cliff. However, people still brought flowers and food and left them in the spot where Jai had fallen.

Sahaj had more important things to worry about. The Crown maneuvered to undermine him, goading neighboring princes to harry his borders. They could not supplant him, however. Anglic power in Bharata had substantially diminished since the insurrection and the loss of the Bridge. Still, it persisted like an invasive weed, thriving in the rich soil of trade, bribes and firepower that still propped up corrupt *ranas*. Mahindra would not have been surprised. He had known what the handshake between the two lands meant. He knew that only a great leader could change that.

Anglic reprisal over Fort Poondras never came to pass. The Crown had at first threatened retaliation, but when ships laden with cannon and troops went down by the dozens on the kraken-infested seas, it gradually became a deferred plan, then an empty threat.

The rope bridge lay before them. Tori and Anand left their cart behind and crossed it, winding once again into the dense jungle that would only fall away once they were climbing the palisades to the cave.

At dusk, they at last came to the foot of the great hillside. They had brought with them their food and a supply of torches. This time there would be no spirit woman to show the way.

Anand looked up at the gaping holes in the cliff face. "You said it was far inside, *mataji*."

"Yes, very far." He would soon take a walk from which he would return quite altered. It was fitting that he hesitate. "Are you sure you wish to enter?"

Before he could answer, a commotion came from just down the talus slope. She and Anand turned in alarm. Three men were quickly picking their way through the rocks toward them. Soldiers. Oh, Tori knew whose.

Behind them, a man appeared from the bush, wearing a finely cut tunic and a blue turban.

So, he had not given up, after all. She watched in consternation as the soldiers drew closer. How comfortable she had become these last years, so assured that Sahaj dared not touch her! But here he was. He had waited for her to come back.

The soldiers came level with them and to Tori's shock, one of them struck Anand, sending him staggering. Then they forced both of them to kneel as Sahaj approached.

"I thought all the Anglics had left my kingdom," Sahaj said. "But here is a woman I banished long ago." He tried to sound perplexed, but he was enjoying himself.

"How do you do, Your Highness," Tori said as evenly as she could.

"I do very well indeed. And I shall do better soon."

"I am surprised you waited for us all this time." Truly, how had he managed it?

"Oh, a *rana* has many duties that would prevent him from noticing you.

But before you received your letter from the school teacher, it was read to me. A foreign letter asking for *Ardha Chandra mahila...*" he shrugged... "attracts attention."

Anand made a noise deep in his throat, one of dismay and surprise.

Sahaj went on. "I knew you would come back one last time. I have decided I would look upon the holy flower. And eat of it. We shall see if it heals. I am curious."

"But evil is not a sickness, Your Highness. It is a choice."

Sahaj's eyes grew hard. He turned to one of his soldiers, a tall one with a deep scar over one eye. He gestured to Anand. "Kill her servant."

The soldier placed a hand on Anand's head, pushing it forward to expose his neck. He raised his sword.

A roar stopped his hand in midair.

Everyone looked up. For a moment a great silver and black cat stood poised on a rock outcropping just fifteen feet above them. Then it was in motion, springing down, crashing among them, and sending Tori falling to one side. Someone screamed. As she scrambled away from the snarling animal, blood splattered her.

The tiger was savaging the soldier who tried to kill Anand. The other two soldiers had gone sprawling on the path. But Sahaj stood his ground.

He drew his sword and slashed down on the tiger, but Anand dove for the *rana's* legs, and he staggered backward, outraged at being touched.

But he had forgotten that there were two tigers. Now the second cat was rushing down the path, taking great slow-motion strides, heading for Sahaj who looked confused to be the apparent target.

As the cat leapt upon him, it carried him off the steep path and partway down the hillside. The tiger ripped out his throat in one efficient pass of teeth over neck. Sahaj lay still, head pointed downhill, his blood forming a gentle, red rivulet.

To their credit, the two remaining soldiers stood ready with their swords, but it was no fair match. Each cat took a man.

It was done. Four lay dead.

Anand and Tori had frozen in their crouched positions against the hillside.

The second tiger stood on the path before Tori, licking its bloodied face. A great paw came up and wiped at its cheek, very efficiently restoring the fur to its pristine silver and white. As Tori and Anand huddled together, the tiger turned and looked at her. She felt she must not look it in the eye, but was helpless to stop. They stared at one another. Once, these cats had slipped through the zenana door to freedom. Now they had come, she felt, to pay back the favor. When the thought had firmly formed in her mind, the great cat finally looked away.

As daylight fell away, it became harder to see. The tiger was joined by its sister, and they sniffed at each other, assuring themselves that no damage had been done.

Then Tori saw that no damage had been possible.

The tigers were fading. She stared most intently, but it could not be denied, even in the heavy dusk, that the animals were losing their form. It was possible now to see right through them, between the stripes. She knew that she would never see them again, and almost—but not quite—reached out for them.

And then they were gone, vanished within feet of Anand and Tori.

"Magic," Anand breathed.

"Yes," Tori said. They had been magical creatures. They'd had no need to follow Tori, if protection had been their mission instead of revenge. However Sahaj had conjured them, he had not counted on them having goals of their own.

She had always thought the tigers were the natural kings of this land, and now, seeing that they were the stuff of magic, it seemed all the more true. This was Bharata, after all. And sometimes knowing real from conjured, or desire from reality was a most challenging matter of being willing to see.

In place of a burial, she and Anand covered the bodies with lengths of cloth from the men's own turbans.

Tori insisted on covering Sahaj herself.

By torchlight they found the scratches on the walls, the signs that Tori had once made to lead her out. Now they showed the way in, faint in the flickering light.

She tried to put away her fear that the lotus would be gone. Over the years she had begun to wonder if the events in the cave had been real. In time its vivid impressions had receded. Faded memories raised doubts. She wondered if Jai had been her lover, as she remembered, or if Ned Conolly had wished to have the lotus for foreign intrigues, or if the great flower had ever floated upon a light-struck pool deep in a cave. But when she looked at her left foot, she was certain that it had all been true.

Still, would the flower be there for Anand?

They entered the great cavern, holding up their torches, but they could not see the ceiling, so dark it was.

"Oh, Anand…" she whispered, "This was the place. I'm sure this was." Her voice took on a strange resonance in the lofty chamber.

Anand put a hand on her arm to steady her.

They walked forward, footfalls echoing. They saw that a pool of water lay just ahead, their torches reflecting on it, filling it with a ghostly light.

But no, it was not their torches. Tori's heart kicked hard in her chest. There, deep below the surface was something stirring, something glowing. It looked like an ember, cooling in the water. Or like a bud.

It rose.

Anand lay prone beside her, at the edge of the pond. He stirred now and then in his dreams, his mind worked upon by the lotus.

The small piece she had hoarded was still effective. If it had not been, they would have had to find a way out to the flower in the pond's center. The little skiff was still there, but beyond repair without Draupadi's magic.

What was Anand seeing in his visions? She had told him what she saw in hers, that all our desires are somewhere true. It was a good thing to know, though it would disappoint people who wanted practical things. It was not a knowledge that could make one's reputation—at least not in Anglica—nor gain one admittance to circles wherein one was deemed inferior. But the lotus could also heal.

Anand would have to come back with supplies to harvest the petals. They had already agreed that he would do so gradually, to see if they grew back.

And what then? They had not discussed it. In some way, left unspoken, Tori was not relevant to what happened next. It was Bharata's legacy.

In her heart she hoped that Anand would become the influence, the inspiration, to make the land whole. Instead of warring states exploited by Anglica, Bharata could become one. It might find a way to use its magic that did not depend upon blood and suffering. Maybe renunciation would be enough. If so, the lotus visions could show the way.

Anand stirred, eyes opening. Tori helped him to sit up.

They sat side by side, gazing at the golden lotus floating serenely in the pond, commanding the cavern and their thoughts.

She thought that Anand, though a simple man, was the one that Mahindra had asked her to look for. That he was worthy to lead Bharata. But it was a far reach, she knew.

Beyond bringing him to this place, she could do more. *Nelumbo aureus* always belonged to Bharata. Whatever came of it now, and whatever Anand could accomplish, it was good enough.

34

April was the month the world should see Poondras, Tori thought. From her survey of Nanpura, she estimated that there might be 15,000 species of flowers in Bharata. All of them were in flower now. *Iridaceae*, the irises, *Abelmoschus manihot*, the hibiscus, even the lowly elephant creeper cascading over the walls of the bazaar.

Heading toward the fort from the bazaar, there was a narrow alleyway that snaked around the craftsmen stalls. Here she passed men sharpening knives against a stone wheel, and others resting in front of towering stacks of cotton cloth, waiting for garment customers. The street was deep in shadow, and she thought this was the cause of the stark chill that came over her, not the fact that a person waited for her on the Ralawindi Bridge. She felt that if her steps slowed she would, like a clock winding down, gradually come to a halt and then she would begin to retreat, falling back into the jumble of stalls, the mud huts, the deep shadows of unknowable Bharata. It was always easy to think that happiness and wisdom lay in the shadows, in places that have never yet been seen. The reasoning was, surely the gods have put truth on earth somewhere, and since it is so difficult to find, it must be in the darker places. She knew the old pull, not just of natural history, but of life, longing to be a deeper red. She still had doubts about going. It was very hard.

Emerging from the alleyway she stepped into blinding sunlight. It was 90 degrees and more on the hot paving stones leading to the bridge. She saw that a woman in a sandy brown dress stood in the very center of it. Her face was hidden in a broad straw hat, but by the set of her shoulders and determined stance, Tori knew it was Elizabeth.

She hadn't recognized Tori yet, but of course she would not be expecting a barefoot woman in a saffron-colored sari. It was not too late to turn back.

Then Elizabeth turned to watch her approach. When she was a few feet away, Tori stopped, wondering what they must say to each other. But Elizabeth had not changed. She charged forward grasping Tori's hands and squeezing them.

"Oh, you have come! My dear friend." She shook her head over and over. "My dear friend. My heart is beating like all the drums of Bharata. I see I have worn the wrong thing, for you look like a queen of Nanpura!"

Tori smiled. "Don't say that, or they will arrest me."

Elizabeth drew herself up. "Nonsense. They shall not." She patted a purse tied to her wrist. "I have brought real rupees and should ransom you!"

Tori hoped no thieves listened about the fat purse of rupees, but no one could squelch Elizabeth Platt. "Well, then, I'm safe."

Even Elizabeth recognized this irony. "I'm being foolish. But I'm so glad to see you, I think I shall break into song."

"I'm glad to see you, too, Elizabeth." Her voice left her, and she whispered, "Very glad." Elizabeth embraced her, kissing her on each cheek.

"What of my mother and sister?"

"Oh, they are well! They miss you so terribly."

"Jessa married, of course."

"Yes. They are so happy. And with four young ones, all boys, the oldest looking so like your father everyone says!"

Tori was pleased to hear it. She had imagined them happy, and now it was true.

Elizabeth turned to watch an ox cart rumble by, bringing rice and vegetables to the bazaar. On its open gate sat a small boy, legs dangling, wearing a little turban and a vest over pajama pants. She watched the cart until it turned into the square.

"A child died here," Elizabeth murmured. "Because of me. He was no more than ten." She looked at Tori, her eyes glistening.

Tori laid a hand on her arm. "Elizabeth. I know. I heard what happened. I don't blame you for it."

Elizabeth turned to her in perplexity. "You do not blame me?"

"I almost killed someone, once. I held a gun to the head of a man who was bound hand and feet. None of us is innocent. And you were fighting for your lives."

Elizabeth looked in the direction of the vanished cart. "But it was a child."

"Yes, a child died. And also many others." Tori took her by the arm and led her to the low wall of the bridge, where they sat together. "Are you still teaching, Elizabeth?"

"Oh yes. I have lately been much preoccupied with the higher education of women. But it is too much to recite just now. There is so much to tell you..."

"And the dangerous journey back here, all on your own!"

Elizabeth took Tori's hands in hers. "I was not alone." She saw the doubt in Tori's face. "Pray do not judge me yet, before I have told all."

Tori waited in growing anxiety.

"You wish to have no pressure, of course. You have fled us because you wish to escape confining society. I would not aid and abet any station other than what you would wish, no matter what it may look like."

"It does not look to me that you would do so, Elizabeth."

"But you see, Edmond has come with me." She looked up to the fort gate, where, absent the old heavy doors, the archway threw a deep shadow. A figure stood there, one hand on the archway, leaning into it.

"He would not hear of my coming by myself. But he does not expect that you will receive him. It is very clear and sensible to him that you do not wish to have any persuasion of him, particularly on matters of the heart."

Tori was now staring at this figure with very palpable agitation. She glanced in consternation at Elizabeth. "Of the heart? Why would my sister's husband have ought to persuade me of?"

Elizabeth took Tori's hands in hers. "Because your sister has been married to the most excellent Mr. Robert Perry for these nine years, a most amiable and well-situated gentleman. My cousin, of course, has never married."

"Has he not?" Tori whispered. She could not contain her shock. Her relief.

"Nor would he expect that you and he would arrange anything but an alliance of equals."

Tori withdrew her hands from Elizabeth's and slowly rose from the stone wall. She began walking toward the gate as Elizabeth's voice followed her. "You must have everything at the Greenhouse Cottage as you will. We will all support you, sparing no good will nor energy for your happiness..."

It was very far to the gate in the noonday heat. Edmond had now understood that she had seen him, and came forward a few steps into the sun. He had not changed in appearance, except that instead of His Majesty's uniform, he wore a light brown country frock coat and pants tucked into Wellington boots. He looked very well. She supposed that no one had ever looked better to her eyes.

He began walking toward her, first slowly, and then striding, perhaps thinking he should cover more of the distance between them, but by then she was running.

And between the Sita Bridge and the gate of Fort Poondras, Tori decided that she would very much indeed like to go home.